WINGS OF THE NIGHTINGALE

D1403437

ON DISTANT SHORES

SARAH SUNDIN
COPY 1

THORNDIKE PRESS
A part of Gale, Cengage Learning

GALE
CENGAGE Learning·

Detroit • New York • San Francisco • New Haven, Conn • Waterville, Maine • London

GALE
CENGAGE Learning®

LIBRARY OF CONGRESS CATALOGING-IN-PUBLICATION DATA

Sundin, Sarah.
    On distant shores / by Sarah Sundin. — Large print edition.
        pages ; cm. — (Wings of the nightingale ; book two) (Thorndike Press large print Christian historical fiction)
    ISBN 978-1-4104-6173-5 (hardcover) — ISBN 1-4104-6173-4 (hardcover) 1. Letter writing—Fiction. 2. Friendship—Fiction. 3. World War, 1939–1945—Fiction. 4. Large type books. I. Title.
PS3619.U5626O5 2013b
813'.6—dc23   2013032568

Published in 2013 by arrangement with Revell Books, a division of Baker Publishing Group

Printed in Mexico
1 2 3 4 5 6 7 17 16 15 14 13

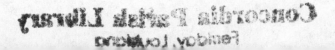

For my husband, David Sundin, Pharm.D., my own pharmacist hero. Your outrage over the plight of our profession in the wartime military showed me I had a story. Your discovery of an outstanding research book aided that story. And your love and support steadied me through the writing of this story.

1

Over French Morocco
July 7, 1943

If only the plane would keep flying over the Atlantic and straight back to Virginia where Georgie belonged.

Flight nurse Lt. Georgiana Taylor spun her gaze from the khaki landscape below to the interior of the C-47 cargo plane. More khaki. And olive drab. And aluminum.

Six canvas litters suspended on aluminum racks. Twelve canvas seats. Eighteen patients in khaki and olive drab. This plane needed a little magenta or tangerine or violet.

Georgie strolled to the front of the plane. She might be the only color in the lives of these poor wounded soldiers, so she'd shine as brightly as possible.

"Good afternoon, gentlemen. I hope you're enjoying your flight." She looked into each patient's face long enough to make him feel cared for, but not long enough to

9

give him the wrong idea about her. "We'll land in Casablanca in an hour. Sergeant Jacoby and I will make one last round. If y'all need anything, please let us know."

A corporal raised his hand and a mischievous smile. "I need Ingrid Bergman to meet me at the airport in Casablanca and kiss me hello like she kissed Bogart good-bye."

The men hooted and hollered.

Georgie cocked her head. "Sorry, honey. She's off fighting Nazis with her *husband,* remember?"

The corporal flapped a hand at her. "Ah, you're spoiling my fun."

"All in a day's work." Georgie knelt in front of the first patient on the left and perused the flight manifest to refresh herself on his condition. Private Joe Carney lost a foot to a land mine in Bizerte, Tunisia, a week after the Germans and Italians surrendered in North Africa. His wound had earned him a plane ride to Casablanca and a cruise home on a hospital ship. A twinge of envy, but Georgie certainly didn't want to pay the same price.

"How are you feeling, Private?"

"Fine, ma'am." The stiffness of his voice contradicted his words.

"Would you like some codeine for pain? You haven't had any today."

His expression turned steely. "Lost my foot almost two months ago. If I don't get off these drugs, what good will I be to my wife and kids?"

She settled her hand on his rigid forearm. "I understand, but I don't want you miserable either. Let me know if you need some."

After she took his temperature, pulse, and respiration, she moved to the next patient, Sgt. Harold Myers. An artillery shell had hit his tank, killed all his crewmates, and left him with horrible burns. Bandages swathed his trunk, one arm, and one side of his face.

His good eye shifted to Sergeant Jacoby. "Say, nurse, is he your brother?"

"You'd think so, wouldn't you?" Like Georgie, the surgical technician had blue eyes and curly brown hair. He hailed from North Carolina rather than Virginia, but she could hardly expect a man with Myers's flat Yankee voice to tell the difference in accents.

"Is he your boyfriend?" Myers's eye twinkled.

Flirting was the favorite sport of most soldiers, but Georgie knew how to end the game. A sweet smile. A dreamy sigh. "My boyfriend's back home. We'll get married after the war."

The twinkle turned to a snap. "Why ain't

11

he fighting like the rest of us?"

Georgie wrapped her fingers around his wrist. If only she'd taken his pulse before it galloped out of control. "Ward *is* fighting. He's raising apples and tomatoes for your rations and to feed the Allies. He wanted to enlist, but the draft board wouldn't let him."

"Sorry, ma'am. Just assumed."

"That's perfectly all right."

"What's he think about his girl wearing a uniform when he can't?"

Georgie froze at the memory of Ward's handsome face in an atypical scowl, but she couldn't blame him. He wanted Georgie at his side, and that's exactly where she wanted to be. In the sweet little farmhouse she hadn't even seen yet, baking ham, sewing curtains, and rocking babies. She winked at the sergeant. "He couldn't be prouder."

Next came Private Bill Holloway. Multiple bouts with dysentery and malaria had reduced him to almost nothing, and the dust of the Tunisian summer had aggravated the asthma he'd concealed from the Army recruiter.

His respiration ran at a steady trot. Two spots of red illuminated his thin, pale cheeks.

Georgie wanted color on the flight, but not this kind. Her own respiration accelerated. "Private Holloway, are you all right?"

"Don't think I . . . got my . . . asthma pills . . . this morning."

She glanced at his orders on her clipboard. "The doctor sent you with a bottle of aminophylline. I'll fetch it." And a syringe of epinephrine to be safe.

She headed for the back of the plane. The engines vibrated through her legs and rattled her heart. The other nurses in her squadron loved the danger and excitement of emergencies, but not Georgie. What if she let her patients down? What if her incompetence harmed one of these sweet boys?

Georgie opened the medical chest and pulled out supplies. After she swabbed the glass ampule with rubbing alcohol, she snapped the thin neck and laid the ampule on its side on a gauze pad. She angled the syringe through the neck and drew up the contents, three two-hundredths of a grain of epinephrine.

Private Holloway had an order for two hundred milligrams of aminophylline. The bottle contained aminophylline tablets, one and one-half grains each.

Georgie groaned. She hated math. Without the help of her best friend, Rose Danilovich, she never would have made it through nursing school.

She pulled a notepad from the pocket of her dark blue uniform trousers. Sixty-five milligrams per grain. One and one-half grains. Two hundred milligrams. She wrote down the numbers and set up the problem. Rose and Mellie and all the other nurses in the 802nd Medical Air Evacuation Transport Squadron could do this in their heads.

Two tablets? Was that right? Georgie chewed on the end of the pencil. Aminophylline was a dangerous drug. What if she had it wrong? She couldn't take that chance.

Georgie leaned down the aisle and beckoned to Sergeant Jacoby, who collected empty ration tins from the patients' lunches.

He ambled back to her, dumped the tins, and flashed a grin. "What's up, Lieutenant?"

"Private Holloway's asthma flared up. I'm giving him epi and his aminophylline. Looks like his morning dose was forgotten in the preflight excitement. Would you please check my calculations?"

He cocked an eyebrow at her. "It's one ampule."

"No, the aminophylline. The order's in milligrams, but the tablets are in grains."

He took the notepad from her. "That's why I like working with you. You ask my

14

opinion. None of the other gals do."

"Thank you." But was that a compliment? The other gals could figure it out themselves.

"Looks great." He winked. "Let's hope you always have someone to consult in a crisis."

Georgie's smile faltered. What if she didn't? What if she faced a true crisis that required her to make her own decisions? She wanted to go home, but not due to failure, not if someone got hurt.

Daddy and Mama and Ward were right. Georgie was in over her head.

USAT *Mexico,* Gela, Sicily
July 13, 1943
Technical Sergeant John Hutchinson coiled his fingers around the rope net, climbed over the side of the troop transport, and anchored his feet in the net.

American naval guns boomed, and shells whizzed overhead to explode behind the town of Gela. The Americans had landed on the southwestern side of Sicily's triangle on July 10 in Operation Husky, and now the 93rd Evacuation Hospital headed to shore, where Hutch planned to set up the finest pharmacy ever seen in a mobile hospital.

15

Two and a half years in the Army, but Hutch had yet to serve in a combat zone. He glanced over his shoulder. The Gulf of Gela held the bluest water he had seen in his life below an equally blue sky. Sicily's hills seemed more colorful than Algeria's, more gold than tan, but maybe that was his imagination. After all, this landing put him one step closer to war's end, one step closer to home and his own drugstore and Phyllis Chilton.

Someone whacked his helmet. "Get moving, boy."

Over the rail of the ship, Capt. Al Chadwick glared at him. "We're not sightseeing. Move."

"Yes, sir." That was all he was allowed to say to the surgeon. Hutch gritted his teeth and worked his way down the net. He had the second highest number of stripes the Army could award, but without an officer's commission, he'd never get respect.

A bachelor's degree. A valuable profession. But in the Army he was "boy."

Thank goodness, that was about to change. Back in Philadelphia, Dad worked hard with the American Pharmaceutical Association. Legislation to create a Pharmacy Corps sat before Congress, bolstered by Hutch's testimony about his Army experi-

16

ences. When that went through, Hutch would become a pharmacy officer.

He grinned. Knowing the disrespect wouldn't last much longer, he could handle it.

Loaded with all his gear on his back, Hutch followed the sailor's instructions, stepped down into the landing craft, and made his way toward the bow. Debris floated past. Was that — his stomach wrenched — it was indeed. A body.

He dropped to his backside along the port side of the boat and closed his eyes. To ease suffering, to heal, to prevent death — that's why he took this position in the first place. With his college degree, he could have applied for Officer Candidate School, gotten a commission, and served in supply, or the infantry, or wherever the Army placed him. But he wanted to use his skills to help people and boost his profession at the same time.

He sat wedged among a couple dozen other hospital personnel — nurses, medics, and doctors. Including Capt. Nels Bergstrom.

Hutch caught Bergie's eye across the crowded boat, made a stern face, and lifted a salute.

Bergie smiled and returned it.

Hutch owed the physician for his nickname, for every fun thing he ever did as a boy, and for introducing him to Phyllis. He even owed him for the transfer to the 93rd. Since Bergie was an officer and Hutch enlisted, they couldn't fraternize, but he still liked having him near.

Next to his friend, a nurse drew her knees to her chest and squeezed her eyes shut. Lt. Lillian Farley, if Hutch remembered correctly.

Poor thing. Had she seen the body too? Even if she hadn't, the roar of artillery, naval guns, and planes overhead would be fearsome enough.

"Berg." He tipped his head toward the nurse. If anyone would know how to distract her, Bergie would.

The physician studied the blonde, gave Hutch a nod of thanks, then peered up as if the blue sky held the solution.

Bergie covered his mouth, puffed up his cheeks, and patted Lillian's shoulder with a wild look in his eyes.

She screeched, yanked him to his feet, and pressed his shoulders over the edge of the boat. But Bergie didn't vomit. He just broke down in laughter.

"Oh, you." The nurse gave him a playful slap on the back. "Should have known."

"Yeah, you should have." Bergie returned to sitting, shot Hutch a grin, and chatted with Lillian.

Hutch settled in for the ride to shore, shifting his gear on his back. Once again his friend's odd sense of humor had saved the day.

The motor on the landing craft revved, and the boat pulled away from the troop transport.

He gazed up as if he could see the truck parked on the transport's deck, packed with half the pharmacy supplies. The personnel and equipment of the 93rd were divided among thirteen cargo and transport ships to minimize the impact on the hospital if one ship sank. Hutch and his truck came on the USAT *Mexico,* while his two technicians rode on another transport.

He tried not to think of the dozens of fragile medication bottles, his scales, his glassware. *Please, Lord, let it all survive.*

Across from him, Bergie's conversation with Lillian verged on flirtation. Why not? He was single and she was cute, even blonder than Bergie.

Hutch pulled out the most recent letter from his own cute little blonde. Well, at five foot eight, she wasn't little, but compared to his six foot two, she was just right.

He unfolded the well-worn piece of paper, addressed to "my darling John." She could never bring herself to write "Dear John," which was fine by him.

Oh, John, how I miss you. New York City should be exciting, but every sight only reminds me of your kiss before you boarded that ship and the love in your brown eyes. Do you still love me, darling? You're so far away, surrounded by exotic sights and beautiful nurses.

My job keeps me occupied. I tell myself that my work at the shipyard will bring you back to me soon. Edwina and Betty Jo say hello — I'm blessed to have such wonderful roommates. They listen to me and keep me busy and amused.

If only we'd married before you shipped out. Then my mind would be at ease.

Hutch puffed out a breath. Yep. If only he'd given in to her pleading and married her. He kept telling her that even if he wanted to date a nurse — which he didn't — he couldn't, because the nurses outranked him. Nothing reassured her.

At the time, a year and a half ago, it seemed practical to wait, kind to wait. Now he regretted it. Marrying her would have been so simple. So pleasurable. And a passionate night or two before his departure would have proved his love and faithfulness.

A trio of fighter planes droned overhead.

A couple of the nurses screamed. Hutch slapped his hand on his helmet and glanced up, heart pounding.

"Ours, ladies," a sailor shouted. "P-38 Lightnings. No need to fuss."

Even Hutch could identify a P-38 with its unusual twin-boomed silhouette.

The landing craft's hull crunched over sand. The bow ramp flopped open and sent up a wall of water. The boat's occupants laughed or cussed or gasped. Hutch laughed. The splash felt great under the growing heat of the day.

"Everyone out." The boat lay a good fifty feet from shore. They'd have to wade.

Bergie slung Lillian over his shoulder and carried her shrieking to land. No doubt Lieutenant Farley would join Bergie's long line of girlfriends. None lasted longer than three months.

Hutch shrugged off his pack, held it over his head, and sloshed through the warm turquoise water. Once on shore, soaked to the waist, he pulled a one-ounce glass medication bottle from his trouser pocket and filled it with Sicilian sand. He'd label it later and add it to his collection — Oahu, Northern Ireland, England, Algeria, now Gela, Sicily.

How many more vials would he fill?

2

"Yerrrrr out!" Lt. Clint Peters tackled Rose Danilovich around the waist, and they both fell to the ground.

Georgie nudged Mellie Blake as they sat in batting order on the edge of the airfield's makeshift baseball diamond. "Since when is tackling allowed in this game?"

Mellie's dark eyes gleamed. "She isn't complaining. You arrange the best birthday parties."

"I do, don't I?" Georgie winked at her friend. Rose loved Clint and baseball, and the officers of the 64th Troop Carrier Group were more than happy to join a game with the ladies of the 802nd. What could be better for Rose's birthday?

Rose got to her feet and brushed dirt from her dark blonde hair. Still a tomboy, even though Georgie had tried to make a lady

23

out of her since first grade. About as successful as Rose trying to make a tomboy out of Georgie.

"Kay, you're up." Grant Klein, a C-47 pilot and one of Kay Jobson's many boyfriends, handed the redhead a bat. "You know how to use it?"

"Why don't you show me?"

Oh brother. Georgie managed not to roll her eyes, but only because brassy Kay and shy Mellie had formed the oddest of friendships lately.

"This was such a good idea." Mellie held back her thick black hair from a sudden gust of wind. "It's taking everyone's minds off Sicily."

It was until Mellie brought it up again. "Yes, well, I'm glad they didn't send us over there on that hospital ship yesterday. It would have messed up my party plans."

"The party's our only consolation." Mellie's wide mouth settled into a hard line. "We should be there. Did you hear? They're flying patients from Sicily to Tunisia without nursing care."

Georgie clucked her tongue. "That's a shame." Did her voice sound convincing?

"This would be a great opportunity for us to show what we can do. We were trained to fly close to the front. Why won't they let us?"

Thank goodness they hadn't. Georgie scrambled to her feet. "I'm up."

Mellie laughed. "Kay's at bat. She only has one strike, one ball."

Georgie wrinkled her nose. Why couldn't Kay hurry up and strike out and end this conversation?

Mellie sighed, and her gaze roamed the airfield as it always did.

"Is he here?" Georgie asked.

"I doubt it. I think he's in Sicily."

Mellie had fallen in love with her anonymous pen pal, an Army engineer. A few months ago she'd met him and figured out his identity, but he hadn't solved the puzzle. Mellie thought that was best, since she was convinced he didn't find her attractive. Just as well. He was the son and namesake of notorious murderer Tom MacGilliver. Who wanted to be saddled with a name like that for life?

A loud crack, and Georgie jumped.

Kay stood at the plate, the bat cocked over her shoulder in a practiced way. The men craned their necks to the sky. Somewhere up there, a little white ball soared.

With a satisfied smile, Kay jogged around the bases, hips swinging. How could she do that even when running?

Clint pointed to the ball and whistled. "Good thing our ships aren't around. They'd shoot that down too."

Grim laughter circled the field, but Georgie shuddered. Two days before, a flock of C-47s flew to Sicily loaded with paratroopers, but word never reached the US Navy. The cargo planes passed over the fleet right on the heels of a German Luftwaffe attack. Twenty-three C-47s fell to American guns.

Georgie crossed her arms over her stomach and trembled despite the oppressive midday heat. They wanted the nurses to fly over there too?

"Georgie!" Rose held out the bat. Her amused smile said this wasn't the first time she'd called.

"Just planning my batting strategy." She turned and almost stepped on someone.

Lt. Cora Lambert, chief nurse of the squadron, sat close enough to hear the conversation. Lambert gave Georgie a long, curious gaze. A penetrating gaze.

Goodness, was Georgie that transparent? Were her fears visible?

"Sorry, Lieutenant." Georgie mustered her perkiest smile. "Did you know Kay was a baseball star? I sure didn't."

The gaze softened. "Who would have

known?"

"Certainly not me." Georgie headed to the plate. "What do you think, Rose? Should I try for a touchdown or a field goal?"

"For heaven's sake." Rose pressed the bat into Georgie's hand. "Just try not to kill anyone."

"I couldn't if I tried."

Her friend's freckled face scrunched into a familiar fond, teasing smile.

"Ready?" the pitcher called.

On the baseball field, men and women relaxed from wartime stress, and her best friend basked in her element.

Georgie settled the bat onto her shoulder and stared down the pitcher in a comical way. If only flight nursing was as easy as throwing a party.

Gela, Sicily
July 15, 1943
Hutch slid the lid off another case and sighed in relief. Everything was intact. He lifted a bottle of magnesium sulfate powder and inspected it for damage. None, thank goodness.

In the first case, several containers of ethanol had shattered, and the tent reeked of booze. How long would it take to get replacement supplies?

27

Dominic Bruno and Ralph O'Shea, the pharmacy technicians, set medications on the counter and dumped sawdust from the case into a crate. They'd need it someday when they relocated. Hutch placed a case upright as shelving and arranged the meds inside.

He stepped back and put his hands on his hips. A trickle of sweat ran down his bare chest.

Pharmacy and laboratory shared a long ward tent, with a canvas flap dividing them. Boxes and bulk bottles rested in open shelving beneath the pharmacy counter, and the cases perched on top for smaller bottles. The clean lines of the steel casing and the neat rows of bottles with their labels lined up just so — something about it felt right and good.

"The scales, Hutch." Ralph bowed and held out the wooden box, as if presenting a gift to a king. His bright green eyes glittered. "I'll let you do the honors."

He smiled at the teasing and took the box. Dad had taught him reverence for the tools of the profession while Hutch did his homework behind the drugstore prescription counter. "Treat your equipment well, and it'll never fail you."

Ralph scratched his head of red hair. "I

don't know, Dom. Has he ever said that before?"

"Nope. He usually says, 'Take care of your equipment, and it'll never fail you.' "

"Ah, that's it. Good, because 'treat it well' makes it sound like I've got to take it to dinner and a movie."

Dom pointed a finger at Ralph. "Don't you dare kiss it on the first date."

"Watch me." Hutch laid a smooch on the wooden box.

From the tent entrance, someone clucked his tongue. "What would Phyllis say?"

Bergie. Hutch gave him a sheepish smile. "She'd probably say I can't be trusted."

Bergie's eyes bulged, and he broke out in laughter. "What? You? Absence makes the heart grow weirder. You've only had two girlfriends, and I had to set you up with both."

Hutch opened the wooden box and set up the scales. "You're here. That's the problem."

"So it's me she doesn't trust." Bergie crossed his arms over his stocky chest and pushed out his lower lip. "I'm going to cry."

The last time Hutch had seen his friend cry was in '35 when the Philadelphia Athletics erected the Spite Fence around Shibe Park to block the free view from the street.

Bergie set his foot on the sawdust crate, his face suddenly serious. "Hey, buddy, she knows you're rock-steady faithful."

"More important, I know it."

Ralph broke out in a fake coughing fit.

"I smell coffee," Dom said in a pointed voice.

Bergie gave Hutch a quizzical look.

"Lieutenant Kazokov. Cough. Coffee." Hutch grabbed his khaki shirt and slipped it on.

Bergie glanced down at his own unbuttoned shirt. "Should I worry?"

"Nah, you outrank him." Hutch did up a button or two.

"Hutchinson! Bruno! O'Shea!" Kazokov shouted.

Hutch snapped to attention. Ridiculous. This was a hospital, not an infantry unit.

Kazokov gripped his hands behind his back, making his portly middle-aged belly protrude. He strode around the pharmacy and stopped in front of Hutch. He glanced at Bergie, then back to Hutch. "Did I hear you fraternizing with an officer?"

He gazed down into the man's little dark eyes. Kazokov accepted only two replies, and Hutch had to be honest. "Yes, sir."

"It's okay. I'm supervising. Ordering him around." Bergie clapped a hand on Kazokov's shoulder and flicked his chin at Hutch. "That shelf is crooked."

Hutch swallowed a laugh and straightened the perfectly straight shelf. "Yes, sir. Thank you, sir." Anyone who attacked Hutch received a full frontal humor assault from Bergie, but Kazokov wasn't armed for defense.

"This is my command. I have it under control." Kazokov's round face turned blotchy.

"Yes, sir." Hutch gave him a reassuring smile. "Ber— Captain Bergstrom is my oldest friend from Philadelphia."

His gaze shifted to Bergie. "But he's an enlisted man."

Bergie's lips twisted. "When we met in first grade, he failed to mention that fact."

Hutch stood tall and rigid as a tin soldier. "I apologize, Captain Bergstrom, sir. Please write me up for insubordination."

"You can count on that."

Kazokov's face turned completely red. "That won't be necessary."

"We haven't been formally introduced." Bergie stuck out his hand, all congeniality again. "I'm Capt. Nels Bergstrom."

"Lt. Humphrey Kazokov." He shook Bergie's hand.

"Swell name. They call you Kaz?"

31

"I should hope not."

Bergie nodded, his eyes lively, his lips pressed together.

Hutch returned to work. If he laughed, Bergie would lose all control.

"So, Lieutenant, what did you do in civilian life?" Bergie sounded interested in the man, but Hutch knew better. He just wanted to mine for more nuggets.

Kazokov sucked in his stomach. "My father and I own the finest florist shop in Kalamazoo."

Hutch shot Bergie a warning glance so he wouldn't break into "I've Got a Gal in Kalamazoo."

Bergie wiped a hand across his mouth. "So you're from the Kalamazoo Kazokovs?"

Hutch clamped his lips together, but across the tent, Ralph gulped back a laugh and covered it with another fake coughing fit.

"You've heard of our shop?" Kazokov's voice brightened.

"I haven't had the pleasure. How did you get from floral work to hospital work?"

"Simple. I majored in business so we could expand throughout the county. When I was drafted, my degree enabled me to attend Officer Candidate School. After my three months' training and commission, I was assigned here."

A "Ninety-Day Wonder." No experience in health care whatsoever. Hutch set the bottle of salicylic acid down too hard on the counter. Bottles rattled.

Kazokov scowled. "Be careful with my medications, Sergeant."

"Yes, sir." Hutch's fingers tightened on the bottle. The man didn't know the difference between salicylic acid and sulfuric acid.

He swallowed his indignation. This was why he came. Without him, the patients of the 93rd would be under the care of Kaz, Dom, and Ralph, with nine months' training between them. Few mobile hospitals had a pharmacist on staff, and Hutch hoped to have a hand in changing that.

In the civilian world, only pharmacists were allowed to fill prescriptions, but the military believed technicians could do the same job. They couldn't, and the pharmacy profession had gathered volumes of stories of compromised patient safety, some of the stories provided by Hutch.

"Are you almost set up, Sergeant?" Kaz said.

"Yes, sir. This is the last case."

"Good." He poked the sawdust crate with his foot. "Put that away, out of sight."

"Yes, sir." That was the plan.

"My work is done here. I'll report to Colonel Currier." Kazokov extended his hand to Bergie. "A pleasure meeting you, Captain."

"Oh, the pleasure's mine. All mine." Bergie's head swiveled to follow Kazokov out of the tent, but his gaze strayed back to Hutch, and one side of his mouth crept up.

"Don't." Hutch pointed one warning finger at his friend.

"Ohhhhhh." Bergie stamped his foot over and over like a dog getting his ears scratched. "It would be so easy."

"Too easy. Where's the sport?"

"You're ruining my fun again."

"That's why we're friends. I keep you out of trouble."

Bergie's grin lit up his tanned face. "And I get you into it."

How many times had they said that? Both Hutch's mom and Bergie's said they were good for each other, balanced each other. Hutch needed that balance.

3

Ponte Olivo Airfield, Sicily
July 17, 1943

In the pressing heat of the tent, Georgie set up the mosquito bar so the netting on its boxy frame encased her cot. As long as she tucked the bottom edge under her bedroll, she'd be protected from mosquitoes and malaria while she slept. She smiled at the four other women in the tent. "Tell yourselves you're sleeping in a romantic Victorian canopy bed."

"Looks like a coffin to me." Vera Viviani shook back her dark hair.

Rose wiggled her fingers near Vera's face. "At least it keeps the Sicilian bugs off."

Alice Olson shuddered and ran her fingers up into her pale blonde hair as if insects had invaded. "Please stop talking about bugs."

Georgie opened her little canvas musette bag and set her photos and mementos on

35

an upturned crate. Thank goodness she'd been raised on a horse farm and felt comfortable with dirt and bugs and the great outdoors.

Kay Jobson picked up the framed photo of Virginia Ham, Georgie's horse. "Mellie and I are taking guesses on how long it'll take you to sew curtains for this place."

Georgie tapped her finger on her chin and grinned. "Do you suppose they'll let me cut out windows?"

A trio of thumps in the distance sent shivers through her shoes. Artillery, and not far away. Her fingers itched for needle and thread and fabric and something, anything, to do.

Lieutenant Lambert poked her head into the tent, letting in a swirl of a breeze. "Ladies, we have evac flights. I need you down at the airstrip immediately."

Georgie's heart flipped like an egg over-easy. She stuffed her mementos back into her musette bag. Wherever she went, her family and Ward and Hammie went with her.

"Georgie . . ." Lambert gave her a slight frown and a patting motion, telling her to sit.

She had nowhere to sit. She sent the chief nurse a curious look.

Lambert repeated the patting motion. "Where's Mellie?"

"She went out a few minutes ago, looking for —" Georgie shut her mouth tight. Looking for her engineer, but no one was supposed to know about him except Georgie and Rose and Kay. "Looking around. You know how adventurous she is."

"Now isn't the time for adventure." The chief nurse leaned out of the tent and looked around. "There she is. Lieutenant Blake! Hurry up! Get to the plane. We've got an evac flight."

Rose, Kay, Vera, and Alice stepped outside, knotting neckties, adjusting garrison caps, and chattering in excitement.

Georgie could work up some chatter. That was her specialty.

Lambert extended her hand back into the tent like a traffic cop telling Georgie to stop. "Head on down, ladies. Captain Maxwell will brief you. Georgie and I have a special project."

A special project? She shifted the mosquito netting so she could sit on the cot.

Lambert came back inside.

"What's our project?" Georgie gave her a big smile.

The chief nurse crossed her arms, gazed toward the tent entrance, and tapped one long finger on her upper arm, ticking, ticking, ticking.

Time to get busy. Georgie unpacked her musette bag and set her photographs in an attractive arch, Ward on the left, Ham on the right, and in the middle Mama and Daddy and her sisters, Freddie and Bertie. In front, she set her sewing kit and the windup alarm clock from Daddy.

"You seem jittery today."

"Pardon?"

Lambert inclined her head, her brown eyes kind. "Are you all right?"

"Goodness, yes. I'm excited to be in Sicily, and I can't wait to fly."

Lambert's mouth pursed, and her gaze meandered over Georgie's face. "Not today."

Could she see through the smile? Georgie let out a disappointed sigh. "Too bad."

Lieutenant Lambert headed out of the tent and motioned for Georgie to follow. "You and I are taking this jeep to the 93rd Evacuation Hospital, just over that rise there. I need to talk with the physicians about the criteria for selecting patients for air evacuation. We could walk, but we have a few crates of meds for pharmacy that came with us from Tunisia. That's your project."

Lambert didn't need Georgie to haul crates. She needed a burly medic. But that wasn't the point. At home, whenever Georgie was nervous or afraid, Mama put her to work in the kitchen or on the sewing machine. Lambert must have suspected Georgie needed busywork to keep her occupied.

The pampering turned up the corners of her mouth. "May I drive?"

"Oh, I don't think so. I'm not even sure I can make this thing go. Now hush, or they'll send a man to drive us."

After they climbed in, Lambert started the engine, and the sturdy olive drab vehicle lurched forward. Georgie grabbed the dashboard and held on tight. Each gearshift made the ladies bounce and laugh.

They drove out of the tent complex surrounding Ponte Olivo Airfield and down a dirt road. Toasty golden hills encircled the plain, and olive trees graced the hills with touches of deep green.

Artillery rumbled, and a putrid smell hit Georgie's nose. By the side of the road lay a dead horse.

She slammed her eyes shut and clapped her hand over her nose and mouth. Why did innocent animals have to pay for man's violence?

Lambert swung the jeep up to another

39

large tent complex. "Be glad graves detail has already come this way."

Georgie nodded. As a nurse, she'd seen plenty of death, but not lying twisted and dismembered on the roadside.

"Here we are." Each tent bore a large red cross in a white circle on its roof to protect it from enemy air attack. A wooden sign with an arrow read "93 EH Information, Registrar."

They passed a clump of pyramidal tents in a neat grid. Living quarters, from the looks of it. A few nurses chatted and washed laundry. They gave Georgie and Lambert strange looks. While the hospital nurses wore belted khaki GI coveralls, the flight nurses wore dark blue trousers and crisp light blue blouses, their dark blue waist-length jackets abandoned due to the heat.

Georgie waved. "Good afternoon, ladies!"

The women smiled and waved back. Some nurses resented the "glamour girls" of medical air evacuation, so Georgie was determined to stamp a friendly face on the image.

The jeep approached the large ward tents, set up like a typical four-hundred-bed evacuation hospital and labeled with wooden signs: two tents marked Receiving, then Bath; Dressing and Dental; Pharmacy and Laboratory; Headquarters and Registrar; and Officers' and Nurses' Mess.

Lambert turned the jeep around and parked it between two olive drab ambulances across the road from Pharmacy and Laboratory. Medics hustled around, carrying stretchers and assisting ambulatory patients. The Americans had made significant progress, but the front lay a meager twelve miles from Gela.

Lambert pointed to her left. "I'll be in HQ. Tell the pharmacy staff to get the crates from the jeep. Ask if they have any aspirin while you're at it."

"Good idea." They had none at Ponte Olivo or at the hospitals in Tunisia.

The tent flaps were tied back, and Georgie stepped in. "Hello?"

A red-haired young man grinned. "Look, Dom. We got ourselves a girl. Tie her up and make her stay."

"I'll get the rope." A wiry, dark-haired man stepped around a makeshift counter of wooden crates and right up to Georgie. He sniffed. "Smells like a girl too."

She laughed. "I'm Lt. Georgie Taylor, one of the flight nurses at Ponte Olivo. Is this pharmacy or laboratory?"

"Pharmacy." The redhead extended his hand and bowed to Georgie. "Ralph

O'Shea, Technician Fourth Grade."

"You can do better than him, toots. Dominic Bruno, Technician *Third* Grade."

Georgie shook both their hands. "You don't get many women in here, do you?"

"It's the neighborhood." By a counter filled with glass bottles, a third man stood, tall and dark-haired, his back to Georgie. He wore five stripes on the sleeve of his khaki shirt, identifying him as a technical sergeant, same as the men she flew with in her squadron.

"That's Hutch," Dom said. "He thinks he's in charge here."

"Maybe it's because I'm the only one working." He shifted glassware around, but a note of humor rang in his voice. He gave Georgie a quick nod, then went back to work.

"I have three crates for you."

"Crates?" Hutch spun to face her, light in his dark eyes.

"Now you're speaking his language," Ralph said.

"What did you bring?" He strode to the tent entrance and leaned out. "Any aspirin?"

"I wish." Georgie led him to the jeep and motioned for the other men to follow. "I hoped you'd have some."

"Nope. I was about to compound some.

Would you like me to double the batch?"

"Compound? You can make it?"

"Sure." He stood a full foot taller than she, and he was quite good-looking when he smiled. "I learned a few things in pharmacy school."

Dom clapped Hutch on the back. "He's a real, live, honest-to-goodness pharmacist."

Georgie patted the side of the jeep. "And you aren't?"

"Me?" Dom snorted and hefted up one of the crates. "I'm a grocer. Ralph's a welder."

"How'd you end up in pharmacy?"

"Simple." Ralph's face reddened as he wrestled out a crate. "The Army gave us tests, threw away the results, and sent us to training school."

Dom headed back to the tent. "Three months to try to teach us what college boy here learned in four years."

Georgie studied the stripes on Hutch's sleeve as he lifted out the last crate. Most college graduates ended up as officers.

He looked down at her, his face serious but still nice-looking. His jaw tightened. "The job of pharmacist is one of few in the Army that requires a college degree but doesn't earn a commission."

Georgie frowned. "How strange. Why is that?"

He marched back to the tent. "History, tradition, a system run by physicians who look down on my profession."

"We nurses have the same prob—" But she wore second lieutenant's gold bars on the shoulders of her uniform. "Well, some doctors look down on us, but we do have commissions even though we don't have college degrees. That's strange, isn't it?"

"That's the Army." Hutch set the crate behind the counter. "They commission you ladies to protect you from the unwashed rabble of us enlisted men."

"Nonsense." Georgie waved him off. "You seem like quite a gentleman for a Yankee."

His laugh had a rich rumble to it. "See? We Northerners aren't all savage brutes, and you Southerners aren't all uneducated hicks."

"Glad we got that straight." Georgie leaned her forearms on the counter. "What does Hutch stand for?"

"John Hutchinson. My best friend came up with the nickname." He pried the lid off the crate. "Good. Ethanol. Dom, Ralph, after you stock that, please make the delivery to pre-op."

The three men bustled around. Hutch had a quiet confidence about him that reminded her of Daddy and Ward. While he wasn't shy, he wasn't flirtatious either. "Hutch, you have a sweetheart at home, don't you?"

Brown eyebrows rose. "How'd you know?"

"I have a sweetheart of my own back home. I can tell these things."

He nodded to his technicians. "Thanks. Why don't you make that delivery? I'll get the aspirin started."

Georgie nestled her chin in her hand. "How do you make aspirin?"

He pulled a bottle off the shelf. "Salicylic acid has the same properties as aspirin, but it's hard on the stomach. Mix it with acetic anhydride and sulfuric acid, let it crystallize, and you get acetylsalicylic acid."

"Aspirin."

"Right. Then I put it in capsules. It takes awhile though. You don't need to wait around."

"I have to wait for my chief anyway. But kick me out if I annoy you."

A slow grin. "I'll do that."

"Tell me about your girlfriend." Asking about a fellow's sweetheart was the simplest way to assure him she wasn't flirting.

"Fiancée. Her name's Phyllis." He lined the pans of a scale with paper.

"Where'd you meet her?"

A pause while he checked something in a handbook. "My best friend introduced us."

"Was it love at first sight?"

Hutch selected weights from a box and set them in the left pan. One side of his mouth twitched. "That would require speed. I don't do anything quickly."

"Slow and methodical. A good trait in a pharmacist."

"Yes." He shot her a glance through lashes too thick for a man. "But not a good trait in a date. If it weren't for Bergie, we wouldn't be together."

"Your best friend?"

"Yep. He's a physician here."

"Right here? In the 93rd? That is so sweet."

"Sweet? We're men."

She laughed and adjusted her elbow on the rough crate. "My best friend's in my squadron, and it's very sweet having her here."

"You're girls." Teasing warped the words.

"You must have little sisters."

"I do." He shook white crystals from the bottle into the right pan of the scale. "I thought you were a nurse, but apparently you're a psychologist as well."

"Oh, I just like people. They're infinitely fascinating. Which brings me back to my first question. Phyllis — what's she like?"

He spooned some crystals back into the

bottle. "She's pretty. Blonde. Kind of tall."

Georgie clucked her tongue at him. "That wasn't what I meant. What's she *like*? Shall I help you? I have a hunch she's a social dynamo who pries your nose out of the books."

"Phyllis? She's even quieter than I am."

"Really?" Ward said he needed Georgie's spirit to coax him into society. "Well, you'll have a peaceful home someday."

"That's the idea." Hutch lifted the paper filled with crystals, folded the edges together, and held it over an Erlenmeyer flask. The crystals slid down the paper chute into the flask.

Georgie settled her chin into her other hand and watched the man pour some stinky fluid into a graduated cylinder. His home wouldn't be peaceful. It would be dull. Too much seclusion wasn't good for the soul.

One of those two would have to become more social, and it would have to be Hutch.

With her help, Rose had gone from school outcast to the girl named most likely to succeed. With her help, Mellie had gone from painfully shy to a well-liked member of the squadron.

A tingly sensation filled her belly. She

needed a new project, and John Hutchinson might be the one.

4

Gela
July 20, 1943

Hutch squinted through the eyepiece of his telescope. Only three days had passed since the full moon, so the night was brighter than he liked for stargazing, but Hutch never wasted an opportunity. The quiet ridge separating the 93rd Evac from the airfield had beckoned.

The binary star Algieba in the constellation Leo winked at him, low on the western horizon.

The cooler night air, the chirp of cicadas, and the stars in their familiar shifting patterns eased the twinges of pain in his stomach.

On his way to the enlisted men's mess for supper, he'd run into Bergie and they'd discussed the heavy patient load. Capt. Al Chadwick, one of Bergie's tent mates, summoned Bergie for an emergency surgery.

After Bergie left, Chadwick gave Hutch a long look. "Don't you have anything to do, boy?"

The pain flared, and Hutch pressed his hand against his rib cage. Dad had served as a pharmacist for almost thirty years, and no one had ever called him "boy."

Something rustled in the grass behind him.

Hutch sucked in his breath. Like all medical personnel, he was unarmed. The Allies had made rapid advances the last few days, but the Germans were famous for leaving troops to wreak havoc behind the lines.

More rustling. Someone walked straight toward him. What could he do? Whack him on the head with his telescope? And what was the parole and countersign for the Husky landings? That's right — "George" and "Marshall" for the Army Chief of Staff. Hutch cleared his throat. "George!"

Feminine laughter greeted him. "Close. My name's Georgie. I'm a nurse."

A sigh rushed out. "Georgie Taylor? What are you doing out at night?"

"Hutch? Is that you?"

"Yeah." He stifled a quick thrill that the cute nurse recognized his voice. "What are you doing out here? It isn't safe."

"When I'm nervous, I can't sleep. And

when I can't sleep, I have to walk. But I stay close, and I know they cleared the area of land mines. Is that a telescope?"

"Yeah. It's a hobby of mine."

"Mind if I join you?" She sat on the blanket next to him without waiting for an answer.

A smile edged up. So much for his quiet evening. He looked into his telescope again. Algieba disappeared below the horizon. "Be my guest."

"Thanks again for the aspirin. I don't know what we'd have done without it."

"You're welcome." She'd already thanked him profusely when he delivered it to the airfield the other day. He liked the way her Southern accent swirled "thank you" into "thankee-you."

"What are you looking at?"

"You're interested? Or are you just making conversation?"

Georgie hugged her knees. She seemed to be wearing pajamas and a bathrobe. "I always liked looking at the stars with Daddy. Orion's my favorite."

"One of mine too, but he won't be out until long after midnight." He rotated the tripod so his telescope faced Cygnus. "You'll like this."

"What is it?"

"Let me get it focused. There we go." He scooted to the side.

She held back her hair and gazed through the eyepiece. "What am I — oh, isn't that pretty? One's blue, one's yellow."

"That's Albireo. It's a double star that forms the head of Cygnus the Swan."

"That's just about the most beautiful thing, isn't it? God is so colorful and creative."

"Yep." He motioned Georgie to the side and readjusted the telescope. "That's one of the reasons I like stargazing. It also reminds me how big he is and how little I am."

"What are you showing me next?" Enthusiasm lit her voice.

"You can see this without a telescope. If you want to see signs of God in the sky, you can't get better than this." He traced a pattern with his finger. "From Albireo, draw a straight line that way, through those two bright stars, then another line that way."

"It's a cross."

"The Northern Cross. The Greeks called it Cygnus. They say Zeus disguised himself as a swan to make Leda fall in love with him." He made a face. Not the best story to tell when he was alone with a girl at night.

"Those Greek gods always made a mess of things, didn't they?"

Hutch chuckled, conscious of the feminine presence beside him. Would Phyllis believe this was innocent? What about Georgie's boyfriend? What would the man think about his girl traipsing about at night?

He readjusted the telescope. "You said you couldn't sleep because you were nervous?"

"I shouldn't have said that." A deep sigh. "I suppose I can tell you. You don't seem like the kind of man who'd blab other people's business."

"Never blabbed in my life."

Georgie didn't speak, which seemed unusual for her, so Hutch tightened the screws on his tripod.

"All right," she said. "I'm a big ol' fraidy-cat. I try to be brave, but I've never been so close to the front, and the flights are more dangerous here than over North Africa. Worst of all, I'm afraid something will happen, and I'll freeze, and I won't help my patients."

Hutch straightened. The moonlight illuminated anxiety on her face.

She hugged her knees tighter. "I don't know why I told you that. Mellie kind of knows, but she thinks I'm over it, and Lieutenant Lambert — she suspects — but I've never blurted it all out before."

He nodded. He had that effect on people.

"I'm quiet. I'm safe."

Her shoulders lowered. "That must be it. My daddy's the same way. He makes me talk more by saying nothing than Mama does with a million words."

Hutch turned his attention to the telescope. What was he going to show her again?

"You must think I'm horrible."

"Horrible?" He snapped his gaze back to her. "Of course not. But I wonder . . ."

"Wonder what?"

"Well, flight nursing is voluntary. Like everything in the Army Air Forces. So how'd you end up in the program?"

"Simple. I followed Rose."

"Rose?"

"She's my best friend. When she found out about medical air evacuation, she had to be a part of it, so I came along too."

Hutch leaned back on his hands, and his gaze followed the bright streak of the Milky Way. "So you did something you didn't want to because of a friend."

"Yes, but it's worth it. We need each other. And I'll do fine. Sicily's nerve-wracking, but I'll adjust."

High overhead, the North Star sat immovable while all the constellations swung around, changing with the time and the season. "Do other people always make decisions for you?"

"Excuse me?" Her voice tightened.

That did sound rude. "It's — you're the baby of the family, aren't you?"

A small laugh. "And you accused me of playing psychologist."

"Well, are you?"

"Yes." She stretched the word around like a piece of elastic.

"I thought so. You remind me of my youngest sister, Lizzie. Everyone's always made decisions for her, and she likes it that way. She's always running to Dad, Mom, me — 'What should I do, John? Tell me.' "

"And you tell her like a good brother."

"I used to. Then I realized she had to grow up and make her own decisions. I give her advice, help her weigh her options, but I refuse to tell her what to do."

Georgie eased back. "Do you think I need to grow up too?"

He'd stepped into that one, hadn't he? "Wait a minute. First of all, I don't know you that well. What's important is — do you think you need to grow up?"

"I am grown-up. I made the decision to come here on my own. Yes, I followed Rose, but my parents and Ward didn't want me to come."

"There's your answer." He returned to the

55

telescope. "Want to see something else?"

"Oh yes." She sprang to her knees and scooted closer.

Hutch caught his breath and edged to the side. "It's a little group of stars that looks like a coat hanger. Right there below Cygnus's beak. Almost as if the swan dropped it in flight."

"Isn't that cute?" She gazed through the telescope while the moonlight cast arcs of light on her curls.

He looked away, down the slight rise to the hospital complex, its tents in perfect military order.

"How'd you end up here, Hutch?"

"Drafted."

"When?"

"First round. Got inducted December of '40. I was only supposed to serve a year, but you know the story."

"Pearl Harbor."

"I was there."

She gasped. "You were there?"

"Well, I was on Oahu. Serving at Tripler Army Hospital. We weren't bombed, but we dealt with the casualties."

"Oh my goodness. Then you transferred to the 93rd?"

A wave of fatigue caught up to him. It had to be close to midnight. "The Army transferred me to the 5th General Hospital at Fort Dix in January '42. Got sent to Northern Ireland, then to England. This May, I got orders to transfer to the 93rd in Algeria. Got off the boat, and there's Bergie. Turns out it was his doing."

"So . . ." A teasing lilt danced through her voice. "Do other people always make decisions for you?"

He laughed. "Okay, I deserved that."

"Yes, you did."

"In the Army, the only decision I made was being a pharmacist, and that was only because my dad has friends in Congress who yanked strings."

"Friends in Congress?"

Hutch drew in his feet to sit cross-legged. "He's a pharmacist too, a leader in the American Pharmaceutical Association. They're working on legislation to create a Pharmacy Corps, so the Army will use pharmacists properly and as officers, and the soldiers will get the same safe care they do at home. The state of pharmacy in the military stinks, so Dad wanted me to provide eyewitness testimony. Which I've done."

"You're a good son."

"Yep." A firm nod. "I'm Isaac."

Georgie's laugh bubbled low like water in a brook. "Isaac? Like in the Bible?"

"My father's like Abraham, a great man and leader, and I'm the 'son of the promise' set to follow in his footsteps. Like Isaac, I even needed help to find my future wife."

"So . . ." There was that lilt again. "Did your daddy ever put you on the altar?"

He laughed. "In a way. I could have taken an officer's commission and served in another capacity, but I chose to practice my profession instead."

"So you went willingly, like Isaac."

"Yes. I sacrificed for a good cause."

Georgie rested her chin on her knees. "That must help you be content."

Hutch screwed the telescope off its tripod. He needed to get some sack time. "Content? Nope. Contentment would mean surrender to the status quo. I'm fighting for a better system."

"Hmm." She rolled the edge of the blanket in her fingers. "Does that require sacrificing your peace?"

Peace? In the middle of war? But after all, wasn't that what God promised? Hutch laid his telescope in its case.

The petite brunette sat beside him in the moonlight. He'd challenged her, and now she challenged him. Beneath that charming vulnerability lay admirable strength.

He held out his hand. "How about a deal?

You learn to make your own decisions, and I'll learn to be content."

"Deal." Her tiny cool hand slipped into his.

He shook her hand and dropped it. Quick. He never ran from a challenge, but he always ran from temptation.

5

Valle dei Templi, Agrigento, Sicily
July 24, 1943

"Can you believe this is 2,500 years old?" Georgie's gaze climbed the columns of the Temple of Hera. The roof was long gone, but columns still soared skyward. "I never thought we'd see Greek ruins in Sicily."

"Mm-hmm." Mellie Blake looked down the sun-baked slope to the Mediterranean.

Georgie and Rose exchanged a worried glance. Only depression could dull Mellie's interest in sightseeing.

That morning, Vera and Alice framed Mellie and made it look as if she'd pulled a nasty prank on them. To top it off, Lieutenant Lambert believed Vera and Alice's side of the story.

Rose hooked her arm through Mellie's. "Don't worry. We believe you."

Georgie cringed. They came on this trip to take Mellie's mind off her troubles, not to focus on them.

Mellie lifted a feeble smile. "I know."

If they were on the subject, they might as well talk it all the way through. Georgie took Mellie's other arm and led the ladies along the ridge toward the next of the seven temples. "I don't understand why they'd do such a thing."

"They're just mean," Rose said.

Georgie shook her head and found the path through the olive trees. "They're nurses and good ones. They care. There has to be a reason, but I can't imagine what it could be. What do they have against you?"

Mellie's chin lifted, and pain flickered through her exotic dark eyes. "I refuse to gossip."

"It's not gossip if you're defending yourself."

"In this case, it would be. Can we talk about something else?"

"You want to talk about Tom?" Rose asked in a gentle voice. A week before, Mellie had evacuated her pen pal to Tunisia with a raging fever. He still hadn't figured out her identity, and Mellie refused to tell him.

Mellie gazed into the distance as if nothing lay before her. "I wish I knew how he was doing."

Georgie patted her arm. "They have us

flying so often, you're sure to get a chance to go to Tunisia. You said he's at the hospital right by the airfield in Mateur."

"True." Some light returned to her eyes. "I'm praying hard for him."

"We are too, honey."

"Yes, we are," Rose said.

"You two are the best of friends. I'm so glad I met you." Her pace picked up. "You and Tom have been good for me. You know a relationship is strong when it makes you grow."

Georgie and Rose murmured their agreement. Georgie had seen that with Clint and Rose as well. And with her and Ward . . .

She frowned and ducked around an olive tree, its leaves fragrant and dusty. Ward helped her grow, didn't he?

"Oh my," Mellie said. "Would you look at that?"

Farther along the ridgeline stood a temple, completely intact, the Temple of Concordia.

Rose shielded her eyes against the afternoon sun. "Why do they call it the Valley of Temples when it's along a ridge?"

"The Ridge of Temples." Georgie cocked her head to one side. "Not very poetic."

"It would be if you said it in Italian."

Georgie smiled at the perk in Mellie's voice.

Before long they stood in front of the Temple of Concordia. Triangular pediments crowned elegant Doric columns with their simple capitals. Hutch would enjoy the Valle dei Templi with his knowledge of constellations and Greek mythology.

A ripple of sadness. She probably wouldn't see the quiet pharmacist again. Although the British were bogged down on the east coast of Sicily, the Americans had cleared the entire western half of the island and seized Palermo on the north coast. Today the 802nd had transferred forty miles north to Agrigento. Who knew where the 93rd Evac would go?

Still, Georgie treasured their short friendship. Hutch had made her uncomfortable when he implied she didn't make her own decisions, but he had a point. Perhaps she needed to change and grow. What if something happened to Ward? To her parents? Where would she turn?

She studied the classic lines of the Greek temple. Concordia meant peace, and Georgie needed to grow to find it.

A bowl of Atabrine tablets sat on a table in the doorway to the officers' mess tent.

Georgie picked out her daily dose, and the clerk checked off her name.

63

She stepped away and stared at the little yellow pill. What if she didn't take it? What if she left a gap in her mosquito netting? A rip-roaring case of malaria could get her sent home.

Heart pounding, she slipped the tablet in her trouser pocket. She didn't belong here. Lieutenant Lambert would welcome the excuse to replace Georgie with a competent nurse.

A medical discharge, and Georgie could marry Ward and settle down on his farm and raise lots of apples and tomatoes and babies. She could still help the war effort at home. With her energy and enthusiasm, she could raise money, gather scrap, and improve morale.

She belonged in Virginia.

Georgie settled on a camp stool next to Rose and Mellie, and gave them a cheery greeting, although the Atabrine tablet sat heavy and hot in her pocket.

"Mail came." Rose passed Georgie a square V-mail envelope.

Georgie sighed and opened the letter from Ward. V-mail was patriotic but not terribly romantic. His single sheet of paper was photographed stateside, the film was shipped overseas, and the letter was printed one-quarter size and delivered. The V-mail system freed precious shipping space for troops, weapons, and supplies, but Ward wasn't required to use it. Why couldn't he send a long letter like Tom sent Mellie?

She smiled and peered at the tiny handwriting. For Ward, V-mail was a long letter.

Dear Georgie,

How are you? All is well here. I have a bumper crop of tomatoes, and prices are solid.

I wish you could be here to see the harvest, but I'm looking forward to showing you the farm soon. You'll like it.

How much longer until you come home? I want to marry you more than ever. It's hard to run both the farm and a house. I had to hire Pearline Gibbs to clean and cook for me. Don't worry though. You alone have my heart.

Myrtle Ferguson came home on furlough last week after training with the WAVES. You wouldn't recognize her, she's gotten so hard and headstrong. That's what the military does to girls, and it isn't natural.

Every night I pray that won't happen to you. I don't want you to change one whit. I want my Georgie back same as she's always been.

Around the tent, nurses laughed and chatted. Nothing hard or headstrong about them. While strong and confident, they remained compassionate and feminine.

Georgie alone lacked strength.

Ward didn't want her to change one whit. But what if she needed to change? Everyone did. Only the Lord was perfect.

Hutch was right. She needed to learn to make her own decisions.

Although she longed for the comforts of home and family, comfort wouldn't help her grow. Perhaps she needed discomfort, a little dirt and danger in her life.

Only one question mattered. What was God's will? Did he want her home with Ward? Or did he want her in Sicily with her friends?

Georgie rested her hand in her lap, on the hard lump of Atabrine. Her plan to get a medical discharge was unethical, and worse — she was trying to manipulate God's will to match hers.

She slipped the tablet out of her pocket and into her mouth. If the Lord wanted her to go home, he'd make a way.

6

On the horizon, the gibbous moon cast pale gray light on the battered landscape.

Hutch poked his arm out the truck window and twisted his wrist until he could see his watch. One thirty. The 93rd Evac convoy had been on the road for ten hours, heading north from Gela through Sicily's rugged heart.

The truck wrenched down into another pothole. Hutch banged his helmet on the roof of the truck. Again. Height had some disadvantages.

At the wheel, Dom Bruno cussed. Beside him, Ralph O'Shea snored. How could the man sleep? And how could the equipment and medication bottles survive the journey?

Dom leaned over the wheel and squinted at the road. The hospital traveled in complete blackout conditions to prevent attack from the air. Their new location at Petralia would be only four miles from the front and twenty miles from Sicily's north shore.

"Not again." Dom stomped on the brakes, and Ralph's head flopped onto Hutch's shoulder.

"Another hairpin turn?" Hutch nudged Ralph away.

"Yeah. This road's more treacherous than Hitler."

"No kidding." Hutch climbed out of the truck to help navigate the tight turn to the right.

Roads built for peasants, mules, and wagons couldn't handle US Army two-and-a-half-ton trucks.

He jogged behind the truck and around to the driver's side. The moonlight illuminated a steep drop-off to the left side of the truck, perhaps a hundred feet, with only scraggly bushes to break the fall. Better that Dom didn't know.

"Ready?" He stood by the left rear tire and shivered in the cool mountain air.

Dom gave the thumbs-up and threw the truck into reverse.

Hutch motioned him backward, watching the road, the truck, and his own step. "More. More. A little more. Stop!"

The vehicle halted about two feet from

the rim. Dom cranked the wheel to the right and eased around the bend. Good. Only one reverse on this hairpin. The last one took three tries.

Hutch ran around and hopped back inside. Ahead, the landscape opened up to reveal the remains of a village. Large dark letters on the first building proclaimed, *"Viva Mussolini!"* But the dictator's name had been crossed out, and it now read, *"Viva Americani!"*

The Italians seemed to have lost all heart for fascism and the war it created, and they surrendered gladly and in droves. The Germans, on the other hand, fought tenaciously.

Many of the village's buildings had been reduced to rubble. A young woman wrapped in a shawl huddled inside a freestanding doorway and watched the convoy. A beautiful woman, sure to attract many GIs.

Hutch wouldn't be one of them. If only he could convince Phyllis. Her last letter reeked of loneliness and anxiety.

He drummed his fingers on the rim of the truck door. Good thing Phyllis didn't know he'd spent a pleasant evening under the stars with a cute little nurse.

As for Georgie, she adored her Ward and wasn't the cheating type. As for Hutch, he'd had plenty of opportunities in Hawaii and Ireland and England, and never once had a girl turned his head. He was committed to Phyllis, and nothing could shake that.

But how to convince her? She'd always been insecure in his love.

Hutch leaned out the truck window and inhaled mountain freshness, tainted by smells of motor oil, dust, and death. He looked up to the stars, but the rough ride bucked the familiar patterns before his eyes.

Phyllis had never stargazed with him. She always had an excuse. Too cold, too damp, too many bugs. She never minded him going by himself, but he wished she'd come. Something about the dark and quiet encouraged deep and intimate conversation.

After the war, Hutch would marry Phyllis as soon as he stepped off the boat. They'd spend quiet evenings at home, reading and listening to the radio. But to break the monotony, they'd need occasional evenings out. She'd balk as always, and he'd coax her. And he'd fail as always. Then Bergie would drag them out.

Hutch sighed and clenched the door rim. He and Phyllis would always need a Bergie in their lives.

Dom hit the brakes. "Now what?"

The line of trucks ground to a halt outside

the village. Truck doors thumped shut toward the front of the line.

Hutch craned his head out the window. An officer approached, one he didn't know.

"What's happening, Lieutenant?"

"A roadblock." He glanced at Hutch's sleeve. "Get out and do your job."

"My job? I'm a pharmacist."

"Listen, pal, I don't need any smart alecks. I don't care if you're a Rockefeller. Get out and remove that roadblock. That lazy bum beside you too. All but the driver."

"Yes, sir. I didn't mean any disrespect." Hutch shook Ralph awake and hopped out of the truck. The last thing he needed was to be written up for insubordination.

Hutch headed for the front of the convoy with the other enlisted men, past trucks filled with equipment and other trucks filled with officers high above the riffraff.

His hands fisted, and his arms swung harder than necessary. He didn't mind manual labor, but he did mind how some men sat and watched while others did all the work.

Wasn't America about democracy and equality? Wasn't that what they were fighting for?

Hutch followed barked orders and grabbed one end of a log while Ralph

71

grabbed the other end. When he became an officer, he wouldn't treat enlisted men like this.

7

Over the Mediterranean
August 7, 1943

Sergeant Jacoby stepped into the C-47 cabin from the radio room. "Landing in ten minutes."

"Thanks, Sergeant." Georgie scanned her flight manifest one last time. Her data was complete, every patient well cared for and in good spirits. Perhaps she could handle this job.

"All right, gentlemen. In a few minutes you'll be in Tunisia." She made her way down the aisle. The fighting had intensified the last few days as the Americans grappled with the Germans for Troina and the San Fratello Ridge, which meant frequent evacuation flights.

A hand grasped hers. "Please, nurse. I'm thirsty. So thirsty."

Georgie smiled at Private Hawkins, who was recovering from abdominal surgery due to a rifle wound. "We'll be in Tuni—"

He was too pale. Restless. His hand chilled her. Georgie leaned closer, her mind tingling with concern. "Are you all right?"

"Thirsty." He rubbed his throat with white fingers.

She wrapped her hand around his wrist to measure his pulse — rapid as she feared. No doubt about it. He was going into shock, probably from postsurgical internal bleeding.

"I — I'll get you some water." Georgie dashed for the back of the plane. She knew the treatment for shock. Keep the patient warm. Put him in Trendelenburg position with feet higher than the heart — but the litter was clamped into aluminum brackets and couldn't be tilted. Plasma and oxygen — but how could she administer them safely during landing?

Sergeant Jacoby sat on the floor behind the litters.

"It's Private Hawkins," she said. "He — he's going into shock."

"Oh wow. Lousy timing."

"What are we going to do?" Her voice edged high.

He got to his feet and gave her a strange look. "Treat him."

"But we — we're landing. How can we —"

Jacoby took her by the shoulders. "Pull yourself together, Lieutenant. The patient comes first."

"I know. I know." She flipped open the medical chest and grabbed a plasma administration set, gauze, and iodine.

"I'll get the oxygen equipment and some more blankets."

"Thank you." She tried to draw a deep breath, but it snagged on her rough throat. *Lord, help me calm down and take care of the patient.*

Georgie hurried back to Private Hawkins's litter, in the midlevel bracket at hip height. The plane's nose tipped down. How long until landing? She and Jacoby would be bounced around like pinballs.

She knelt, ripped the tape off the cardboard box, and pulled the string to lift out two tin cans. Although her hands shook, she pried the key off the first can and opened it. Fluffy white plasma flakes filled the glass bottle like snow in a snow globe.

"Water?" Hawkins groped for Georgie's arm.

"Oxygen." Jacoby wedged a portable tank between Hawkins's hip and the fuselage, and he fitted the rubber oxygen mask over the patient's face.

The second tin can yielded a bottle of sterile water and the IV administration set. After she wiped the rubber stoppers of both bottles with iodine, she inserted a double-ended needle into the water bottle. With lips tucked between her teeth, she stilled the needle long enough to thrust it into the plasma bottle's rubber stopper. Thank goodness the vacuum didn't break, and water streamed over the plasma flakes.

"I'll dissolve it." Jacoby eased the bottle out of her hand and looked her firm in the eye. "You're the only one who can start the IV."

The IV. What would happen if the plane landed while she was inserting the needle? She had to hurry. She had to relax.

Daddy would tell her to roll her shoulders. Mama would tell her to pray. Georgie did both.

Patient care — she was good at that. She smiled at Hawkins while she swabbed the inside of his elbow with iodine. "We believe in only the finest service on this flight. The highest-quality fluids, delivered by IV, so you don't even have to swallow. What do you think of that?"

Bushy eyebrows twitched, but he didn't make a noise behind the oxygen mask.

Lethargy was common in shock.

So were collapsed veins. Georgie palpated the antecubital area. "There. I found a vein."

Jacoby set the end of the tubing, with needle already attached, in Georgie's hand. "You can do it." He didn't sound convinced.

Georgie's shoulders stiffened. She wasn't sure she could do it either. The plane's vibrations blurred the pale blue line of the vein, and the needle wiggled in her shaking grasp. She pulled his skin taut, rested the needle on the surface, and slipped it in. She missed. "Oh no."

"Come on, Lieutenant." Jacoby's voice strained.

"Okay. Okay." She switched hands, stretched out her fingers to relax them, and massaged the patient's vein. Before the shaking could resume, she plunged in the needle. "Got it."

"Good." The word poured from Jacoby's mouth as the life-giving fluids poured into Hawkins's body.

The plane leveled off. A mild floating sensation.

"The flare before landing." Jacoby looped his arm around a litter support while holding the plasma bottle high. "Hold on. Watch out for that tank."

Facing the back of the plane, Georgie

grabbed a stirrup-shaped foot under the litter and leaned across his body to secure the oxygen tank. *Lord, keep us safe.*

The landing crumpled her knees, pitched her forward, wrenched her fingers around the stirrup. Pain shot through her fingers. "Ow!"

"You all right?" Jacoby hadn't even budged.

She got her feet back under her and stretched her sore hand. "I'm all right."

"Here. Hold this." He thrust the plasma bottle at her. "I'll open the door."

Georgie grimaced from the pain and transferred the bottle to her good hand.

Fresh hot air and African sunshine flowed through the open door. Jacoby returned with a ground crewman and showed him how to unclamp the litter from the brackets. They rushed Private Hawkins off the plane, and Georgie followed alongside with the plasma elevated.

A physician stood outside the receiving tent, hand lifted to shield his eyes from the late morning sun.

Georgie flagged him over. "Doctor! We have a patient in shock."

While she reported the private's condition, Sergeant Jacoby recruited other men to unload the plane. Medics whisked Hawkins to the shock ward to prep him for surgery, and Georgie discussed the remaining cases with the physician.

Half an hour later, the patients had been sent to the appropriate wards.

Georgie's hand throbbed but hadn't swollen. Good. She'd almost finished sewing a sundress for Mellie, and she needed to hurry. If her plan didn't succeed, Mellie Blake would go home soon.

In front of the next tent, Vera Viviani and Alice Olson stood talking. The two nurses formed a vital part of Georgie's plan, but she could barely stomach speaking to them after how they'd treated Mellie. Nevertheless, she set a warm smile on her face.

Daddy said privilege came with responsibility. The Taylors were blessed financially, and they had a responsibility to give financially. Georgie was blessed socially, and she had the responsibility to embrace outsiders. Vera and Alice were blessed with fine minds and gorgeous faces, but they used their privilege for power over others.

That rubbed Georgie the wrong way.

"Hi, ladies," she said with a sweet smile. "How were your flights?"

Alice's perfectly plucked blonde eyebrows sprang high. Vera glanced at Georgie, then down and away. Probably surprised at

Georgie's friendliness and ashamed of their own behavior, as they should be. "Fine," Vera mumbled.

"I'm not surprised, since you two are such talented nurses." Georgie ladled out Southern charm as thick as syrup. "That's why Mellie wanted you to stay in the 802nd, because you're so gifted."

Color rose in Alice's cheeks, and Vera stared at the tarmac. After the dirty trick they'd played on Mellie, they deserved to be uncomfortable. When Lieutenant Lambert had discovered the truth, she decided to send Vera and Alice home, but Mellie pleaded for Lambert to give them a second chance — and to send her home instead. Mellie's sacrifice sang of mercy, but insecurity fueled the decision.

Georgie planned to rectify it.

She pulled a sheet of paper from her trouser pocket. "Speaking of Mellie, I knew you two would want to be involved in this."

"With — with what?" Vera's gaze darted to Georgie.

"A petition." She handed Vera the paper with a flourish. "To keep Mellie in the squadron. You know what a good nurse she is — so brave and caring and smart. And you know how she helps us with her knowledge of living in the field. She's such an asset, don't you think?"

"Yes." Alice didn't raise her head. No one whined about Mellie's survival tips more than Alice.

Georgie pressed her hand over her heart. "She's kind and giving, which is even more special since she was so shy when she joined us. She's changed so much, don't you think?"

"She has." Vera chewed on her full lips as she read the petition.

"As you can see, you two are the only ones in the entire squadron who haven't signed it yet. I wanted your signatures to be last, big and bold like John Hancock himself. Only fitting after all Mellie's done for you." She tipped her head to the side and raised her sweetest smile.

Vera blinked in a flurry of long black lashes. "I — I still don't understand why she did that."

Georgie's heart softened, and she rested a hand on Vera's stiff forearm. "Because she loves the Lord, and she shows her love by being merciful to others."

Alice crossed her arms and hunched her shoulders. "It doesn't make sense."

"There's another reason. She honestly thinks she doesn't belong in the squadron, that everyone wants her to leave. I can't imagine why she'd think that." Georgie gave them an exaggerated puzzled look. Vera and Alice had done everything possible to make Mellie feel unwelcome from the first hello.

In tandem, the two beauties glanced at Georgie, at each other, then down at the ground.

Georgie wrestled down a triumphant smirk. A little guilt would do them a lot of good.

She waited a moment to let the guilt sink in, then tapped the petition in Vera's hand. "See? I left a big space at the bottom for you. Feel free to add a personal note. Most everyone did." Was it wrong to enjoy this so much?

Vera and Alice signed the petition and handed it back.

Georgie tucked it in her pocket. "Thank you. You don't know how much this means to me, and how much this will mean to Mellie. She deserves to know she's loved." A bit much, but it was fun to watch Vera and Alice writhe.

She headed for the mess tent to grab lunch before the planes headed back to Sicily, loaded with supplies.

"One question," Alice called out.

"Yes?"

Alice frowned. "There can only be twenty-four nurses in the squadron, twenty-five if you count the chief. Two replacements have already arrived. So . . ."

So one nurse would have to leave. The selfish little twerp, still only concerned with her own job.

Regardless, she smiled. "We'll leave that to Lieutenant Lambert."

A single lightbulb dangled over Lieutenant Lambert's field desk and illuminated the faintest lines around the corners of her eyes.

Georgie clasped sweaty hands before her stomach and waited.

"No one told me a chief nurse needed juggling skills." She flipped through papers. "Mellie volunteers to go home, Sylvia needs to go home to recuperate from her malaria, you bring me a petition demanding Mellie stay, Wilma — oh, for heaven's sake. Now this complaint from Sergeant Jacoby."

"Yes, ma'am." The words stumbled over Georgie's thickened tongue. "I failed today. I'll take Mellie's place. Please let her stay. She's an excellent nurse."

A harried expression crossed the chief's face. "Now you're volunteering to leave?"

Georgie nodded, but a heavy sensation pressed on her heart. Why? Wasn't her deepest longing to go home?

Lambert gathered her papers into a pile. "It's not that simple. Wilma came in earlier. She and her husband are expecting a baby. She'll take Mellie's place. You'll have to stay."

"Oh." The pressure on her heart eased, then bore down again. What would happen the next time she faced a crisis?

"I don't know what to do with you." The chief rubbed her forehead. "You're such a good nurse, but you're jittery. I can't have you endangering patient lives."

Shame drifted down on her, dark and suffocating. "I understand, ma'am."

"I'll ground you for a while, give you other duties, maybe some easy flights, see if you adjust."

Georgie straightened her shoulders. Something deep inside her wanted to find the strength to adjust.

8

93rd Evacuation Hospital, San Stefano, Sicily
August 10, 1943

Hutch could compound terpin hydrate with codeine cough syrup in his sleep, but for Dominic Bruno's benefit, he'd work from the book.

"Elixirs . . ." Hutch flipped through the War Department's *Technical Manual TM 8-233: Methods for Pharmacy Technicians.* "Elixir Terpini Hydratis et Codeinae."

Dom leaned against the counter and huffed. "Figures. All I got out of high school Latin was *'veni, vidi, vici.'* "

"Appropriate. You *came* to work, you *saw* the recipe, and you'll *conquer* it."

"I expect the Medal of Honor for this."

"Kaz will nominate you."

"Not if he hears us call him Kaz."

Hutch laughed and pulled out the 1,000-cc Erlenmeyer flask. Good thing Lieutenant Kazokov wasn't around today to hear his nickname. Poor man had been sick with dysentery since the 93rd left Petralia for San Stefano three days earlier. "Okay, Dom. Study the recipe. Gather your ingredients."

"What are you baking today?" A feminine voice skipped into Hutch's ear.

He turned and smiled. "Lieutenant Taylor. What are you doing here?"

She wagged her finger at him, a cute scolding look on her face. "Call me Georgie, or I'll write you up for insubordination."

"Yes, sir. Ma'am." He snapped a sharp salute, a bit too glad to see her. A little sister. She was like a little sister to him. "What are you doing in San Stefano?"

"We're based in Termini now." She adjusted the dark blue garrison cap pinned over her brown curls. "My chief nurse told me the 93rd had moved to the north coast not far from us and asked me to toddle over and see if y'all had any candidates for air evac. I jumped at the chance."

Hutch sorted through her pile of words and gave Georgie half a smile. "Sorry, but we don't have any candidates for air evac, do we, Dom?"

"Speak for yourself. I'll volunteer. Where do I sign up, baby?"

Hutch tapped the bottle of terpin hydrate.

"Weigh out seventeen grams."

Georgie leaned her forearms on the wall of crates that kept people out of the main pharmacy area. "I have another reason for coming, and this one's a good one."

"Yeah?" Hutch tore his gaze from her pretty smile, poured 425 cc of ethanol into his largest graduated cylinder, and bent to inspect the fluid level. A few more drops.

"Don't you want to know what it is?"

"I figured you'd get around to telling me." His mouth twitched.

"If you're going to tease me, I won't —" A dramatic sigh. "Oh yes, I will. I have the best plan. You're going to love it. You know victory in Sicily is just around the corner."

"Any day now." He glanced at the scales. "Seventeen grams?"

"Yeah." Dom poured the terpin hydrate into the Erlenmeyer.

"Twenty cc tincture of sweet orange peel."

"I'm throwing a party." Georgie's shoulders lifted. "On the beach by the airfield at Termini on the day after the island's secure. We'll have barbecue, and music, and swimming, and games, and all sorts of fun."

"Sounds great." Hutch poured the ethanol into the Erlenmeyer and swirled the flask to dissolve the terpin hydrate.

"I figured out a way to get you there,

Hutch."

"Me?" He set down the Erlenmeyer so he wouldn't drop it.

"Yes, you." Her big blue eyes sparkled with excitement and a hint of mischief. "You can bring your telescope and show everyone the constellations and tell their stories. Won't that be fun? Because you're officially an entertainer, you can come even though it's a party for officers, and you'd be free to enjoy a whole day at the beach."

Hutch groped for the bottle of glycerin. How long had it been since he'd gone to a party? Since he'd had time to relax?

He steeled his jaw and poured 400 cc of glycerin into the large graduate. "I can't take a day off. This is the Army."

"That's why I got permission from your CO, Colonel Currier." Her smile might break through to her ears if she weren't careful.

"You . . . you got me a day off?"

"Two." She chewed on one side of her lower lip, making the other side pooch out. "Are you angry with me?"

"Angry?" He shook off his shock so his smile could rise. "Are you kidding me? A day on the beach? Barbecue?"

Her face brightened again. "Oh, good. This is going to be fun. I have so much to celebrate now that I found out Mellie can stay in the squadron, and I can too. Oh, I can't wait for you to meet my friends."

Could she possibly get any cuter? Excitement animated her entire face.

Dom nudged him. "I added the orange stuff. Five cc spirit of bitter almond?"

"Yes." Hutch spun away and studied the recipe as if he didn't have it memorized. His heart thudded. What was he doing? An entire day with this girl?

"I'm glad you can come. The colonel will send you with an ambulance load of patients, then you'll catch an empty ambulance back the next day. Bring your telescope and swim trunks and a towel."

And a book. He'd lie on the beach and read. Georgie would get bored and go chat with her friends because she couldn't stay quiet for five minutes straight. Then he wouldn't be tempted. Even if he were, he wouldn't do anything. He loved Phyllis. He was committed to her.

"Mail call." A corporal stepped into the tent. "Got a letter and a magazine for Hutchinson. Two letters for O'Shea."

"Thanks. O'Shea's in the sack. He's working the night shift." Hutch scanned the cover of *The Journal of the American Pharmaceutical Association.* Good, more about the research on that wonder drug, penicillin. It promised to save a lot of lives. He set the journal on the counter, as well as an envelope addressed in his father's neat handwriting.

"Don't mind me." Georgie waved her hand at him. "Read the letter."

"Didn't want to be rude." He gave her a smile of gratitude and opened it.

July 12, 1943

Dear John,

I'm afraid this will be a short note. My mind is too consumed with good news to write much, but I wanted to inform you immediately.

The legislation for the Pharmacy Corps passed both the Senate and the House unanimously, and today President Roosevelt signed it into law. Resolutions from the American Legion and twenty state legislatures in favor of the bill definitely helped us. We're still waiting on the details, but the deal is done. As soon as I know what you need to do next, I'll inform you.

Your hard work has paid off, son, and now you'll reap your reward. Soon I'll address a letter to Lt. John Hutchinson.

90

Hutch stared at the letter. It was real. It was done. It would finally happen. Something built inside him until it exploded. He let out a whoop.

Georgie stared at him, jaw hanging open.

He laughed and whooped again. If he could, he'd grab her and spin her in a circle. This occasion called for spinning. "Roosevelt signed it. The Pharmacy Corps. It's happening."

Her eyes widened. "That's what you've been working for all these years. I'm so happy for you."

He held the letter high like a victory torch. Finally he'd get an officer's commission. Finally his profession would be taken seriously. Finally the soldier on the front would get the same quality care he did at home.

"I've got to tell Bergie."

"And Phyllis," Georgie said. "She'll be happy for you."

"Yes, she will." His grin escaped fully. He'd return stateside for Officer Candidate School and marry her immediately. No. He wouldn't. He'd wait until he could marry her in his officer's uniform.

"Bitter almond?" Dom said.

Bitter? Nothing bitter about this day.

Dom raised one thick dark eyebrow at him.

Oh yeah, the elixir. "Yes, then add the glycerin. I've got to tell Bergie."

Dom gave him a paternal smile. "You'll need a hall pass in case you run into an officer. Let's finish up this terpinius Brutus maximus, and you can deliver it."

"Yeah. Great idea."

"I'm leaving." Georgie waved. "The ambulance is probably loaded. I'll see you at the party. Now you have something to celebrate too."

"I certainly do." He waved good-bye, then whirled to the elixir. "Glycerin?"

"Added." Dom pointed to the scales. "While you chatted with Shirley Temple, I weighed out two grams codeine."

"Great." Hutch measured 100 cc simple syrup in the graduated cylinder. "Wonder if she tap-dances."

"Ask her at the party. But you'll want to tango instead." Dom marched an imaginary partner down the length of the tent and threw her into a deep dip.

Hutch rolled his eyes. "I won't dance with her. She's like a little sister. And I'm a happily engaged man."

"Doesn't mean you can't have your fun."

"Yes, it does." Hutch poured the simple syrup into the Erlenmeyer. "Line a funnel with filter paper."

"Ah, she wouldn't tango with you anyway. You're the most boring man in the world."

Hutch added the white codeine powder to the flask. "Thank you."

After they filtered the elixir, they poured it into 250-cc bottles for the wards, and Hutch affixed the labels he'd typed earlier.

"Hold down the fort." Hutch loaded the bottles into a cardboard box and left the tent. The midday sun blazed in his eyes, and he squinted. The wards that needed terpin hydrate lay ahead of him, but he detoured to his right toward the receiving tent where Bergie worked today.

Hutch strolled past Dressing and Dental, and past Bath. Someone shouted ahead of him. More yelling. Nurses and medics stopped outside Receiving and stared at the ruckus inside.

A loud cry. A helmet rolled out of the tent, and everyone gasped.

Bergie was in there. What was going on? Hutch strode forward.

"I ought to shoot you myself, you whimpering coward," a man shouted.

They needed help in there. Hutch made for the doorway.

An officer stomped out, holstered a pistol, and turned back to the tent. "I meant what I said about getting that coward out of here.

I won't have these cowards hanging around our hospitals."

Hutch tried to step back, but the man bumped into him. A steely gaze pierced him through. The man stood as tall as Hutch. He wore three stars on his helmet. He could only be one man. General George S. Patton, commander of the US Seventh Army.

"Sir," Hutch stammered. He saluted. "General Patton, sir."

Patton's gaze swept Hutch up and down, then he stormed past, grumbling about how psychoneurotics didn't belong in hospitals with brave wounded men.

Hutch fingered his necktie. Thank goodness he was wearing it. Patton levied heavy fines for men caught with an open collar.

But what on earth had just happened? He ducked inside the tent.

Col. Donald Currier stood next to Major Etter, the receiving officer. He shook a finger toward the tent entrance. "I don't care who he is. No one treats one of our patients like that. I'll write him up."

A dozen patients lay on cots. Everyone focused on a soldier who lay curled in a ball, sobbing.

Bergie knelt next to him and smoothed his hair. "Private? Are you all right? Don't worry. He left."

"My nerves. My nerves," the patient cried.

A nurse standing next to Hutch clucked her tongue. "I can't believe it. I can't believe the general slapped a patient."

Hutch sucked in a breath. Everyone knew what Patton thought of cowardice, but a hospital should be a safe place.

"The private's shell-shocked, poor thing," another nurse said.

Fire flashed in the first nurse's eyes. "I have half a mind to go slap the general myself."

Hutch didn't blame her. Combat fatigue had nothing to do with courage or lack thereof.

"You. Medic." Captain Chadwick flung a hand in Hutch's direction. "Go get the psychiatrist."

Hutch suddenly felt out of place. "I — I'm not a —"

Chadwick scowled. He grabbed Hutch's elbow and marched him out of the tent. "Hutchinson? What on earth were you doing in there? You're in the way. Go back to your drugstore and count your pills."

Hutch had a couple of inches on the doctor, and he pulled himself to his full height. "I'm delivering medications. And with all due respect, sir, there's more to pharmacy practice than counting pills."

95

"Is that so?" Chadwick crossed his arms and narrowed his gray eyes. "My uncle says otherwise."

"Your uncle?" Hutch said. "Sir."

"He's with the surgeon general's office. He says Army pharmacy is simple, and any intelligent boy who can read a label can do it."

Hutch's hand tightened around the box of elixir. He'd heard those words before, quoted in a furious letter from his father. They'd been spoken in November in congressional hearings on the Pharmacy Corps bill.

"Recognize that statement, don't you?" Chadwick's thin upper lip crept up. "Thought you might. Your father's that druggist rabble-rouser, isn't he? My uncle told me about him."

"My father —" Hutch pressed his lips together. He refused to forfeit his future by snapping up this man's putrid bait. "Sir, my father advocates patient safety. Now, if you'll excuse me, sir, I need to get back to my drugstore and count pills."

"Go ahead, boy." He waved him off. "For the record, three comes after two."

Hutch spun away and headed for the wards that needed his expertly compounded elixir. A spasm of pain ripped through his

96

stomach, and he pressed his hand over it.

"It doesn't matter. It doesn't matter." And it didn't. He had Dad's letter as proof.

The spasm subsided, and a bounce entered his step. After he got his commission, he'd watch Chadwick eat his words. Hutch would count the words as they went down.

9

Termini Imerese, Sicily
August 18, 1943

Georgie hugged herself, savoring the soft pink cotton of the sundress she'd sewn. This party couldn't get any better.

The officers based at Termini Airfield frolicked on Sicily's north coast, splashing in the impossible turquoise of the Tyrrhenian Sea, lounging on the sand, and playing games. The delectable smell of barbecue already filled the air. They'd eat around six, before sunset, and then the band would set up. Too bad the imbalanced ratio of nurses to men would limit dancing.

The sand caressed her bare toes as she strolled across the beach. She'd thrown a similar party the night before for the enlisted men, with the officers doing the work. Thank goodness the news of the Axis surrender in Sicily came before noon so she had time to set up.

The sense of peace and victory made the party perfect. She shoved aside the knowledge that the war was far from over and another invasion had to follow.

"Great party, Georgie." Kay Jobson sashayed past with a man on each arm and more in her wake. She wore a green two-piece swimsuit that complemented her green eyes and strawberry blonde hair. As if she needed any help.

Georgie wiggled her fingers in a wave. "Thanks, Kay. Have fun."

"I always do."

Once Kay was past, Georgie shuddered. The woman had no shame.

"Cold?" A masculine voice sounded behind her.

"Hutch!" Georgie spun around and grinned at him. "I was afraid you wouldn't make it."

"Can't rush the Army." He wore a khaki shirt and trousers, much smarter looking than the gray-green herringbone twill fatigues the men lived in. "Where should I put my telescope?"

Georgie led him down the beach. "We have a tarp in the band area to keep sand out of the instruments. Oh, I'm glad you're here."

"Thanks." He didn't smile, and his gaze

99

darted around the crowd.

She recognized the look. He didn't know anyone but her and didn't make friends quickly. "I can't wait to introduce you around. There's so much to do here. You can swim or play volleyball or baseball."

"I brought a book."

"A book?" She stopped and stared him down. "You're at a party. You're supposed to have fun."

He cocked half a smile. "Reading is fun."

She threw back her head and groaned. "Not today. Not at a party. You can read any old day. Today you play."

His smile grew. "Those of us with imaginations can play in our heads."

"Is that so? Why use your imagination when all this fun lies before you?"

He laughed. "All right. You win."

Georgie led him to the band area. "What do you want to do first? Swim? Volleyball?"

"In this heat? Swim." He set down his telescope case and a satchel. "But you don't have to entertain me all day."

"I want to swim too. Clint and Rose are playing in the surf, so I can introduce you."

Hutch unbuttoned his shirt. "Once I get these stripes off, I'll fit in better."

"You fit in fine." She turned away and slipped off her sundress from over her swimsuit. At least she wouldn't have to worry about him being attracted to her. Phyllis was a quiet, tall blonde, Georgie's opposite in every way.

"I may need your help to meet people, but I don't need help to find the water." Hutch strode across the beach on long muscular legs.

Oh dear. He looked mighty fine in swim trunks.

Georgie shook herself and followed. She'd thought of him as a skinny city boy, perhaps even scrawny, an illusion based on his height. He might be lean, but he certainly wasn't scrawny.

"Like a brother. A big brother," she mumbled.

Hutch plunged into the ocean, ducked beneath the surface, and shook water from his hair. "Feels great. It's got to be ninety degrees today."

"At least." Georgie stood at water's edge, and a wave crept forward and nibbled at her toes. "Is it true what they say? That the general slapped a patient at your hospital?"

"Wow. Rumors spread fast."

"Oh, good. It's only gossip."

Hutch kicked at the water. "No, it's true. I was there."

Georgie gasped and stepped in up to her

knees. "It's true? You saw it?"

"Not the actual slapping incident. I was heading into the tent to see Bergie — he saw the whole thing. But I did see Patton himself, almost ran into him."

"Oh my goodness. And the patient? Poor thing. Is he all right?"

"Bergie says he's shaken up. The psychiatrist confirmed the diagnosis of battle fatigue. But the patient was actually begging to return to the front. He's no coward. Patton returned the other day and apologized to him and to the hospital staff."

"That's good." Georgie trailed her hands through the water. "Why would he do such a thing?"

"He confused battle fatigue with cowardice." Hutch shrugged. "But I think there's more. We got hung up at Troina and San Fratello, finally broke through, but he wanted to get to Messina, and he wanted to beat the Brits to the prize. Frustrated goals can make a man snap."

"Hmm. What do you think Eisenhower will do with Patton?"

"Do? Nothing. We're at war. He's our best general, a military genius. The men like how he wins battles, even if we don't like his necktie rule." He patted his bare chest and grinned. "Maybe I should put my tie back on."

An officer ran into the waves, snatched a football out of the sky, and another man tackled him into the surf.

Saltwater rained down on Georgie. She cringed and laughed.

"About time you got wet." Hutch floated on his back and kicked water at her. "That's a swimsuit, not a stand-around suit."

Georgie smiled at the brotherly teasing. "Your little sisters must hate you."

"They love me. Teasing's good for them. Better than coddling." Mischief lit his smile.

She sloshed toward him. "Coddling? What makes you think I was coddled?"

"Weren't you?"

She tilted her head and raised one shoulder. "Only because I deserve it."

"I thought so." He stood in water up to his waist and grinned at her. A smattering of dark hair formed a *T* on his chest, emphasizing his broad shoulders. "Spoiled rotten."

"Humph. Spoiled perfect." Georgie teetered on the brink of flirtation and she didn't like it. She stepped backward and looked for Clint and Rose. A group would help, or a volleyball game.

"So, your parents spoil you, and your big

sisters spoil you. Does Ward?"

"Shamelessly." Her smile rose in relief. Nothing flirtatious about discussing their sweethearts. "You'd better spoil Miss Phyllis too."

"No." Hutch paddled parallel to the beach. "But I treat her well."

"You'd better." Georgie crouched low in the water, so nice and cool.

"There's a difference between being good to someone and being good for someone."

"You mean like helping each other grow?" A wave knocked Georgie onto her backside. She scrambled to get up before the water went over her head and made her hair frizzy.

"Mm-hmm." He swam along, oblivious to her clumsiness. "My parents have a great marriage, filled with love. But they can be hard on each other when necessary. They balance each other."

Was Ward good for her? Or just good to her? Georgie stood, shivered, and renewed her search for Rose.

What was she worried about? Daddy spoiled Mama, and they were the happiest couple ever. "Remember, every woman likes to be treated like a princess."

"Ah, Phyllis can be a princess on our wedding day. And that's coming soon." Hutch swam back with a big wet grin.

"Because of the Pharmacy Corps?"

"Yep. Still need details, but when I go home for Officer Candidate School, I'll marry her."

"That's so romantic and exciting. All your dreams coming true."

"Now I can be content."

She opened her mouth to remind him that contentment came from God not circumstances, but she pressed her lips together. The job of being good for Hutch belonged to Phyllis. "I'm glad everything's going your way. I'd hate to see you become bitter."

He shot her a glance, something dark in his eyes. Anger? Fear? Conviction?

Guilt washed through her, and she raised a hesitant smile, which he returned.

A splash behind her. Arms wrapped around her waist. Down she went, face-first into the surf. She spluttered to the surface. "Rose Danilovich! How dare you."

Rose sat in the water beside her, bursting with laughter. "Clint! Did you hear her scream? Like a little girl."

"I am a girl, and I'm not ashamed of it." Georgie stood and wiped water off her face. Now her hair would explode in a mass of unruly curls. "Any sign of Tom and Mellie?" Getting those two together had been the first success of the day. Tom had flown in,

105

Mellie had revealed her identity, and it was so romantic.

"Right behind you." Mellie stood at water's edge in her swimsuit, holding hands with Tom MacGilliver. Both glowed. They couldn't be more different — Mellie with her dark exotic beauty, and Tom with his blond boy-next-door good looks.

Georgie cocked her head. "Looks like you two had a nice — long — bike ride."

"We did." Mellie raised a hand to cover her wide smile, then dropped her hand.

"They deserve it." Clint helped Rose to her feet.

"True." Georgie's heart swelled with the joy of knowing she had a hand in their happy ending. But her day's work wasn't done yet. She stretched her hand toward Hutch. "Everyone, this is John Hutchinson, the pharmacist at the 93rd. Hutch, these are my friends, Rose Danilovich and her boyfriend, Clint Peters. Clint's a C-47 navigator. This is Mellie Blake and her — boyfriend?"

"That sure sounds good." Tom shook Hutch's hand. "Tom MacGilliver. Yes, I'm his son."

Georgie cringed. She'd meant to warn Hutch that he was about to meet the son and namesake of the notorious executed murderer.

"Nice to meet you." Hutch's face registered only the slightest shock. "Read about you in the *Stars and Stripes.*"

Clint chuckled and draped his arm over Rose's shoulder. "He's a better man than the article said, but nowhere near as heroic."

Tom led Mellie into the water. "Don't know about the better-man part, but I agree with the not-as-heroic part."

Mellie whispered in his ear, and he gave her an adoring smile.

Georgie glanced at Rose so she could roll her eyes and mouth the words she was certain Mellie had spoken — "You're *my* hero." But Rose gazed just as adoringly at Clint. Oh dear, it would be a long day with two pairs of lovebirds chirping around her.

"Where are you from, Hutch?" Clint asked.

Georgie smiled as a wave slurped sand from beneath her feet, glad Hutch could make more friends.

Rose tugged on Georgie's arm, a fake smile on her face. "May I talk to you for a minute?"

"Sure. Excuse me, everyone." She followed Rose through the shallow waves and glanced over her shoulder. Hutch said something about the Athletics, and Tom countered about the Pirates. Why did men enjoy arguing about sports?

"What is going on here?" Rose's voice hardened.

"What do you mean?"

"Hutch. You made him sound like a pathetic little thing, afraid of his shadow."

"What? I just said he was lonely and unhappy."

"You didn't say one word about him being tall, dark, and handsome."

Georgie couldn't deny that little truth. She shrugged. "He's engaged and getting married soon, and I have my Ward."

Rose glowered over the water toward the pharmacist. "I don't like this."

A long sigh blew through her lips. Rose had a teenage crush on Ward, which only dissolved a few months ago when she fell in love with Clint. She probably still wanted to protect Ward. And Georgie too.

She patted her friend's arm. "Don't worry. You know I'd never hurt Ward. And I trust Hutch. Besides, Mama taught me right. If that man lays even a pinky finger on me, I'll slap him across the Mediterranean."

"You would, wouldn't you?" Rose's smile returned. She gathered her dark blonde hair over her shoulder and wrung out seawater.

"Let me know if you do, because I want to watch."

Hutch's laughter rolled into her ear, deep and infectious. Thank goodness he'd never give her the chance to slap him. Thank goodness she'd never have to test her resolve to do so.

10

"To see Pegasus, you have to picture the great winged horse lying on his back." Hutch pointed out the constellation for the dozen men and women gathered around his telescope. "Those four stars — that's his body. Coming out from the lower corner, stretching this way, that's his neck and head."

"I don't see his wings," Georgie said.

Hutch smiled, but she wouldn't be able to see it in the dark. "For that, you'll have to use your imagination. You do have an imagination, don't you?"

"Funny."

"I thought so. You want to hear the story?"

"Of course. I love Pegasus." With her accent, she couldn't sound anything but delighted.

Hutch had picked the constellation for her horse-loving sake. "Pegasus couldn't be tamed. Wherever he struck the earth with his hoof, springs of water gushed forth. One day Athena gave Bellerophon a golden bridle, and he sneaked up behind Pegasus and captured him. Bellerophon rode the great horse into battle with the Chimera, which he defeated. But then the hero got too full of himself and tried to ride Pegasus up to Mount Olympus. The horse threw him to earth and continued on alone to Olympus, where he served Zeus."

Georgie sighed. "I don't think anything could be more beautiful than a winged horse, do you, Rose?"

"Oh! And rainbows! And daisies! And kitty-cats!" Rose's voice rang with affectionate mockery.

"You're such a tomboy." Georgie giggled.

Hutch adjusted the eyepiece of his telescope. "Who wants a closer look?"

Clint stood and helped Rose to her feet. "Later. We're heading back to the dance floor, if you can call it that."

The first chords of "String of Pearls" tickled his ears. If Phyllis were here, he'd dance too. "Have fun."

"We want more *vino*." A group of men stood and brushed sand from their trousers. "Thanks, Hutch."

"You're welcome."

Only Georgie remained. Hutch winced.

111

She wouldn't abandon him, but spending more time alone with her wouldn't be wise. Even though she'd put her sundress on again. He could still see her sweet figure in her swimsuit, still see her graceful arm draped over her knee as she sat on the beach, still see the sand clinging to the curves of her legs.

He squeezed his eyes shut, trying to burn his fading image of Phyllis back in place. A year and a half since he'd seen his fiancée.

"Oh dear," Georgie said. "I'm sorry they left. I'm sure they'll come back."

"That's okay." Now to release her to celebrate with her friends. "You don't have to —"

"May I ask you something?" She slid closer. But not too close. "It's been on the tip of my tongue all evening, but I didn't want to ask in front of the crowd."

"All right. What is it?" One question. Then he'd excuse her. She'd have more fun without him anyway.

"You know a lot about the constellations. So tell me. Why do people trust in the stars? In astrology? It seems silly to me."

He chuckled. "It is. The idea that the position of a ball of fire halfway across the universe determines the course of our lives."

"So they'd rather look to the stars than to

the God who made them. Why do people do that?"

"It's about control. God doesn't tell us everything we want to know. On purpose. So we learn to lean on him and trust him. People don't want that. They want quick answers. Astrology gives them that illusion."

"And why do you watch the stars?"

He grinned at the teasing in her voice. "Because they're beautiful. Because I know God made them. Because the stories are interesting."

"All right. You pass. Now may I see what you have in your telescope?"

So much for excusing her. But he had promised. "It's set up. The Andromeda Galaxy, right near Pegasus."

Georgie peered through. "When I was little, I used to imagine my horse had wings. It certainly felt like he did."

"Mm-hmm." He dug his bare toes into the warm sand. "You don't have to stick around on my account. I have my telescope, and the moon doesn't come up for another hour."

A soft sigh. "I don't want to dance. It wouldn't be right."

Hutch gazed to the expanse of the Mediterranean, lit only by pinpricks of reflected starlight. "Me neither."

"If you don't mind my company . . ."

"Of course not." What else could he say? "So how long have you and Ward been together?"

"Forever." She pulled back from the telescope, her voice perky again. "We were childhood friends, then high school sweethearts. He never officially proposed. We always knew we'd get married."

Just what Hutch needed to hear. "Why aren't you Mrs. . . . ?"

"Mrs. Manville. You know how it is. I wanted to get married right out of high school, but he wanted to save money to buy his own farm. So I followed Rose to nursing school to pass the time. He still wasn't ready, so Rose and I joined the Army Nurse Corps. Then the war came, and I was committed for the duration plus six months."

He let out a wry chuckle. "I definitely understand that."

"Now he has his own farm, and I'm over here."

"Mm."

She drew her knees to her chest and rearranged her skirt. "I know what you're thinking. I let other people make my decisions."

Hutch leaned back and burrowed his hands into the sand. The sound of the sea

114

added to the music. "What do you think? Are other people your stars?"

"My stars?"

"The ancients looked to the stars to tell them what to do. You look to other people."

"Oh." Her voice dove, and she lowered her chin to her knees. "I do, don't I? I just . . . I don't trust my own judgment."

He pointed up. "You see the North Star? It's only one degree from true north. It barely moves. But God never moves. He's always the same."

A sad laugh. "I'm like the other stars, going around in circles."

"The Lord will help you make decisions, you know. In the book of James, it says if you lack wisdom, ask God, and he'll give it to you. 'But let him ask in faith, nothing wavering. For he that wavereth is like a wave of the sea driven with the wind and tossed.' "

"Unwavering. I want to be like that. I'm tired of being tossed around by the wind."

"You can be. I know you can." Something about advising her made him feel manly again, made his chest feel full and his arms like iron.

"I'd like to see the North Star closer. Would you please show me?"

"Sure." Hutch realigned his telescope to

focus on Polaris.

The band started playing "The Story of a Starry Night." Too romantic for his taste and for his peace of mind.

"It's ready."

"Thank you." When she scooted forward, her bare arm brushed his bare arm. "Sorry."

"Sorry." But the flame of desire licked deep down into his body. He should have put his shirt back on. Most of the other men wore their shirts again, but not him. He didn't want to flash his enlisted man's stripes. Pride and desire. Twin vices. He had only himself to blame.

And Uncle Sam. Over a year and a half since he'd held a soft feminine body and kissed moist willing lips. Was the Army trying to kill him?

"The North Star barely moves?"

"That's right." He jolted his vision to that unwavering star and his thoughts back to his unwavering God.

"How about you and Phyllis? You said you met in college. Why aren't you married?"

Thank you, Lord. That topic would definitely help. "Bergie introduced us my last year of pharm school. I wanted to work awhile after I graduated, save money, get to know her better. We were supposed to get married Christmas of '41, but you know

116

the rest of the story. Duration plus six months."

"Trapped." She sighed in commiseration. "Have you seen her since you were drafted?"

"Yeah. She moved to New York when I was stationed at Fort Dix. She wanted to get married then."

"Why didn't you?"

Hutch groaned and leaned back on his hands. A breeze contributed to his cooling-down process. "I didn't want to rush things. I didn't want a hurried wedding and honeymoon. I wanted to do things right."

"So you stood your ground. Unwavering."

He shook his head. "That was one time I should have wavered."

"You're kind of a bulldog, aren't you?"

"Suppose so."

"I found your constellation." She pointed to a region near the North Star. "Four stars for his body, short stubby tail. It's the Bulldog."

He chuckled. "That's the Big Dipper."

"Mm-hmm." Laughter choked her voice. "Yes, the Big Dip."

"Hey, now."

"See, the Milky Way is his leash. He needs one, you know."

He made as if he were going to stand up and walk away. "Fine. Go ahead. Stab me in the back."

She convulsed in laughter. "You are so much fun to tease."

He grinned. Receiving the teasing was a lot of fun too. "You're not far off calling it a bulldog. It's called the Bear, Ursa Major."

"Hmm." Starlight glimmered on her curls. "The Bear. That fits you better than a bulldog. Slow moving, steady, single-minded."

"Furry. Hibernates for the winter. Growls when he doesn't get his way."

She giggled. "Do you?"

Hutch growled, as rough and rumbly as he could.

Georgie laughed and leaned closer, as if she were going to nudge his shoulder. She stopped short, thank goodness.

His heartbeat resumed.

She smoothed her hair. "I'm glad you have Phyllis to soothe you when you're growly."

He frowned. When he got growly, Phyllis got even growlier. They were so much alike. That's why Bergie introduced them.

"Oh, look!" Georgie cried. "Mellie and Tom are coming. I can show them Pegasus and the North Star and the Bulldog. Mellie! Tom!"

"Good." The word flowed out. He didn't want to ponder the differences between

118

quiet, serious Phyllis and social, light-hearted Georgie. Or which type of woman was best for him.

He didn't think he'd like the answer.

11

Termini Airfield, Sicily
August 26, 1943

"It's not fair." Rose marched, swinging her arms hard.

"It's fine." Georgie pointed in the other direction — toward the airstrip. "Y'all had better get going. Don't want to miss your flights."

"We have half an hour," Mellie said. "And Rose is right. It isn't fair for Lambert to ground you."

Georgie continued down the dirt road between rows of khaki tents. "I'm not completely grounded. She said I can fly sometimes. Meanwhile, I have an important job."

"Screening patients." Rose harrumphed. "That's Captain Maxwell's job."

She held her chin high, although Rose told the truth. "I reassure the patients, help them understand what to expect. It's important."

Sparks flew in Mellie's dark eyes. "Yes, but it isn't right. We worked hard to earn the right to fly. Now this."

Georgie gave her a reassuring smile. How could she say the right to fly meant little to her, when it meant the world to them? "I'm fine. Really, I am. I'm sure it's temporary."

"How can it be temporary?" Dust kicked up behind Mellie's shoes. "How can you prove yourself as a flight nurse if you can't serve as a flight nurse?"

Rose crossed her arms over her pale blue blouse. "Lambert's gone too far. First the nonsense with Mellie, now —"

"No, she's right this time." Georgie hardened her voice. Behind the airfield a rugged mountain rose, dotted with Sicily's odd mixture of olive trees and cacti. As odd a mixture as Georgiana Taylor and a combat theater. "A flight nurse needs to keep her head in a crisis. I don't. And I've faced only itty-bitty crises. What would I do in a big one? And a flight nurse needs to think for herself, not ask her tech's opinion every five minutes."

"I know you can do it." Mellie put her arm around Georgie's shoulders. "You're as smart as any of us, you care for the men, and deep inside you're stronger and more capable than you think."

She fought the urge to roll her eyes. "There's the ambulance. I'll see y'all later. Thanks for cheering me up."

"Just a minute." Rose tugged on her arm. "Maxwell's not there yet. And it's time."

Mellie reached into her musette bag.

"Time?" Georgie peered over.

Rose formed a triangle with Mellie and Georgie. "We made something for you. I hope you don't mind that we raided your fabric scraps."

"My fabric scraps?" She frowned at Rose, who hated sewing even a button.

Rose tucked a wayward blonde lock behind her ear. "Mellie's great at drawing, especially birds, and I'm okay with needle and thread. You could do a better job yourself but — well, show her."

A stuffed bird nested in the palm of Mellie's hand. "It's a nightingale. You may not see yourself as a flight nurse, but we do. You're a true nightingale bringing mercy on wing."

Georgie's eyes watered. "That's so sweet."

"And it represents our friendship." Mellie stroked the bird's back. "We made the body from the yellow fabric you used for Rose's dress, because Rose is the backbone of this group."

"She sure is." Georgie had relied on her

since childhood.

Rose flapped the bird's turquoise wings. "We used the fabric from Mellie's sundress for the wings, because of her love of adventure and flight nursing. She lifts us up."

"She does." Georgie gazed at her newest friend through blurry vision.

Mellie slid one finger away to reveal a pink heart. "That's from your sundress, because you're the true heart of this group, of this whole squadron."

Her throat too thick for words, Georgie took the little bird and clutched it to her chest.

"We know you can do it," Rose said, and Mellie nodded.

She dropped her gaze to the gift. Her friends were right about her heart, right about their friendship, but wrong about her becoming a good flight nurse. A true nightingale needed heart and wings and backbone.

Georgie traced the little pink heart on the bird's chest. She was nothing but heart. Nothing.

The ambulance swayed and jostled over the rough road that hugged Sicily's north coast. Georgie sat as close to the passenger door as possible so she wouldn't bump Captain

Maxwell in the center seat.

Something about the man made her nervous. For a married man and a father, he spent too much time with the nurses, especially Vera and Alice. Those two certainly didn't mind, shameless as they were, since the physician was rather handsome.

Georgie didn't think too highly of Kay Jobson, but at least the redhead kept her distance from married men.

She unfolded Ward's most recent letter, hoping it wouldn't make her angry the second time she read it. After her first starlit conversation with Hutch soon after arriving in Sicily, she confessed her fears and insecurities to Ward. Seemed only right after spilling her heart to a stranger.

But Ward's response . . .

Dear Georgie,

Your letter of July 21 alarmed me and confirmed my suspicions. Sweetheart, I appreciate how you try to be brave, but thanks for telling the truth.

We've got to get you home where you belong. Resign immediately. A combat zone is no place for a lady, not even for those hard females who think they can handle it. But my sweet Georgie never belonged over there. When I think of what your beautiful eyes have had to see, it breaks my heart. No woman should have to endure that. No woman should deliberately be put in harm's way. How can we claim to be a civilized country?

Besides, you're needed here on the farm something fierce. Pearline put up curtains for me. It's nice to have a woman's touch around the place, but it should be your touch, not hers. She makes a good rhubarb pie, but nowhere near as good as yours. She knows I'm lonely for you, so she keeps me company over supper most evenings. I appreciate her efforts, but I'm still lonely for you.

Now I'm not just lonely but worried. Go to your commander right away and resign.

Georgie scrunched up her nose. So Miss Pearline wanted her Ward. As far as Georgie was concerned right now, the girl could have him.

The road curved around a rocky bay, and Georgie's mind frothed like the waves on the stones. Rose and Mellie and even Hutch wanted her to grow, to face her fears, and to become a good flight nurse. They believed she could change.

Ward, on the other hand, wanted her to

give up, to remain stagnant. He didn't believe she could change.

Besides, what was he thinking? This wasn't an ordinary old job she could up and quit. This was the Army. Sure, she could resign from the flight nursing program because it was a voluntary service, but the Army Nurse Corps owned her for the duration. The only way out was a medical discharge.

However, if Lieutenant Lambert continued to find her wanting, the chief would send her stateside. Georgie would still be in the Army, but they probably wouldn't send her overseas again, and she'd be safe, and she could marry Ward and visit home occasionally.

She sighed and leaned closer to the open window to pull in a breath of fresh air. What did she want? Whom could she ask for advice?

The ambulance turned down the road to San Stefano. It hit a bump, and Georgie's shoulder banged against the door.

She already knew whom she could ask — the only One she should ask. *Lord, what do you want me to do? Do you want me to become a good flight nurse, to be here for Rose and Mellie, to take care of the wounded and serve my country? Or do you want me to accept my weakness, go home, and be there for Ward and my family?*

The first choice made her uneasy, as if groping her way in a dark and perilous cave. The second choice felt too easy, like cuddling up in Daddy's lap — at her age!

Perhaps today she'd have time at San Stefano to visit Hutch. Thank goodness his tent pharmacy was far less romantic than a starry night at the shore. But he was a good listener and wise. He'd help her weigh her choices without deciding for her.

"That's odd," the driver said.

Captain Maxwell peered forward. "This is the spot, right?"

"Yes, sir."

Georgie studied the area. Yes, this was where the 93rd Evacuation Hospital was. Or where it used to be.

A void formed in her chest, as empty as the land before her. Dry grasses lay flattened by tents and trampled by feet and trucks. Dirt clods littered the ground, yanked up by tent pegs. "Where did they go?"

The driver shrugged. "Beats me. This is the spot."

Captain Maxwell huffed. "No one thought to telegraph us at Termini? That's what's wrong with the Army. Too much paperwork and too little communication."

"I don't see anyone around to ask," the driver said.

"Head on back."

Georgie grasped the dashboard as the truck lurched through its U-turn. She gazed back at the hospital site. Where had they gone?

Rumors of an upcoming invasion infested Sicily. They might head to Italy, to Sardinia, to Corsica, even to Greece. Had the 93rd packed up for the next landing?

Georgie's heart throbbed in the void in her chest. Would she ever see Hutch again? She didn't have his Army Post Office number, so she couldn't even write him.

How could she already miss him? His quiet way of listening, his intelligent analysis, his gentle sense of humor, his warm brown eyes.

Georgie gave herself a good shake. He loved Phyllis, and Georgie loved Ward, even if his most recent letter annoyed her. They had a history and shared dreams and goals.

Perhaps it would be best if she never saw Hutch again.

12

Cerda, Sicily

Hutch rolled down his sleeves as he walked from the enlisted men's mess tent to pharmacy. Sunset signaled relief from the day's heat but also the necessity of covering up from malarial mosquitoes.

An orange glow washed over the hospital complex. Today's move had been accomplished with record speed, and new patients already filled the wards of the 93rd.

Hutch pulled Phyllis's latest letter from his pants pocket. Since the beach party, he'd read all her letters over again, determined to rekindle the spark of romance, the warmth of love. But the letters made things worse. Her melancholy fed his worry for her, and her concerns about his faithfulness irritated him. What right did she have to make him feel guilty? He had no choice about being overseas and he'd resisted temptation.

He focused hard on her airy script. For now, he'd shove his feelings aside and rely on commitment and prayer to stay faithful. Feelings were deceptive and a lousy basis for decisions. However, once he got home, he'd give the relationship a thorough appraisal. Was Phyllis good for him? Was he good for her? Was marriage God's will for their lives?

"Oh, Hutchie-kins, my darling!" A falsetto voice warbled behind him. Bergie looped his arm through Hutch's and batted his blond eyelashes. "How I pine for you, my love. Without you, I am naught but a pool of tears, quivering from the dire ache of loneliness."

Hutch laughed and shook off his friend. "How dare you read her letters?"

"Seriously? That bad?"

He held up the page. "She quoted the entire lyrics from 'I Don't Want to Walk Without You.' "

"Oh boy." Bergie whistled a snippet of the wistful tune. "At least it proves she needs you."

"Yep." His voice came out stiff.

"And it proves you two sorry souls need me to drag you out for nights on the town."

"Yep again." But what if Phyllis needed more — someone Bergie-like to lift her

130

moods on a daily basis and provide a little fun? Hutch wasn't that kind of man.

Bergie slapped him on the back. "You look as glum as your girl. This is my prescription — one dram of quit-worrying, six minims of smile-a-little, and a gallon of prayer."

Hutch wrangled up a smile. "I can fill that."

"Good man." He nodded to Pharmacy and Laboratory. "All set up?"

"Nice and neat."

Bergie leaned closer. Pale stubble ringed his jaw. "You didn't hear it from me, but don't get too cozy."

"Not planning on it." The tension in Sicily reminded him of North Africa right before the Husky landings in July. They were going somewhere. Soon.

"I've got to get back to the ward. Thank goodness for twelve-hour shifts. Sure beats working till you fall unconscious."

Hutch waved good-bye. Pharmacy might not get as much respect as medicine, but at least he worked better hours.

He ducked inside the tent. Kazokov rummaged through a crate, and Ralph O'Shea stood behind the lieutenant, red-faced. Ralph gave Hutch a wild-eyed look and mouthed something.

What was wrong? Crates lay around with

131

bottles inside. Boxes sat on top of the counter. Shelves sat partly empty.

What on earth happened? He'd set this place up hours ago. Who had done this? Why?

Blood tingled on its way out of his face. What kind of cruel joke was this? Kaz would think he hadn't done his job.

The lieutenant straightened up. "I'm glad you're back, Sergeant."

The last thing Hutch needed was a black mark on his military record. "Honestly, sir. I didn't leave it like this. I don't know what happened. It was set up. Perfectly set up. Right, Ralph?"

Kaz chuckled and pulled up the waistband of his khaki trousers. Dysentery had decreased his belly. "You had it set up, all right, but now it will be *perfectly* set up."

Hutch gazed around. Complete disorder. Why would anyone do this to him? It would take hours to put things back right. In the meantime, how could he accomplish his regular work? "What do you mean?"

Kaz wore a smug smile. "I've been studying this operation. The inefficiency and disorganization appalled me. I'm putting my business education to use and making this streamlined and modern."

Streamlined? Modern? What on earth? He

nudged his feet forward. A bulk bottle of antiparasitic tablets he rarely used was on the center-front shelf on top of the counter — but the scales were down on the bottom shelf. "What did you do?"

"I don't know why you never thought of this. Everything is now alphabetical. Your productivity will soar. You'll be able to find things much faster."

"I've never had a problem finding things. This was organized like my dad's pharmacy, like every pharmacy I've ever seen."

Another chuckle. "Is that so? Maybe I can hire out my services."

Hutch surveyed the damage, the heat of anger blurring his vision. "I don't think so, sir. We group medications and chemicals by type — tablets, injectables, liquids. We alphabetize within each category."

"Willy-nilly. No logic at all."

"No, sir. There's logic." He tightened his throat so he wouldn't raise his voice and get accused of talking back to an officer. "We put the items we use most frequently up where we can reach them and lesser-used items down below."

"Don't fuss. It takes time to undo bad habits. You'll see the merit of better organization."

Better? Tall bottles lay on their sides on

the narrow top shelf. A drop of liquid fell from one and sizzled on the metal counter. Hutch gasped and yanked the bottle off the shelf. "Sir, this is glacial acetic acid."

Kaz peered at the label. "Acetic acid, glacial. It belongs with the *A*s."

"No, sir. It must be upright. It was dripping. This is a dangerous acid."

The lieutenant sniffed. "Fine. Put it under *G* for glacial. But screw on the lid more carefully this time."

Behind Kaz, Ralph mimed pouring something over Kaz's head.

Hutch glanced away so the tech's rightful mockery wouldn't stoke his fire. "I will, sir."

Kaz set a bottle on a bottom shelf — sodium hydroxide. In the same compartment as sulfuric acid.

"Um, sir. You can't put sodium hydroxide on that shelf."

The lieutenant's little dark eyes snapped at Hutch. "It's an *S.*"

"Yes, sir, but it's a base. It's next to a strong acid."

"So?"

"So it's a volatile combination." Like Hutch and Kaz.

"They're in bottles." He shook his head as if the pharmacist were a bit dim.

Hutch swallowed hard. Hot saliva burned

down his throat and into his stomach. "Yes, sir. But as you know, each shelf also serves as a packing crate. When it's time to move, we just add sawdust and slide the lid on."

"I know that."

He nodded slowly so anger wouldn't pollute his words. "Every single move we've made, we've had damage. If those two bottles broke in the same crate, we could have a dangerous situation."

Kaz crossed his arms and narrowed his eyes. "One thing I've learned about you, Hutchinson, is you're a pessimist, a downright worrywart."

His hands clenched, damp with sweat. "No, sir. I'm practical. And knowledgeable."

"Knowledgeable? You're not calling me stupid, are you?"

"No, sir!" He stretched out his fingers and rubbed his palms down his trouser legs. If he didn't calm down, he'd get reprimanded and lose his chance at the Pharmacy Corps. "Not at all, sir. You know business, and you know it well. But I know chemistry and pharmaceuticals, and this is an accident waiting to happen."

"Ridiculous." He spun back to the crate, pulled out two pasteboard boxes of capsule shells, and put them under *C,* rather than right under the counter where they be-

longed. "This is a solid plan. I'm modern-
izing this operation."

His hands coiled in on themselves again.
"Sir, a pharmacist is always — always — in
charge of his own pharmacy."

Kaz thrust a finger in Hutch's face. "Not
in the Army. I'm in charge here, and you'll
do as I say. Do I make myself clear, Sergeant?"

In the Army, he couldn't even argue like a
man without being charged with insubordination.

"Yes, sir." The words charred his tongue.

Kaz pointed to the crates. "Put everything
in proper order. If you don't know where
something belongs, ask. You do know your
alphabet, don't you?"

"Yes, sir." What else could he say?

And what else could he do? Go whining
to Colonel Currier? He'd get in even worse
trouble for going over the head of his commanding officer. Maybe he could ask Kaz
to put the order in writing to protect himself
if something went wrong. Why not ask to be
demoted to private? That's what would happen.

He set the second bottle of sodium hydroxide beside the sulfuric acid. He closed
his mind to the potential chemical reaction.
Sure, they neutralized each other, but after

an exothermic reaction producing heat and gas.

Ralph placed the diodoquin under *D* in prime center territory. They rarely dispensed the antiprotozoal tablets. The tech slid a furtive glance to Hutch as if the pharmacist might explode.

He couldn't afford to explode. He had to keep his stopper in tight.

Hutch blew off a heated breath. Soon he'd be an officer and he wouldn't have to put up with this nonsense ever again. But when? Dad's last letter referred to bureaucratic delays.

How much longer would he have to wait?

Pain jabbed below his ribs, and he winced. If he couldn't be in charge in his own pharmacy, what good was he?

13

Licata Airfield, Sicily
September 8, 1943

A ghostly half-moon hung in the pale late-afternoon sky while several dozen C-47s circled Licata Airfield on Sicily's southwestern coast. Rose's fingers cut off the circulation in Georgie's arm.

"They'll be all right, honey." Georgie patted her friend's hand.

"Rome," Rose whispered. "So far away."

"We don't know that for certain," Mellie said from Rose's other side.

Georgie murmured her agreement, but the grim faces of the paratroopers of the 82nd Airborne Division confirmed Rose's fears. The men slouched toward the C-47s, loaded down with gear and resignation.

On September 3, the British Eighth Army landed in Calabria on Italy's toe. That same day, the 802nd MAETS transferred down to Licata. They'd left Termini Imerese bustling with landing craft and cargo ships being loaded for the next phase of the invasion. It couldn't be much farther north than Calabria since an amphibious landing needed to be in range of fighter planes based in Sicily.

Georgie didn't know anything about military tactics, but dropping paratroopers at Rome, several hundred miles ahead of the main landing force, didn't make sense.

"Isn't that good news about the 807th?" Mellie said with a stiff smile. "They just arrived in Tunisia, I heard."

What a sweetheart, trying to distract Rose. "Oh yes. With a second air evac squadron in the Mediterranean, we can help so many more patients."

"There's Clint!" Rose broke away and dashed into the arms of her boyfriend.

Mellie smiled at Georgie. "We tried."

Clint cupped Rose's face in his hands. "It'll be okay. Remember? We'll be together forever."

She nodded, her face red. "I just . . . I couldn't —"

He silenced her with a long kiss. "I'll see you in the morning. You won't even know I was gone." He turned to Georgie and Mellie. "Take good care of my girl, you hear?"

"Yes, sir," Georgie said with a smile and a salute. Rose had waited so long for someone to love her, and Clint had waited so long for Rose to return his affections. Either would be devastated by the loss of the other.

Clint gave Rose one last kiss then headed for his plane. The crew members in leather flight jackets and crush caps stood out from the paratroopers with their combat jackets, baggy trousers tucked into high buckle boots, steel helmets, and full field packs.

One man stopped and gazed around the airfield, drinking it all in — friendly territory and sunshine and life — as if he knew he'd never see any of it again. His expression ripped Georgie's heart open.

The paratroopers wouldn't return to Licata, but if all went well, the men of the 51st Troop Carrier Wing would return by morning. If the unescorted cargo planes weren't ambushed by the Luftwaffe. If antiaircraft fire around Rome didn't shred them to pieces. If mechanical problems didn't plunge them into the Mediterranean.

Georgie fought off a shudder and put on a pleasant expression for her friends' sakes. Mellie didn't seem concerned about Tom, although the aviation engineers would certainly go ashore with the invasion force to build or repair airfields. But Tom had been in danger the entire length of their relationship, so perhaps she was used to it.

Evacuation hospitals would be needed in Italy too. Would the 93rd be shipped over there? If so, when?

"Unwavering," she whispered. She had to learn to be unwavering. *Lord, calm my fears.*

Not far away, Kay Jobson kissed Grant Klein, one of the C-47 pilots, then strolled over to Mellie, grinning. "Six men. Six kisses for good luck. My job is done."

Mellie shook her head and laughed. "Good luck? Not if they start fighting over you."

"But I like it when they do that." Kay crossed her arms and made a fake pout.

Georgie struggled to maintain her pleasant expression. The woman had no shame.

A gleam entered Kay's eyes, and she squinted across the tarmac, where Clint headed for his plane with his pilot, Roger Cooper, and copilot, Bill Shelby. "Shall I try for seven? Hey, Coop! Roger Cooper!"

Roger stopped and turned slowly, a wary look on his face. "Yeah?"

"Want a kiss for good luck?"

"No, thanks. Don't need luck. I've got the Lord." He walked away.

Georgie grinned. She knew she liked that pilot. He had brains.

Kay just laughed. "Such a fuddy-duddy. I love rattling his cage."

Mellie gave her a teasing smile. "You know it bothers you. He's the only single male who doesn't roll over at your feet."

"Proof there's something wrong with him." Kay's mouth tightened. Just a bit. Was that evidence of the hurt Mellie claimed lurked behind Kay's brazen exterior? Or just wounded pride that she couldn't have her way with any man she wanted?

The engines on Clint's plane started up, adding to the din. About four dozen of the olive drab, two-engine planes droned above the field and streamed northwest. More C-47s taxied on the tarmac, while others surged down the runway and lifted into the sky.

"What's that?" Mellie pointed to a plane approaching from the north.

A twin-engine plane, much smaller than a C-47. A current of fear raced into her heart until she noticed the RAF's roundel on the fuselage. "Thank goodness. It's British."

"That's a Beaufighter." Rose spent too much time with her aircrew buddies.

A red flare sprang from the fighter, and Georgie gasped.

Red flares meant an emergency, wounded on board. Around the field, ground crewmen and officers pointed, shouted, and jumped to action. The plane needed to land immediately. C-47s taxied away from the runway, clearing it for the British plane.

"Come on, ladies." Rose headed toward the end of the runway. "If it's a medical emergency, we can help."

"Of course." Georgie followed, her chest tight with fear, her gaze fixed on the olive drab plane and its heartbreaking red flares.

The Beaufighter landed, a flurry of dust behind its propellers. As soon as it stopped, a man leaped out and sprinted for the headquarters tent — an American officer in full dress uniform. "General! General Ridgway!"

Georgie swatted the cloud of dust and exchanged a confused look with her friends. Gen. Matthew Ridgway commanded the 82nd Airborne. And no one seemed to need medical care.

She leaned to one side and peered across the runway and into Headquarters. A heated discussion, men in motion, a man barking orders into the radio.

"What's going on?" Rose's fingers dug into Georgie's arm again.

"I don't know."

The Beaufighter taxied off the runway. C-47s on the ground turned around and

143

went back the way they came. Engines shut down. Overhead, the planes spiraled lower and lower. They were returning.

"It must be a recall," Mellie said.

"A recall?" Rose's voice shook. "They're not going?"

"Looks that way, honey." She rubbed Rose's hand. The release of the afternoon's tension made her friend more nervous than the tension itself. Typical for Rose.

An officer jogged past, wearing the patch of the 82nd Airborne on the sleeve of his khaki shirt — the letters *AA* in a blue circle on a red square.

"Excuse me, sir," Georgie called. "Do you know what happened?"

"Operation's cancelled. Don't know why yet."

"Thank you, Lord." Rose wobbled, so unlike her.

Georgie wrapped her arm around her friend's waist so she wouldn't fall. "Let's go home now that you know Clint's safe. I'm sure he has plenty of work tonight."

The ladies headed down the tarmac toward the road that led to the sea. All around them, paratroopers disembarked from cargo planes, laughing and joking.

One young man kicked at a rock. "Swell. Now they won't have time to switch plans and drop us somewhere else. The invasion will go on without us."

"Make up your mind." His buddy jabbed him in the side with his elbow. "You whined because we were jumping, and now you're whining because we aren't."

Georgie's breath caught. The invasion was going on without them? That meant even now the convoys sailed for Italian shores. Hutch's face flashed in her mind, serious but warmhearted. *Lord, keep him — keep them all safe.*

Something about the sunset over the Mediterranean seemed more colorful that night. The four ladies stood at the base of the Licata lighthouse, its round concrete tower thrusting 131 feet into the orangey-pink sky.

Georgie couldn't imagine a more romantic place to be based. Twelve of the nurses of the 802nd were billeted in the light-keeper's home, while the remainder stayed in Palermo on Sicily's north shore. If only Ward were here to share the romance. If only she could sit on the beach snuggled beside him and watch the colors shift and the stars come out.

Stars? Georgie spun away from the ocean. If she weren't careful, Hutch would nudge Ward out of her fantasy, and that wouldn't

145

be right. She looked at her wristwatch — almost seven o'clock. "We should go in. Our dinner's already cold."

The ladies headed home. Overhead, the lighthouse was dark, no beam to light the way for raiding enemy aircraft, no beam to warn friendly ships off shore.

Sailors depended on lighthouses to guide them, and Georgie depended on people. She had to remember to turn to the Lord's light for guidance. She was determined to do so.

"What's going on in there?" Kay asked. "Sounds like a party, and we're missing it."

Georgie tuned her ears toward the house. Laughter and music flowed from inside. "Come on, girls. Let's find out what's happening."

Mellie swung open the door, and the ladies stepped inside.

A party, all right. A scratchy version of "Beer Barrel Polka" played on an old phonograph, almost drowned by singing and stomping feet. Pairs of nurses whirled around in an exuberant polka.

"There you are, duckies!" Mary "Goosie" Gerber grabbed Georgie around the waist and led her in the polka.

Georgie laughed as she fought to keep up with the tall frizzy-haired blonde. "What's going on? Why the party?"

"Haven't you heard?" Goosie leaned back her head and let out a raucous peal of laughter. The girl belonged on the vaudeville circuit. "Eisenhower was on the BBC. The commanding general himself."

"Italy surrendered!" Vera Viviani shouted and twirled Alice Olson under her arm.

"Italy surrendered?" Georgie narrowly missed polkaing into a chair.

"Yessirree, little missy!" Goosie tripped on a threadbare rug but didn't slow down. "It's over! It's over!"

Rose met her gaze from across the room, where she danced with Mellie. "We won't have to fight in Italy. That must be why the airborne mission was cancelled."

The realization blossomed in Georgie's heart, and she laughed with joy. Clint and Tom and Hutch and all the other good men would live. With Italy in Allied hands, they could march over the Alps and kick down Hitler's back door.

Lieutenant Lambert leaned against the wall, arms crossed, a slight smile on her face. But the tilt of her head and the softness of her brown eyes spoke of sadness. Why?

"One down, two to go!" Rose cried. "Only Germany and Japan left."

The thought snagged Georgie's feet and her heart. Germany had fought hard for Sicily, and almost their entire force escaped to Italy. Other Nazi troops had to be on the peninsula as well.

"What about the Germans?" Mellie asked.

The dancing paused. Georgie panted from exertion.

The chief nurse's smile faded.

No, the Germans wouldn't give up easily. They never did.

"Don't be so gloomy," Alice said. "Haven't you heard? The Brits aren't having any trouble in Italy. They sit around eating spaghetti and drinking *vino*. The Germans are running away."

Running away to a better defensive position, more likely.

Vera lifted the phonograph arm and returned the needle to the outer edge of the record. "Germans or no Germans, we still have reason to celebrate. Mussolini is overthrown. Italy surrendered. Benito is *finito*. Let's dance, ladies."

"Beer Barrel Polka" resumed, and so did the dancing, but in a more subdued tone.

No way in God's little green earth would Adolf Hitler let the Allies polka their way up the Italian boot.

14

Paestum, Italy
September 15, 1943

In the morning sun, Hutch stood by the railing of *LST-350*. Salerno Bay curved before him as the giant gray landing craft lumbered like a hippopotamus toward Yellow Beach. The Army insisted LST stood for Landing Ship, Tank, but the men believed it stood for Large Stationary Target.

"Heads up!" someone shouted.

Hutch's breath clumped in his throat. He dropped to a squat.

The men and women of the 93rd Evacuation Hospital crouched low, their helmets paving the deck like steel cobblestones.

Hutch peeked up. With his height, he couldn't get as low as the others. A trio of fighter planes swooped down from the north. The LST's antiaircraft guns opened up, walloping Hutch's eardrums. He pressed his ears shut and hunkered under his helmet. If he had a pistol, at least he could shoot back.

After a thunderous minute, the Navy's guns did their job and scared the Luftwaffe away.

Hutch unfolded himself to standing and drew a long breath. On the broad Salerno plain, six fighter planes rose close to the waterfront. The good guys.

The US Fifth Army and the British Tenth Corps had landed six days earlier, on September 9. The day after the Italian surrender, the Germans occupied Italy and disarmed the Italian army. The Nazis fought viciously at Salerno. Rumors were, the other day they'd almost shoved the Allies back into the sea until the 82nd Airborne dropped reinforcements on the beachhead.

No one knew what the 93rd would find on shore.

The LST slowed to a stop. A loud grinding sound vibrated the entire ship, and enormous doors in the bow of the landing craft eased open.

His bones rattling from the vibrations, Hutch peered over the heads of the men in front of him. A pontoon causeway led to the LST's door.

Down in the belly of the hippo, truck engines roared to life, exhaust fumes spewed from the open mouth, and vehicles rolled onto the causeway. Dom Bruno would drive the truck loaded with pharmacy equipment. About half a mile north at Red Beach, *LCI-14* would land the other half of the 93rd's personnel, including Ralph O'Shea. Colonel Currier liked to divide each department to minimize the impact if one landing craft was sunk.

Not the cheeriest thought.

A high whistling sound overhead. Hutch dropped to the deck with the others, his pulse racing. The artillery shell sent up a plume of water several hundred feet out to sea. The sooner they could get off this floating bull's-eye, the better.

After the vehicles disembarked, Hutch joined the mass of personnel snaking off the LST. The causeway rocked and bounced underfoot, but a dip in the warm blue calm of the Mediterranean didn't seem like a bad idea, even so early in the day.

Hutch stepped onto the relative safety of the Italian mainland. He worked his way to the edge of the group, pulled a one-ounce medication vial from the pocket of his field jacket, and scooped up soft fine beige sand. He had a nice collection now, including the beach party at Termini.

Memories of the party intruded. Laugh-

151

ing and splashing with Georgie, sitting in the warm sand and stargazing.

He huffed out a breath. Good thing he hadn't seen her since the party. He missed her a bit too much, kept thinking of things he wanted to tell her or show her.

Guilt lengthened his letters to Phyllis.

Hutch wrenched his attention to the scene around him. Rugged hills ringed the Salerno plain, which stretched flat several miles inland. The village of Paestum stood straight ahead, and Salerno lay about twenty miles north.

Even the throbbing motors of landing craft couldn't conceal the sounds of battle. Artillery boomed and fighter planes roared — American P-40s this time. A few miles ahead, smoke rose in spots and red tracer fire zipped through the air. The Allies hadn't secured the beachhead.

The 93rd Evac was in for a tough time of it.

Some of the hospital personnel looked nervous, but most laughed and chatted as if out for a day at the shore. Even the nurses. Hutch smiled, pleased with how the ladies handled themselves with courage and grace. Georgie could do the same, but he was glad she didn't have to test herself.

"All right, folks. Let's move on out."

The trucks led the way northwest along a dirt road parallel to the beach. Hutch followed on foot with most of the enlisted men. Tan dust swirled around his feet and coated the inside of his mouth with grit.

A squat round tower stood to the right of the road, maybe fifty feet tall. Looked medieval. Weeds poked out from between the stones, and fresh divots marked battle damage. Wouldn't be surprising if German snipers had favored the lookout.

Now a couple of GIs stood watch. A wolf whistle floated down from the perch. "Dames! Look, a bunch of dames! Real live American dames!"

The nurses of the 93rd waved and shouted their greetings.

The medic marching next to Hutch elbowed him. "How come they're not excited to see us, huh?"

"It's all in the hips. You've got to wiggle them."

The medic grinned, stuck one hand behind his head and the other on his hip, and sashayed down the road, hips careening from side to side. "Hiya, fellas!"

The guards jeered. One of them threw something. A K-ration tin bonked off the medic's helmet.

"Knock it off, Carter." The next man over

punched the medic in the shoulder. "You're gonna get us killed."

"You're just jealous 'cause they didn't give you a present." Carter waved the ration tin at the guys in the tower. "Thank you, handsome!"

"Disturbing," Hutch said with a grin. "Truly disturbing."

The convoy entered a beachside village, the mottled plaster on the houses revealing brick and stone walls beneath. Two small boys peered through laundry hanging from a wrought-iron balcony.

Hutch waved. The boys squealed, ducked inside, and slammed wooden shutters closed. Poor things probably didn't know whom to trust.

The road bent inland onto a paved road pocked by shell fire and fenced by a tall ancient wall. He trailed his fingers along the porous gray stones covered with black and yellow lichen.

"Sergeant Hutchinson!" Bergie jogged down from the front of the convoy. "I need Sergeant Hutchinson. Anyone seen him? It's an emergency."

He frowned, stepped out of formation, and raised his hand. What kind of emergency needed a pharmacist?

Bergie beckoned. "Get up here, Sergeant.

154

Make it snappy."

Snappy? That word wasn't in Bergie's vocabulary.

"Yes, sir." Hutch jogged forward to meet his friend. "What's up?"

"Follow me. Faster." Bergie broke into a full run, passing personnel and trucks.

Thank goodness Hutch's long legs allowed him to keep up.

Bergie turned onto a road to the left, then ducked behind the wall while the convoy continued straight ahead.

"What on earth is going —" Hutch's jaw dropped. A temple. Ancient. Greek. And another. And farther down a third. "What on . . ."

"Yeah, I thought you'd like it. Come on, we've got to keep moving."

Hutch crossed a lawn spotted with low brown and green grass. "They look Greek. But this is Italy."

"Didn't you pay attention in Latin? The Greeks colonized this area."

"That's right." The first temple had lost its roof, but fat columns still formed a rectangle. Plain capitals hinted at its antiquity. "What do you think? About 2,500 years old?"

"More. Early Doric." He threw his arms out wide. "You may now thank me."

Hutch shook his head in wonder. "You spotted this —"

"From the back of our truck. Knew old Kaz would never give you time off to see it."

"Guaranteed." The convoy rumbled along on the other side of the wall. "Know where the hospital site is?"

"On the far side of that wall there. We'll take the scenic route."

The men strolled toward the temple, its columns rising high to their left, while umbrella-shaped pine trees lined the wall to the right. Away from the road, the air smelled piney, almost herbal. The constant chirp of cicadas thrummed in the warm air.

Hutch filled his lungs. "Wonder which god they worshipped here."

"Don't know. They didn't exactly give us a guidebook when we landed."

"Nope." He turned in front of the temple and gazed deep inside. "Just think, thousands of years ago, people went in there to make sacrifices to their gods — gods in their own image."

Bergie took off his helmet, rubbed off sweat, and made his hair stand up in spikes. "Gods in their own image. Yeah, that's about right."

"Mm-hmm. The fullness of the Lord

156

Almighty broken into tiny manageable chunks."

"Preeeeeach it, Brother John." Bergie waved his hands in the air.

Hutch laughed at the thought of his friend acting that way in their proper home church, of the reaction of the proper congregation.

Then he stopped. The next temple was more complete with both triangular pediments intact. But soldiers and officers strode in and out on official-looking business.

"Uh-oh," Hutch said. "Looks like HQ."

"Big brass, I'm thinking."

After his encounter with Patton, Hutch had no interest in an encounter with Gen. Mark Clark, commander of the US Fifth Army. He turned around. "Let's go."

"Are you kidding?" Bergie grabbed his arm. "We're not leaving."

Hutch stared down his friend. "We're not supposed to be here."

"You know my motto. If you don't belong someplace, act like you do."

"That motto always gets us in trouble."

Bergie clapped him on the shoulder, his broad face spread with its familiar grin. "That motto has enriched your life. And now it'll allow you to see all three temples."

"I have no choice."

"You never do. I outrank you. Follow me, or I'll write you up."

That joke had grown annoying long ago, but Hutch wrangled up a smile. "Yes, sir. Lead on, sir. We get in trouble, you take the blame, sir."

"Now you're talking." Bergie marched across the grass. "Look purposeful. Try not to gawk. You're here on official business."

"With my field pack."

"With your field pack. Believe it, and they'll believe it."

Hutch matched his stride to his friend's. Once again, balancing each other. Bergie talking Hutch into adventures he needed to take, and Hutch talking Bergie down from his crazier schemes.

But this was one of Bergie's better schemes. The classic beauty of the temples captured him, the connection with history and mythology and astronomy. Without Bergie, he never would have seen it. He would have heard about it, and the inability to see the site would have festered in his stomach.

They marched past a clump of officers in front of the temple. Salutes were exchanged, but not second glances. They were getting away with it. "You're a genius, Berg."

"Remember that next time you try to keep

me out of trouble."

"But that's where my genius comes in."

Bergie laughed. "Just march and look purposeful."

They marched purposefully down a dirt path and left the soldiers behind. The third temple stood several hundred yards away. A maze of foundations lay on both sides of the path, hinting at the town that existed thousands of years earlier. Sandal-clad feet had trod the same path, and the sounds of ancient Greek seemed to echo in the air.

A shiver ran up Hutch's arms. He wanted to take pictures, movie footage, something to remember every moment, every stone and column.

"What's up with Kaz?" Bergie said. "I heard him grumbling about you."

Now it was Hutch's turn to grumble. "Why do you have to ruin a perfect day?"

Bergie stood in a wide stance, planted his fists on his hips, and tilted his face to the sky. "Ah yes, a perfect peaceful autumn day."

Naval shells whined overhead and burst toward the base of the hills, and farther north a squadron of medium bombers dropped their loads.

Hutch lifted half a smile. "Granted."

"So what's this I hear about you being poky?"

"I told you he alphabetized my pharmacy, right?"

"Yeah . . . ?" He squinted, his familiar "what's the big deal" expression.

Hutch pressed his lips together tight. "All right, when you do a surgery, you have your equipment on a tray. How do you want your stuff arranged?"

"In the order I need it."

"Not alphabetically?"

"Okay. Understood."

"Mm-hmm. So you need your scalpel, but it's way on the far side of the tray under *S*. That's my problem. My scales are on the bottom shelf under *S* when they belong on the counter. Everything takes twice as long."

"Can't you explain to —"

"Don't you think I've tried? All I'm allowed to say is 'yes, sir,' 'no, sir.' " Hutch studied a semicircular wall to his right. "We tried keeping the fast-movers on the counter to save steps, but Kaz got on my case about the mess. He wants things neat. As if I didn't."

On the LST, Hutch had finally had time to transcribe the details of the incident in a long letter to his father. Testimony like that would help the pharmacy leaders smash

160

bureaucratic walls. He'd give the letter to Bergie for censorship. Not to Kaz.

"I'll see what I can do," Bergie said.

"Don't." He thumped his friend in the arm. "You'd make things worse. And don't you dare say something to Currier. I'll just look whiny and insubordinate."

"Aren't you?" Bergie grinned and thumped him back. "Hey, look! It's an amphitheater."

"Sure is." He peered through an arched doorway in the center of the semicircular wall.

Bergie whooped and ran through the gate. "Too bad we don't have swords."

Hutch ambled after him. "Only tent pegs."

"Tent pegs!" His eyes gleamed. "Give me one."

"You're kidding."

"You know I'm not." His fingers opened and closed in demand. "We're in an ancient amphitheater, for crying out loud. Every boyhood gladiator fantasy brought to life. Prepare to defend yourself, Johnius Hutchicus."

He rolled his eyes, but he shrugged off his field pack and found two tent pegs. After all, Bergie had a point.

The men circled each other, sizing each other up, knowing each other's strengths

161

and weaknesses all too well.

Bergie lunged first, as Hutch knew he would, always impulsive.

Hutch blocked him and swept his feet from underneath, as he usually did. He scrabbled on top of his friend and held the tent peg a safe distance from his throat. "Gotcha."

Blue eyes narrowed and a grin lifted. "Assaulting an officer?"

What would happen if the brass strolled past? He could be thrown in the brig for years. He'd never get in the Pharmacy Corps. His gaze hopped to the archway.

Before he knew it, he was on his back. Pinned.

Bergie rapped his tent peg on Hutch's helmet, making it ring. "Fighting's in the mind. That's where you lose."

Always. Hutch sighed and closed his eyes as the cicadas laughed from the cypress trees. Worries. That's where he always lost.

15

*93rd Evacuation Hospital, Paestum, Italy
September 16, 1943*

Planes thundered overhead, artillery rumbled in the distance, and cries of wounded soldiers pierced Georgie's ears. A detachment from the 802nd MAETS had landed at Sele Airdrome on the Salerno beachhead that morning, and the trembles wouldn't leave her alone. But nothing made her insides shiver like Rose's glare.

After Captain Maxwell stepped out of the jeep, he helped out Georgie and Rose. Her chaperone. Never before had Rose accompanied her on a hospital visit, but when she heard the 93rd was in Paestum, she insisted on it.

"Come along, Rose." She put on her cheeriest voice and headed for Receiving. Usually she stopped at Pharmacy and then joined the flight surgeon. But not today. Not with Rose skewering her with her gaze.

It would be rude not to stop by and see Hutch. She hadn't seen him for almost a month. What was the best way to convince Rose of the innocence of the friendship? To not visit Hutch? Or to visit him and show Rose firsthand?

"Coming through." Two medics rushed past with a litter. A man writhed on top, a shock of red on his gray-green field jacket.

Another medic assisted a soldier who clutched his twisted, bloodstained arm to his chest.

Georgie took a deep breath. Compared to the ravages of battle, her concerns were nit-picky.

"Georgie? Lieutenant Taylor?"

She spun around. "Hutch, it's so good to see you."

He looked great, tall and tanned and happy and whole, his sleeves rolled up and his collar open, a cardboard box in one arm. With every step toward Georgie, his grin collapsed. "What are you — you ladies — doing here?" He nodded to Rose. "Hi, Lieutenant Danilovich."

"Hello." Frost coated the word.

He shot her a confused glance, then gazed overhead, where a fighter plane zipped past. "I know the airstrip's open, but the beach-head isn't secure. I can't believe they flew you in."

Georgie gave him her steadiest smile. "The generals declared it secure this morning. And besides, you have nurses here at the hospital, don't you?"

One corner of his mouth crept up. "Yeah."

"And I'm supposed to be unwavering, right?"

The other corner joined in. "Yeah."

He was too adorable. In a brotherly way. "So here we are. How have you been?"

"Busy. We landed yesterday morning, set up, opened at 1800. It hasn't slowed down since."

"How's Phyllis?" Now she'd show Rose.

"Good." He rubbed the back of his neck. "Hard at work at the shipyard, making wedding plans."

Georgie couldn't have put better words in his mouth. "How exciting. Are you going back soon?"

"Don't know." The luster left his brown eyes. "Army's dragging their heels on the Pharmacy Corps."

"I'm sorry. I'm sure it'll work out."

Rose tugged the sleeve of Georgie's blouse. "We need to go. Captain Maxwell's waiting. Good-bye, Sergeant."

Somehow Georgie kept her annoyance off her face. Why did Rose have to be rude?

Hutch glanced over his shoulder. "I should get back to work too. Better not be seen fraternizing."

"Silliest rule ever." Georgie stanched the urge to pat Hutch's arm. "Well, we're stationed at Sele. Maybe I'll see you again."

"I hope so. Bye, ladies." Warmth deepened his voice.

Georgie's heart disobeyed her and did a little hop. She waved and followed Rose. Not easy, because Rose kept up a brisk pace. What was *she* angry about?

"Have you told Ward about him?" Acid fried the last word. "Wonder what he'd think."

"Don't be ridiculous. Hutch is just a friend. He knows how much I love Ward, and he's crazy about Phyllis."

"All I know is what I saw."

Georgie hated fighting with Rose, but she hadn't started it. She stopped in her tracks and put her hands on her hips. "What exactly did you see, Miss Danilovich?"

The fire in her eyes could have set the pharmacy tent aflame. "I saw that he cares too much for you. I saw that he didn't want to talk about Miss Phyllis. And I saw your face when he called your name. Lit up like a Christmas tree."

"Nonsense." Her cheeks heated under that

fire. Had she really lit up?

"You never look like that when you see Ward."

Georgie glanced to the side and crossed her arms. "For heaven's sake. I saw Ward practically every day of my life. You watch me when I see him next. I'll make a Christmas tree look dull."

"Will you?"

Her hand twitched. "If I weren't such a lady, I'd slap you."

Rose's cheeks reddened, blotting out her freckles. "I'm the one who should do the slapping. Slap some sense into you."

"How dare you? I don't think of Hutch that way. And he doesn't think of me that way either."

"Guess again, sister."

Never in her life had she wanted to slap Rose more. "He's an honorable man."

Rose sniffed, her nose high in the air. "See how long *that* lasts. Mark my words, he'll make a move. And I have a hunch you won't mind."

Her hand sprang through the air.

Rose blocked it. She always did.

"Ladies? Is something wrong?" Captain Maxwell leaned out of the receiving tent.

"Of course not, Captain." Georgie flung off Rose's grip and put on her most charming smile. "We're coming."

"Good. I certainly don't want any more female histrionics in this squadron." He ducked back inside the tent.

"This isn't over," Rose grumbled behind her.

Georgie wheeled and gave her most imperious glare to her friend. No, her former friend. A true friend would never malign her character. "Oh yes, it is most definitely over."

Boccadifalco Airfield, Palermo, Sicily
September 17, 1943
In preparation for landing, Georgie tightened the strap across Corporal Gonzales's chest. Today she learned the name was not pronounced "gon-zales."

Mirth still lit up the man's deep brown eyes. *"Gracias, señorita."*

He said that to taunt her. He spoke perfectly fine English. She winked at him. *"De nada.* See, I'm learning a lot from you Texans today."

"Aye yi yi! The *gringa* translated the secret code of the 36th Division." From the litter above Gonzales, Sergeant Alvarez spoke in an exaggerated Mexican accent.

Flurries of Spanish and English floated around the plane.

Georgie laughed. "Settle down, gentlemen. We'll land in a minute."

She headed to the back of the plane past a mix of white and brown faces. Growing up in Virginia, she'd only seen people in white or black, but this war filled in the spectrum in the middle.

Georgie sat on the floor behind the tier of litters and slung her musette bag across her chest. Sometimes she was glad she'd come to the Mediterranean, glad she'd followed Rose.

A bitter taste filled her mouth.

Rose. The traitor.

They hadn't spoken since their fight at Paestum, and Georgie would be perfectly happy never to speak to her again. Thank goodness Rose and Mellie left Sele on evac flights an hour before Georgie. She didn't have to endure Rose's presence or Mellie's questioning.

How could Rose not trust her? How could she think she'd betray Ward?

Truth took an edge off the bitterness but left a sour sensation behind. Yes, she found Hutch attractive. Yes, she enjoyed his friendship a bit much. Yes, she felt cozy in his presence.

Georgie sighed and leaned her head against the cold aluminum litter bracket.

The 802nd had followed the 93rd from shore to shore, but that wouldn't happen forever. One of the units would transfer or Hutch would leave to join the Pharmacy Corps.

That should make Rose happy.

Perhaps Clint Peters was the one who should worry about faithless hearts. Rose said she loved Clint, but she acted as if she still carried a torch for Ward Manville.

Too bad that thought hadn't occurred to her during yesterday's argument. Oh, to see the look on Rose's face when she said it!

Georgie pressed a hand over her cheek. Rose would have slapped her and she wouldn't have missed.

The plane leveled off and floated to the ground. A perfect landing.

But where was the rapid deceleration? The protesting screech of brakes?

She shot a glance across to Sergeant Jacoby and found her worry mirrored on his face.

"Brace yourself," he said in a low voice.

Georgie's heart sprang into her throat. The brakes. The brakes must be out. She wrapped her arms around the litter supports and clasped her hands together. What good would that do? At least the patients were secured. "Oh Lord, keep us safe."

The plane sped along, and alarmed voices shouted in Spanish and English. They knew. They knew something was horribly wrong.

A sudden jolt. A series of rough bumps. Her cheek banged the litter support, right where Rose would have slapped her. A warm trickle slid down her face.

Terror tightened every muscle, stopped her heart. They'd taxied off the tarmac onto the grass. That would slow them down, but how far could they go before they ran into something?

Another jolt. Smoothness. Tarmac again?

Metal crunched on metal. The plane bucked like a furious horse.

Georgie screamed. Her head smacked the litter support. She flew back, her arms scraping against the brackets. She landed in a heap on the floor.

Screams and shouts filled the plane.

Georgie lay still, breathed hard, felt her head. Intact. Blood on her cheek. She was alive.

"Lieutenant! You okay?" Jacoby leaned over, his lower lip bloody.

She nodded. She couldn't find her voice.

"We hit something. Gotta check the crew." He gave her a hand, pulled her to standing, and dashed down the aisle toward the cockpit.

Georgie's head whirled. She sank to the floor and hugged the litter supports for safety. Her breath pounded in beat with the burning pulse in her cheek.

She could see the scene as from afar, as in a movie. The crumpled aluminum walls of the plane. The smell of aviation fuel and smoke. The men strapped in their litters, calling for help. Her sitting there, helpless as a baby.

"Lieutenant! Get up here! Klein and Singleton — they're badly wounded."

The pilot and copilot. They needed help.

Shock locked her limbs. Her breath came out in quick puffs.

"Lieutenant! What's wrong with you?" Jacoby cried. He turned to a patient. "You there. Can you help?"

"Yes, sir." A few of the ambulatory patients joined the tech.

The cargo door flew open behind her. Two men climbed onto the plane. "The other plane's on fire! Evacuate immediately."

Evacuate. Immediately. Her breath stepped up its pace, a racehorse driving for the finish line. She wasn't wavering. Not at all. She couldn't even move.

Jacoby carried a man by the shoulders, while one of the ambulatory patients carried the man's feet. Looked like Grant

Klein. Hard to tell with all the blood on his face.

"Lieutenant! Georgie! Pull yourself together." Jacoby gave her a light kick as he passed. "You fellows, get the patients out of here. Now."

The movie scene whirled around her. Men rushing, shouting orders. Patients calling out, limping down the aisle.

"Get off the plane." Standing outside, Jacoby tapped her back. "If you can't help, get out of the way."

She stared at him over her shoulder, her arms clamped around the brackets.

"Useless girl." He cussed, grabbed her around the waist, and dragged her to the cargo door. The broken grip wrenched pain through her wrists. Georgie screamed, but he slung her over his shoulder like a sack of feed, hauled her away from the plane, and plopped her on her bottom. "Stay out of the way."

The asphalt burned her backside. Her breath trotted at a steady pace. She pulled her knees tight to her chest.

The nose of the C-47 was folded up, smashed into another C-47 where the wing met the fuselage. The other plane's wing bent high and crooked. The engine had been shoved inside, right into the radio room.

Flames shot up, orange and yellow. Black smoke curled high into the twilight.

The other plane sat motionless in the flames, shocked by the impact, as paralyzed as Georgie. No patients screaming or medics scurrying. Empty.

Back at her own plane, men inside passed litters to men outside, who shuttled them to safety. A good system.

She should be a part of it.

She was a flight nurse. That was her job.

Her breath wouldn't behave. If she could make it behave, then maybe . . . maybe . . .

Rose would slap her. That's what she needed.

She unlocked her hands from around her knees, unfurled frozen fingers, and slapped herself across the cheek.

Her bad cheek. Pain galloped through her. Her chest heaved and filled with air. Her head lightened. Her thoughts focused.

She had to help.

Georgie pushed to her feet and stumbled toward the plane. The earth rolled as if she'd just stepped off a boat. "Lord, help those men. Get them off the plane."

At the cargo door she waited for medics to help an ambulatory patient off, then she climbed inside.

Flames snapped. An explosion rocked the plane. Smoke seeped through cracks in the fuselage.

Her mind sharp and clear, she grabbed the flight manifest on its clipboard by the cargo door and made her way down the aisle.

Eighteen patients on the manifest. How many had already been evacuated? If she'd had her wits about her earlier, she'd know. The litter supports were empty. All six evacuated.

Jacoby assisted a wounded man down the aisle. He glared at Georgie. "Get out of here. You're in the way."

"I'm fine now. I can help. How many left? I have the manifest."

"Get out. Only three left. All taken care of." He passed her. "Completely useless."

Her heart crumpled. She was. She was completely useless.

Three pairs of medics and patients headed down the aisle. "Get off the plane, ma'am. Any minute she could blow."

"That's everyone? You're sure?"

"Yes, ma'am."

Georgie headed for the cockpit, determined to check. Everything empty — the seats, the smoky radio room, the flaming cockpit. She dashed back to the cargo door and jumped out.

"All clear." She ran over to check the patients, gathered a hundred feet away.

"Listen up, boys. Roll call." Georgie called each name, looked each man in the eye, checked off each line on the manifest.

"Thank you, Lord." All saved in spite of her failure. Her legs shook and almost buckled. She turned to Sergeant Jacoby. "We need to examine them for injuries, do TPRs."

Suspicion flashed through his blue eyes. He reached for the clipboard. "Why don't you let me do that?"

She found her smile and set it in place. "We'll work together, same as always."

Dozens of people watched from a respectful distance. Four figures burst out of the crowd. Mellie, Kay, Vera, Alice, all carrying first aid kits.

Mellie swept Georgie into an embrace. "Oh, thank God! Thank God, you're all right. We heard the crash, heard it was an evac flight, saw it was your plane."

"I'm all right." But her voice quavered.

Mellie pulled back and looked her hard in the eye. "You need to sit down."

"No, I need to examine the patients, make sure no one's hurt."

Kay plucked the manifest from her hand. "Let us do that. You sit down. Mellie will give you first aid." She exchanged a strange glance with Mellie.

Georgie let her friend guide her a short distance away and get her seated. For once, the flight of six nurses fully pulled together and worked as a unit.

Almost all of them. A flash of irritation. "Where's Rose?"

"Oh, she's . . ." Mellie's gaze skittered over the tarmac. "We can't find her."

Too consumed by smug self-righteousness to help Georgie in an emergency. The friendship was over, and she wouldn't miss it. "Off with Clint, most likely."

Mellie chewed on her full lips and opened her first aid kit. "Let me clean that wound."

Georgie turned her head to let her friend work. Before her, firemen sprayed down the planes. A column of flame and smoke rose in front of Monte Cuccio, as if the conical volcano were erupting.

Through the flames, the white triangle on the tip of the victim plane's nose identified the squadron. Nose art, unusual on C-47s, showed Hitler's head in the shape of a drum, with red, white, and blue drumsticks poised above.

"Coop's plane." Roger Cooper was a

drummer.

"Uh, yes." Mellie turned Georgie's head away from the scene. She dabbed the wound on her temple with a gauze pad.

Georgie winced and looked out the corner of her eye. Coop sat a safe distance from the nose of his plane, his head in his hands. Shelby paced in front of him, twisting his cap in his grip. Pilots mourned their planes as normal people mourned family.

Surprising that Clint wasn't there, but then he was off smooching with Rose. "They should be here. Clint and Rose."

Mellie groped in the first aid kit as if she couldn't find what she was looking for, as if blind.

Lieutenant Lambert approached Coop and Shelby, asked them something. Coop pointed to the plane, his mouth distorted in a grimace. Lieutenant Lambert clapped a hand over her mouth.

An uneasy feeling slithered in Georgie's stomach.

The chief nurse knelt in front of Coop and laid a hand on his shoulder. He nodded, big slow nods. Then they looked over at Georgie, eyes enormous. Stricken.

The slithering congealed into a nasty knot.

Mellie turned Georgie's head again. "You have to look over here." Her voice shook.

Redness lined her eyes.

"What's going on?"

Mellie dabbed iodine, stinging iodine, on Georgie's cheek. "Let me clean this up."

"No one's on that plane, right? Where's Clint? Where's Rose?"

Lieutenant Lambert walked over, her hands clasped in front of her stomach. She wore a neutral expression. But she was pale. Too pale.

When Georgie was ten years old, her horse, Biscuit, had broken his leg. Daddy had him put down. Daddy wore that same expression when he gave Georgie the news.

The knot in her stomach squirmed around, vile and putrid. "What's wrong? Tell me."

Lambert knelt in front of Georgie and took her hand. She laid her other hand on Mellie's shoulder.

Mellie gulped, a strange sound, almost a sob. She pressed both hands over her mouth and doubled over at the waist.

Georgie's whole face tingled. Her lips parted. No words came out.

Lambert squeezed her hand. "Honey, please listen to me. I need you to be strong."

Strong? Why did she need to be strong?

Another gulping sob from Mellie.

Lambert rubbed Mellie's back, her brown

eyes hurting, compassionate, but firm. "Lieutenant Cooper says that after they landed, Clint Peters remained on the plane to work on his log."

He always did that. Georgie's gaze sprang to the flames. To the radio room, the compartment shared by the navigator and the radio operator. He couldn't still be in there. *Oh God, please no.*

"He — he never came off."

Oh no. Her mouth drifted open. Her chest convulsed. He couldn't be dead.

Mellie's shoulders shook.

Clint couldn't have survived. The crash. The engine. The flames. *Oh God, no!*

Poor Rose. What would she do? She'd shatter. She'd break into a million pieces.

Her cheek stung fresh as if saltwater had leaked into the wound. Her vision blurred over. She set her free hand on the pavement to push herself to standing. "Rose. I need to find Rose. She needs me."

Lambert tugged her hand, made her sit. Tears formed watery trails on her cheeks. Lambert was crying? She never cried.

Mellie straightened, her face red and puffy. She scooted around and hugged Georgie's shoulders. "She isn't anywhere to be found."

"Lieutenant Cooper —" Lambert's voice

broke. She lifted her chin. "After the flight, after the patients were transferred, Rose went back to see Clint. Cooper left the plane a few minutes before the accident. They were — they were both still on the plane."

No. It couldn't be. Not Rose. Her head wagged from side to side. It couldn't be.

"I'm so sorry, honey." Mellie laid her head on Georgie's shoulder. "I'm so sorry."

No! No! The knot in her stomach jolted, unlashed. "No! It can't be!"

"I'm sorry, sweetie," Lambert said. "We're certain."

"No. No." She shook off Mellie and Lambert, stumbled to her feet. "No. Not Rose. It can't — it can't be."

Mellie and Lambert stared up at her, faces twisted with grief and concern. Cooper and Shelby sat together, shoulders hunched in manly mourning. Not for a plane. For a friend. For two friends.

The flames cackled in macabre laughter.

Georgie stepped back. And again. She turned. She ran.

She'd never run like that before, hard and fast, knees high, stride long, like Rose ran. Rose used to laugh at Georgie when they raced, flapped her hands in imitation of her feminine gait. But never mean. Always affectionate.

Her best friend. Forever.

Her chest heaved with each step, heaved out sobs. How could Rose leave? They did everything together. Rose was the backbone. Georgie was the heart. They needed each other.

And the last time — the last time Georgie saw her — the last time she talked to her . . .

Her legs collapsed. She skidded to her hands and knees, felt the heat of skinned flesh.

She should have said good-bye, should have told Rose how much she loved her. She folded in two, down over her knees.

"Did she know? Did she know, Lord?" She died thinking Georgie hated her.

An image pounded her brain. Rose screaming, dying. In that crash. In those flames. In that hideous smoke.

Georgie pressed the heels of her hands against her eyes so hard they hurt. Tears stung her skinned flesh. Still the image scorched her mind. "Lord, no! Not Rose!"

And Clint. Poor Clint.

At least Rose wasn't alone. She was with the man she loved. They'd died together. In each other's arms.

A sob bruised her ribs with its forceful-ness. The night Clint met Rose, he said

they'd be together forever.
He was right.

16

93rd Evacuation Hospital, Paestum
September 23, 1943

Hutch felt the mortar containing mercury and oleate of mercury. "It's cool enough. Add the petrolatum mixture, about twenty-five grams at a time. Triturate it well."

"Triturate." Dom Bruno scooped up a blob of petrolatum with a spatula and plopped it into the mortar. "Who comes up with these words?"

"Same people who named this Unguentum Hydrargyri Forte."

Dom ground the pestle around inside the mortar. He was a fast learner and already had excellent technique. "My Latin ancestors. Can't wait to march into Rome and thank them."

"Maybe by Christmas." That's what everyone was saying now that the Allies had forged out of the Salerno plain.

Another blob of petrolatum. "Strong

184

mercurial ointment. Can't imagine smearing this —"

"Exactly." Hutch cut him off before he got crude. "That's why you stay away from the women. Seems like syphilis puts more men in the hospital than battle." But lonely men didn't always think straight.

Hutch gathered dirty glassware for cleaning. Loneliness certainly skewed his thinking in Georgie's direction, but lately he couldn't help it. When he'd heard a flight nurse had been killed in an accident in Palermo, his heart had seized. Then a moment of joyous relief that Georgie was safe, followed by guilty grief.

Rose Danilovich might not have liked Hutch — and he had a sneaky suspicion his attraction to Georgie was the reason — but she was Georgie's best friend, and Clint Peters was a great guy. They'd made a good couple.

A swirl of air stirred up the stuffiness in the tent. Hutch turned to the entrance and saw the object of his thoughts. "Georgie."

She looked tiny and vulnerable, her face pale, her eyes dull. A bandage covered one cheek.

He stepped to the counter. "I'm so sorry. I heard about Rose and Clint."

"Thank you." She closed her eyes and

185

lowered her head. "I came to say good-bye."

"Good-bye?"

"Say, boss," Dom said. "Finished that ointment. Want me to deliver it?"

"Yeah, sure. Thanks." He gave his tech a grateful smile, not just for the delivery but for the privacy. He turned back to Georgie. "You have a minute? Want to talk?"

She nodded, her face contorting.

"Come on." He motioned her around the counter and offered her a crate to sit on.

"No, thanks. I feel like standing." She twisted her hands together.

"Good-bye?" he said in his gentlest voice. "What do you mean?"

"My flight of six nurse — no, five —" Her voice hitched. "We're going back to Bowman Field in Kentucky. Our formal training was cut short last year, so Lambert's rotating us home. Six replacement nurses have arrived."

Hutch leaned one elbow on the counter, determined to focus on her needs, not the fact that he'd miss her. "Are you coming back?"

She shook her head. "The other girls will be assigned to a squadron after training, maybe the 802nd, maybe another. But Lambert expects me to fail. She thinks it'd be best if I failed."

"I find that hard to believe."

"No. She said so just this morning. She told me she can't have me putting patients' lives at risk. I used up my second chance." Georgie met his gaze, her eyes hollow and reddened. "After the crash, I just sat there in shock. I couldn't move. I couldn't pull myself together. I didn't help. My tech had to carry me off the plane like the helpless baby I am."

Hutch resisted the urge to take her hand. "You're not a baby. You're not helpless."

"As a flight nurse, I am. I'm not strong enough. I wish I were, but I'm not." Heart-wrenching grief swam in her blue eyes.

"You could be. I'm sure you could. Wait, I know." He rummaged in a box on the floor behind him. "I was going to give this to you before I returned stateside, but I guess you'll beat me."

He picked out the tin disc and handed it to Georgie. "It's your constellation."

Her face softened, and she traced the smooth round edge. "What is this?"

"It's a hobby. I learned tin punching in shop in junior high. I do constellations. This one — it's the bottom of a plasma tin. Hold it up to the light to see the design."

She lifted it to the daylight coming through the tent entrance. "Which constellation is this? Pegasus?"

"Nope. Made this one up." He pointed to the design, careful not to stand too close. "Those are waves, and above them, a nightingale. I know you ladies call yourselves nightingales."

"Mercy on wing," she whispered.

"Yeah, and you're above the waves. Unwavering. Not driven with the wind."

"James 1:6."

So she'd looked it up. "Yeah. To remind you God can give you wisdom and strength."

Georgie clutched the tin to her chest. "I'll miss you."

He dug his hands into his pockets so he wouldn't draw her into his arms. "I'll miss you too."

She glanced down at the tin punch. "Everyone — everyone back home sees me as I am and doesn't want me to change. Lieutenant Lambert — she sees me as I am and doesn't believe I *can* change. Rose —" She choked on the name.

Hutch's hand flew from his pocket. He squeezed her shoulder.

Georgie drew a deep, shaky breath and pulled herself taller. "Rose saw me as I should be and couldn't understand why I wasn't already there. But you . . . you're the only one who sees me as I really am and believes I can become the woman I should be."

Something warm and powerful surged inside him, and he opened his mouth to tell her what an amazing woman she was, but he slammed it shut before he said too much.

"I — I made you something too." She pulled a piece of cloth from her pocket. "We were thinking along the same lines. It's a handkerchief. I embroidered it."

"You did?" He stretched out the white square. In one corner she'd stitched dark blue stars, which she'd connected with pale yellow lines to show the constellation. He smiled. "It's the Bulldog."

"And the North Star because you said it was constant, like the Lord, so you can keep your eyes on him."

"What's this?" He traced some darker yellow lines around the belly and along the tail.

"Oh, I thought this section looked like a mortar and pestle. How appropriate — part of your constellation, like pharmacy is part of you."

"Thank you." He looked her in the eye. "I'll never blow my nose in it."

A shaky laugh. "That's what it's for, silly."

He shook his head. Nope, too special for that.

Georgie slid the tin punch into her trouser pocket. "We're flying home, so I'll be stateside in a week. Is there anything you'd like me to take along and mail stateside? It'll arrive much faster."

"Could you?" Sometimes letters took weeks to get home.

"Of course."

He tucked the handkerchief in his shirt pocket and returned to the crate. "I have letters for my parents and sisters, a package for Phyllis. I was going to the PX after my shift." Too bad he didn't have time to write a set of letters free from censorship.

"I'd be glad to mail them." She took the pile and studied them. "She's in New York?"

"Phyllis? Yeah. She got a job at Bethlehem Steel on Staten Island when I was stationed at Fort Dix. She stuck around."

"We're flying into New York. I could deliver it in person. I'd like to meet her."

Hutch's breath stopped at the thought of the two women meeting. But he hadn't done anything wrong, and knowing Georgie, she'd gush about how much Hutch talked about his fiancée and how she couldn't wait to go home and marry her Ward. He wrestled up a smile. "That'd be nice. You two would like each other."

She looked up at him with watery blue eyes. "Is there anything I can send you? Anything you miss from home?"

"Steak. Medium rare."

Her smile was so flimsy, he wanted to gather her in his arms and smother her pain. "How are you really doing?" His voice came out low and throaty.

"Honestly? I'm a mess." She blinked, and moisture glistened on her eyelashes. "All the girls in the squadron are mourning, and I want to comfort them, but how can I be strong for everyone else when I'm falling apart?"

Compassion swelled and shoved aside reason. He touched her forearm, gave her a soft smile, and beckoned her. "Come here. Fall apart on me."

Her face turned red and blotchy. She set the mail on the counter, flung her arms around Hutch, and pressed her head to his chest. Her shoulders shook in silent sobs.

He held her tight, hushed her, rubbed her back, so little and frail, and laid his cheek on her soft curls.

She needed him. In a week, she'd have her father and Ward to hold her, but now he was all she had, and he'd hold her for their sakes. For hers.

For his sake too. He tried to ignore how nice she felt in his arms, how her head nestled perfectly under his cheek, how her hair smelled like grass and flowers, how it felt smooth and slippery under his lips.

Under his lips? What was he doing? He twisted his head to the side, his heart racing. Georgie had turned to him for comfort, not so he could make a pass. What a jerk he was.

He should let go, but she clung to him. At least the crying had tapered off to sniffles.

"I don't know anymore." Her words blew hot on his chest. "I just don't know anymore."

"Hmm?" He zoomed his focus back to her words. "What don't you know?"

"All my life, everything's been smooth and easy. My family loves me, lots of friends, I never wanted for anything. Nothing bad has ever happened to me. I knew God loved me. But now . . ."

"He still loves you, sweetheart." Hutch winced, and his cheeks flamed. Why on earth did he call her sweetheart?

"I know. But I've always been good, and my life's always been good, and now . . ."

"Now your life stinks."

She lifted her face to look at him, so close he'd barely have to move to kiss her. He wouldn't mind the taste of tears.

"It does stink." She buried her face in his shoulder again.

"And you haven't stopped being good."

"No. I know the Lord doesn't make bargains like that. I know good people suffer and the wicked prosper, but I always thought . . ."

Hutch sighed and rubbed her back. "You always thought you were the exception."

"It sounds stupid."

"No. It was a reasonable assumption based on observation."

Georgie sagged in his arms. "I also thought God spared me because I'm weak. He knows I can't handle tragedy."

"Well, then." He gave her a squeeze. "This tragedy shows you what I already know. You are strong enough. This is hard, the hardest thing you've ever gone through, but you can handle it if you lean on God. You'll come through stronger and wiser and even more compassionate because of it."

"Thank you. You're such a good friend." Her arms loosened around his waist, and she pulled back slightly, staring at his chest. "I should get going. I just wanted to say good-bye."

"This place won't be the same without you." A surge of manliness and affection and loneliness, and he pressed his lips to her forehead. Warm and silky.

A brotherly kiss. Just a brotherly kiss.

She raised her face, her eyes soft and liquid.

His heart slammed to a stop. She was going to kiss him. And he'd kiss her back, long and hungry and so, so sweet.

But she didn't. She ducked to the side and kissed his cheek. Every muscle in his body ached to turn and meet her lips, and every fiber of his will fought the urge. His will prevailed.

He released her from his arms, from the danger of his desire.

She picked up the letters and package — the package for his fiancée. "I'll never forget you." And she dashed out of the tent and out of his life.

Hutch rubbed his hands down his heated face and groaned. More than anything, he needed to forget Georgie Taylor. And fast.

17

Prestwick Air Base, Scotland
October 1, 1943

How sad to visit Scotland for the first time in her life and not enjoy it. Georgie's eyes registered the green hills and rolling sand dunes, the wooly clouds and quaint stone houses, but her heart didn't delight.

Everything dimmed in the gray haze of grief.

The five nurses followed Captain Maxwell and hauled their gear across the windy tarmac toward a C-54 Skymaster. The large four-engine transport plane would take them across the North Atlantic to Newfoundland, to Maine, and then to New York.

On board, Georgie stashed her barracks bag in the back and extracted her overcoat and blanket for the chilly flight. She found a seat toward the front of the plane beside Mellie, with Kay Jobson on Mellie's other side. Vera and Alice sat across the aisle to the rear of the plane with Captain Maxwell.

The rest of the seats were occupied by Eighth Air Force flyboys who had survived their combat tours and were headed home. A couple of the airmen tried to flirt with the nurses as they passed, but stopped short. The women's slowed movements and dull expressions had to be as obvious as full black mourning clothes.

Georgie hugged her musette bag to her stomach. Almost a year of trials and triumphs failed to bring this group together, but Rose's death united them. Would the unity last?

One by one, the four engines started, the sound foreign to her ears. So different from the familiar C-47.

She closed her eyes during taxiing and takeoff, her heart pounding. Perhaps it was best they were flying home instead of sailing, all these little hopping flights, all these takeoffs and landings. As an equestrienne, she firmly believed the adage about getting back on your horse.

Still, the sensations of the crash, the fire, the plume of vile black smoke before the volcano wouldn't leave her, the mental image of Rose sitting on Clint's lap, the engine plunging into the radio compartment, the instant of terror. The quick and horrible death.

Georgie's eyes ached from tears, from dryness, from being squeezed shut too much for too long.

The plane leveled off for its long trek. In a few days she'd be home for a ten-day furlough before training started at the School of Air Evacuation. Home, where memories of Rose would assault her from every hill and dale.

Not so long ago, home promised safety. Now she knew the promise was false. Daddy and Mama couldn't keep her safe. Ward couldn't keep her safe. Even God wouldn't necessarily keep her safe.

He allowed tragedy. For a reason. For a good, if unfathomable reason, but he allowed it.

All her life, safety and security had been her goal. Rose's death showed her she shouldn't aim for safety but for strength to stand in an unsafe world.

Through the khaki canvas of the musette bag, she felt the hard metal disc Hutch had given her. He believed she could change and be strong with God's help, and that spurred her to believe it too.

In her mind she could hear the deep timbre of Hutch's voice, see the kindness in his eyes, feel the strength of his embrace, smell the medicinal scent of his shirt, and taste his rough cheek under her lips.

Georgie shivered and wriggled into her overcoat. Thank goodness she'd meet Phyllis soon. Once she saw her as a human being and a friend, she'd be able to kill the silly crush she had on the woman's fiancé. When she went home and savored Ward's kisses, she could bury the crush forever.

Beside her, Mellie shifted, and her head slumped forward in sleep. Rose's death had been hard on her. Rose had been one of her first friends ever.

And Rose had been Georgie's best friend ever.

Although they'd parted on poor terms, truth drove away guilt. How many fights had she and Rose come through? They always made up. Always. Their love overpowered their differences. Rose knew how much Georgie loved her.

Georgie hugged the musette bag tighter. Perhaps it was her imagination, but she heard the letter crinkle. Rose's last words to her.

When they'd arrived in Algeria in February, Lieutenant Lambert made the nurses write "just in case" letters to family and friends.

She hadn't had the courage to read it yet. Two weeks had passed. It was time.

With a deep breath, she opened the flap of her bag and found the envelope. Rose never had pretty handwriting, but what did things like curlicues and frilly dresses and girly games matter? She was everything a friend should be.

Georgie had coaxed Rose from her shell. Rose had coaxed Georgie from her shelter.

She unfolded the letter.

Dear Georgie,

If you're reading this letter, it means I beat you to heaven. No big surprise. I always beat you in footraces. Of course, you always beat me in horse races, but that's more to the horse's credit than yours. As always, you know I'm kidding. It takes great skill to be an equestrienne. See, I even used the prissy spelling.

Okay, now I'll be serious, because that's the purpose of these letters.

Since that first day of school, when you befriended the shy tomboy, you've been an anchor for me. You helped me make friends and even trained me to be a proper Southern lady. Yet you still loved me when I was quiet or had dirt on my knees. You helped me become a better version of me.

I've always loved your warm heart, your happy spirit, and your ability to turn any occasion into a party. Life without you would have been dull.

I hate that Lambert made us write these stupid letters because it makes me think of what I'd do without you — and what you'd do without me.

Now, listen. I know I'm the only reason you came to Africa. You hide your fear well, but I know you're scared and you'd rather be home. I never said anything because adventure is good for you. That's always been my job, to push you to push yourself.

But if God's taken me home, it means I've finished my job and so have you. Go home, honey. Find some way and go home. We both know you belong in Virginia, close to your parents, in Ward's farmhouse, with a sunny kitchen and lots of sewing projects and horses in the barn.

Please don't mourn me. Well, maybe a little. Then get up and move on. Mellie needs you, and so do all the other lonely souls you can rescue. You're so good at that.

Thank you for loving me, believing in

me, and helping me grow.

All my love, Rose

A sob gurgled in Georgie's throat, but she swallowed it back down.

She had permission to go home and seek the security she craved. Yet somehow Rose's death was having the opposite effect on her, as if her friend had left behind a trace of her feistiness and determination.

Rose had been a great flight nurse, and her death left a hole in the squadron. Georgie wanted to do something in her memory. A new goal swelled in her chest — to do something big and brave and bold. To honor Rose by being a bit more like her.

Lieutenant Lambert had sent Georgie to Bowman Field to fail and exit gracefully.

But what if she applied herself at Bowman? What if she could learn to be an excellent flight nurse? What if she leaned on God for courage in crises and wisdom in decisions?

Georgie opened the musette bag and slipped the letter inside. Her fingers brushed the soft cloth of the little stuffed nightingale. The backbone of the group had departed, leaving wings and heart unsupported. Georgie would have to become backbone too.

"From Rose?" Kay Jobson stared at the musette bag.

"Pardon?"

"The letter? Was it from Rose?"

Georgie nodded. "She wrote me a 'just in case' letter."

Kay let out a long breath. "I don't understand."

Irritation sparked. How could Kay understand deep friendship? All her relationships were superficial. She never mentioned her family, never exchanged any letters. She enjoyed the company of Vera and Alice, and she had a boyfriend on every air base. "Rose and I were best friends." Her tone came out snippier than intended.

Kay flashed her a glare. "Not that. I understand that, believe it or not."

What was it about this girl that rubbed her wrong? Oh, she knew perfectly well. While Georgie tried to be good, Kay seemed to try to be bad.

Yet, she sought out Mellie as a friend. And Georgie rarely gave her a chance. She might not understand the girl, but she could at least be kind. "I'm sorry. I shouldn't have jumped to conclusions. What did you mean?"

Kay gave her a long hard look, and Georgie raised an encouraging smile.

With a flip of her wrists, Kay pulled her blanket over her head like a peasant. For once, she looked small and ordinary. "I meant, why Rose?"

A question Georgie had asked herself a dozen times. "I don't know."

"It doesn't make sense. Rose and Mellie and you — you're so good."

"And bad things don't happen to good people?"

"They're not supposed to. They're supposed to happen to bad people."

"They don't always."

Kay waved one blanket-encased hand. "Vera and Alice, they're not good. And me — you know what I am." Her words puffed up with her usual defiant pride, but something quivered in them. Fear. Hurt.

Georgie's heart crushed. A dozen phrases came to mind, but she rejected them all. Too contrite. Too judgmental. Too naïve. But a question hovered in the corner of her mouth, and she let it slide out. "What are you, Kay?"

The blanket came up higher, obscuring the shiny strawberry blonde hair. "It should have been me. Not Rose."

If Mellie weren't sleeping in the seat between them, Georgie would have put her arm around the girl. "No, it shouldn't have

203

been you."

Kay peeked around the edge of the brown Army blanket. "What? I'd think you of all people would agree."

Georgie's cheeks heated. Of course Kay would think that, not just because Georgie loved Rose but because she thought little of Kay — and Kay knew it. She had a lot of making up to do with Miss Kay. Perhaps the Lord was giving her a new project — her most challenging ever.

"You honestly think it's better that Rose is dead rather than me?"

Georgie studied the curved ceiling of the fuselage. "I think God took Rose home because he'd done everything he wanted to do with her on earth. But you — I think God has more he wants to do with you. Lots more."

Kay shuddered and snapped her gaze to the side. "Why would he? He's never wanted anything to do with me. And I certainly don't want anything to do with *him*."

Something quiet in Georgie's head told her to let it go, to wait, and she obeyed and stifled her pretty words.

The temperature drop in the cabin made her shiver. She found Mellie's blanket on the floor and tucked it around her friend's lap and shoulders, and then she wrapped herself in her own blanket.

She sneaked a glance at Kay. Reaching the redhead would be far more difficult than teaching a tomboy to skip rope or a shy nurse to smile. But it might help her see God's reason for Rose's death.

18

93rd Evacuation Hospital, Montella, Italy
October 2, 1943

"Pitch tent!" Lieutenant Kazokov shouted.

As the other men from pharmacy and laboratory rolled out the tent, Hutch pulled eight short tent pins from a canvas bag and distributed them — one to each corner marker, and two for each door.

The air rang with calls of men at work, canvas flapping in the wind, and blunt ends of axes clanging on tent pins.

Rain pattered on Hutch's helmet and mackinaw, and damp brown grasses squished underfoot. The field would be a muddy mess by the end of the day.

Behind the veil of rain, steep green mountains soared around him, capped by castles, convents, and tiny villages. Montella lay north of Paestum, east of Naples — which the Allies had entered the day before — and only ten miles south of the front. The way the Army charged for the Volturno River, the 93rd would soon be far to the rear.

"Hoods and storm guys out!" Kaz called as if the men hadn't already done this seven times since arriving in the Mediterranean.

The men stretched out the canvas flaps and tossed the anchoring lines toward the front of the tent area.

Either Hutch or Technical Sergeant Paskun, the head laboratory technician, was supposed to supervise, but Kaz insisted on doing it, probably to ensure that Hutch and Paskun didn't undo his "modernization."

The reorganization irked the lab guys too.

"Keep your eyes open." Ralph O'Shea shifted the ax closer and nodded to the crowd of locals watching.

"Mm-hmm." Hutch pulled his corner of the tent taut and stretched the loop over the pin.

Theft was a serious problem in Italy, not that Hutch could cast blame. The country hadn't been rich to begin with, and Mussolini had impoverished the nation with his foolhardy entry into the war. Now the Germans left a path of devastation in their retreat, slaughtering or stealing all the livestock, confiscating all vehicles, blowing up aqueducts, and ruining food supplies.

"Good afternoon, Lieutenant." Why was

207

Bergie talking to Kaz?

"Captain Bergstrom, what a pleasure. What brings you here?"

Bergie stood with his back to Hutch. "Thought I should pass on the good news. I overheard Colonel Currier talking about you."

"You did?" Kaz's voice lit up. "What did he say?"

"Didn't hear much. Not polite to eavesdrop, you know. But I might have heard something about him looking for you."

"Oh!" Kaz peered at the tent space next door for Headquarters.

"He's not there. Saw him over by Morgue." Bergie shot an imaginary basketball. Morgue sat at the far opposite corner of the hospital complex. "Say, I could take over here if you want to find him."

"Could you? Thanks." Kaz scurried away.

Bergie grinned at Hutch. "You can thank me now."

"Liar."

"Not a lie. I did hear Currier talk about him. Something about a report ten times longer than necessary. And I didn't say the colonel *was* looking for him. Just that he *might* be."

"Well, Captain, I'll thank you." Ralph stood and swept a deep bow. "We are forever in your debt, kind and gracious sir."

"Hear, hear!" one of the lab guys shouted.

"See, Hutch?" Bergie clapped Ralph on the back. "That's how you show gratitude."

"Gratitude, huh?" Hutch stood, crossed his arms over his soggy mackinaw, and gave Bergie half a smile. "You said you'd take over. Ever pitch a tent before?"

"In Boy Scouts." He raised a three-finger salute. "On my honor —"

"A big old Army ward tent?"

"Nope. But I'm willing to get dirty. What's mud compared to the blood and guts I usually swim in?"

Hutch turned to Paskun. "Why don't you supervise? Ralph can take your spot. I'll put the captain on my team and mess up his pretty officer's manicure."

"Heavens to Betsy!" Bergie said in a falsetto, inspecting his fingernails. "I just had them done."

Hutch let out a laugh. He gathered a fistful of short pins and handed them to Bergie. "Set one on the ground by each wall loop."

"Just like Boy Scouts."

Pitching a tent alongside his best friend did bring back scouting memories, mostly of extra KP duty as punishment for Bergie's pranks.

Hutch took a long tent pin and measured off four and a half pin lengths from the wall. Paskun laid alignment ropes between Hutch's pin and Dom's at the next corner to mark the placement of the guy ropes.

"How's Phyllis?"

"Fine." Hutch pointed to a short tent pin and picked up the ax. "Point it straight down. I'll drive it in. We hook over the wall loops later."

"Payback time, huh? Watch out for my precious surgeon's fingers."

"It'd be a shame if the ax slipped in the rain." He pounded the stake into the ground with the butt of the ax.

Bergie set another in position. "Does Phyllis miss her Hutchy-poo?"

Thank goodness she never called him that. "Too much."

"No such thing, buddy."

Hutch shook his head and hammered away. Letters from home were supposed to raise your morale, not your blood pressure. How many stateside women were in the same position as Phyllis, with loved ones overseas? The vast majority bucked up and made do. If only Phyllis would do likewise. If only his words reassured her.

Maybe a hand-delivered package from Georgie would help.

But his stomach twisted. Phyllis had always been the jealous sort. What would she think when a female friend of Hutch's showed up at her apartment door? A cute female friend.

Hutch drove in the last pin on his side. Why worry? Georgie had a way about her, friendly and disarming and engaging. By the end of the visit, those two would be fast friends, and Phyllis would be convinced of Hutch's love.

Phyllis needed someone like Georgie in her life.

A parallel thought made him scrunch his eyes shut. No, he did not need someone like Georgie. He needed Phyllis. His fiancée. The beautiful willowy blonde who wore his ring and pined for him, because she loved him so much she couldn't imagine life without him.

"What's next?" Bergie gave him a strange look.

"Long pins, right outside the alignment ropes, angled at thirty degrees toward the tent." Hutch stepped behind the rope. "Speaking of women, how are things with your nurse?"

"Lillian's the best thing that ever happened to me. Sweet and gentle and thoughtful. She's the one."

"She seems like a great girl." Hutch hammered in a tent pin. He knew to stay out of Bergie's love life. His pal specialized in the three-month romance, and he'd been dating Lillian Farley since he carried her to shore in Sicily. Heading on three months. Poor Lillian.

Bergie swiped rain off his face. "Remember how you always said the day would come when some gal would break through and make me think of forever? Lillian's the one."

Hutch paused to gaze into Bergie's blue eyes. Serious for once. "We'll talk in November."

He cuffed him in the arm. "I'll show you, and I'm looking forward to it."

"Come on. Let's finish before Kaz gets back and I'm in trouble."

"Nonsense. I'd be the one in trouble, but I outrank him. Ha! The man's blinded by the blazing glare of my rank."

"Just hold the pin."

He did so. "Giving me orders, Sarge?"

Hutch's mouth tightened, and he pounded the stake deep into the ground.

"Relax. You'll be an officer soon."

"Dad's not so sure."

"Why not? He thinks you're the hero of your profession."

More pounding. "Got a letter this morning, right before we left Paestum. More details on the Pharmacy Corps. Turns out Congress only authorized seventy-two officers."

"Seventy-two? That wouldn't staff a fraction of Army hospitals."

"I know." Hutch wiped his hands on his trousers, but they were just as wet as his hands. "They appeased us, offered a lollipop when we need steak and potatoes."

"What are you going to do?"

Hutch stood and looked down at his friend. "I'm going to be one of the seventy-two."

A grin. "If anyone will, you will."

He stretched the guy ropes toward the long pins and showed Bergie how to loop them over the second notch. A sour feeling ached in his stomach. Dad said it might be harder to get in the Corps since he was overseas. But he'd fight. The Corps was the whole reason he went overseas in the first place.

Hutch inserted the front tent pole through the ring in the roof — still flat on the ground.

"Now's the fun part." He lifted the tent entrance, ducked under the damp canvas, and led Bergie to the number one pole.

"Okay, Berg. You hold the bottom part in place. I raise it."

Hutch tilted the pole up about four feet and gained relief from the weight of canvas on his back. Flecks of mud and grass drifted down around him. The rest of the men came inside and partially raised the other three poles. Now they'd wait for Paskun to check the hoods and guy wires at the top of the poles.

"Say, Hutch, I always wondered why you chose pharmacy."

"Why?" He glanced down to his friend through the dim khaki-colored light. "Don't you know? Saw what Dad did. Loved it. Wanted to do it too."

Bergie put on his pensive face. "Sure. But I'm surprised you didn't go to med school with me. You got me through college, helped me with math, chem, bio."

Hutch shrugged. "You're smart enough. You just needed discipline."

"That's what I mean. You're smarter than I am."

"Don't ever forget it."

"All right, men," Paskun called from outside. "Looks good. Are you ready?"

"Number one ready," Hutch called.

"Number two ready."

"Number three ready."

"Number four ready."

"Raise!" Paskun shouted.

As one, the four teams hefted their poles to the vertical. Canvas snapped and more grass rained down.

"Bergie, take my spot. Hold the pole." After he did so, Hutch headed outside and tightened the corner guy ropes to hold the poles steady. Meanwhile, Paskun made sure the four central poles were aligned.

Bergie came out of the tent, brushing grass from his field jacket. "What's next?"

"Pull the wall loops over the pins. I'll tighten the guy ropes." Hutch tugged the first one taut.

Bergie anchored a wall loop and glanced over his shoulder at Hutch. He still wore his pensive face. "I just never understood it. You're smart enough to be a doctor."

Hutch's blood went chilly. "What's that supposed to mean?"

"Just that. You could have been a physician."

He took a couple of deep breaths, but the chill remained. "Why would anyone want to be a pharmacist when he could be a physician?"

"That's not what I said."

"Exactly what you said."

Bergie snorted. "I just meant that in

retrospect, it seems a shame. If you'd chosen medicine, now you'd have the commission you want so badly."

Hutch tugged a rope too tight. "But if I had, I'd have to associate with arrogant jerks who think they're better than everyone else because they have two extra letters after their names."

"Are you calling me an arrogant jerk?" Fire crackled in Bergie's voice.

"Not what I said."

"That's exactly what you said."

Hutch faced his friend and raised one corner of his mouth.

Bergie rolled his eyes to the leaden sky. "All right. I maligned your profession, and you maligned mine. Are we even now?"

"Even." He offered his hand. "Don't do it again."

"Same to you." Bergie slapped his cold wet hand into Hutch's cold wet hand.

In the distance, truck engines rumbled. The crowd of locals backed off the road.

Bergie cocked his head. "Ambulances coming. I'd better get to Receiving."

"I can handle the rest. We're almost done here. Go save lives."

Bergie trotted away and tipped Hutch a salute. "You too."

Hutch erected a pole to hold up the front

corner of the tent, while the sourness in his stomach turned to burning pain.

The truce didn't erase the truth. Deep inside, Bergie didn't respect his work.

19

Manhattan
October 4, 1943

Apartment 315. Georgie lifted the door knocker and paused.

Hutch said Phyllis worked the swing shift, so Georgie came in the morning to make sure the woman was home. She needed to meet her.

After a quick prayer, she rapped the door knocker and stepped back and gazed at Hutch's neat square handwriting on the package. This would be her last connection to him. She'd memorized his Army Post Office number without wanting to, but she would never write him.

The door swung open. A tall brunette in a red suit looked Georgie up and down. "Yeah?"

The girl needed a demonstration of good Southern manners. Georgie set her most charming smile in place. "Good morning. Is

Phyllis home?"

"Phyllis? She hasn't lived here in over a year."

Georgie frowned. How could Hutch be using a year-old address?

"That for her?" The brunette tapped the brown paper. "She comes by every day to pick up mail. She moved up to the fifth floor when she got married."

"Married? I must have the wrong address, the wrong Phyllis." She glanced down the hallway. "I was afraid I'd get lost in this big ol' city, and I guess I did."

The girl peered at the package. "Nah, that's right. Phyllis Chilton. Well, it's Phyllis Richards now."

Georgie stared, her mouth drifting open, her face tingling. That couldn't be. How could she be married? She was engaged to Hutch. To poor . . . poor Hutch.

"What's the matter?" The brunette squinted at the writing again, then up to Georgie with understanding in her brown eyes. "It's from him. He keeps writing, the poor sap. You know him?"

"We served together in Italy. He — he doesn't know she's married."

"You all right, miss? You want to sit down? Have some coffee?"

Georgie managed a faint smile at the sign

219

of manners. "No, thank you. How long ago did she get married?"

"Let's see, June of last year." She leaned against the doorjamb. "Ted was her supervisor at the shipyard, lives here in the building. They started dating about a month after your pal there shipped out. Edwina and I had it out with her. She said Ted made her laugh and forget her troubles. It sure didn't take long for her to flip blonde head over high heels."

Georgie traced Hutch's handwriting on the package, her heart aching for him. "They've been married over a year?"

"Baby must be about four months old."

"Baby?" She clapped her hand over her mouth. "Poor Hutch."

The brunette crossed her arms. "Edwina and I told her to tell the man, but she wouldn't listen. She read some magazine article saying nothing's more dangerous on the front lines than when a man gets a Dear John letter. She thinks it's her patriotic duty to keep up morale."

To keep up morale? Through lies? How could adding betrayal to heartbreak be good for Hutch's morale?

The brunette motioned to the package. "Want me to take that? She'll come by later."

Tingles transformed to sparks. How dare the woman treat sweet, steady Hutch with such contempt? "You said she lives in the building. I'll deliver it myself."

"Apartment 534." Her voice perked up. "Ooh, I wish I could watch."

Georgie lifted her chin. "Dear Mrs. Ted Richards is about to get a dose of Southern charm at its most lethal."

The brunette grinned. "I hope it's more effective than New York brass."

"Much more effective." Georgie strode down the hallway. She took all her heartache for Hutch, her righteous indignation, and her outrage, and stirred them in her heart until they formed the gooiest, sweetest, deadliest syrup.

At Apartment 534, Georgie whacked the door knocker. She could still see Hutch sharing his photograph of Phyllis, the love and pride in his eyes.

Footsteps approached, and the door opened. "Yes?"

Tall like Hutch said. Pretty and blonde like in her photograph. A bit plumper in the face, and she'd cut her hair from shoulder-length to just below her chin.

Her last hope for a case of mistaken identity crumbled, but she bolstered her spirits and flung on a grin. "Phyllis, honey!

221

Oh my goodness! It's wonderful to see you."

Alarm flashed in her eyes, quickly replaced with the polite stiff smile of someone who can't remember the name of a friend.

Good. Georgie hugged her. "You look great. Motherhood suits you. And I love your hair shorter like that. Just darling." She pulled back and fluffed Phyllis's hair.

"It — it's wonderful to see you too." Her gaze skittered around Georgie's face, desperate to recognize her.

She sashayed into the apartment, which was tastefully and simply decorated. "So where's that little sweet baby of yours?"

"The baby? He — he's napping."

"Isn't that a shame? Well, maybe he'll awake by the time we finish catching up. Oh, we have so much to talk about, don't we, honey?" Georgie settled into a sage-green sofa and set the package beside her. "Is Ted at work?"

"Uh, yes. He's at work." Phyllis lowered herself into an armchair, perched on the edge, and smoothed the skirt of her bottle-green shirtwaist dress. She coordinated nicely with her furniture, although her phony smile made the scene less picturesque.

"And you?" Georgie leaned forward and shone her most winsome smile. "Are you still working at the shipyard?"

"Not since — not since we got married."

Another lie she'd told Hutch. "I'm so glad you can be a good wife and take care of your husband. It's what you always wanted."

"Yes." Creases formed in her forehead, and she twisted her hands in her lap. "And look at you. A nurse. In the . . . Navy?"

If she hadn't broken Hutch's heart, Georgie would have felt sorry for her discomfort. "Army Air Forces. I'm a flight nurse."

"Flight nurse? How exciting. I read an article about that. And you've always . . . well, I'm sure that's exciting for you. I — I hadn't heard."

Georgie tilted her head. "No, I suppose you wouldn't have."

Phyllis's upper lip twitched. "No, I hadn't heard."

"I'm sure you're surprised." Georgie crossed the room to the fireplace. "But can you imagine how surprised I am? After everything Hutch has said, and here I find you married with a little ol' baby. Heavens!" She picked up a framed photograph of a light-haired young man. "Is this Ted? Oh, he's handsome, isn't he?"

"Hu— Hutch?"

"John Hutchinson." Georgie cocked her

head and smiled. "Remember him? Your fiancé?"

"You — you know John?"

She pressed her hand to her cheek. "Didn't I mention that? Silly me. We served together in Sicily and Italy. He sent that package over there with his *love.*"

Phyllis's face went ghostly white. "It's not —"

"You know how much that boy talks about you?" Georgie flapped her hand. "He's simply crazy about you. He talks about how much he loves you, how much he misses you, how he can't wait to come home and marry you. Isn't he in for a big ol' surprise?"

"You — you don't understand."

"You're right, I don't." Georgie planted her fists on her hips. "Sugar, I don't know how y'all do things up here, but down South where I come from, bigamy is illegal."

Twin spots of red bloomed on her cheeks. "I'll tell him when he comes home."

"Oh no. You'll tell him now."

Phyllis gasped. "I couldn't. I can't tell him in a letter. That would be tacky."

"Tacky? Tackier than marrying one man when you're engaged to another?"

"You don't understand." She stood and turned to the window, facing another apartment building. "I was so lonely when John shipped out, so sad and worried. And I was angry at him for not marrying me. Ted asked me out dancing to keep up my spirits, just as friends. We didn't mean to fall in love. We just did."

"And it simply slipped your mind to inform Hutch about your change of name, address, and marital status?"

Phyllis swiped away a tear and glared at Georgie over her shoulder. "I'm not completely heartless. I do care about him. That's why I didn't tell him."

Georgie gazed over at the lamp. Ugly fringed thing. "You're right. When I want to show my boyfriend I care, I lie to him."

"Don't you understand?" She wheeled around, a panicky look on her face. "Don't you know how dangerous a Dear John letter is? I read an article that said soldiers are twice as likely to be wounded after they receive one. I couldn't do that to him. And letters are the biggest factor in morale. Don't you know that? John says my letters are the best part of his life. How could I take that away? The one thing that makes him happy? The Army's stripped him of everything else that brings him joy."

Georgie stared at the sincerity on the woman's face. She honestly believed she'd done the right thing. She'd acted out of patriotism and concern.

But none of that excused her actions. Not only had she cheated on Hutch, but she'd lied to him for over a year, teasing him with the dream of one life while happily living another life.

Georgie raised a smile dripping with syrup. "Aren't you patriotic, writing the boys overseas? Your hubby must be proud of you."

Her gaze darted to the sofa. "I — he doesn't know."

"Hmm." Georgie crossed her arms. "Well, sugar, you have yourself a decision to make. Today you'll 'fess up to Hutch or 'fess up to hubby."

"Oh, I couldn't do either."

"But you will. You'll write to Hutch and tell him the truth. Or I'll make myself comfortable and wait until dear Ted comes home so I can tell him his wife is still exchanging love letters with her fiancé."

Phyllis stared Georgie down. "Who do you think you are? Marching into my home and ordering me around?"

"I'm a friend. A friend of a man who's been nothing but faithful all his life." She sauntered over to a desk. "Is this where you wrote all those romantic letters to Hutch? The letters saying how much you love him and miss him and can't wait to marry him?"

"That's quite enough."

"You're right. It is. Now make your choice. Tell Hutch or tell Ted." She opened a drawer. "Look. Isn't that the prettiest stationery? Here, I'll set up for you. Your stationery, an envelope, your pen. Have a seat, sugar pie. Time to write one last masterpiece."

Phyllis stomped over and sat so hard the chair creaked. "If anything happens to John, it's your fault."

"Yes, you keep telling yourself that." Georgie sat on the edge of the desk and smoothed her dark blue uniform skirt over her knees. "Oh, don't mind me, sweetie pie. You just write your little ol' letter. I'll help you start . . . 'Dear John —' "

She gasped. "I never start my letters that way."

"How else would you start? 'My dearest darling'? That wouldn't be appropriate." Georgie waved her hand over the paper. "Go ahead. Don't let me make you nervous."

"Fine." Phyllis put pen to paper.

"Oh dear. It's not October 3. It's October 4."

Icy blue eyes. "Do you mind?"

"Of course not. I don't mind at all. I love

to help people." She batted her eyelashes.

Phyllis wrote hard for several minutes in chilly silence. "I told him this was your idea. Some friend you are, breaking his heart and crushing his morale."

"Please tell him that. And tell him Georgie said hi."

"Be quiet so I can finish." A few more lines and she folded the paper.

"I'd better proofread that for you." She snatched it from the blonde's fingers and scanned the letter, finding nothing but the truth, although in shaky handwriting.

Phyllis stood and held out her hand for the letter. "You may leave now."

"Address the envelope." Georgie slipped off the desk. "I'll mail this myself. We wouldn't want you to misplace it or have the baby drool on it, would we?"

Phyllis pursed her lips and scrawled Hutch's address on the envelope. "I don't know who you are, but I don't like you very much."

"Aren't you the sweetest thing?" Georgie took the envelope. "The feeling is mutual."

"I'm sure you can find your own way out."

"How kind of you. Thank you for your gracious hospitality." She headed out the door before she could hear a retort.

As she trotted down the stairs, her hands

began to shake. She paused on the second landing, leaned against the wall, and stared at the two pieces of paper. With a heavy heart, she slipped the letter inside the envelope and sealed it shut.

Sealed Hutch's fate. Phyllis was right about one thing. The Army had stripped away everything that gave him joy. This letter would steal his last dream — the dream that had been snuffed out over a year earlier without his knowledge.

Georgie pressed the letter to her chest. "Lord, be with him."

20

93rd Evacuation Hospital, Montella
October 5, 1943

Hutch slorped through the mud toward Bergie's tent. Even the gooey mud couldn't pull his spirits down. Snuggled inside his field jacket, his application for the Pharmacy Corps and his most recent letter from Phyllis warmed his heart.

For the first time in months, Phyllis sounded cheery. She and her roommates, Edwina and Betty Jo, had spent a country weekend in Connecticut with Edwina's family, picking apples and glorying in the fall leaves. Edwina's sister had a four-month-old baby boy, and Phyllis described his antics.

She'd be a great mother, gentle but firm, and maybe he'd have the honor of ushering her into motherhood in the near future.

Phyllis was his destiny. Georgie was a distraction, cute and perky and present, a crush issuing from his starved heart. But Phyllis was Rebekah to his Isaac.

And Bergie was Abraham's faithful servant. Bergie had met Phyllis at the soda fountain, the modern equivalent of the well. He knew right away, deep in his heart, that she was the woman for Hutch, and he introduced them.

Hutch knew it too. With Georgie gone, he could see clearly again.

Still, he prayed for Georgie — for God to see her through her grief and guide her decisions. Knowing she'd be home with her family and Ward eased his concerns. She'd be loved and supported, as she deserved.

Hutch counted the pyramidal tents in the officers' area. Back in Philly, he didn't have to knock to enter the Bergstrom home. But in Italy, rank separated him from his best friend.

He peered inside the tent. Bergie lounged on his cot, and Capt. Al Chadwick lounged on his. No barging in. "Captain Bergstrom, sir? Permission to enter, sir?"

Bergie laughed, sat up cross-legged, and set down his magazine. "Granted, of course. Come in. Sit down."

"Thank you, sir." He stepped inside and over the slit trench that served as drainage ditch and air raid shelter. He shot a glance at Chadwick. "I'll stand."

An almost imperceptible curl of the lip, and the man disappeared behind *The New England Journal of Medicine.*

"What's up?" Bergie asked.

Hutch would have preferred to ask when Chadwick wasn't present, but he didn't want to waste any time. "I received the application for the Pharmacy Corps. Dad's asking for reference letters from the dean of the Philadelphia College of Pharmacy and from my first employer, but I need some from Army contacts. Colonel Currier agreed to write one, and I have to ask Lieutenant Kazokov. Would you be willing to write one, sir?"

"I'd be glad to. But what's it worth? Sure, I can tell them what a great fellow you are, but honestly, how can I evaluate your work?"

"Threefold. First, you can account for my character. Second, you can describe how I relate to physicians. Third, you can evaluate how my work affects your practice."

Bergie laughed. "Typical methodical Hutch."

"Methodical is good in a pharmacist. Put that in." He grinned. "Sir."

"All right, then." Bergie swung one leg over the side of the cot and slipped on his combat boot. "Since you've got my letter written for me, tell me how your practice affects mine."

Didn't he know that? Hutch shifted his weight from one leg to the other. "Don't I always get you the meds you need, properly prepared, in a timely manner?"

A snort from behind *The New England Journal.* "Except aspirin. Remember that?"

Hutch snuffed out a spark of annoyance. "Sir, if you'll remember, that was a theater-wide shortage. All hospitals were affected. And I compounded aspirin from scratch as soon as we settled in."

"What? One part asp, two parts rin? Must be difficult." Chadwick laughed and glanced at his fellow doctor.

Bergie smiled and tightened his bootlaces.

Another spark. Alarm this time. But he put on a pleasant smile. "It is. It's tricky. The instructions aren't in the Army manual, but I learned it in school."

Now Bergie smiled at Hutch. "Say, that's good. I'll put that in the letter."

"Thanks." He stepped closer. "See, that's why we need the Corps. The pharmacies in most mobile hospitals are run by technicians with three months of training. Back home it's illegal for anyone but a pharmacist to fill a script. Don't our patients deserve

233

the same level of care they'd get at home?"

"Puh-reach it, Brother John! When do you need the letter?"

"By the end of the month. The earlier, the better."

"Will do. Say, Chad, ready for supper?"

"If you can call it that." He set down his journal and lifted his nose at Hutch. "You're dismissed, Sergeant."

A jab in his stomach. "Yes, sir." He stepped out of the tent into the dimming daylight and plodded through the mud toward the administration tent Kaz shared with three other staff officers.

What was wrong with Bergie? He'd jumped on Kaz for condescending to Hutch, but he let Chadwick get away with it?

Hutch pulled a metal pillbox from his trouser pocket, flipped it open, and chewed a sodium bicarbonate tablet to neutralize the acid in his stomach.

Only one more letter, but this would be the most difficult. And the most necessary. Ivor Griffith served as both the dean of Hutch's alma mater and the president of the American Pharmaceutical Association, so his letter would shine with authority. Mr. Hancock from Liberty Bell Drugs would trumpet Hutch's skill, Currier's letter would carry weight, and Bergie's would lend authenticity. But the Army would look most closely at the letter from his current CO, supposedly the most familiar with his work habits.

Hutch stepped inside the administration tent. Kaz sat at a field desk, typing away. The typewriter belonged in pharmacy and lab for labels and reports, but Kaz kept it in his office so he wouldn't have to share one with the other officers. The way the man churned out reports, sharing probably wasn't an option.

"Good evening, Lieutenant Kazokov, sir."

His shoulders sagged. "You need to type labels *again*?"

"No, sir. I have a favor to ask."

"What do you need?"

Hutch stood straight and tall. "I'm sure you've heard me mention my interest in joining the new Pharmacy Corps. I received my application and I need letters of recommendation."

"You want one from me?" One thin dark eyebrow hitched up.

He swallowed hard. "Yes, sir. Colonel Currier and Captain Bergstrom have already agreed, but I need a letter from my immediate commanding officer."

"Need? Or want?"

235

"Um, need, sir."

"No, you want it." He stood and clasped his hands behind his lower back. "There's a difference between needs and wants, Sergeant."

"I know that, sir. But —"

He held up his hand to block Hutch's argument. "I'm a busy man with important work, and unless this is official Army business, your personal favor will go to the bottom of my pile."

"Yes, sir." He chewed on his lips. He needed to try a different angle. "I would appreciate the help, sir. Only one short letter, but it will carry a lot of weight in the Army. They'll be impressed with your concern for the men under your command. And think, if I join the Corps, I can spread your ideas for modernization." He'd spread them as ideas of what *not* to do, but Kaz didn't need to know that.

Kaz cocked his head and pushed out his lower lip in thought. "I'll see what I can do."

"Thank you, sir."

"You're welcome. You may return to duty."

"Thank you, sir. O'Shea's working the night shift. I'm off now."

"I know the schedule. I set it."

A sigh leached past his fake smile. "I'm

thankful for it, sir. Good night."

Hutch marched outside into the twilight.

Begging to use a typewriter. Working in an alphabetized environment. Giving respect when he received none in return. He'd better be accepted into the Corps.

21

Charlottesville, Virginia
October 6, 1943

"Georgie, it's beautiful," Mellie said from the backseat of Daddy's Chrysler. "I see why you love it so much."

Kay Jobson murmured her agreement.

Georgie leaned against the car window and drank in home. The rolling green hills outside Charlottesville, the Blue Ridge Mountains to the east, and dots of fall color as the leaves started to turn. Crisp white rail fences divided properties, and horses cavorted in the pastures. Best of all, the large white house that had been in the Taylor family for a hundred years. "Home."

Daddy guided the car onto the gravel driveway. "It's where you belong, sweetie pie."

"I know." Her goal. Her greatest longing. Fulfilled. Why didn't it warm her to the core?

The front door of the house swung open, and Mama dashed onto the porch, waving with one hand and wrestling off her apron with the other.

Daddy threw the gearshift into neutral. "Go to her, Georgie. Introduce your friends. I'll bring in your bags."

"Thanks, Daddy." She flung open the car door and ran up the porch steps and into Mama's arms.

"Oh, baby. My baby." Mama's voice swam with tears. "I'm sorry. I'm so sorry about Rose, sorry you had to go through that."

"Thank you." Georgie breathed in the scent of lavender soap, accented by ham and the faint dusty smell of flour.

"I can't believe she's gone. She's so much a part of this place, of your life."

"I know." Georgie squeezed Mama's just-plump-enough middle. How could home be home without Rose banging open the front door and begging Mama to make rhubarb pie?

"Let me take a look at you." She grasped Georgie's shoulders and raised a flimsy smile. She wore her barely graying curls rolled at the hairline and gathered in a little bun at the nape of her neck. Fashionable but mature. A lady, as always.

"Look at my baby." She clucked her

239

tongue. "So beautiful. I'm glad you didn't have to wear those hideous trousers. I can't believe they make you wear those things."

If only Mama knew how hard the flight nurses campaigned for the right to wear trousers.

Mama put on her best company smile. "Please introduce me to your lovely friends."

"May I introduce Mellie Blake and Kay Jobson? Mellie and Kay, this is my mother, Olivia Taylor."

"Mrs. Taylor, it's a pleasure to meet you." Mellie shook her hand.

Kay did likewise. "Thank you for having us."

"It's our pleasure." Mama ushered them into the house. "Where are you from, ladies?"

Mellie smiled. "California mostly, but I spent half my life on botanical excursions with my father in the Philippines and East Indies."

"Oh my!" Mama pressed her hand to her chest. "And you, Kay?"

Kay's gaze darted around the entryway with its dark wood, white trim, and framed etchings of horses on the walls. "Me? From everywhere and nowhere."

"Oh? What do you mean by that?"

"We . . . moved around a lot. Oklahoma,

Nebraska, Kansas, Missouri, wherever."

"Isn't that interesting?" Mama's smile fluttered. She stood in the home she'd lived in since her wedding day, in the county where she'd been born, in the state she'd never left.

Georgie chewed on the inside of her cheek. She hoped Kay wouldn't embarrass her this week, but she could hardly abandon the poor thing. She headed up the staircase. "Let me show you to your rooms."

Mama waved them along. "Mr. Taylor will bring in your things. Supper will be ready in an hour. Y'all lie down and take a rest now." She headed through the door to the kitchen, releasing the scent of baked ham and apple pie.

"Real beds?" Mellie followed Georgie upstairs. "That sounds heavenly. How long has it been, girls?"

"Forever," Kay said. "If I lie down on a real mattress, I may not get up until 1944."

"Here are your rooms." Georgie smiled at the cross-stitch samplers on each bedroom door — Winifred, Alberta, and Georgiana — lined up in birth order down the hallway. "Kay, you'll take Freddie's room. Mellie, you're in Bertie's room. The bathroom's at the end of the hall."

Kay gazed around. "I've never had a room

to myself. What on earth will I do?"

"You'll sleep." Georgie smiled at her and showed her where the towels and extra blankets were stored, then showed Mellie her room. "Don't worry about missing supper. Mama makes a ruckus with the bell."

Georgie took a deep breath and entered her own room. Late afternoon sun slanted through the windows and cast a golden glow over the warm woods and the pale pink bedspread. She sat on her bed under the ruffled canopy. How many times had she and Rose huddled on this bed and played games and told tales and laughed together?

Pink ruffles blurred in her damp vision, and she stood. She yanked out bobby pins and set her garrison cap on the dresser.

Daddy's footsteps clomped down the hallway, and he set Georgie's gear inside her door. "Your mama said you're to lie down for a spell. You've had a long trip."

"Actually, I'm not tired. I'll go help in the kitchen."

"No, you won't, young lady." He smiled with warmth in his blue eyes. "That was a direct order from the general herself."

Georgie fiddled with the hem of her waist-length jacket. All her life she'd done what Mama and Daddy said. Except when she joined the flight nursing program. They knew she couldn't handle it. They knew what was best for her.

But she did not want to lie down. "Thanks, but I'd like to help with supper."

"Are you going to deal with the general? Because I'm not doing KP for you, missy."

She raised her sharpest salute. "I'll take the punishment. You are relieved of your responsibility, soldier."

"We'll see about that," he said in a mock dark tone.

Georgie patted his arm and went down to the kitchen, where Mama stood at the counter, her wooden spoon thumping in her big glass mixing bowl.

She gasped. "You're supposed to be resting, baby."

"I'm not tired. May I help?"

Mama pointed her batter-coated spoon toward the door. "You can help by taking a rest. The ham's in the oven, the peas are shelled, I'm mixing the biscuits, and the pie's out to cool. Made from Ward's apple harvest. He'll be here for supper, of course."

"Good." The sooner she saw Ward, the better. She'd hoped her encounter with Phyllis would empty her mind of John Hutchinson, but it had the opposite effect. In a few weeks, he'd receive that letter and mourn, and she wouldn't be there to comfort him as he'd comforted her. Now she needed to fill her eyes and her mind with the man she'd marry.

Mama turned to her mixing. "I've taken care of everything. Go rest. Let me pamper you."

Georgie glanced around. "May I set the table?"

"Pardon?" Mama gaped at her. "This is not like you, young lady."

"I know. I just want to keep busy."

Understanding softened her features. "All right. Set the table."

Georgie pulled a stack of plates from the cupboard. "Thanks for letting my friends visit."

"You know they're welcome. Did I understand your telegram right? They have nowhere to go?"

She carried the plates into the dining room, leaving the door open for conversation. "They could go to Bowman Field, but the program doesn't start till Monday."

"I suppose California's too far."

Georgie set the plates at Daddy's place and returned to the kitchen. "Mellie's father was in the Philippines when the Japanese invaded. He's in a prison camp, poor thing."

"Oh! How horrible." Mama turned, and a glop of biscuit dough fell to the floor unnoticed. "A prison camp? What about her mother?"

"She passed away when Mellie was little."

"The poor dear." Mama gazed up, as if she could send a big old hug right through the ceiling to Mellie. "What about Kay?"

Georgie grabbed a handful of silverware. "She never talks about family. I think they're estranged."

"Oh dear." Another penetrating upward gaze, but this one carried concern laced with suspicion. "Whatever for?"

"I don't know. We aren't close, but I couldn't abandon her, and she and Mellie are good friends."

"That's just like you, sweetie. Always caring for strays."

Like Rose and Mellie and even Hutch. Georgie distributed silverware at the dining room table, already laid with Mama's creamy damask tablecloth and matching napkins.

A pan clanged onto the counter. "Thank goodness on Monday this nightmare will be over."

"Over?"

"Of course. You said flight nursing was a voluntary program, and now with Rose . . . gone, you have no reason to stay. On Monday you can resign."

Georgie clutched forks in her hand and stared at the open door. "I — I haven't decided."

"Haven't decided? What do you mean?"

She laid a fork on each napkin. "I haven't decided whether I'll resign."

Mama stood in the doorway. "Of course you will. It's too dangerous. Now you know for certain."

Georgie grabbed the knives and circled the table again, cheeks warm, head down so Mama couldn't see the redness. "Even if I left the flight nursing program, I'd still be in the Army Nurse Corps for the duration. I can't just quit. And they could send me anywhere."

"But you've already served overseas. They'll keep you stateside."

"Maybe. Maybe not." Although inside she agreed with Mama.

"They'll keep you stateside." She returned to the kitchen. "Yes, Monday you'll resign."

Georgie groped blindly for the spoons. Her parents wanted her to resign. So did Rose. So did Lieutenant Lambert. Then why did the urge to stay in the program gain strength each day? Why did prayer make the urge stronger?

No matter what, quitting outright struck her as wrong. If God wanted her out, he'd let her fail. And failure wouldn't be a stretch at all.

The front door creaked open. "Hello! Is my Georgie home?"

Ward. Georgie's heart flipped, more in apprehension than anticipation. She hadn't seen him in ten months. So much had happened since then. In Paestum, she'd told Rose the next time she saw Ward she'd make a Christmas tree look dull. But would she?

Mama beckoned Georgie back into the kitchen, her eyes alight. She smoothed down one of Georgie's curls. "You're lovely. Don't make him wait."

Georgie opened the door to the entryway. "I'm home."

Ward wore his good brown suit and the softest smile. He swept off his fedora and set it on the hall table without breaking his gaze with Georgie. "It's been too long, baby."

She nodded and went to him. His hazel eyes shone with his lifelong love for her, and he took her in his thick arms and folded her to his solid chest, strong as an ox. Even at five foot eight, he towered over her.

He pulled back and kissed her, sweet as the apples from his own orchard and about as exciting. Less like the Fourth of July and more like Thanksgiving, warm and homey. But what did she honestly expect after nine years together?

Still, disappointment dimmed the kiss.

Ward led her by the hand into the parlor. "Saw your daddy out with the horses. We'll have some privacy before supper." He settled into the big brown leather armchair and pulled Georgie into his lap.

After she arranged her skirt properly, she snuggled into his embrace. While he played with her curls, she ran her hand over his smooth sandy hair, motions as familiar and comfortable as her favorite pair of slippers.

Ward blinked too many times. He eased Georgie's head down so their foreheads touched. "Can't believe Rose . . . can't believe she's gone."

"Me neither." The mutual grief made her eyes water, and she tightened her arms around his neck. "It was hard over there, but being home, seeing all the old places without her . . ."

"Her parents — they took it hard. They worried about their boys — never thought they'd lose their girl."

"I'll call on them this week."

"That'd mean the world to them." He looked her in the eye. "Now, don't you worry. They really will be glad to see you."

"I know." They weren't the type to hold Georgie's survival against her. "I also need to give them Rose's . . . her things."

Ward pressed her head down to his shoulder. "Baby, no. That's too much for you. Go call on them — that'll be hard enough. I'll make the delivery later."

A few months ago she would have jumped at his offer, the escape from a heart-wrenching experience. Now his pampering, even the pressure on the back of her head bothered her. She resisted and sat up. "You're very sweet, but it's my duty. I need to do this."

"No, it'd be too painful. You're not strong enough."

Her jaw tightened. "I am. And I'm doing it."

His eyebrows pinched together, and he studied her for a long moment. "If it means that much to you, I suppose it'd be all right. I'll come along for support."

"Thank you, sugar." She rewarded his compromise with a kiss on his forehead. "You'll see. I've been through a lot the past few weeks, but I'm doing fine."

Ward traced the scar on her cheek. "Now you're doing fine, baby. Now you're home."

"Mm-hmm."

"Now this nonsense is over."

Georgie tensed. "You want me to resign."

"Why wouldn't you? I've thought this through. Monday you resign from the flight nursing program. In a few weeks we'll get married. I'd marry you tomorrow, but you and your mama will want the whole big wedding, right?"

"Right," she whispered, her throat closing in.

"Once you're in a family way, the Army will discharge you."

She could only nod. Wilma Goodman in the 802nd had gotten married in North Africa and was discharged for getting PWOP — "Pregnant Without Permission." She'd told Ward about it in a letter. Maybe she shouldn't have.

"Simple solution." Ward's voice deepened with assurance. "Then we'll both have everything we've always wanted."

Yes, everything she'd always wanted. Virginia, marrying Ward, living on his farm, raising his children.

So why did it taste wrong? Like pepper instead of cinnamon in the apple pie.

22

Castelvetere sul Calore, Italy
October 11, 1943

The truck lurched over bumps and slipped in the mud. Dominic Bruno cussed the narrow curving road, and Ralph managed to snooze, but Hutch focused on Phyllis's handwriting. With all the transfers and the difficulties of delivering mail in a combat zone, the letter was already a month old. But no less welcome.

I'm so proud that you're joining the Pharmacy Corps. You'll look handsome in an officer's uniform! Even if the odds are long, don't be discouraged. Don't give up. Don't settle for less than you deserve.

Phyllis knew what he needed to hear. They shared the same perspective, the same goals. He'd told Georgie he'd learn to be content, but how would being content drive him forward? Sure, the Bible talked about contentment, but it also said to "press toward the mark."

The truck slammed to a stop, and Hutch braced himself on the dashboard. Dom waved his fist out the window and shouted a long string of Italian at an old man pushing a handcart across the road.

The old man raised his own fist and voice, and walked even slower.

When the road was clear, Dom revved the engine and sprang forward.

Hutch folded the letter. "Impressive language skills."

"I probably told him his mother's giraffe danced on the blue icebox. Gran tried to teach me, but Mom and Pop insisted a good American boy didn't speak-a the old-a language."

"Yeah." Yet the old language fit the old country, with its rustic villages and ancient castles, its rugged hills and treacherous roads, its olive groves and vineyards. But Hutch had never pictured Italy as such a rainy place.

Finally the rain let up enough to allow the 93rd to escape from Montella to Avellino, about fifteen miles to the west. The Germans had bombed the bridges over the rain-swollen rivers and isolated Montella from the world, but now the US Army Engineers and their lickety-split bridges reconnected them.

The convoy of trucks and patient-laden ambulances wound through a village of red-roofed stone houses — and piles of rubble. On Hutch's side of the road, a line of raggedy children sat on a stone retaining wall, bare feet hanging over the edge, calling and reaching to the hospital personnel. For food. Money. Attention.

If only they could stop and help each child.

A boy threw something into the road. It landed behind the previous truck.

A little girl screamed, hopped off the wall, and darted for the object.

"No!" Hutch's foot stomped imaginary brakes.

Dom stomped the real brakes.

In an eternal moment, the child paused, stared at the truck with gigantic eyes, and lunged to the side.

A sickening bump.

The three men yelled and spilled out of the truck. Hutch got to the girl first. She lay on her back, behind the front tire, screaming, writhing, her legs twisted and mangled.

He grabbed her hands. "Ssh. Ssh. Hold

still. You'll be okay. Ralph, get a doctor!"

Ralph took off running.

Big brown eyes fixed on him, terrified and full of pain. *"Mi fa male. Mi fa male."*

"It hurts, she says." Dom knelt beside her, his face contorted. "It's all my fault."

"It's okay." Hutch squeezed the girl's clenched hands. "You couldn't help it. You tried to stop. You didn't have time."

The street urchins gathered around, crying out and chattering all at once. The girl screamed and twisted.

"Calm down," Hutch said, as much to Dom as to the child. "Say something to her. Tell her to be still. Ask her name."

"Um . . . um . . ." He closed his eyes. *"Tranquillo. Come si chiama?"*

But she still screamed, staring at Hutch. *"Aiuto! Mi fa male!"*

"Tranquillo, tranquillo." He leaned closer, trying to soothe her with his voice. *"Come si chiama?"*

She clamped off her cries, her chest heaving. "Lucia." She said it "Loo-*chee*-a."

Hutch gave her a soft smile. "Lucia. *Bella* Lucia. Brave Lucia."

An older boy squatted down, his dirty face stricken. He asked something long in Italian.

Dom motioned him back, yelled at the

254

crowd, motioned them all back. They obeyed.

"Dov'è la mia bambola?" Lucia whimpered. *"La mia bambola."*

"What's she saying?"

"Let me think." Dom clapped his hand behind his neck. "She's asking where's her doll."

One of the children ran to the object in the road that caused the accident and thrust it at Lucia. She clasped it to her chest and sobbed. A filthy cloth doll. She'd run into the street for a doll. Poor kid. Probably the only toy she owned.

Hutch stroked back the hair from her face. A pretty little thing under the grime, with long tangled black hair. The other girls wore braids. "How old is she?"

"Quanti anni ha?" Dom asked.

"Sette." Lucia's arms shook.

The pain had to be severe. Where was that doctor? For heaven's sake, this was a hospital. "Where's the doctor? And where's her family? We've got to get her family."

"She's seven." Dom sat back on his heels and grimaced. "Should have paid more attention to Gran. Um . . . *Dov'è la tua famiglia?*"

Lucia rolled her head to the side and closed her eyes. Tears dribbled over her cheeks. Her grip on Hutch's hand intensified.

The crowd talked all at once, adults pushing their way in front of the children. Dom held up his hands to slow them down and shouted questions until they spoke in turn. After a long exchange, the crowd fell silent.

"It's bad." Dom's voice dipped low. "They're all dead. Mom and little brother and a baby killed in a Luftwaffe bombing a month ago. The Germans tried to take the dad away for slave labor, the devils. He insisted he needed to stay for Lucia. He was all she had. They shot him. Right in front of the girl. She's been living on the streets."

She had no one. Hutch's throat thickened, and he stroked her matted hair. She didn't even have anyone to braid her hair. "Poor little thing."

Lucia opened damp brown eyes and latched onto Hutch. *"Come il mio padre. I suoi occhi."*

"What was that?"

"You remind her of her father. Something about your eyes."

Like a vise on Hutch's throat. For her father's sake, Hutch would do his best for her. And the way her arms and body shook, she needed pain medication and lots of it. "Where's that —"

"Out of the way!" Bergie shouted. "Come on. Everyone out of the way."

"Where have you been?" Hutch didn't leave Lucia's side, not that he could have anyway. For such a tiny creature, she had a stranglehold on his hand.

"You guys kind of caused a roadblock, and half the country came to see." Bergie opened a small medical chest. "We'll get her stabilized, then move her out of the road. Got to get the convoy moving."

Two medics set up a litter and a pair of leg splints, while Bergie's girlfriend, Lillian, knelt beside Lucia, tucked a blanket over the girl, and cooed to her.

Lucia stared at the medical chest, shrank back, and sobbed.

Hutch turned her chin so she faced him. "Don't think she likes doctors."

"We're used to being the bad guys. And she'll really hate me now. Here comes the morphine. Don't let her see."

Hutch leaned closer and sang "Mary Had a Little Lamb," the only children's song he could think of.

Bergie wiped a clean spot on her thigh, then sank in a syringe

Lucia screamed bloody murder. While Hutch sang and squeezed her hand, a river of words flowed from Lucia's mouth. She pointed at the plasma bottle in Lillian's hands and screamed more, her eyes wild. The only thing Hutch could make out was *Tedeschi,* the Italian word for the Germans.

"Uh-oh," Dom said. "We've got a big problem."

Bergie continued his examination. "Bigger than compound comminuted fractures in both legs?"

"Yeah. Seems some German doctors took care of her brother after their house was bombed. They hung fluids, just like that, right before he died. She thinks they murdered him."

"She needs plasma," Bergie said. "She'll go into shock."

Lillian laid her hand on Bergie's shoulder. "Can we wait? The morphine will put her to sleep soon. Then we can hang the plasma."

He turned to her with a frown, but then his face softened. "Yeah, sure. We can wait."

One corner of Hutch's mouth twitched. Maybe they'd last longer than three months after all. "Good idea, ma'am. We have to convince her we're on her side."

Bergie helped the medics lift the girl onto the litter. "If she panics at the sight of an IV, giving her sulfa will be fun."

"How about oral?" Hutch didn't let go of Lucia's hand.

"Oral? She can't be more than fifty pounds. Even if she could swallow a tablet, it'd be too much for her."

How could he not laugh? "Have you forgotten your friendly neighborhood pharmacist? I can make a suspension for her."

Bergie's face lit up. "Of course. You saved the day."

"Put that in your letter."

"My letter?"

"For the Pharmacy Corps."

"Oh yeah. Forgot about that. Sorry, pal. I'll get on it."

Hutch's abdominal muscles stiffened. It meant everything to him and nothing to his best friend.

The medics, Bergie, and Lillian applied traction, elevated Lucia's legs, and bound them with muslin strips to angled metal rods that served as splints. The child sobbed, her gaze locked on Hutch.

He clutched her hand to his chest. "*Tranquillo. Bella* Lucia."

An elderly villager approached, speaking in an authoritative voice. Dom stood to talk to him. With every word, Dom's face got redder and Lucia's grew paler.

He wheeled away. "That's the mayor or

some-such. They don't want her back. She's an orphan, has no family. They don't have enough food as is, and now she'll be a cripple. They can't take care of her."

"Sono invalida," Lucia whispered. *"Sono invalida."*

Dom lowered his head and scrunched his lips together. "She says she's a cripple."

"No." Hutch drilled his gaze into her. "No *invalida.* Captain Bergstrom's a great doctor. He'll fix up your legs better than new. You'll be walking and dancing and running into streets again real soon."

Bergie nodded and smiled at the girl, but his hand clenched onto Hutch's forearm. "Don't make promises I can't keep."

23

School of Air Evacuation
Bowman Field, Louisville, Kentucky
October 11, 1943

A year before, Georgie had stood by the same green lawns and utilitarian white buildings, smiling over her fears.

All those fears had been realized. She'd experienced the first great tragedy of her life. She'd lost her best friend. She'd let down patients under her care. She'd been proven helpless and incompetent.

Yet she stood.

Beside her, Mellie sighed. "Bittersweet memories."

Georgie strode toward HQ, reminders of Rose everywhere. "Yes." This was also where she met Mellie. A friendship with a shaky start but now a source of joy and comfort.

"It's good to be back. I can't wait to see what they have to teach us." Mellie hooked her arm through Georgie's. "Have you

261

decided? Your family sure wants you to re-sign."

"I'll give it a week, since I've come so far. I'm sure I'll fail by then, and the Army Air Force will decide for me."

Mellie squeezed her arm. "Nonsense. You won't fail."

A groan collapsed Georgie's chest. "But then I'd have to decide, and I don't know what to do. My family and Ward want me to resign and get married. When we start a family, the Army will discharge me, and I can go home where I belong. But that seems unethical, don't you think? Taking marital vows for the purpose of breaking military vows?"

"Mm."

"Then I think of Rose. I think of the men fighting so hard in Italy and getting sick and wounded, and my heart goes out to them, and I wonder if I have it in me to be the flight nurse they need."

"Mm-hmm."

She stopped and faced her friend. "What should I do?"

Mellie shook her head, and her dark curls lashed from side to side. "Oh no. If I can learn to make friends, you can learn to make decisions. I learned right here, and you can too."

Georgie tipped her head to the blue sky. A fleet of C-47s roared by and drowned the sound in her head of Hutch's rich voice speaking similar words. Then she batted her eyelashes at Mellie. "Remember, honey. I helped you learn."

The corners of her exotic dark eyes crinkled. "I can help you too. I'll listen and help you weigh your options, but I will *not* tell you what to do. I won't baby you like your family does."

"That obvious?"

"They even call you baby."

The pet name used to feel like a snuggly blanket, but now it suffocated her. "I just want to make everyone happy."

"You sound like the old Tom." Mellie spoke in a love-softened voice. "But he learned — and you will too — that you can't and shouldn't make everyone happy. Do God's will, not man's."

If only the Lord would rearrange the wispy white clouds to spell out his will. He wrote sixty-six books in the Bible. Certainly he could spare one word for her.

No amount of frowning at the clouds changed their formation.

Feminine laughter floated up the walkway ahead of them. Six nurses approached, all wearing the official gray-blue flight nurse trouser uniforms. The women eyed Georgie's and Mellie's uniforms and whispered to each other.

Georgie felt frumpy in the old dark blue Army Nurse Corps service jacket she'd refashioned to waist length and the trousers she'd bought at J. C. Penney's. They'd shipped to North Africa on too short of notice to be properly outfitted.

"Oh for heaven's sake, I'll ask." A nurse with light brown hair stepped forward. Her wide-set eyes sparkled with determination and a hint of fun. She saluted Georgie and Mellie. "Excuse me, ladies. I'm Louise Cox. A rumor's floating round that nurses who really, truly flew in North Africa and Italy are here."

"Some rumors are true. We're from the 802nd." Mellie held out her hand with a warm smile, such a different woman than a year before. "I'm Mellie Blake."

Louise squealed as if Mellie had said she was Katharine Hepburn. "Really? You flew? What's it like?"

The other women gathered around, faces bright. Questions and answers and introductions flitted around like fireflies on an August night.

A firefly glow built in Georgie's chest. These women longed for what Georgie had.

They'd worked hard to be accepted into the School of Air Evacuation. They shared her passion to help the boys overseas.

Louise, obviously the ringleader, filled them in on the rigorous curriculum — aeromedical physiology, crash procedures, ditching procedures, neuropsychiatry. While the new girls were halfway through a six-week program, the women of the 802nd would study for only three weeks, filling in gaps in their original training.

Georgie didn't need the clouds. God's will was as plain as the glow on Louise's face. She must apply herself and stretch herself.

In her mind, she could see Hutch nod his approval, his brown eyes warm and serious.

Georgie shook off the thought. She shouldn't consider Hutch's opinion, only Ward's.

"No," she murmured under her breath. She should only consider God's.

Charlottesville
October 16, 1943

"Good solid crop this year, and the War Department paid well." Ward clicked his tongue at his horse, Clyde, and urged him forward through the orchard.

"I'm glad." Georgie stroked Hammie's ebony mane, the long stiff hairs welcome to her touch.

The sun blinked in and out through the branches of the apple trees, leafy but plucked bare of fruit. Scents of soil and fresh air swirled together in autumn crispness, and Hammie's gentle gait rocked her, lulled her.

Ward talked on and on about the fall apple crop and the summer tomato crop and his plans for winter. Why couldn't she concentrate? This would be her life.

Her thoughts glided back over the Appalachians to Bowman Field. The bereavement leave for the nurses offered generous travel vouchers. Every weekend she could catch a C-47 from Bowman to Richmond, Virginia, and back again.

The past week, she learned so much at the School of Air Evacuation, and she didn't fail. Not at all.

Rather the training energized her. She saw how it could be applied in the field, and something deep inside her wanted to apply it.

A branch stuck out in her path, the leaves as dusty and old as her fears, and she swept it aside.

How could she bask in the glory of a Virginia October when men suffered in New Guinea and the Solomons and Italy? And

Hutch would suffer very soon. Two weeks had passed since Georgie had mailed Phyllis's confession.

She nuzzled Hammie's russet ears and cooed to him as if it would comfort Hutch too. The poor man. All his dreams dashed.

"Glad it's over." Ward headed out of the orchard and toward the stable. "Can't stand seeing the Yankees win."

"What Southerner could?" Georgie managed a smile, although talk of the World Series dredged up memories of how Rose and Ward argued sports, great heated joyful discussions, and Georgie would sit back and laugh.

"Four games to one. The Cardinals couldn't pull it off for us."

"Well, St. Louis isn't really in the South anyway."

"More than New York." He spat out the last two words with disgust.

Georgie had met too many Northerners in the past year to share his contempt any longer.

Ward approached the stable with its shiny coat of white paint and its white rail fence, pretty as could be. "Hammie will like his new home."

Something lurched in her chest. It wasn't Hammie's home yet, not until they married. But she gave Ward the smile he expected. At least he'd thought of her.

After they dismounted, they led the horses into the corral to graze. Georgie fed Hammie one of Ward's gorgeous red apples, savoring the tickle of horse lips on her open palm. She pulled the horse's head down so she could lean her forehead against his, the warmth of his brown velvet eyes assuring her. "I don't suppose you'd decide for me either, would you?"

He puffed air out through his nostrils.

"No, I didn't think so."

"What was that?" Ward waited by the gate.

"Telling him what a wise old horse he is."

Ward cracked his familiar grin and reached for her. "Come see the house."

"I can't wait to see inside." She took his hand. The farmhouse didn't have the grandeur and scope of the Taylor home, but the simple, trim lines appealed to her.

"Four up, four down, and plenty of room to add on if we need it. And I hope we need it." He squeezed her hand and gave her a shy smile.

Georgie's cheeks warmed, more aware than ever that they weren't chaperoned. Mama had given her a strict one-hour deadline before she sent out the cavalry. Ward had always been a gentleman, but

268

men were men.

A broad shady porch, a narrow entry, a cozy parlor. Yellow curtains hung in the windows, and Georgie flipped the fabric to inspect the stitchery.

"Pearline made those." Ward dug his hands in his trouser pockets, without a trace of telltale red in his cheeks. "I told her yellow since it's your second-favorite color after pink."

"Mm-hmm." Miss Pearline had cheap taste in fabric and second-rate seamstress skills. "May I see the kitchen?"

Ward grabbed her hand. "Come see. You'll love it."

She did. Sunshine streamed through ample windows over wide counters and modern appliances.

Ward stroked the icebox. "The previous owners put in new appliances a few years ago. Thank goodness, since you can't buy any with the war on."

"It's beautiful." Georgie leaned over the sink. The window overlooked a grassy slope toward the orchard, with the stable to her left.

"We both know you belong in Virginia," Rose had written in her final letter, *"close to your parents, in Ward's farmhouse, with a sunny kitchen and lots of sewing projects and horses*

269

in the barn."

Her throat clogged shut. All of that lay before her.

He set his hand in the small of her back. "Do you like it?"

"Of course. It's perfect." She spun away and out onto the porch, where she gulped a deep breath.

Ward leaned his thick forearms on the porch railing beside her.

The blue sky and green grass and neat white buildings. The rustle of trees and nickering of horses. The earthy smells and the taste of autumn in the air. It was all she'd ever dreamed of. "Ward, have you ever wanted to travel?"

"Travel? Out of Virginia? Why? It's perfect here."

"Yes, it's perfect, but there's so much more in the world." She looked into his puzzled eyes. "This past year I ate coconut in Florida, sailed past the Statue of Liberty, shopped in a Casablanca bazaar, traipsed the streets of Algiers, swam in the Mediterranean, strolled down winding Sicilian streets, and explored ancient Greek temples. I heard people speak French and Arabic and Italian and Spanish and even German. It's all so fascinating."

Ward's mouth compressed. He stared

down at his clasped hands, one thumb tapping the other. "I was afraid of this. Afraid going away would make you discontent with plain old home."

"I'm not." She covered his hands with hers. How could she word it? "I'm not discontent with home, but now I like other things as well. My horizons have expanded."

He wouldn't look at her. He cleared his throat. "Have they expanded past me?"

"No. No, honey, no." She squeezed his hands hard.

His Adam's apple bobbed up and down. "So why are you going through this training program? Why didn't you resign on Monday as we agreed?"

"*We* didn't agree. I never said I'd resign."

"I don't understand. It's the only way to get you out of this crazy mess."

Georgie waved her hand eastward, toward the Mediterranean. "What if this crazy mess is exactly what I need to grow?"

He rubbed her back as if she were a toddler needing a nap. "Baby, you don't need to grow. You're perfect the way you are."

"But I want to grow. I need to learn how to make decisions."

"Why? Your family and I — we'll always be here for you. We'll always take care of you."

"Will you? Can you honestly make a promise like that? What if something happened in the house with a half-dozen children, and you were off in the orchard, and I had to make a decision? What if you got hurt and I had to help you?"

He coiled one finger into her hair. "See, the war's made you into a worrywart. That's not like you, baby."

She resisted the urge to swat his hand away. "I'm not a worrywart. I'm just more realistic. I need backbone."

"Why would you need backbone if you're surrounded by people with backbone?"

"I want it. I want to be decisive."

His hazel eyes softened into the most infuriating condescending look. He pressed a kiss to her forehead.

Georgie's face tingled as the blood drained from her face and the confidence drained from her soul. "You don't think I can do it."

"Nothing wrong with that, baby." He nuzzled her cheek. "That's like a thoroughbred trying to be a big old draft horse. It's not in your nature, and that's okay. I love you the way you are. Backbone would ruin you."

The fog of his words blurred her vision. Hutch thought she could learn to make decisions, but what did he know? The people who knew her best knew she couldn't do it.

24

Volturno River
October 24, 1943

Unlike the US Fifth Army, Hutch crossed the Volturno River backward. While the Allies crossed under machine-gun fire eleven days earlier, Hutch rode in a jeep, turned in the front seat to face Lucia. Her litter was strapped across the backseat, while two more litters were strapped on the hood, a makeshift ambulance. The 93rd would be the first Allied hospital on the north bank of the Volturno.

Under an overcast sky, the jeep rattled over the Bailey Bridge, an engineering marvel that could span a river in hours.

A furrow raced up Lucia's forehead, and she clutched her *bambola* even tighter. Bergie's girlfriend, Lillian, had finally convinced the child to let her bathe the doll, and the nurses had fashioned a miniature hospital gown and bathrobe and braided its hair to match Lucia's clean shiny locks.

The nurses fussed over Lucia, but she only ever asked for her Signor Oo-chay. She couldn't say the letter *H* and she tacked a vowel at the end of most words, so "Hutch" became "Oo-chay." Dom said the Italians would spell it Ucce. Hutch liked that.

Time for his treat. "I have a gift for you. For Lucia."

She'd picked up a lot of English in the past two weeks, and he'd picked up a smattering of Italian. She tilted her head. *"Non capisco."*

He pulled a tin disc from the pocket of his field jacket and handed it to her. "For Lucia."

She ran a finger over the pinpricks, and he showed her how to hold it up and shine a flashlight behind it. He hadn't learned the word for *stars*, but he knew Lucia's name had to do with light, and *notte* meant *night*. *"Lucia di notte."*

Her grin rose, revealing two missing teeth in the lower row. *"Stelle."*

"Si. Stelle in Italiano. In English, stars."

"Star-zay."

"Stars." He clamped his lips together in an exaggerated manner to show her how to cut off the final vowel.

"Star-zay." She clamped her lips shut.

Hutch laughed, met with her bubbling giggle. She was impossibly cute, lit from within. Her name fit. Something about her reminded him of a tiny Italian version of Georgie. He understood why Georgie's family had coddled her, because he felt a strong urge to coddle Lucia.

The convoy halted in the middle of the bridge. Jim Fleischer, the driver, stopped the jeep. "Cute kid. What's wrong with her?"

Hutch glanced to the clouds and tensed. The Luftwaffe loved to target bridges, especially bridges loaded with vehicles. "Got hit by one of our trucks. Two broken legs."

Fleischer cut himself off mid-cuss, for Lucia's sake, most likely. "What about her parents? They're fine with us hauling her halfway up Italy?"

"They're . . . gone. The war, you know."

"War is — well, you know what it is."

"Yep." War was bad enough when men shot each other to pieces, but it defied understanding when little girls lost entire families and got maimed.

That little girl tugged his sleeve. *"Il orso!"*

Not just cute but smart. She'd figured out the constellation on the disc. He gave her a deep throaty bear growl.

She giggled and held out her little hand. *"Per favore. Vorrei il orso."*

Hutch pulled out Lucia's favorite thing, the handkerchief Georgie had embroidered with Ursa Major.

Lucia compared the handkerchief and the disc and chattered in delight.

Fleischer inched the jeep forward. The Bailey Bridge rocked with the river's flow. "I hate to ask, but what'll happen to her?"

Hutch studied the cast-bound legs, out of traction only for the ambulance ride to the new hospital site. "The surgery went well. Now we wait and see how well she recovers."

"After that?"

"The Red Cross wanted her in a hospital in the Naples area, but when they saw how attached she is to the staff of the 93rd, they decided she should stay with us until she recovers."

"And then?"

Hutch drew in a deep breath, marred by exhaust fumes. "She has no family left. She'll go to an orphanage near Naples."

"Too bad." He wrestled the gearshift, and the jeep lurched forward and up onto the north bank. "She sure likes you. You married?"

"Engaged."

"You gonna adopt her after the war?"

"I've thought about it."

Lucia had tied the handkerchief over her *bambola* like a peasant's scarf, and she showed the doll the constellation on the tin disc like a teacher with a student.

The war had ripped Italy to shreds. This country would be no place for an orphan after the war, especially one who couldn't walk or couldn't walk well. What kind of future would she have? But in the United States, she'd have a chance.

Tonight he'd write Phyllis and broach the subject. She couldn't wait to have children of her own, but would she want to adopt a seven-year-old who didn't speak English and might never walk?

He hesitated to bring it up. Phyllis had been acting odd lately. Her most recent letter told a funny story about her roommates and mentioned an accident at the shipyard — both stories identical to ones she'd told months earlier.

She didn't realize how often he read her letters. Repetitions popped out at him, and they'd increased in frequency. As if she didn't have any fresh stories. As if she weren't getting out with her friends. Worry for her slithered in his stomach.

He needed to go home, but for the first time in years, he didn't want to go quite yet. If the Pharmacy Corps could hold off until Lucia was discharged from the 93rd, that would be best.

"*Grazie,* Signor Ucce." Lucia held out the disc, flashlight, and handkerchief.

He took the hankie but folded her fingers around the disc and flashlight. "For Lucia."

She cried out, clutched the gifts to her heart, and unwound a long ribbon of Italian.

He couldn't make out a word, but he understood her just fine. "*Prego, la mia* Lucia."

"*Grazie, grazie, grazie.*" She hunched her shoulders and closed her eyes with a look of such bliss that no one in their right mind would guess she'd lost her entire family and the use of her legs in less than two months.

Such resiliency. Such grace. He patted her arm. *"Canzone?"*

"*Si! Si!* Yes-ay!" She loved songs.

He launched into "Twinkle, Twinkle, Little Star" and folded the handkerchief. Georgie made it to remind him to keep his eyes on the Lord. But the more he studied it, the more he realized the bear, just like the real Ursa Major, didn't actually look at Polaris.

Hutch traced the mortar and pestle she'd worked into the design of the bear. It was almost as if the mortar and pestle weighed the bear down and took its eyes off the North Star, as if the burden of Hutch's profession pulled his eyes off the Lord.

He tucked the handkerchief into his jacket pocket. Nonsense. He read too much into it. Didn't the Lord want him to do his best work? To strive for the best?

The Army interfered with proper pharmacy practice and good patient care. Hutch could help more people in the Corps, where he could reform the system. Of course it was God's will.

"Again-uh? *Per favore?*" Lucia's dark eyes begged him.

Hutch sang "Twinkle, Twinkle," this time with hand motions, and Lucia imitated him and tried to sing the words.

" 'Like a diamond in the sky.' " That was his goal. The Pharmacy Corps, marrying Phyllis, and adopting Lucia. A glittering dream.

25

School of Air Evacuation
October 25, 1943

If Georgie was going to fail, today was the day.

The top half of a C-47 cargo plane lay by the side of a pool for ditching practice. They'd had lectures and seen a training film, but today they'd put it into action and work with a flight crew to evacuate a plane.

Georgie shuddered, and not from the brisk breeze. The situation reminded her of the crash that took Rose's and Clint's lives, of her own paralysis under pressure.

"You'll do fine." Mellie stood beside Georgie next to the pool, where Kay Jobson and Alice Olson assisted mock patients into inflatable life rafts.

"Thank you." She had no reason to panic. Unlike in a real ditching, the plane couldn't sink, she'd be within easy reach of dry land,

and no lives would be at risk. "You did great."

"Thanks. Louise made a good partner. I like her."

The nurses worked in pairs, one in place of the technician. Georgie clamped off a comment about having to work with Vera Viviani. Mellie didn't tolerate gossip.

Besides, Vera stood only a few feet away, arms crossed tight over her chest. Was she nervous? Georgie stepped closer. "Ready, Vera?"

"Ready for our performance, you mean?" She glared across the pool, where Captain Maxwell stood with his wife and two darling little daughters, who were staying at Bowman this week. "I do not appreciate being on display. Honestly, this is a training exercise, not a ballet recital."

"Hmm." Georgie hiked up one eyebrow. She thought it was sweet that the flight surgeon was showing off to his family. And Vera never avoided the spotlight.

Mellie cleared her throat and beckoned her.

"Yes?" Georgie returned to her friend.

"I think . . ." she whispered. "I think it's that time."

Of the month? Why hadn't she thought of that? Vera certainly had been cranky today.

"By the way," Mellie said in full voice, "thanks for bringing us home with you again last weekend. Kay and I had fun."

Georgie chuckled. "I'm surprised Kay didn't break her neck horseback riding."

"I am too. But it was so relaxing after a week at Bowman."

Relaxing? Not for Georgie. She sighed and brushed a curl out of her face. At least her friends had served as a buffer.

"Are you and Ward all right? Things seemed tense."

Georgie tried to concentrate on watching the ditching practice, but how could she? "He has a friend in city hall who'll bend the rules for us. He wants us to get our marriage license next weekend and get married as soon as we legally can."

"Next weekend? So soon?"

"We've been dating since the ninth grade."

"Yes, but it seems . . ."

"Rushed. It's rushed. He wants me in a family way and out of the ANC."

Mellie pulled her full lips between her teeth and searched Georgie's face. "What do you want?"

"More importantly, what does God want?"

"Mm-hmm. Any thoughts?"

She jutted out her chin. "For the first time in my life, it bothers me that someone wants to make a decision for me. For the first time in my life, I want to push myself, to grow, to —"

"Lieutenant Taylor, Lieutenant Viviani." The officer running the drill read from a clipboard.

Georgie headed over and tossed one more comment back to Mellie. "And I honestly believe I could do good things as a flight nurse."

A smile crept up Mellie's face, and she shooed Georgie off.

She entered the half-fuselage, set up with men strapped to litters and lounging in their seats, sporting various fake injuries.

Vera nudged her. "You play the technician. I'll be the nurse. I'd like to pass."

Georgie gave her a stiff smile. Some women ought to go into hiding once a month.

It didn't matter who played which role anyway. They'd have to work in unity at lightning speed, taking care of patients and medical supplies while the crew dealt with the plane, rafts, and emergency equipment. The nurses couldn't interfere with the crew's work or ask for help.

"Prepare for ditching."

Georgie's heart lurched, and she hated the fact that it did so. Vera dashed to the front of the plane and talked over the ditching procedure while she helped the ambulatory patients into their life vests. Georgie wrestled life vests onto the litter patients, checked their securing straps, and spoke words of comfort.

Meanwhile, crewmen tied down life rafts and other equipment by the cargo door, and Georgie scooted to allow them to pass.

The bell rang six times.

Georgie and Vera took seats near the back of the plane, put their heads between their knees, and clasped their hands under their thighs. The aerial engineer and navigator mirrored their positions on the other side of the aisle, closest to the cargo door.

Georgie put on her cheery voice. "Any of y'all done this in real life?"

A smile cracked the navigator's long face. "No one does it and lives."

The engineer grunted. "Baloney. Heard of a fellow who ditched off Guadalcanal, got his whole crew off in time. Another plane ditched off the Pacific Coast. The C-47 never did sink. The only fellows who died had chosen the water rather than the rafts."

"Yeah." The navigator jerked his head back toward the patients. "They didn't have to evacuate eighteen incapacitated folks."

Vera looked up, swung her dark hair off

her face, and gave them a coy smile. "They didn't have a trained flight nurse."

The men's eyes rounded in appreciation.

Oh brother. How could Vera make a simple sentence sound flirtatious?

One long ring of the bell. "The plane has hit the water. Evacuate."

The men got to their feet and flung the life rafts out of the cargo door into the pool and inflated them. While they loaded the emergency equipment into the rafts, Georgie and Vera recruited the most able-bodied ambulatory patients to help those bound to litters, and sent the rest to the rear to enter rafts when available.

Georgie unclamped litters from supports, carried them down the aisle, assisted men out of the plane, and lashed litters across the rafts.

When it was her turn, she stepped gingerly into the boat and tied down one litter in front of her and another behind her. She rowed out a few feet, still anchored by rope to the plane.

Vera, the copilot, and the pilot evacuated into the last three rafts with two more patients each. They cut the rafts loose from the plane, all tied together in a giant circle.

The man lying on the litter in front of Georgie reached his hand into the pool and

286

splashed her, a mischievous look on his face.

She laughed and wiped her cheeks dry. "If you're feeling so chipper, you should have gotten up and helped."

He rolled onto his side and propped his handsome face in his hand. "I'm feeling chipper, all right. What are you doing Saturday night?"

"Going home to marry my boyfriend." She batted her eyelashes at him, even though she'd told a whopper of a lie.

A whopper indeed. She waved to Mellie on the pool deck. Mellie applauded and gave her a thumbs-up.

Georgie returned her grin. She'd succeeded. Of course it wasn't a true emergency and no lives were at stake, but she'd made decisions and acted quickly, and now she knew exactly what to do in a real emergency.

Mellie was proud of her. Would her family be proud? Would Ward?

She tipped her face to a sky speckled with clouds. None of it mattered. She felt the Lord's approval.

26

93rd Evacuation Hospital, Piana di Caiazzo, Italy
October 26, 1943

Rain pelted the Pharmacy tent, and Hutch snugged his helmet into place for the dash to Mess. After dinner, he'd visit Lucia, then head back to his tent to write letters.

He sent Ralph a good-bye nod. "You should have a quiet night. Tons of casualties, but Dom and I got a lot done today."

Ralph winced. "Are you trying to jinx me, saying that Q-word?"

"What Q-word?" Hutch winked. "Quiiiiiet?"

The tent flap flipped open, splattering droplets over the damp dirt floor. "Who wants mail?" Corporal Blevins reached into a leather satchel. "Let's see . . . Hutchinson and O'Shea?"

"Right." Hutch passed mail to Ralph and took some for himself. The latest *Journal of the American Pharmaceutical Association* with news on the trials of penicillin in US Army hospitals in Britain. His sister Mary had written, so had Grandpa Hutchinson, and Phyllis too.

He took off his helmet and sat on a crate. He'd rather read here under the lightbulb than in the crowded mess. And he needed to read Phyllis's letter, although he really didn't want to. Her repetitions and melancholy concerned him, and her pleas to stay faithful irked him.

He opened the envelope and unfolded the letter. Shaky handwriting made his skin prickle. What was wrong?

"Dear Hutch," she wrote.

Hutch? She never called him Hutch. She disliked the nickname.

Some woman is here, a nurse who claims to be a friend of yours. But how can she call herself a friend, when she's forcing me to do something horrible?

Something horrible? His frown deepened. That had to be Georgie. What on earth had happened? What had Georgie done?

First, I want you to know that everything I did, I did because I care about you. I believe high morale is vital, and writing to you is the best way to keep up your morale. Your so-called friend cares nothing for you, and is forcing me to deliver bad news via letter. Not only is that poor form, but I'm concerned the news will cause you to put yourself in a dangerous position. I planned on telling you everything when you came home.

Acid dribbled into Hutch's stomach. Bad news? Concerned? A dangerous position? He read as fast as he could.

I do hate to tell you this way. You see, after you abandoned me to go overseas, I was so sad and lonely. My boss, Ted Richards, often took me out dancing to cheer me up. He was kind to me and made me smile and laugh. You must understand that neither of us intended for this to happen, and I certainly didn't want to tell you in a letter, but Ted and I fell in love. We were married in June 1942, and our dear little Donald is now four months old.

You mustn't worry about me. Ted is a good man with an important job at the shipyard, so he's exempt from the draft. We have a lovely flat, I don't have to work anymore, and he treats me like a queen.

But I do worry about you! Please take care of yourself and don't do anything dangerous! I feel horrible that you have to hear this way. I vowed to keep writing, to keep up your morale out of patriotism and my concern for you. After all our years of friendship, it was the least I could do.

I'll always treasure our years together. If it weren't for the Army, things might have turned out differently.

If it weren't for the Army?

If it weren't for the Army, *he'd* have Phyllis, *he'd* have the good job, *he'd* have the baby.

The acid roiled in a full-blown storm in his belly, and his chest heaved from the force of it. The Army had stolen everything — his marriage, his career, his masculinity, every single shred of respect.

"Hutch? You all right?"

He jerked his gaze to Ralph, to the pharmacy shelves in their blasted disorder. This was no way to work, no way to live. "No. But I'm going to make things right."

He bolted from his seat and behind the counter. He yanked bottles off the top shelf.

"Hutch, what are you doing?"

"I'm making things right." He cleared the top shelf, started on the next one down. She was married? She had a baby?

A firm hand clamped on his forearm. "I don't know what's going on, but you can't do this. You'll get us both in trouble."

Hutch wheeled on Ralph. "This is *my* pharmacy. I will not practice like this anymore. I refuse to."

"But Kaz —"

"Who cares about Kaz?" Or Phyllis either. She'd betrayed him. She'd lied to him. He grabbed two more bottles off the shelf.

"Why don't you get some dinner, think this through on a full stomach?"

"I don't need to think this through. I'm sick of this. Either help me or get out of my way."

Ralph backed up, hands in front of his chest. "I ain't taking the blame for this."

"I'll take the blame. It's my pharmacy." The one place he needed to be in control, deserved to be in control. All his years of education and training. He would not let a florist order him around anymore.

"So I should wait to make that terpin hydrate?" Ralph eased himself down onto the crate.

"Yes." The same blasted crate where

Hutch read that stinking, blasted letter. She'd duped him, made a fool of him. She'd been married since June of '42? That was a year and — July, August, September — four months? Almost a year and a half. She'd been writing all that time, saying she loved him, saying she couldn't wait for him to come home.

Saying she worried about him cheating on her.

Pain doubled him over.

"Hutch? You okay?"

He straightened up and motioned Ralph away, while his stomach tangled into a bigger mess than the pharmacy shelves.

All those letters, so worried about him cheating on her, when she was married to another man, kissing him, sleeping with him, bearing his son.

A groan issued from the mess in his stomach. She'd made a fool out of him. He grabbed the boxes of capsule shells. They belonged under the counter. *Under* the counter.

Someone coughed loudly on the lab side of the tent, behind the flap of canvas that divided the two departments.

"Hutch! Cough. He's coming."

Cough. Kazokov. A chill shot up his arms and froze his thoughts in place.

293

The lieutenant shoved aside the flap. "Good evening, O'Shea. Hutchinson, shouldn't you be off now?" A frown narrowed his tiny eyes. "What are you doing?"

The chill iced up his plans, his one remaining dream. He needed Kaz's letter to get into the Pharmacy Corps. Worse, if he received a reprimand, he'd lose Currier's recommendation, lose his chance entirely.

"I — I —"

Kaz stepped closer, his frown deeper. "You're not demodernizing, are you?"

"De— no, sir. No, I'm — I'm cleaning. It's dirty here. It's not sanitary."

"Yes, sir, we're cleaning." Ralph sprang to his feet. "Hutch likes things spic and span. The Army way."

Kaz brightened, and he clasped his hands behind his back. "That's what I like to see. A young man who keeps a clean shop."

"Yes, sir." Bile filled his throat. A pharmacy was more than a shop.

Kaz surveyed the tent with a series of nods, then headed outside into the rain. "Carry on."

Hutch pressed his hand over his stomach, and his eyes drifted shut.

"I won't say it." Ralph returned bottles to the shelves. "But I told you so."

He turned back to the counter, weak in defeat.

Phyllis was right about one thing. Her bad news caused him to put himself in a dangerous position.

27

School of Air Evacuation
October 29, 1943

"I love this system. It's much better than
the aluminum litter brackets." Georgie
unbuckled the web strapping holding the
last litter in place, and she and Mellie
slipped the litter pole out of the loops.

Two medics took the litter and carried it
off the C-47.

"It solves all our problems." Mellie unhooked a length of strapping from a pole on
the floor. "The parts stay on the plane
permanently. How many patients did we
have to turn away because of lost parts?"

"Too many." Georgie rolled up strapping
so it looked like a snail. "And it weighs next
to nothing. The C-47 crewmen will like
that, won't they?"

"Especially since the straps are stored up
here. More space for cargo." Mellie stood
on tiptoe and tucked her roll into a canvas

bag on the ceiling.

"I can't wait to use this in the field."

Mellie shot her a glance, a half-smile. "Is that right?"

"If I pass." Georgie headed down the aisle. "Let's see how we did."

"We did great. You did great. Why on earth wouldn't you pass?"

"I'll fail if God wants me to fail, but not because I didn't try." Georgie hopped to the ground.

"Excellent job, ladies." The officer showed them his stopwatch. "All patients unloaded in six minutes, forty-eight seconds."

Mellie hugged Georgie's shoulders. "See, I knew you could do it. You're so speedy."

Sadness settled like gray fog over her heart. She knew firsthand the necessity of speed in evacuation.

Kay sauntered over, flipped back her strawberry blonde hair, and winked at Georgie. "You're just trying to make the rest of us look bad."

"My goal in life." She returned the wink. This furlough had given her new appreciation for Kay Jobson. Something about the Taylor farm brought out vulnerability beneath the girl's brass. Last weekend she'd heard sobbing from Kay's room and Mellie's soothing voice. She hadn't stayed to eavesdrop, as much as she wanted to, but something was stirring in the redhead, and Georgie wanted to be ready and available.

She followed the ladies back toward the classroom building, where they'd receive their final marks.

This entire furlough she'd been praying hard. When she prayed, she felt a squirming unease about going home, and a peace and rightness about staying in flight nursing. When she'd talked to Pastor Reeves after service on Sunday, he'd told her to heed the sense of peace.

Too bad the sense of peace didn't cover telling Ward and her family.

Georgie climbed the steps into the classroom building and sat beside Mellie. The harder she'd worked the past three weeks, the more she caught the passion for flight nursing, and the more she wanted to put this training into practice and aid the sick and wounded. And this might be her last chance to see the world. Mellie made the Pacific islands sound exotic and enticing. England had always intrigued her. And Italy had so many charms.

Not Hutch. The memory of her little crush on him sent a shard of shame into her heart. But she knew the opportunity to see him again didn't sway her opinion, since he'd return stateside to join the Pharmacy Corps.

"I'm so worried," one of the new girls said in the seat ahead of Georgie.

Louise Cox patted the girl's hand. "No need to worry. The hard part is getting in. I heard no one failed in the last class."

Georgie's shoulders relaxed too. She wanted to pass, wanted it more than anything. The roughness, the muddiness, the sharpness of life in the field would prod her to keep growing. If she went home, she'd be tempted to settle back onto the pillow of pampering.

"Well . . . ?" Mellie gave her a gentle smile.

What a dear friend Mellie had turned out to be. They complemented each other — in a different way from how she and Rose had complemented each other — but in a very good way.

She looped her arm through Mellie's. "Remember that stuffed nightingale you and Rose made me?"

Mellie's smile wobbled, and she blinked. "Mm-hmm."

"You're the wings, and I'm the heart. We'll be backbone for each other."

"So you . . . ?"

The chief nurse passed out envelopes that would declare their paths.

Georgie held her envelope tight. "I want to pass. Oh Lord, I want to pass."

*93rd Evacuation Hospital, Piana di Caiazzo
October 30, 1943*
Lucia shifted on her cot, but she couldn't roll over with both legs up in traction. Tears wet her cheeks. *"Sono invalida."*

"No. *No invalida.*" Hutch squeezed her hand, but nothing he did or said today cheered up the little girl. How could he convince her she wouldn't be an invalid when the doctors still didn't know? Until the casts came off in a few weeks, his promises were vapid.

And how could he lift anyone's spirits when his lay in the mud?

A new dimension to Phyllis's betrayal punched a fresh hole in the raw meat of his heart. As an unmarried man, he wouldn't be allowed to adopt Lucia. Thank goodness he'd never discussed his dream with the child, or Phyllis's letter would have broken two hearts.

"She's been restless and depressed today." Lillian Farley came beside Lucia's bed and clutched a clipboard to her chest. "Even Signor Ucce isn't working his magic."

Hutch managed a wan smile. "Signor Ucce is all out of magic."

300

Lillian patted his shoulder and gave him a sympathetic smile. "You deserve better than that floozy anyway."

"Thanks. I'm glad I'm not stuck with her. Any woman who can maintain a deception like that for a year and a half, and wave the flag to justify her actions — well, she can't be trusted." The more he said it, the more he'd believe it.

And deep down, he did believe it. Being betrayed and duped and humiliated took a big chunk from a man's pride, but when he peered through his anger, the truth shone through. For months he'd doubted her suitability for him. For months her letters had been a source of irritation rather than joy. He'd seriously considered breaking up with her.

In a way, he was free.

But her decision still caused painful repercussions. Namely with one sad little girl.

What seven-year-old liked being cooped up inside for weeks on end? He trained his ear to the roof of the tent. No rain tapped. "Say, Lieutenant, could I take Lucia outside for a bit?"

"Great idea." Lillian unhooked the traction apparatus. "A change of scenery would be good for her. She can be off traction for

301

half an hour or so."

Lucia asked a series of questions in Italian that Hutch couldn't pick up.

He whipped out his handkerchief and dried her cheeks. *"Lucia no invalida. Lucia è ballerina."*

"I no ballerina. I *invalida.*"

"No more of that talk." He scooped her up into his arms, the casts weighing as much as she did.

Once outside, Lucia tilted back her head and drew a deep breath. The poor thing hadn't been in the fresh air since they'd come to Piana di Caiazzo almost a week earlier.

Hutch headed for the edge of the hospital complex. The road wound before them between steep green hills, and patches of blue sky repaired the torn gray fabric overhead.

He bowed his head to the girl. *"Balle con mi?"*

"Si." A little smile pushed up her cheeks.

Hutch hummed "The Blue Danube Waltz" and whirled her around. Her braids swung out, and her smile rose. Before long, she waved her free arm in time to the music and giggled. That giggle sounded more beautiful than a full orchestra.

He waltzed her around and around, sang

out louder and louder. Lucia was the only girl in his life now. All the nurses were officers and off-limits, so he couldn't date until he joined the Corps or the war ended. The way the US Fifth and British Eighth Armies plodded their way up Italy, hill by bloody hill, the war wouldn't be over for years.

Besides, the only woman who interested him was thousands of miles away and wouldn't come back. A shame. Her family's pampering, on the heels of Rose's death and her own failure, might set her back.

Hutch dipped Lucia low, bringing up a shriek of delight. What was he thinking anyway? Georgie's heart belonged to Ward, and she'd never given any indication she was attracted to Hutch. Even if she were, he'd never steal another man's girl. Besides, she must think him a fool, knowing what happened with Phyllis.

Nope. For the time being, Lucia was his girl. But thanks to Phyllis, that time wouldn't be long enough.

He swung Lucia in the opposite direction. *Lord, please let her walk again. It's her only hope.*

Hutch's only hope sat on the desk of a florist. The letters of recommendation needed to be mailed by November 1. Two days from now.

He stepped inside the tent where Kaz kept his office. "Good evening, sir."

Kaz typed away. "Do you need something, Sergeant? I'm busy."

"I understand, sir. I was wondering if you'd had the opportunity to write the letter of recommendation for me. Monday is the deadline."

"Letter of recommendation?"

That didn't sound good. Hutch shifted his weight to his right leg. "Yes, sir. For the Pharmacy Corps."

Kaz realigned the paper. "I'm busy, and anyway, I can't in good conscience support such a scheme."

"Scheme, sir?"

"Yes, scheme." He smoothed his thin graying brown hair and frowned at Hutch. "You almost had me fooled, but Captain Chadwick enlightened me. Stripping away the rights of physicians indeed."

"Stripping away . . . ? No, sir. That's not what it's about." What rubbish had Chadwick fed to Kaz?

The officer attacked the typewriter keys. "The whole thing implies that hospitals aren't doing their job. It's an insult to the Medical Corps. They know what they're doing."

"Yes, sir. They know how to practice medicine, but not pharmacy."

Kaz tilted his head and gave Hutch a thin-lipped smile. "I've seen what you do. Bruno and O'Shea do the same tasks with only three months' training. It's silly to slap a commission on something so trivial. It devalues the commissions we officers worked so hard for."

Hot coals smoldered in his stomach. The commission Kaz worked so hard for? What? In *his* three months of training? Why did Kaz's college degree — in business — mean more in a hospital than Hutch's degree?

Kaz waved toward the doorway. "If you don't have anything important to ask, you're dismissed."

Flaming, destructive words burned in his throat. He didn't trust himself to open his mouth, even for the required "yes, sir." He marched outside, his hand pressed over his steaming belly.

All the years he'd aimed for this goal, all the work he'd put in, all the disrespect he'd endured — wasted.

Jerks like Chadwick and Kazokov and Ted Richards wrecked everything he worked for, everything he longed for.

28

Charlottesville
October 30, 1943

Plates and stories and laughter circled the supper table. Mama's best cooking filled Georgie's heart with contentment, as did Ward's cheer and the presence of Freddie, Bertie, and all six of her nieces and nephews. From the way Freddie's face turned greener than the peas when the vegetable bowl passed, Georgie guessed a seventh grandchild would soon join the table.

Gus's last furlough from the Navy was in July, if she remembered correctly. He'd root for a son, since Freddie had given him three adorable daughters so far.

Family talk ruled the table — the children's shenanigans, Gus and Freddie's grocery in downtown Charlottesville, Carl and Bertie's crop, Ward's crop, and Daddy's newest filly. Georgie hadn't had a chance to say one word about the School of

Air Evacuation, which suited her fine. She'd enjoy the peace while it lasted.

Mama set a gigantic pumpkin pie in front of Daddy and smiled at Georgie. "Enough suspense, sugar. We can't stand it any longer."

"Stand what?" Did they want to hear about her final marks? Their faces were far more eager than she would have expected.

Donna Lou, Freddie's four-year-old, climbed into Georgie's lap. "Uncle Ward says you have 'citing news."

"Exciting news?"

Ward draped his arm over the back of her chair and grinned. "I thought it would be fun to tell you in front of your whole family."

Around the table, faces grew even more eager.

All Mama's good cooking congealed in her stomach. "Tell me what?"

"It's all set, baby. Bobby Lang from city hall will meet us after church tomorrow, let us sign for the marriage license. I imagine you have loose ends to tie up with the Army this week, but we can get married next Saturday. Pastor Reeves is avail—"

"Excuse me? You made plans without asking me, without even asking about my deci—"

307

"Baby." Ward jiggled her shoulders, and his smile stiffened. "I know you like when plans are settled."

Mama lowered herself into her chair, her face white. "Georgie, what's going on?"

She couldn't look Ward in the eye, so she played with Donna Lou's plump fingers. "Why would you make plans before you heard how I did at the School of Air Evacuation?"

Bertie gave her a sad smile, overflowing with sympathy. "You got your grades back."

They thought she failed. They all thought she failed. Georgie sat up straighter and hefted up a smile. "Y'all will be happy to know I had some of the highest marks in my class. The chief nurse was impressed with my performance and said my patients would receive excellent care."

Silence hovered over the table. Even the children stilled, staring at the adults.

Ward shifted in his chair. "You're not saying —"

"I am." She'd made her decision, and now she had to be strong enough to defend it. She stroked Donna Lou's fair hair. "The five of us asked to stay together and return to the 802nd if possible. I'm willing to go wherever they send me, but they said they'll try to keep us together after all we've been through."

"After all you've been through?" Daddy pushed the pumpkin pie away, his eyes swirling with confusion. "After all you've been through, I'd think you'd want to come home where you belong."

"Where I belong is where God wants me."

Ward balled up his napkin in his lap. "God wants you at home."

"After the war, yes. But not right now. I have skills and training, and I want to use them to serve."

Ward's cheeks reddened. "Since when has serving at home meant nothing?"

"Oh goodness." Mama fanned herself with her hand. "I never thought you'd turn headstrong on us."

Georgie groaned. "Headstrong? Because I made a decision? Nonsense. You and Freddie and Bertie make decisions all the time."

"That's different." Freddie exchanged a knowing glance with Bertie.

"Why?" Steam filled her head. "Because I'm Georgie, and I'm too silly to know my own mind?"

Daddy leaned his forearms on the table. "That's not what your sister said."

"It's what she meant, what y'all believe." She drew a long breath so she could keep her voice calm and low. "I prayed for wisdom, for God to show me his will. At first I didn't want to be a flight nurse. I just wanted to be with Rose. But this is where God wants me, and he changed my heart, and now that's what I want more than anything."

"More than marrying me?" Ward's voice came out like gravel.

"I do want to marry you — after the war."

"After the —" He stood and tossed his napkin onto the table. "Excuse me, folks, but Georgie and I need to have a little discussion in private."

"Pardon me, sweetie." Georgie slid Donna Lou off her lap and left the dining room without looking at her family. She followed Ward through the house, across the porch, and down to the stables.

Her breath hitched at the sight. The sun had descended behind the Blue Ridge Mountains, and soft purple light bathed the autumn trees, the rolling hills, and the beloved stable. Ward brought her out here, not just for privacy but to show her what she was leaving.

Unwavering. She'd prayed for wisdom and she'd received it.

Ward rested his elbows on the white rail fence around the stable. "I've never been so humiliated in all my life. How could you make a decision like that without talking to me?"

Georgie leaned on the fence a good six feet from him and crossed her arms. "I could ask you the same thing."

"That's different." A scowl marred his handsome face. "I made a decision for us. You made a decision for you alone."

An uneasy feeling blurred the edges of her determination. Had she made the decision for selfish reasons? "For me? No. That's not true. If I were being selfish, I'd come home."

He ran one hand through his sandy hair. "What? You think staying home is selfish? That doesn't make sense. Staying home is smart and right."

"Not now."

"Come on, baby. It's a fine plan. We get married, start a family, and the Army has to let you out. You'll have fulfilled your duty."

A sliver of a moon dangled over the horizon, as flimsy as her arguments. "It doesn't seem right."

"Of course it's right. Starting a family is more than right."

Her sigh disrupted the still air. "Not this way. Not for that purpose. That'd be like Bertie telling Carl in New Guinea to stop taking his Atabrine so he'll get malaria and

311

come home."

"That's silly. Completely different."

"Is it? Freddie and Bertie miss their husbands. They need their husbands at home. But they're not demanding Gus and Carl get sick or wounded just to come home."

Ward's mouth curled up on one side. "You can't compare —"

"Why not? Because they're men and I'm just a woman?"

He pounded his finger on the fence rail so hard the vibrations reached Georgie. "Because your rightful place is at home. You're abandoning it. It isn't natural."

Images of Africa, Sicily, Italy floated through her mind, images of men ill and mutilated and afraid. "War isn't natural. We all have to make sacrifices."

"Not you, baby. You don't have to."

"I've chosen to. Gus and Carl are sacrificing to serve our country. Freddie and Bertie are sacrificing by doing their husbands' jobs plus their own. Daddy and Mama are working harder than ever with hired help so scarce. And yes, you and I have to put our dreams on hold."

Ward's jaw shifted forward. His gaze focused on a point far behind Georgie. "So that's that. You're willing to sacrifice me."

"Sacrifice you?" A chill flowed up her arms and not from the evening air. "I'll only be gone for the duration."

His gaze zoomed back to her, hard and dark. "Why should I wait?"

The foundation of nine years together crumbled beneath her. But instead of collapsing in a heap, she felt a floating sensation. "Are you breaking up with me?"

He blinked once, then returned to his stony expression. "If you're asking me to wait, I am. Why should I wait when I don't even know what sort of girl will come home?"

The chill produced nothing but cooling relaxation, not what she would have expected. "I'll be the same Georgie, but stronger and wiser and better able to handle life."

He huffed. "You're getting hard and headstrong, just as I feared. I don't like who you're becoming."

She held her chin high. "That's too bad, because I do."

Ward angled his head toward town. "You wanted to make a decision, did you? So make one. If you stay, I'll marry you. If you leave, I won't wait. Plenty of girls around here would be happy to take your place."

Georgie's mouth tightened. She'd never

been more certain of a decision in her life. "They want to take my place? Let them."

He whipped his gaze back to her, his shock and pain visible even in the dim light.

But she didn't waver under the wind of his emotions. "If you value your own will higher than God's will, then you aren't the man for me."

Ward straightened, stepped closer, and shook a finger at her. "If you honestly think God wants you to leave your rightful place at home, then you're deluded. And you definitely aren't the woman for me."

"No. I'm not. Good night, Mr. Manville."

He rocked, as if caught in a high wind. Then he spun away, banged open the corral gate, and marched to his horse. "Good riddance, Miss Taylor."

"That's *Lieutenant* Taylor." Georgie strode back to the house.

When she reached the porch steps, the sounds of her family's conversation burrowed into her ears.

Her legs quivered, and she grasped the porch railing for support. Oh goodness, what had she done? She'd driven off Ward, flung away her lifelong dream, and earned her family's reproach.

For what? For something she couldn't wait to escape only months before. For an uncertain future.

Hooves clomped down the drive.

Georgie turned to watch her dreams ride away, around the bend, out of her life. Above her the sky had turned purplish black. A handful of stars poked through.

Polaris. The North Star. Always constant, always present, like the Lord himself.

She filled her lungs with cool autumn air, filled her mind with certainty. She'd done the right thing.

29

Piana di Caiazzo
October 31, 1943

Rough-hewn men's voices sang out "Praise to the Lord, the Almighty," graced with a handful of high notes from the nurses. Sunday morning services were the only time officers and enlisted mixed. Hutch shared a hymnal with Bergie, his friend's off-key bass a reminder of home.

> Praise to the Lord, who o'er all things so
>   wondrously reigneth,
> Shelters thee under His wings, yea, so
>   gently sustaineth!
> Hast thou not seen
> How thy desires e'er have been
> Granted in what He ordaineth?

Hutch prayed the verse for Georgie, to see the Almighty's hand in her life, to be sheltered under the Lord's wings, for God to grant her wisdom and strength.

> Praise to the Lord, who doth prosper thy
>   work and defend thee;
> Surely His goodness and mercy here daily
>   attend thee.
> Ponder anew
> What the Almighty can do,
> If with His love He befriend thee.

The verse grabbed Hutch's voice and shook it. *Who doth prosper thy work and defend thee?* That's what he needed — for God to prosper his work and defend him. The Army certainly wouldn't do so.

He sang the final verse mechanically while his soul called out to God. *I need your help. I need that letter to get into the Corps, and I know it's your will for me to join. Show me how to change Kaz's mind. Prosper my work. Defend me.*

After the chaplain spoke the closing prayer, Bergie settled his hand on Hutch's shoulder. "How're you doing, buddy? Five years is a long time."

Five years? Oh, Phyllis. Hutch cracked a smile. Only five days had passed since her Dear John letter, but it felt like a lifetime ago. "Actually, I'm fine about that. Relieved, in fact."

Bergie's blue eyes homed in on him. "Yeah? Glad you found out her character before you were married?"

"Definitely. But more than that. I've had second thoughts for a long time. We weren't good for each other."

"Too much alike," he said in a matter-of-fact tone, as if he'd noticed too.

"Wasn't that why you introduced us?"

"Yeah." He led the way down the aisle, past the crates that served as pews, but he stepped to the side before the tent entrance, where the ranks divided again.

Bergie crossed his arms over his field uniform, his Bible in one hand. "When I met Phyllis, she reminded me of you. I thought you needed someone like you. But now I have Lillian."

"Mm-hmm. You broke the three-month barrier."

"You know why? Because she's nothing like the girls I usually date. I've always liked them fun and lively, but it never worked out. Lillian's gentle and peaceful. She's good for me, and I think I'm good for her too."

Hutch ran his thumb along the black leather spine of his Bible, the gold lettering long gone. "You're strong where she's weak, and vice versa. Phyllis and I were both weak in the same areas. That's not what I want."

"You need someone more like . . . me." He grinned.

Hutch rubbed his jaw. "A girl who needs a shave?"

Bergie laughed and clapped him on the shoulder. "You seemed down earlier today, but you'll be fine. I see that now."

He winced and glanced around the tent, mostly empty. "I'm not down because of Phyllis. It's Kaz. Your pal Chadwick gave him the line about the Pharmacy Corps being unnecessary and worse — usurping physician authority. Kaz refused to write the letter."

"You're kidding? What'd you say?"

"Nothing. Would've said something rash and shot myself in the foot." Pale, cloud-filtered sunlight slanted through the tent entrance, a reminder he needed to complete his mission. "I'm going to talk to him now. As long as I'm respectful and logical, he'll listen."

"Kaz?" Bergie wrinkled his nose. "The same man who listened to logic after he alphabetized your shelves? I don't think so. You need help."

"What? No." The last thing he needed was a Bergie scheme. "I can do this myself."

Bergie stepped outside and strode down the path.

319

Hutch jogged to catch up. "Berg — Captain, really. I can do it myself."

"You shouldn't have to." He nodded to a trio of nurses. "If he only listens to physicians, he needs to hear another side of physician thinking. I have a plan."

Hutch stopped. His head flopped back, and he closed his eyes. "Not one of your plans."

"Who's on today? Dom? Ralph? Go get the other one. I'll get Kaz. Meet me in Pharmacy." He marched away. "Trust me."

How many times had he heard that phrase? How many disasters had it preceded?

Hutch stared at the thick gray sky. "Lord, so gently sustain me."

"Have a seat, Lieutenant." Bergie pulled up a crate for Kaz. "Hutch won't toot his own horn, so we'll do it for him."

Hutch tugged the hem of his service jacket. He'd worn his dress uniform so he'd look like officer material. "Pardon me, sir. This was not my idea."

Lieutenant Kazokov shot him a skeptical look.

"It wasn't." Bergie set his foot on another crate and leaned his forearms on his knee. "Captain Chadwick gave you his opinion on the Pharmacy Corps, and I want to give you another physician's opinion. As a man of integrity, I'm sure you'll listen to both sides."

"Of course." Kaz sniffed, then wiped his nose with his handkerchief. "I pride myself on my open-mindedness."

"Understandably so." Bergie nodded. "Did you know only a few mobile hospitals have a pharmacist on staff?"

"Yes. I'm aware of that."

"Great. We take Hutch for granted, but I had no idea how good we had it. Recently a number of physicians transferred here from other evac and field hospitals. They say we have the best pharmacy in the theater. Sergeant Hutchinson anticipates our needs, meets our orders, and answers our questions. Always professional and caring."

"Thanks," Hutch said. "Just doing my job."

"Doing it well." Bergie pointed at him. "Say, Lieutenant, remember when we arrived in Sicily, and no one had aspirin? Hutch made it from scratch, even made some for other hospitals and the air evac squadron."

"We couldn't have done that." Dom waved the pharmacy technician manual. "It's not in here."

"No, sir." Ralph straddled a crate and rapped his knuckles on the wood. "When we have shortages — and we always have shortages — he knows what to substitute."

Bergie's eyes shone as they always did when his plans rolled along. "And that little Italian girl? She refuses to let us put in an IV. Terrifies her. Hutch puts her sulfa in a suspension, a different flavor each day, just for fun."

Hutch smiled. Lucia's favorite flavor was orange.

"He also teaches us." Dom tapped the manual into his open palm. "Not only how to do stuff, but why it works the way it does."

Hutch slid his hands into his trouser pockets. "You two are good learners. You're smart and fast."

Ralph glanced up at him. "We couldn't do it without you. Just imagine. Most hospitals have to get by with clods like us." A wink. Ralph was laying it on thick.

"You're not clods. Not by far. But . . ." Time to press his own case. "But Lieutenant Kazokov, sir, that's my point. The purpose of the Pharmacy Corps is to ensure that all hospitals, all patients have the best care."

Bergie flicked his chin at Hutch. "John

Hutchinson is the man to do it. The Army needs him in the Pharmacy Corps — which is already signed into law, by the way, so why fight it? Not only is he a good pharmacist, but he has three years' experience in Army hospitals. He knows what works and what doesn't. Plus, he has connections, friends in high places . . ."

Kaz regarded Hutch, one eyebrow hiked high.

Hutch gave him a slow nod. "I need to make one thing clear, sir. I have no desire to usurp physician authority. Good pharmacy practice works alongside good medical practice, a team."

"No doubt about it." Bergie clapped a hand on his knee. "The Pharmacy Corps needs him. It wouldn't be fair of us to keep him here."

"That's the only bad part," Dom muttered. "It'll just be Ralph and me."

A twinge of guilt. The patients here needed him. But the Corps was bigger and promised to bring the same level of service to all hospitals. It was his duty and purpose.

Bergie motioned with his thumb toward the tent entrance. "Chadwick's a great physician, but he's old-fashioned, not a forward-thinking modern man like you, Lieutenant. Most of the docs agree with me.

Ask them. Colonel Currier agrees. That's why he wrote Hutch a glowing letter. Ask him. But please write this letter for Hutch. Please don't stand in the way of progress."

No one — no one could lay it on thicker than Capt. Nels Bergstrom.

Kaz's gaze circled the men and landed on Hutch. His eyes narrowed ever so slightly.

Hutch swallowed hard. "Please, sir. I would never forget your kindness."

Kaz slapped both hands on his thighs and stood. "All right then. You'll have your letter tonight. I pride myself on my progressiveness."

All the wind rushed from Hutch's lungs. "Thank you, sir. I'm forever in your debt."

After Kaz left, Bergie turned glittering eyes to Hutch. "Forever in *his* debt?"

"And yours. And Dom's and Ralph's. And God's." His cheeks hurt from the breadth of his smile. " 'Ponder anew what the Almighty can do' — with a little help from Bergie."

30

Piana di Caiazzo
November 6, 1943

Georgie stepped carefully along the logs of a "corduroy road" through the 93rd Evacuation Hospital. Even so, mud oozed up between the logs.

What happened to sunny Italy?

She stopped and gazed around. Capped with fuzzy clouds, steep green hills jutted up around the village of Piana di Caiazzo. The hospital seemed busier than ever, with patients arriving by ambulance, jeep, and mule.

She forged ahead. Ralph O'Shea said Hutch was probably doing laundry on his day off.

So much had changed in the past month. The 802nd was now stationed near Naples, conducting air evac for the US Fifth Army along Italy's west coast, while the 807th covered the British Eighth Army along the east coast.

Georgie was disappointed when Lieutenant Lambert sent her up to Capua with Captain Maxwell. She wanted to fly and prove herself. But when she found out the 93rd was stationed across the Volturno River from Capua, she changed her mind.

Why was Hutch still in Italy? What was holding up the Pharmacy Corps? Was he doing all right after Phyllis's betrayal? What if he hadn't received the letter yet? And if he had, would he be angry with Georgie for her role?

She chewed her lower lip and paused on the pathway that divided the wards from the enlisted men's tents. Up a short ways, a giant Lister bag full of disinfected water hung from a wooden tripod, and half a dozen men gathered around, shaving and washing faces and scrubbing laundry.

One man sat on a camp stool, his back to her, long and lean, and he swiped a comb through wet dark hair.

Hutch.

In that moment the fullness of her crush flooded back into her, stronger now that both of them were unattached, the double barrier dissolved.

She gave her head a good strong shake. Very recently unattached. After long relationships. And his had a frightful ending. Besides, he liked tall serene blondes, not short bubbly brunettes.

But he was a friend. The dearest, big brotherly friend, and she longed to know how he was doing.

She came up behind him and cleared her throat. "Hutch?"

The comb paused. His head turned, and a smile enveloped his face. "Georgie."

He sprang to his feet, moved closer as if about to hug her, then stopped short. But his smile didn't falter. "You're back. What are you doing here?"

My, he looked good, towering over her, clean and shiny with his wet hair slicked back. She had to clear her throat again. "I could ask you the same thing. I hoped you'd be gone. Well, not that way. I hoped you'd be away with the Pharmacy Corps."

"It's moving along as slowly as the US Fifth Army." His field jacket hung open over his bare chest.

Oh my. Her cheeks warmed, and she wrenched her gaze back up to his face. "That's too bad. I know you want to join."

He fumbled with his jacket buttons and gave her a sheepish smile. "Sorry. Just showered. I'm washing my shirts." He nodded toward his helmet on the ground, filled with sudsy water.

"No need to apologize." She could mention she'd seen his bare chest before, but ladies didn't speak of such things. Or think of such things.

"I turned in my application. Dad says the next step is a test. So I wait." His eyes grew warmer than hot chocolate. "Wow, it's good to see you."

Oh dear. A man with a broken heart wouldn't be in such a good mood. Phyllis's letter must not have arrived yet. "Have you . . . have you heard from Phyllis lately?"

His mouth pursed as if he were deep in thought. "Yeah. Something about being married, having a baby, and a mean nurse who made her tell the truth. Sound familiar?"

"You're not angry with me?"

"Angry? Are you kidding? I'm grateful. Sounds like she wanted to string me along for the duration."

"She did. I'm so sorry."

"Don't be. I'm glad I found out."

She studied him. He looked relieved, as if lightened of a load. "You don't seem upset."

He rubbed his jawline, still pink from shaving. "I was when I got the letter, but it didn't take long to put my head back on straight. After all, she saved me the bother."

"The bother?"

"Breaking up. We weren't well suited to each other." His gaze dropped, then bounced back up. "Say, you haven't told me why you're here. Last I heard, you weren't coming back."

She stood up tall and straightened her treasured gray-blue jacket, now emblazoned with gold flight nurse's wings. "You were right. I can do it. I prayed for wisdom and strength, and I passed with flying colors. They said I was a model flight nurse."

"I knew you could do it. Your family — Ward — they must be proud of you."

A wry chuckle. "You've never met them. They say it's too dangerous, that my rightful place is at home."

"They want to protect you."

"I suppose. But isn't the best protection the ability to handle life? They can't shelter me. No one can. Rose's death proved it. Tragedies and trials will come, and I want to be prepared."

A damp lock fell over his forehead, and he raked it back. "Give them time. They'll see you made the right decision."

"I don't know about that." Her smile wobbled more than she liked. "My family thinks I made a huge mistake. First big decision I made for myself, and it cost me Ward.

They say it proves I can't make decisions."

His eyebrows pinched together. "It cost you . . ."

"Ward. My former boyfriend. I broke up with him. Or he broke up with me. I'm not really sure, since it was definitely mutual."

"But you . . . how many years?"

"Nine. Apparently a few too many." Georgie tucked a stray curl behind her ear. "We're not . . . we're not well suited to each other."

Hutch's gaze steadied, intensified, and stole her breath clean away. Was he thinking the same thing she was? That *they* were well suited to each other?

Nonsense. She was being silly, just as her family said. Why would he be attracted to her? And even if he were, it was far too early for either of them.

So why hadn't he broken his gaze?

Before she could do something idiotic like throw herself into his arms, she glanced at her watch. "Oh dear. I need to be back in Receiving."

"Yeah. Yeah." He stepped back and rubbed his hand down his cheek. "Too bad. We've got a lot of . . . a lot of catching up to do."

"I know. So much has happened since I saw you last."

"I haven't even told you about Lucia." A

smile crept up his face.

And hers crept down against her will. "Lucia?"

"Lucia Benedetti. My girl."

A local woman. Why did she feel like all the air had been sucked out of her chest? Somehow she kept her smile in place. "Your — your girl. My goodness, that was — fast."

The corners of his eyes crinkled. "She's seven. She's a patient here. Prettiest little thing you've ever seen."

Seven. She laughed and whapped him lightly on the arm. "Why, you. I should have known you liked them young."

"Your face. Priceless."

Not as priceless as his grin, or the knowledge that he was teasing her, or the delight of seeing his mischievous side. "I wish we had more time to chat."

"Me too. Will you be back?"

"We're stationed at Pomigliano Airfield outside of Naples. We'll be up to Capua and Caserta —" An idea slipped into her mind, the sweetest idea she'd had in ages. The 802nd was being honored at a dinner at the palace in Caserta the following Saturday. Right across the river. With a little finagling . . . "When's your next day off?"

"Next Saturday. A week from today. Why?"

She planted her fists on her hips and gave

him her fiercest drill sergeant look. "You, sir, are under strict orders not to eat dinner that evening. You have volunteered yourself for the most dangerous mission of your life, soldier."

"I have?" The curve of his lips said she didn't look fierce at all.

Georgie deepened her scowl. "Five o'clock sharp. You'll accompany me on a special assignment. You will bring your telescope. You will endure my silly chatter. You will eat my campfire cooking. No questions. No complaints."

"No, ma'am!" He snapped a sharp salute, taller than ever. "No complaints, ma'am. Absolutely none."

"Good." She returned to Southern belle and gave him her most charming smile. "I'm looking forward to it."

"Me too." He might not have any complaints, but dozens of questions flitted through his eyes. "See you next week."

"Next week, then." She fluttered a wave and turned toward Receiving. She'd need the week to ponder the answers.

31

Piana di Caiazzo
November 13, 1943

The jeep barreled over the countryside, and Hutch braced himself against the dashboard. "Sure you don't want me to drive?"

Georgie laughed and shook back her curls. "Where's your sense of adventure? I made it all the way from Caserta to the hospital to here."

A solid bump jolted through his tailbone. "I can't believe they let you have a jeep."

"You'd be amazed what a little Southern charm can do."

He grinned and looked away to the olive trees dotting the hill slope. He knew all too well what Southern charm could do. He hadn't felt this good since he'd been drafted. Perhaps longer.

On the drive from the hospital complex, they chatted about Georgie's experiences at Bowman Field and Hutch's at the 93rd.

Normal conversation between friends. So why couldn't he shake the feeling that this was a date?

He'd showered and shaved and worn his khaki shirt and trousers instead of herringbone twill fatigues, although with the good old Parsons field jacket on top. Didn't want to look too conspicuous. Or too eager.

As much as he liked Georgie, the timing couldn't be worse. Less than a month before, both of them were set to marry — or assumed they were. And thanks to fraternization policies, he wouldn't be allowed to date her until he became an officer, and then he'd head stateside anyway. If she even wanted to date him.

Lousy timing.

The jeep bounced to a stop. Hutch banged his knees and almost slid off the seat.

"What do you think?" Georgie said. "Do you like this spot?"

He rubbed his knees. "If it means our ride's over, I love this spot."

"Aren't you just the funniest man in the world?" She climbed out of the jeep. "Well, I think it's lovely here."

Hutch got out and stretched his legs. They stood on a grassy slope a couple of miles west of Piana di Caiazzo, with a ramshackle stone wall behind them up the slope to the east. To the south, the Volturno made a hairpin loop in its journey across Italy's shin, and directly before them, a stream worked its way to the river, lit by the sun low on the horizon. And for once, a clear sky.

Georgie pulled a cardboard box out of the backseat.

"Let me get that for you." Hutch took the box, loaded with food and a portable stove. What was for dinner?

"No peeking." Georgie tossed a blanket over her shoulder and pointed to a level spot. "How about over there?"

Hutch set up the little cylindrical Coleman stove and lit it while Georgie spread out the blanket and poked around in the box.

"Shoo." She waved him to the side, sat in front of the stove, set a frying pan on top, and unwrapped a paper bundle.

"What's for din—"

She laid a bright red slab inside the pan.

He scooted closer, and the blanket buckled between them. "Is that what I think it is?"

"Steak? Yes, it is. Before I left, you said you wanted steak, medium rare."

His nostrils and soul filled with the scent. "How? Where?"

Georgie flattened the steak with a fork.

"The 802nd was invited to a big fancy dinner tonight at the palace in Caserta."

"Really? Fifth Army HQ? You didn't go?"

She flapped her hand at him. "The entire month of October I feasted on Mama's home cooking. She used up a wad of ration stamps. I had steak and fried chicken and ham. Nothing they serve at the palace can compare to Mama's biscuits."

He studied her face in profile, the rounded cheeks and tiny chin. "But you —"

"This afternoon I went down to the palace kitchen and told them I couldn't attend, that I was meeting a friend who hadn't had a nice meal in ever so long, and could they possibly send me with a box?"

"You did what?"

"A little eyelash batting, and here you go. One steak, soon to be medium rare, and a loaf of crusty Italian bread, and a can of peas. Sorry about that — not terribly fancy. But the chef liked me so much he threw in two slices of cake."

"Cake?" He closed his mouth so drool wouldn't slither out.

"Mm-hmm." She flipped the steak.

Hutch stared at her. Now it really felt like a date because the only words that came to mind were "I think I'm in love." But he kept his mouth shut.

She sent him a sidelong glance. "I thought you'd be pleased."

"You have no idea." He leaned forward and inhaled so long he felt dizzy. "May I say grace now so I don't have to wait once this comes off the fire?"

She clucked her tongue at him. "Oh, all right. Nothing wrong with blessing the food before it's ready."

"Definitely not." He closed his eyes. "Heavenly Father, thank you for this bountiful feast and for the friend who procured it and prepared it. Amen."

"Amen." Georgie poked the steak. "You prayed too fast. It isn't ready."

"On second thought, rare would be fine."

"No, you don't. Why don't you get out the plates, slice the bread?"

By the time he followed her orders, the steak was ready. Over his protests, she sliced off only a bit for herself and gave him the rest. Then she placed the can of peas on the stove to warm.

Hutch stared at the meat on his tin plate. Part of him wanted to gulp it down in one bite, and the other part wanted to leave it on the plate forever and savor it like fine art.

In compromise, he took a thin slice and set it on his tongue. His eyes drifted shut.

This was what beef was supposed to taste like, not that hash they slopped on his tray in the mess.

He squeezed the morsel between his teeth, and the juice caressed his taste buds. Finally he gave in and swallowed.

"At this rate, you won't finish that steak by daybreak."

Hutch opened his eyes and gave her half a grin. "Most likely."

She settled her plate on the blanket in front of her. "You seem to be doing well. I have to admit I was worried."

"Because of Phyllis?" He shrugged and sliced another piece. "Nah. The more I think about it, the more I know I didn't love her anymore. Not sure I loved her in the first place."

Georgie tapped him on the arm with the back of her hand. "Don't do that. Don't chalk off your years together because it ended badly."

Hutch took his time with his mouthful of steak and with his answer. "I'm not. Bergie set us up. Before I knew it, she was my girlfriend. I thought she'd be a good wife and mother. Apparently I was right." He winked.

Her eyes rounded, and she laughed.

He mopped up juices with his bread. "It

was never like people say, when all you can think about is her, when you can't think straight in her presence." Like he felt with Georgie.

She turned a circle of bread in her hands. "It wasn't like that with Ward either. I didn't decide to be with him. I just *was*. He embodied everything I wanted — home, safety, security."

"Then when you changed what you wanted . . . ?"

A soft smile. "Then he didn't want me, and I didn't want him."

"He's a fool." His voice came out too husky, so he shoved in the last bite of steak. After he set aside his plate, he stretched out on his back and laced his hands behind his head, his stomach full and happy. "We both had a busy month or so, didn't we?"

"Sure did." She twisted to face him. "It's good to see you and know you're all right. I'm glad I came back."

"I'm glad you came back too. That was the single best meal I've had in my life."

She whacked his knee and laughed. "You men are all alike. Always thinking about food." She scooted down to the edge of the blanket by Hutch's feet, poured water from the canteen into the frying pan, and scraped at burnt bits with her fork.

Hutch let out a contented sigh and enjoyed her curvy silhouette against the colors of the setting sun. "You know what they say. The way to a man's heart is through his stomach."

"True."

Something bold and new surged in his chest. "If I didn't know better, I'd think you were flirting with me."

Georgie paused. She gasped. "Goodness' sake. What a thing to say."

The boldness gained strength and pumped through his body. He wasn't mistaken. She could have gone to that posh dinner at the palace, but she chose a picnic with him. She went through all this effort for him. And she hadn't answered his question.

"Well?" He tapped her knee with his toe. "You *are* flirting, aren't you?"

"John Hutchinson! What a thing to ask a lady." She scraped even harder at the pan without facing him. "You ought to be ashamed of yourself. I thought you were a gentleman."

"Just a simple question. Which you haven't answered."

"Some questions don't warrant an answer. Besides, a lady would never flirt with a man so soon after breaking up with her boyfriend, especially when the man also . . .

it'd be too early."

"Maybe." But something deep inside disagreed. It might be too early, but with the war on, it might soon be too late.

She raised one shoulder and sniffed. "If *I* didn't know better, I'd think you were flirting with me. All these questions and such."

Hutch had seen newsreel footage of paratroopers lined up to jump from the airplane. Each man paused at the doorway. To jump or not to jump?

"Well? Are you?" Scrape, scrape, scrape.

He hovered at the threshold, one massive barrier between them. "I know better than to flirt with an officer."

"You'll be an officer soon. And you haven't answered my question. Are you?"

He didn't have much experience with women, but he recognized an invitation, and he flung himself into open sky. "I am."

Georgie drew in a sharp breath and sat up straighter. Then she resumed her attack on the frying pan.

Somehow her nervousness made him feel even bolder. Now was the moment. He sat up and slid down to the edge of the blanket beside her.

Scrape, scrape, scrape.

"You're going to put a hole in that thing." He placed his hands over hers — they trembled — and he took away the pan and fork and set them aside.

Her laugh came out thin, and she twisted her hands in her lap.

What should he say? Should he hold her hand or embrace her or kiss her without hesitation?

He leaned closer until their shoulders touched. She softened into him, welcoming him.

His pulse thrummed in his ears, and he studied her face in the dusky light. The curves of forehead, cheekbones, chin. The fluttering brown eyelashes over flushing cheeks. The way she pulled in her lips between her teeth until they popped out again, pink and moist.

He raised his hand toward her cheek, to turn her face and read her expression before he made a move that couldn't be undone.

She leaned forward a bit. Away from him. "Ours or theirs?"

"Hmm?" His hand fell. His gaze rose to her eyes, now focused far away, toward the final crescent of sunlight. He couldn't think over the thrumming of his pulse.

"The plane?" She pointed west over the stream. "Ours or theirs?"

The thrumming. It wasn't his pulse. It was an engine. A fighter plane, a black outline in the sky.

He was no aircraft expert, but he'd seen enough Messerschmitts over Sicily and Italy, Me 109s that loved to attack at dusk, loved to attack out of the sun, loved to strafe bridges over the Volturno. "Theirs! The stove!"

"Oh no!" Georgie grabbed the cylindrical cover and clapped it over the stove, snuffing its light.

Hutch scrambled to his feet and pulled her to standing. "We've got to get to shelter."

"The jeep!"

He sprinted up the slope, slower than he wanted but faster than Georgie probably wanted. "No, they'll target the jeep. Go to the wall."

The plane aimed right at them, he could hear. His breath came hard, he stubbed his toe on a rock, Georgie stumbled, he kept going, the wall locked in his sight.

The plane pock-pock-pocked, and bullets thumped into the ground behind them.

Georgie screamed.

"Turn right!" He yanked her hand, angled their path away from the bullets, parallel to the wall. They could maneuver faster than a fighter plane.

The engine sounds shifted. Hutch didn't

look behind him, but the plane had to be turning.

"Turn left!" He aimed straight for the wall. "Can you jump it?"

"Yes." She tugged her hand free, planted both hands on the wall, and vaulted it.

He hurdled over, found her hunched against the wall, crouched over her, shielded her body with his.

The plane whined overhead. Two bullets chinked into the stone wall about ten feet away.

He pressed Georgie close to the wall. *Please, Lord, don't let him come back.*

"More?" Her voice muffled into his chest.

Yes. More engine sounds to the west, but different. He stretched up and peered over the top of the wall. Those planes he knew and liked. "Ours. Three P-47s. That fellow won't be back."

Hutch sank to the ground facing Georgie and pulled her to his chest. Their hearts raced in rhythm, her breath puffed into his neck, his breath huffed into her hair.

He held her tight. If anything would drive her away from him, drive her back stateside, this would be it. She'd told him how she panicked after the plane crash when Rose was killed.

Eventually, her breathing quieted.

344

Hutch leaned back to see her face. "How're you doing, sweetheart?"

Her blue eyes shone in . . . triumph. "I didn't panic."

"No." He wiped a smudge of dirt off her cheek. "No, you didn't. You put out the stove. You ran. You jumped this wall like one of your horses."

"I did. And I only screamed once."

A smile edged up. "When those bullets flew, I almost screamed myself."

She giggled. "Did you?"

"I would have, but I'm trying to impress you."

The glow of her smile showed him he'd succeeded. He'd impressed her. She was attracted to him. And he wanted her in his life more than anything.

Right then, nothing mattered. Not timing, not rank, not the war. Only Georgie mattered.

He swooped in and pressed his lips to hers, her body to his.

A soft gasp, then she melted into him, her hands climbing his back, her lips searching his.

He swept one hand into her hair, so silky, drawing her closer and deeper, her lips willing and pliant beneath his. He'd never kissed a woman that hard before. Never.

Was it too hard? Was he scaring her?

He broke off the kiss, breathing hard.

Her eyes fluttered open, and her parted lips curved upward. "Oh, Hutch. You can flirt with me any time you like."

"Yeah? I will." He wove his fingers into her curls. "Any time you cook me a steak dinner."

She laughed. "I'm learning all sorts of things about you today. You have a mischievous side. I like it. And oh my goodness, that kiss! It was the Fourth of July, New Year's Day, Christmas, Thanksgiving, and every other holiday rolled up in one."

How could he resist? He kissed her again, softer this time but no less passionate, exploring her cheeks, her chin, her warm neck, and those lips, back to those lips.

She sighed and rested her cheek on his shoulder. "I can't believe this is happening. It seems so fast."

Hutch rubbed her back, and honesty spilled out. "I have to admit, I've wanted to do that almost since the day I met you."

"Really?" She eased up and looked him in the eye. "You never let on."

"Wouldn't have been right."

"You're faithful." Georgie settled her cheek down to his shoulder again. "While we're confessing, I have to admit I had a little crush on you too."

She'd never let on either. Because she was faithful.

The words "I love you" poised halfway between his heart and his tongue, but he held them back for now.

He laid a kiss on her forehead. "I think, Miss Georgie, that we're well suited."

32

Caserta, Italy
November 14, 1943

"I wish Tom were here," Mellie said. "It's so romantic."

At the Caserta palace, Georgie sat on the edge of a fountain, and the cool water caressed her fingers, much as Hutch had the previous evening. She imagined strolling the gorgeous gardens with him, kissing by the ornate Baroque fountains, exploring the marble extravagance of the palace arm in arm.

Kay swished her hand through the water. "Now you know Tom's at Foggia. It's not too far."

"I wish he were on the west coast instead of the east, or that we could switch places with the 807th. They're at Foggia. But Tom's due for a forty-eight-hour pass in Naples."

"That'll be nice." Georgie had to remind

348

herself to stay in the conversation, because her mind and heart floated several miles away to a hillside outside of Piana di Caiazzo.

Mellie dried her hand on her handkerchief. "One thing he likes about Foggia — and his little dog likes it too — fewer air raids than in Sicily or North Africa."

Air raids. "Did I tell y'all . . ." Georgie clamped her lips between her teeth. So far she'd sidestepped questions about the picnic. Last night she'd returned to quarters before the rest of the girls, so she pretended to be asleep.

"Tell us what?" Mellie gave her a careful look.

"About last night?" Kay's green eyes gleamed. "For you to miss a dinner like that, he must be some man. And since you're so quiet and dreamy and mysterious, it must have been some date."

Georgie got to her feet and headed toward the palace, down the mile-long path that paralleled a chain of three long pools separated by fountains. "I told you. Hutch is a good friend, and I felt sorry for him. He's eaten nothing but Army chow for three years."

Mellie caught up with her. "That was very kind of you."

349

"Kind?" Kay laughed and fell in beside Mellie. "A charity mission wouldn't make her blush. A date would."

Georgie's hand flew to her warm cheek. "You'd blush too under interrogation."

"I doubt that." Kay's hips swung more than usual. "I can't blame you. He's a nice-looking fellow. I see why you broke up with Ward."

Georgie gasped and stopped in her tracks. "Heavens, no. I broke up with Ward because of Ward. For goodness' sake, I never thought I'd see Hutch again. And he certainly didn't break up with Phyllis for me. She married another man. He was always faithful to her, and I was always faithful to Ward. We didn't even know we were attracted to each other until last ni—" She clapped a hand over her mouth.

Kay crossed her arms and gave Mellie a knowing look. "I told you it was a date."

"It wasn't meant to be."

Mellie's dark eyes swam with concern. "You — you're a couple now?"

"It's not that simple." Georgie gazed down toward the palace's massive marble elegance and beyond to the Bay of Naples. "Since he's noncommissioned, we can't officially date, and we could get in trouble for fraternizing, especially him. Please don't say anything."

Kay arched her perfectly plucked eyebrows. "Ooh, he kissed you well."

"I said no such thing!"

"You don't have to. Your face shines like Moses coming off the mountain."

Georgie never thought she'd hear a biblical allusion from Kay Jobson's mouth. And what a time for her to choose one.

Mellie laid her hand on Georgie's forearm. "I don't know Hutch well, but he seems like a good man. But isn't it rather soon for both of you? It hasn't even been a month, has it?"

Barely over two weeks for each of them. "Maybe, but we've known each other since July, and he's a close friend, and neither of us was undone by our breakups."

Mellie pursed her full lips. "I'm just concerned. You were with Ward for so many years. You're used to having a boyfriend, and I hope you're not —"

"Filling a hole? Definitely not." Georgie shook off her friend's hand and strode toward the palace.

"Be careful, honey. That's all."

"Leave her be, Mellie. Let her have her fun. There's a war on."

"It's not just for fun." How could she

explain that her connection with Hutch ran deep and strong, with a ribbon of rightness to it? How could she explain she was already falling in love?

They hadn't talked about love or the future, but her mind went there anyway — and snagged.

The path rolled over a slight rise and revealed the next pool, sparkling in the sunshine.

If she and Hutch married, what then? He was a Yankee, a big city boy. She was a Southerner, a country girl. Could she adjust to the north, to a city without horses and grassy hills, to being far from her family? But how could she drag him away from his family and best friend and the city he loved?

Oh dear. This was complicated.

"You know, Georgie, that's a swell idea." Kay tipped her head to the clear sky. "I never considered dating an enlisted man. You outrank him. You can tell him what to do."

Georgie grimaced. That held no appeal. Not a man in the world would like that. She would never boss Hutch around, never even joke about it. But still, would it bother him? After all, a woman outranking a man in a relationship wasn't natural.

Hutch had better get his commission and soon.

Georgie wrestled down Captain McCurdy's arms while Sgt. Enrique Ramirez forced him back into the seat. Apparently the captain was a poor candidate for air evacuation.

"What are you waiting for, men?" McCurdy called out. "Jump!"

He'd been in a catatonic state for weeks due to battle fatigue, but the flight from Pomigliano to Tunisia made him snap. Back in September, while the US Fifth Army hunkered on the Salerno landing beaches, his unit of the 82nd Airborne had dropped behind enemy lines at Avellino. Scattered, poorly supplied, and harassed by the enemy, not many men had returned.

Sergeant Ramirez planted his knee on the man's lap and gripped both of the captain's wrists in his big hands, locking him in place. "I got him."

"I'll get the med." Georgie dashed down the aisle, past all the patients craning their heads to get a good look. Her breath raced, and she stretched her fingers, sore from battling a man twice her weight.

Part of her had hoped for a crisis so she could prove herself to Lieutenant Lambert, but this emergency required more physical strength than emotional strength. Still, she hadn't stopped praying since Captain McCurdy started shouting.

"Go! Go! Go, men. Go!"

She flung open the lid of the medication chest. A roll of gauze bandages to use for restraints, scissors, a bottle of phenobarbital.

Ramirez cried out. Shouts rang from the front of the cabin.

Georgie spun around.

Captain McCurdy charged down the aisle toward her. "Green light! Move it, men. Follow me."

Oh my goodness! What could she do? The man believed the C-47 was on an airborne mission, not a medical evacuation mission.

She stepped in front of him. "Sir, you don't have your parachute, your helmet."

Wild eyes focused on the cargo door. He tugged his bathrobe collar and rapped his skull. "Got them. Let's move on out."

Georgie grasped his arm. "But Captain, look. The light — it's red. It isn't time yet."

"It's green." He shoved past her and took hold of the door handle.

Oh no, if he jumped from a thousand feet

over the Mediterranean . . .

At the front of the plane, Ramirez got up to his knees and wiped blood from his face with the back of his sleeve. McCurdy would be gone before Ramirez could help.

If only she could convince him not to jump. She tossed her supplies onto the nearest litter, grabbed the interphone headset, and jammed it over her ears.

McCurdy shoved the door, the slipstream flung it open, and cool air billowed onto the plane. He motioned with his arm. "Go! Go! Go! After me!"

"Wait, Captain!" she yelled. "It's General Ridgway. The mission's recalled." She tapped her earpiece and flipped the switch to connect her to the radio room.

"What?" Frenzied light eyes homed in on her.

"Yes, General Ridgway, sir?" She covered the earpiece and backed away from the door to hear better. "The mission's recalled?"

"Excuse me?" the C-47's radioman-navigator said into the interphone. The Twelfth Air Force Troop Carrier Command had eliminated the position of navigator.

She beckoned the paratrooper to her, away from the open door, as far away as the headset cord allowed. "That's right, General Ridgway. I have Captain McCurdy of the

82nd Airborne back here, ready to jump. Would you please speak to him, tell him the infantry has already reached the drop zone, and the mission has been recalled?"

The radioman cussed. "Pardon my French, ma'am. You're serious?"

"Yes, I am, General Ridgway, sir. The door is open. He's ready to jump."

"Holy Toledo."

"Thank you, General. You can explain to Captain McCurdy. Here he is." Georgie held out the headset with a smile.

He stared at it, then pulled it over disheveled dark hair. "General Ridgway, sir?"

Sergeant Ramirez sneaked up behind the paratrooper, arms outstretched to tackle him.

Georgie held up one hand and shook her head. Better to talk the man down than to force him down.

"Yes, sir." The captain nodded. "That's good news indeed. Glad the infantry did their job for once."

Ramirez edged past McCurdy and Georgie to the open door, but he'd never be able to pull it closed against the slipstream.

McCurdy handed the headset back to Georgie. His hand shook, and blood outlined his knuckles, from Ramirez's teeth most likely.

"What good news. You can have a seat now." Georgie settled the headset back on its hook, grabbed her supplies, and led McCurdy toward the front of the cabin. "Does your hand hurt? That looks painful."

"Yuh — yuh — yes." He stared at his hand, in full tremors.

She had to restrain him and get that phenobarb down his throat. "Let's get you seated, then I'll give you a pain pill and bandage you up."

"Th— thanks." He collapsed into the seat, between two terrified-looking patients.

Georgie opened the medication bottle and pulled out two tablets. A whole grain should get him to sleep. "This will help with the pain."

He reached for the pills, but his hand shook violently.

"Open wide." She smiled and popped the pills into his mouth.

Ramirez knelt by her side. "Let me fasten your seat belt for you."

"I'll take care of that, Sergeant. Why don't you bring me some iodine for his wound?" Georgie hooked the two ends together and studied her patient's face. Confusion replaced the wildness. "Where are you from, Captain? Your accent sounds Western."

"Wa— wa— Wyoming, ma'am."

She lifted her shoulders in delight. "Are you a real live cowboy?"

His eyes barely focused on her. "Ra— ra—"

"Rancher?"

He nodded, and his whole torso rocked forward, over and over. Far from stable.

"How interesting. My family raises horses, and I love the great outdoors, don't you? Nothing like the open sky and fresh air."

Rocking, rocking, rocking.

Sergeant Ramirez returned with a canteen, the iodine, and another roll of gauze.

"Thank you." Georgie moistened gauze with water and wiped the wound clear. "Let's put some iodine on that to prevent infection, shall we?"

McCurdy rocked his assent, and Georgie disinfected the moving target of his hand.

"Let's bandage that up." She wound gauze around his knuckles. "It's important to completely immobilize this hand so it can heal properly." She stacked his injured hand on top of his good hand and wound gauze around both, binding them together. "I learned this in training last month. See how nicely it immobilizes the wound. You'll be better in no time at all."

"Th— thank you, ma— ma'am."

"You're welcome. Sergeant, why don't you

use some gauze to anchor his elbows to his seat belt? That'll aid the immobilization and the healing. He's shaking so badly, poor thing."

Ramirez shot her a look full of humor and admiration. "That's some training program you had, Lieutenant."

"Yes, it was." She sat back on her heels while Ramirez finished restraining the patient. Although the crisis had been dangerous, breaking out of catatonia meant the poor man had a chance of returning to normal. She laid her hand on McCurdy's bound hands. "You'll feel better soon, sir. I know you will. The Lord bless you and keep you."

Deep inside his light blue eyes, something registered. "B— bless you too, ma'am."

She prayed for the man right there, long and hard, her hand clasped over his, begging the Lord to heal his mind and spirit, to cleanse him from the haunting memories, to reach into his soul and remind him who he was, brave and strong and capable.

Sergeant Ramirez touched her shoulder. "It's over. He's asleep now."

She eased up her head, her neck stiff. How long had she been praying? "Thank you."

"No, thank *you*." He raised a salute.

The radioman stood in the doorway to his

compartment, leaning against the door frame, and he saluted her too. "General Ridgway here. An inspired bit of acting there, Lieutenant."

A light laugh slipped out. "Thank you."

All around her, fabric rustled and arms lifted in salute.

"We'd cheer, ma'am." The patient next to McCurdy pointed his thumb at the sleeping captain. "But we don't dare wake him."

Georgie gazed around at all the appreciative faces. She'd done it. God gave her wisdom, and she did her job.

She couldn't wait to tell Hutch.

And Lieutenant Lambert. And her family.

33

Piana di Caiazzo
November 22, 1943

"One bag of oranges." Georgie plunked a paper sack on the pharmacy counter.

"Thank you, Lieutenant." Hutch peered inside at the shiny fruit. "Lucia doesn't need antibiotics anymore, but I mix up an orange drink for her every day with beef extract and multivitamins. Bergie's order to get nutrients into her."

"Delicious."

"It is." But not as delicious as the dreamy look on Georgie's face. He probably looked just as besotted.

Her gaze darted to Dom, hard at work behind Hutch, and she stretched her hand forward on the counter. "I wish I had time to meet her today. I have to be in Receiving in five minutes."

He slid his hand toward hers until the tips of their fingers touched, connecting them, but not close enough for his taste. Too bad he didn't have a good excuse to dismiss Dom. He tilted his head in Dom's direction, rolled his eyes, and blew Georgie a kiss.

She giggled and blew one back.

First time he'd seen her since the picnic, and he couldn't even tell her how much he missed her. True, even if he were an officer, he wouldn't kiss her in public, but they could at least hold hands.

"Say, Lieutenant." His voice came out too gravelly, and he swallowed to moisten his throat. "I'm off for lunch now. I'll walk you to Receiving."

"All right." Somehow she kept her voice nonchalant even though her face lit up.

"See you in half an hour, Dom."

"Sure thing. Enjoy the hash."

"I'd rather have beef extract and multivitamins." He held back the tent flap for Georgie. Outside in the drizzle, he took off his helmet and settled it over Georgie's curls. "Here. Keep your hair dry."

She peeked up at the leaden sky. "I've given up all hope of looking cute in this weather."

He leaned as close as he dared. "You look beautiful."

"I sure missed you." Her low voice did

funny things to his insides.

"Missed you too." He ambled down the pathway and shoved his hands into the pockets of his field jacket so he couldn't take her in his arms.

"A secret romance. Exciting, isn't it?"

"Suppose so." He shot her a grin, liking her attitude even if he didn't share it.

"Here." She slipped him an envelope. "We can be open in letters. No law against us writing."

He tucked it in his trouser pocket. "I'll give mine to Bergie to be censored, let him in on our secret. Certainly can't give the letters to Kaz. Bergie handles the mail I send to Dad, since I'm detailing the problems in the system."

"Oh my. I didn't think about censorship. I'll be careful."

"Thanks."

"Ooh, I know. We can come up with secret codes. This could be fun."

He wiped drizzle off his forehead. "Secret codes? Like 'I wish I had a steak' means 'I want to hold you and kiss you until the MPs cart us home'?"

She glanced up at him from under her eyelashes. "I would love some steak."

Hutch drew a deep breath and watched his step on the muddy corduroy road. "Lead me not into temptation."

"Oh!" Her foot slipped to the side.

Hutch grabbed her so she wouldn't fall in the mud. For half a second he relished the feel of her warm body against his, but he released her.

The look on her face said she wished he hadn't let go. "Steak," she whispered.

All he could offer was beef extract — the flavor of romance without the substance.

Two physicians strode out of the receiving tent — Bergie and Chadwick.

Bergie waved. "Hey, Hutch. Hello there, Georgie. Maxwell said you were here."

She smiled at Hutch. "Delivering oranges to our pharmacist for Little Miss Lucia."

"Sure appreciate it, Lieutenant." Hutch tried to keep the adoration out of his eyes.

She turned to the doctors. "How are things here at the 93rd?"

Bergie and Chadwick exchanged a laugh.

Chadwick nodded to Receiving. "A week ago, General Clark ordered a two-week break in the fighting for rest and reinforcement. You wouldn't know it to see our caseload."

"Yep." Bergie crossed his arms. "Still getting casualties from up at the Winter Line, plus the weather's taking its toll. Saw our first cases of frostbite from troops up in the mountains, even some trench foot."

Treatment of frostbite and trench foot didn't require many meds, but Hutch would make sure he had a good stock of sulfanilamide powder and lanolin.

"Say, Hutch, any word on when we'll get penicillin?" The glint in Bergie's eyes said he was giving him a chance to impress Chad.

He'd rather impress Georgie, but he looked at Bergie instead. "We have a limited supply in the theater now, at a few general and station hospitals to the rear."

Chadwick huffed. "We deal with the most critical patients. We need it more."

Hutch needed to proceed with care. "In theory, that's true, sir. But in practice, the supply is short, and the Army wants us to stick with sulfa antibiotics. If the patient's resistant, they'll give him penicillin."

"Sounds like an excellent plan." Georgie tipped Hutch a smile and handed back his helmet. "Well, gentlemen, I need to find Captain Maxwell. Thank you for loaning me your helmet, Hutch. Wish I could give you a nice big juicy steak to show my gratitude."

A chuckle escaped. "Nothing I'd like more."

She disappeared into the tent, leaving him hungry.

Captain Chadwick gazed at the tent entrance, one eyebrow raised. "She's a honey. Say, Berg, you know if she has a boyfriend?"

Yes. She did. But Hutch imprisoned the words in his mouth, where they rotted and left a foul taste.

Bergie whapped Hutch in the arm. "What do you say? You know her."

Very well, but he hadn't told Bergie yet.

Chadwick narrowed his gaze at Hutch. "Well? Does she have a boyfriend?"

For the first time in his life, Hutch understood why Isaac in the Bible told Abimelech that Rebekah was not his wife. Because the truth would have cost him. Just as the truth could cost Hutch his goal.

"No, sir." His voice sounded choked.

"Good news." A smile put actual dimples in his stupid chiseled cheeks. "That's about to change."

"She — she had a boyfriend for years — childhood sweetheart. They just broke up, not even a month ago."

Chadwick shrugged off the reasoning as easily as Hutch had. "All I hear is she's available."

Bergie gave Hutch a funny look, probing and curious.

Hutch saluted. "Excuse me, sirs. I need to get to the mess before my lunch break is over."

"You're dismissed." Chadwick waved him away. "And Berg, I'll catch up with you later. I have some flirting to do."

The foul taste ate its way down to Hutch's stomach. He headed for the mess and dug in his pocket for his pillbox. Where was it?

Must have left it in his other pair of trousers. And he needed bicarb now.

He marched past the mess and toward his tent. His deception stabbed as sharply as the injustice of the system that forced him to lie. A system that kept him apart from his girlfriend because he wore stripes on his sleeve and she wore bars on her shoulder.

"Stupid, stinking system." He kicked a glob of mud.

He'd lied just to save his own skin. Isaac's lie put Rebekah in danger. Hutch's lie didn't endanger Georgie but put her in Chadwick's crosshairs. Sure, he trusted her faithfulness, but she shouldn't have to fend off the doctor. Hutch should have told the truth and protected her. That's what a real man would do.

He kicked another glob. "Stupid, stinking me."

Three boys burst out of a tent, arms full.

Local boys, stealing.

"Hey, you! Stop! *Fermi!*" Hutch chased them.

The boys cried out in Italian and scattered in different directions, off into the woods beside the hospital. Hutch ran after them, into the trees, but the boys disappeared.

Breathing hard, he returned to the hospital complex. If only the boys had asked. He would have given them whatever they needed. The hospital couldn't feed all the locals, but Hutch slipped the children some rations occasionally.

A crowd had formed, most of the men cursing the locals. Hutch weaved through. He barely had time for lunch now.

The crowd centered around his tent. Hutch worked his way to the entrance.

"Your quarters?" a medic asked. "Sorry, pal."

Sorry? Why?

Hutch ducked inside — to chaos. The tent he shared with three other men had been ransacked.

Blankets gone. Easily replaced. What else was missing?

A void at the foot of his cot.

Oh no. Not that.

His stomach worked into a knot no sodium bicarbonate could unwind. He peered under his cot, the other men's cots, groped in his barracks bag.

No use. He sank onto his bed.

It was gone. Stolen. Soon to be sold to some unsuspecting GI.

His telescope.

34

Piana di Caiazzo
November 26, 1943

Georgie stood in the aisle of the ward tent, clutching her present under her raincoat, her heart aching with love for Hutch.

He hadn't seen her yet. He sat on a camp stool beside a girl with casts enveloping skinny legs up in traction. Together they sang "Twinkle, Twinkle, Little Star" with hand motions.

Someday Hutch would be a wonderful father, wise and loving and gentle and firm. If only she could have the privilege of sharing the joys of parenthood with him. She shouldn't think of such things so early in their romance, but how could she help it?

After the song, Georgie stepped forward. "Hello, Hutch. May I meet your friend?"

"Geor— Lieutenant Taylor." He grinned and got to his feet so fast the camp stool fell over. With a sheepish smile, he set up the stool again. "It's good to see you."

"It's good to see you too." Nothing was better than looking up, up, up into his smiling face. Unless it was kissing that face.

"Lieutenant Taylor, I'd like you to meet my friend Lucia. *Lucia, vorrei presentarle la mia amica Signorina Giorgiana.*"

Oh, he sounded so romantic speaking Italian. "Hello, Lucia. It's nice to meet you." She leaned over and held out her hand to the little girl.

Lucia's smile had several charming holes. "It's-a nice-a to meet you too."

"Your English is so good. Hutch told me how fast you're learning."

He scooted the stool toward Georgie and motioned for her to sit. "Much faster than I'm learning Italian, but I'm trying."

"Sounds fabulous to me." She unbuttoned her raincoat. "This should help — your Thanksgiving present."

He took the book from her. "An Italian-English dictionary. Wow. Where'd you get this?"

"In Naples." She sat on the stool.

"This is swell." He perched on the cot next to Lucia's pillow and flipped through the dictionary. "Look, Lucia. Let me show you. *Italiano . . . Inglese. Il orso . . .* the bear. Grrr."

She giggled. "*Stelle* . . . star-zay."

"Stars." He chomped off the end of the word.

"Star-zaaaay."

They laughed together, and Hutch smiled at Georgie. "She does that just to bug me."

Warmth filled her heart. "You don't look annoyed. You look smitten."

"Times two." A lightning flash of a wink, then he tugged Lucia's long dark braid. "She can't read yet, but we're working on it. When the nurses have quiet moments, they teach her. So do I. She knows her alphabet now."

"Alphabet-a." Lucia lifted herself on her elbows and gave Georgie a bright-eyed smile. "I sing-a for you?"

"Please do." She leaned her elbows on her knees.

"A, B, C, D, E, F, G, 'ow I wonder what you are." Her big brown eyes twinkle, twinkled.

Hutch burst out laughing and ruffled her hair. "You little rascal."

"She's a mischievous one, isn't she?"

"Maybe teaching her English wasn't my smartest idea."

"A brilliant idea from a brilliant man."

"Careful." His voice lowered, and he glanced around the ward. "People will get the wrong idea."

Or they'd get the right idea, which would be a problem. She gave him an understanding nod. "Are you teaching her astronomy too?"

He winced. "That'd be difficult. Someone stole my telescope."

"Oh!" She shut her mouth before a dozen endearments escaped. "Oh dear. You must be so upset. I know what it meant to you."

"A whole lot." He raised a sad smile. "I keep telling myself it'll help feed a couple of urchins for weeks."

Admiration added new facets to her love for him. "Not just brilliant but compassionate."

He rolled his eyes and looked at his watch. "It's getting late. Gotta get back and let Ralph take his lunch. Would you like to walk with me, Lieutenant?"

"I'd be glad to." She tried to sound casual.

After they said good-bye to Lucia, Hutch and Georgie left the ward tent. Georgie flipped up the hood of her raincoat. She had to restrain herself from taking Hutch's hand. "Lucia's absolutely adorable. I see why you're smitten."

"Yeah." He tucked the dictionary inside his field jacket. "I worry about her though. The casts come off in a few weeks. We can't keep her here forever. The Red Cross will place her in an orphanage in the Naples area. They'll take good care of her, but after the war . . ."

"An orphanage. What a shame." She burrowed her hands in her pockets to keep them somewhat dry.

"I can't stand the thought of her growing up like that. After the war she'll be one of thousands of orphans in this country, and even worse off if she can't walk well."

An idea swirled in her head, but it involved marriage and the future, places she didn't dare approach yet. "She's very attached to you."

He nodded, and droplets splattered off his helmet. "I'm hoping to . . . I'd like to adopt her."

She turned up her face to him, not caring about the rain, only wanting him to know she shared his thinking. "That's your most brilliant idea ever."

A flash of a shy smile. He got the message. "Watch your step. It's muddy."

Georgie wrestled back a laugh. Just like a man to change the subject.

He nudged her with his elbow. "Thanks for that letter. Why didn't you tell me in person you saved a man's life?"

"I didn't have time. And I didn't save his

life. General Ridgway did."

Hutch faced her. The dictionary in his jacket made him look as if he had a potbelly — kind of cute, actually. "Do you have any more doubts that you made the right decision about flight nursing? That you can be strong and still be incredibly attractive and feminine?"

"No." In Hutch's presence, she felt stronger than Rosie the Riveter and cuter than any pinup girl. "I'm right where the Lord wants me."

"I'm glad the Lord and I are on the same side." He motioned down the pathway. "Come on. I can hear Ralph's stomach grumbling from here."

She followed him into Pharmacy, greeted Ralph, and thanked him for telling her Hutch was with Lucia.

After he dismissed the tech for lunch, Hutch took off his helmet. A glint entered his eyes. "We're alone."

Her heart flipped around. "We are, aren't we?"

He beckoned her with one finger. "Come here. Wait, let me take off my wet jacket."

"Me too." She fumbled with the buttons on her raincoat and suppressed a giggle. If her mother could see her now. Disrobing so she could kiss a man — a man who wasn't

Ward Manville.

She shrugged the coat off her shoulders and reached out to drape it over the counter, but Hutch threw his arms around her waist and kissed her breathless.

"Sweetie," she mumbled against his warm and giving lips. "Let me put down my coat."

"Go ahead. Don't let me stop you." He nestled his mouth into her neck instead.

She laughed, feeling woozy, and tossed the coat onto the counter. Her attention and her kisses returned to the man in her arms. The previous summer, if she'd ever let herself imagine what his kisses would be like, she would have imagined something cozy and sweet. Never could she have imagined the delightful passion in this quiet man.

He settled a kiss on her forehead. "When you said they were letting you fly now, I thought I wouldn't see you up here again."

"Special request." Georgie straightened his necktie. "Lambert thinks it's good for me to come up here and orient the patients before their flights. And deep inside she has a romantic heart. She understands I want to see my boyfriend."

Hutch's face drew long. "You told her?"

"Don't worry. I didn't say who. Only Mellie and Kay know it's you, and they can keep secrets. But everyone can tell I have a new man in my life. Everyone knows I'm in love." She clapped her hand over her mouth. Oh, why couldn't she ever keep her mouth shut? She'd ruin everything, talking like that.

His gaze riveted onto her. The knot on his necktie wobbled.

Georgie slid her hand over her eyes. "Oh no. Why'd I say that? What must you think of me? The man's supposed to say that first, and it's far too early, and —"

"Georgie."

She peeked over her fingers.

He wrapped his hand around hers and held it to his chest. "I love you."

"Sugar, you don't have to say that to make me feel better. I know it's too early."

He kissed her forehead. "I . . ."

And her nose. "Love . . ."

And her lips. "You."

She studied the depths of his brown eyes. He wasn't the kind of man to toss around his affections or his words. "Oh, Hutch."

"Someday I hope to hear those words from you."

He already had. What a gentleman to pretend he hadn't. "Why, I do think I'm in love with you, John Hutchinson. Now say my name in Italian again."

"You like that, huh?" He leaned close. His lips hovered over hers, and his breath mingled with hers. *"Ti amo, Giorgiana."*

The minuscule distance between them — she couldn't bear it, and she eliminated it.

His kisses would be her undoing. Her thoughts whooshed together into a delicious mess. All she could think of was the warmth of his body against her, the strength of his arms around her, and the passion of his love flowing through her.

Someone on the other side of the tent broke into a loud coughing fit, but a canvas divider shielded them from curious eyes.

Hutch set his hands on her waist and pushed her away. Why? Ralph wouldn't return for at least fifteen minutes, and who knew when they could be alone together again?

"Not yet, sweetheart." She pulled his head down and kissed him.

He stiffened and stepped back, alarm in his eyes. "Georgie, no."

"Sergeant Hutchinson!"

Georgie spun around.

A short, middle-aged officer stood by the flap that separated pharmacy from lab. His face reddened. "What is the meaning of this?"

Oh goodness. What now? Georgie

smoothed her hair, mindful that her face was probably flushed.

Hutch's shoulders slumped, and he stepped away from Georgie. "Lieutenant Taylor, may I introduce my commanding officer, Lieutenant Kazokov?"

His commanding officer? She'd gotten him in trouble. And the look in his eyes broke her heart. Frustration. Resignation. Defeat.

"She's an officer." Kazokov marched right up to Hutch. "Fraternizing with an officer? That violates military regulations."

"It's my fault, Lieutenant." Georgie offered him an apologetic half-smile. "I threw myself at —"

"Georgie, don't." Hutch closed his eyes.

Kazokov glared at him. "Calling an officer by her first name? Don't you know anything about military courtesy? Look at me, boy."

Hutch obeyed. "I apologize, sir. It won't happen again."

It wouldn't? Georgie frowned. Would he break up with her over this? Or would the Army force them apart?

Kazokov clasped his hands behind his back and paced in a circle, giving Georgie a glance as he passed. "To think I actually wrote that letter of recommendation for you. Fraternizing with an officer, and on

Army time. I'll have to write you up."

"Please!" Hutch held up one hand, his eyes frantic. "Please don't write me up, sir. Discipline me. Make me do KP, latrines, midnight guard duty, whatever. But please don't write me up, sir."

Georgie's face tingled. A disciplinary infraction would destroy his chances of getting into the Pharmacy Corps, wouldn't it? "Oh, please, Lieutenant. You know what the Pharm—"

Hutch cut her a short, hard gaze, silencing her. "This isn't your battle, Lieutenant Taylor."

Yes, it was. If she'd let him push her away, Kazokov wouldn't have seen them kiss. Time for some Southern charm. "Lieutenant, this is his first infraction, isn't it?"

"I suppose so."

Hutch groaned. "Lieutenant Taylor, don't —"

"Please, let me speak." Georgie focused her charm on Kazokov, but guilt twanged on her heartstrings. In essence, she'd ordered Hutch to be silent. Any arguments he raised could be considered insubordination.

She'd apologize later. Right now, she had to undo the damage she'd wrought. "Since it's his first infraction — and his last, I'm certain — mercy is in order, don't you think?"

His small dark eyes glanced away. "The Army isn't designed for mercy."

"Oh, but you are, sir. I see it in your eyes. You look like a kind and merciful gentleman. I know your wife would be pleased to see you turn your head — just this once — for the sake of young love."

His mouth shifted to one side. "I'm not married."

"You're not?" Georgie widened her eyes. "What is wrong with the women in your hometown? If you came to Virginia, I could find you a wife in the blink of an eye."

He softened slightly. "Thank you, ma'am. That's very kind, if not completely true. For your sake only, I'll let this slide. One time."

"Oh, thank you! I appreciate it so much."

"Yes, thank you, sir." Hutch's voice sounded strained.

"Very well." Kazokov strode to the tent entrance, held open the flap, and motioned to Georgie. He certainly wouldn't allow a good-bye kiss.

She fetched her raincoat and slipped it on. "Good-bye, Hutch."

"Good-bye, Lieutenant." He turned away without meeting her eye, one hand pressed over his stomach.

Georgie's heart drifted low in her chest, but she managed a polite nod to Kazokov as she exited.

"Pardon me, ma'am," he said in a low voice. "Heed my advice and be more careful whom you associate with."

She ignored the boiling sensation in her head, tilted her chin, and smiled. "How kind of you to be concerned about my welfare."

Georgie pulled up her hood and headed into the rain. Such disrespect. Honestly. How could anyone treat her sweet Hutch that way?

35

Piana di Caiazzo
December 5, 1943

"Are you trying to kill my patients?" Capt. Al Chadwick slammed the medication bottle onto the counter. "What kind of operation are you running here?"

Lieutenant Kazokov stood beside Chadwick, his face purplish red. "This better not have been a pharmacy error."

Although his pulse skyrocketed, Hutch kept his voice calm and addressed the physician. "Would you please tell me the problem, sir?"

"The problem? You almost killed my patient."

Hutch inspected the amber glass bottle. The handwritten label said it contained elixir of codeine, 0.8 percent. Ralph's handwriting. Dated December 4 — Hutch's day off. "Tell me about the patient."

"He's in pain, you idiot. Why do you think

he needs codeine?"

A long, slow breath helped, but barely. "And he can't swallow a pill and you —"

"I wanted an elixir." Chadwick leaned closer, right in Hutch's face, except Hutch had a few blessed inches on the doctor. "And my patient almost died. Should have known better than to trust a druggist."

Kazokov tugged the hem of his field jacket. "You'd better have an explanation for this."

First Hutch had to figure out what happened, which required methodical thinking, not gut reactions. He unscrewed the lid and sniffed the med. Smelled fine. "What happened to the patient?"

"He went into respiratory shock. Thank goodness I was working and saved his life."

"Yes, thank goodness." Hutch dipped his pinky into the solution and tasted it. Too bitter.

Ralph stood backed against the medication shelves, whiter than a bleached sheet hung to dry in the sun. "I didn't want to fill it, Hutch."

He nodded. "May I see your calculations?"

"Of course. I wrote everything down like you taught us." He opened the box of prescriptions and flipped through. "It wasn't in the manual, and I hate doing calculations, you know I do. I asked Captain Chadwick to wait until your shift, but he said no. Then I asked to go fetch you, even though it was your day off, and he said he needed it stat."

"If Captain Chadwick needed it stat," Kaz said, "then he needed it immediately."

Hutch stiffened. Yes, that was what *stat* meant. But what was so urgent that he couldn't wait an extra fifteen minutes? For a prescription that took Ralph fifteen to thirty minutes to fill? For an oral pain medication that took half an hour to work anyway? If the patient needed immediate pain relief, a shot of morphine would have been far more effective. Heat simmered in his chest.

He joined Ralph at the back counter and looked over his work. "Okay, 0.8 percent means . . . ?"

"Ah, I hate percents. I worked from the dose instead."

"That's fine. He wanted half a grain per teaspoon."

"Yeah, and half a grain is 32 milligrams. And he wanted two ounces, which is 60 milliliters. And 32 times 60 is —"

"Five times too much." A sigh leached out with all his hopes that Pharmacy hadn't made an error.

"Five times . . ." Ralph's green eyes flicked back and forth between Hutch's eyes.

He tapped the script. "It's 32 milligrams per teaspoon, per *five* milliliters. You made it 32 milligrams per milliliter. Five times too potent."

Ralph cussed and ran his hand over his mouth.

"Did you numbskulls figure it out?"

Hutch tensed at Chadwick's tone. As a professional, he had to admit the error. He returned to the front counter, a nasty taste in his mouth. "Yes, sir. We made a calculation error. The solution was five times stronger than it should have been. I am so sorry, sir."

"Sorry? You almost kill a man, and you're sorry?"

"I can't believe this." Kaz grabbed the bottle and stared at it, as if he knew one whit about what was inside.

Chadwick raised his square chin. "You druggists want commissions for shoddy work like this? Disgusting. You ought to be shot."

"On the contrary, sir." Hutch kept his voice even and steady. "This is the direct result of Medical Corps policy."

"Excuse me? You're trying to blame us for

your mistake?"

Hutch slid the prescription over the counter toward Chadwick. "You said any intelligent boy who could read a label could practice pharmacy in the Army. Well, this is what happens when intelligent boys are handed a prescription they didn't learn to fill in training. This is what happens when intelligent boys aren't allowed to ask for help from a licensed pharmacist. This is what happens when intelligent boys are ordered by an officer and must obey despite their better judgment."

Chadwick's gray eyes narrowed to steely daggers. "Are you questioning my orders, boy?"

Best avoid that. Hutch smoothed out the prescription. "Your medication order is fine. If I — or any pharmacist — had worked that shift, this would have been properly compounded, even if a tech had filled it. I always check their calculations."

"You can't shirk responsibility." Chadwick rapped his fist on the counter. "You're in charge. It's your fault."

A smile threatened, but Hutch reined it in. He shifted his gaze to Kaz. "But I'm not in charge, sir. As Lieutenant Kazokov reminds me almost every day, he's in charge, and I'm not."

Kaz's chin jutted out. "Are you blaming me? That's preposterous."

"I'm blaming the system, sir. Ralph was given a direct order to fill a prescription he wasn't qualified to fill. This is the Army, and he isn't allowed to refuse a direct order. If this pharmacy were set up properly, with a pharmacist in charge, with checks and balances —"

"A windbag like your father. You almost killed a patient, and now you're blaming a physician — and an officer — for your mistake. Currier will hear about this." Chadwick stormed out of the tent.

Yes, he would. But Colonel Currier was a reasonable and fair man, and Hutch welcomed the chance to explain the situation to him.

Kazokov stomped around the counter and right up to Hutch. "I can't believe what I heard. 'Lieutenant Kazokov is in charge, and I'm not.' '*If* this pharmacy were set up properly.' Appalling. Blatant disrespect for your commanding officer."

"Sir, I didn't —"

"After all I've done for you. Writing a letter of recommendation, choosing to look the other way when I caught you necking with that nurse."

Hutch's stomach clenched. He hardly

called giving him a solid week of KP looking the other way.

"That's another week of KP for you. And for you too, O'Shea." He shook a finger at Ralph. "You started this. And look at this place. A mess."

A mess? The mortar and pestle sat on the counter for the ointment Hutch had been preparing. The scales too. "Sir, we were in the middle —"

"You were in the middle of making a mess as usual." He picked up the scales and jammed them in their wooden box.

Hutch cringed at the rough treatment of the delicate equipment.

"How many times do I have to tell you? Scales go under *S.*" Kaz shoved the box onto the bottom shelf.

Glass shattered. Fluid sprayed into the air, foamed, crackled.

Kaz screamed, dropped to the ground, and grabbed his arm. Holes formed in the sleeve.

What chemical was it? "Don't touch it! You'll burn your hand too. Ralph, get a doctor!"

Ralph took off running.

Hutch ignored Kaz's screams, grabbed a rag and leaned down, avoiding the wet, sizzling patches on the ground. With the rag, he pulled the scales off the shelf so he could read the labels of the broken bottles. Sodium hydroxide. Sulfuric acid.

A base and an acid. Either substance alone caused damage, but in combination, the reaction produced heat and worsened the chemical burns.

He grabbed the liter bottle of water and knelt beside Kaz. "Hold still. Don't touch it." He poured water over Kaz's arm and hand. Through holes in the olive drab fabric, the skin looked red and blistered.

"If you'd cleaned up your mess," he said through gritted teeth, "this wouldn't have happened."

Hutch continued pouring water, but he pointed with his free hand to the shelf. "Remember? On the day you alphabetized the pharmacy, I told you sodium hydroxide and sulfuric acid didn't belong side by side. I told you it was an accident waiting to happen. Today it happened."

Kaz sucked in his breath.

Hutch turned his gaze to the man in pain. "But I'm very sorry it happened to you, sir. I know this must hurt like crazy."

He scrunched his eyes shut and nodded.

Ralph rushed in with Captain Sobel and a couple of medics. Thank goodness it wasn't Chadwick.

The doctor asked questions, cut off the sleeve, and washed away more of the chemicals. Then the medics helped Kaz to his feet and assisted him out of the tent to the wards.

Hutch turned his attention to what was now an actual mess. He wiped off the scale box, slightly pitted, but the scales themselves were all right.

Had he been disrespectful to Kaz? Nonsense. What did Kaz know about disrespect? Hutch had lived with it for over three years. "Disrespect? The Army's disrespect caused this disaster."

"Disaster?" Ralph picked up shards of glass with ragwrapped hands. "Don't you mean dis-kaz-ter?"

Hutch let out a chuckle in spite of himself. "No matter what, I don't want you to feel bad about any of this. You did your job fine. Maybe — maybe this will help Kaz see the truth."

"You ought to feel vindicated."

"Yep." He'd write a long letter to his dad tonight, which would be valuable, since it proved every point they'd made for years.

So why did frustration still churn inside?

36

Naples, Italy
December 13, 1943

Never before in her life had Georgie felt alone in a crowd.

She stood on Naples's waterfront overlooking the busy bay under a clear sky. Vesuvius loomed black to the east, not far enough away. At least in the daytime she couldn't see the ominous red glow from the crater.

All around her, people chatted and laughed. Mellie hung on the arm of her boyfriend, Tom MacGilliver — the first time they'd seen each other since September. Louise Cox had found lots to talk about with Lt. Rudy Scaglione from Tom's Engineer Aviation Battalion. Kay flirted with — yet managed to keep her distance from — pilot Grant Klein, recovered from the crash that killed Clint and Rose. And Vera and Alice giggled at Captain Frank Maxwell's joke.

Vera's mood had improved as soon as they boarded the plane taking them away from Kentucky. Taking Captain Maxwell away from his wife.

What a horrible thing to think! Just because gorgeous Vera never dated, just because she simpered in the physician's presence, just because Georgie didn't like her — none of that justified her catty thought.

The cool sea breeze lifted Georgie's curls. She smoothed them and forced her mind to contemplate Christmas. The holiday was coming in less than two weeks, her first without Rose's off-key carol singing. Somehow she had to overcome her grief and make the holiday special for the nurses and patients. And for Hutch too. Their first Christmas. She wanted to find him the perfect gift.

"All right, folks. Let's keep moving." Captain Maxwell showed the way down the waterfront road.

"Stay close, ladies." Grant put his arm around Kay's waist. "We men have our sidearms to keep you safe."

Kay laughed and wiggled free. "Until the pickpockets steal your pistols."

As they headed down the road, Georgie tucked herself between Tom-Mellie and Rudy-Louise. If only Hutch could be there.

Mellie looked over her shoulder and beckoned Georgie. "I don't want to abandon you."

She came alongside her friend. "Nonsense. You two deserve some time together."

Tom straightened his service cap over his sandy hair. "We have an entire evening of dining and dancing ahead, just the two of us. Now's a good time to get to know Mellie's friends." He had an appealing smile and a friendly personality. For the son of a convicted murderer, he didn't seem like such a bad fellow.

"How are things at Foggia?" she asked.

"Busy. Seems like new fighters and bombers come in every day. They need runways and facilities, which keeps us engineers busy. It's worth it when I see those big birds head for Nazi targets in northern Italy and Austria."

"If only they could help us break the Winter Line. I've lost count how many times we've attacked San Pietro." Mellie tucked thick black hair behind her ear.

"It won't be long. We'll break through."

She leaned against her boyfriend. "One of the many things I love about you — your optimism."

He gazed at her in pure adoration, and Georgie felt completely out of place. Was this how Rose had felt with her and Ward all those years? Even worse, since poor Rose once had a crush on Ward.

Georgie's eyes prickled, and her throat swelled. To distract herself, she stopped and focused on the massive structure across the street.

The Castel Nuovo looked less like a new castle and more like a medieval fort, with high walls to repel invaders and round crenellated towers at each corner to provide good vantage points for defenders — like Italy's many steep hills favored German defensive fighting.

"Impressive, isn't it?" Tom said.

"Yes, it is." Georgie mustered a smile and turned — but Tom and Mellie faced the waterfront, where throngs of men unloaded Liberty cargo ships.

Mellie held back her hair. "Is it true this port gets more traffic than New York City?"

"Sure is." Tom pointed to the nearest dock. "The Germans did everything in their power to prevent it, confiscated every boat in Naples, then sank them to clog the harbor."

"That's where engineers come in, isn't it?" Mellie snuggled close.

He grinned and led the way down the road. "Sure is. They had a big job. The Nazis blew up the sewers and aqueducts and electrical plants, yanked up railroad track, ignited the coal stocks, planted time bombs throughout the city. They know starving people riot. So we had to provide food and water and basic safety. We still have a long way to go."

Georgie passed street urchins clustered around a couple of GIs who passed out sticks of gum. The poor things looked like they hadn't had a solid meal in weeks.

Mellie motioned for Georgie to catch up with them. "Have you heard from your family yet? They were so kind to us."

Georgie clutched her shoulder bag across her stomach as she stepped around a trio of skinny teenage boys. "I received a big ol' stack of letters last night. They must have written two, three times a week since I left. All of them."

"And . . . ?"

She sighed. "They think Ward and I just had a misunderstanding. They say Ward didn't mean to break up with me, only to change my mind. He's beside himself, and Pearline has her sights set on him. They say I'd better act fast and win him back. Why can't they see I don't want him back?"

"Have you told them about . . . ?" Mellie glanced around, lips tucked in. Only she and Kay knew about Hutch.

"Not yet."

Tom gave her a soft smile. "Mellie told me. Don't worry. I'm good at keeping secrets."

They followed the group into a dark stairwell guarded by a white-helmeted MP, and voices echoed off the stone walls as they climbed. Hardly the place to discuss Hutch.

The group emerged into the sunshine and headed into the wide open Piazza del Plebiscito, according to the chatter from Captain Maxwell and Vera and Alice farther ahead.

Mellie led Tom and Georgie away from the crowd to the center of the piazza. Long, ornate three-storied buildings anchored three sides of the piazza, but the west side featured a church with a low dome and a semicircle of colonnades reaching out in an embrace.

Mellie turned serious dark eyes to Georgie. "Why haven't you told your parents about Hutch?"

Georgie rolled her purse strap in her fingers. "It's so soon. I'm afraid they'll think I broke up with Ward because of Hutch, which isn't true and wouldn't be fair to Hutch. It'll be hard enough for my family to accept any man who isn't Ward."

"You two were together a long time,

weren't you?" Tom asked in a low voice.

"Nine years, and my parents have all but adopted him. And here comes poor, sweet Hutch with his Yankee accent. I want my family to adore Hutch, but I don't know if they ever will. At this point, I just hope they'll be civil."

Mellie looped her free arm through Georgie's. "I can't imagine your family being anything but civil. And it won't take long for them to see how good he is for you. They're reasonable people. They'll come around."

"I hope so. I'll tell them when he gets his commission. He's taking his test for the Pharmacy Corps next month." If he could figure out a way to get to Naples for the exam.

"Then they won't be upset with you for breaking the fraternization rules."

"That too." Georgie shielded her eyes from the sun glinting off marble columns. "And it buys time. Hutch won't hear back until February at the earliest, so my letter wouldn't arrive until March. That'll make over four months since I broke up with Ward."

"No, grazie," Tom said to a shoe shine boy and lifted his well-shined shoe as proof. "What's Hutch think of it?"

"Hutch would get a shoe shine."

Tom laughed. "I meant about not telling your parents."

"I know. He agrees. He's waiting to tell his family for similar reasons."

"Come along, folks," Captain Maxwell said. "The ladies want to do some shopping."

Georgie certainly did. Maybe the perfect present would erase the melancholy she read in Hutch's last letter. If only she could give him a commission for Christmas.

Off the piazza, the road narrowed and the sun seemed to disappear. Three-storied buildings rose on each side, crowned by iron balconies festooned with laundry and flower boxes. Bombs had sawed some of the buildings in half and reduced others to rubble.

Before the Italian surrender, Naples suffered from Allied bombing. After the surrender, the city suffered from Nazi fury.

The store windows on Via Roma held none of life's necessities but an odd assortment of luxuries.

"Interesting things in here." Grant led Kay into a small shop.

Georgie stepped into the dim, musty-smelling store. Ramshackle cases displayed all sorts of goods, from watches to clocks to binoculars.

"Hello! Hello!" The shopkeeper waved them inside, a balding man in his sixties with a scruffy gray mustache. "Ah, so many beautiful American girls."

"You have excellent eyesight," Grant said. "And very good English."

"Ten years in New Jersey. Came back here in '35 to care for my mother. Should have brought her to America instead."

"I'm so sorry." Georgie scanned the cases. Would Hutch like a new watch? A pair of binoculars? Would that be a good substitute for his beloved telescope?

Tom fingered a wristwatch and showed it to Mellie. "What do you think? For my mom?"

"It's lovely."

"I have more." The shopkeeper pulled out a long narrow box and opened it. "I still have many beautiful watches because I am smart. When the Neapolitans rose up against the *Tedeschi* late in September, the Nazis struck back. So I buried the best merchandise in my basement, left the cheapest things in the cases, then smashed up my own store, broke my windows."

"Oh my!" Georgie tried to lean on the case, but it didn't have any glass.

"*Si.* When the *Tedeschi* came, they thought they'd already looted my store and left it

400

alone. Now the Americans come, and I make good money, take care of my whole family."

On a high shelf over the shopkeeper's head, a telescope was set up.

Georgie gasped. "Sir, is that telescope for sale? May I see it?"

"*Si.* It is very nice." He scrambled onto a stool, brought down the telescope, and presented it to Georgie.

It looked smaller than Hutch's, but newer. The shopkeeper talked about magnification levels and refraction and the wonders of a telescope made in Italia, the homeland of Galileo himself.

All Georgie understood was restoring joy to Hutch's face, returning a relaxing diversion to his life. "I'll take it." She hadn't looked at the price and she didn't care.

"For Hutch?" Kay said.

Georgie winced. She spoke his name so openly. "Yes."

"You can give it to him at the dance up at the 93rd next Saturday."

"Yes and no." She counted out liras for the jubilant shopkeeper. "I can give it to him, but not at the dance. He can't go, poor thing. Just for officers."

Kay ran a finger along the smooth leather telescope case. "Meet him behind the tent and dance your heart out."

If only they could. She'd never danced with Hutch. "I don't dare get him in any more trouble."

Kay set one hand on her hip. "I need to give you lessons in sneaking around."

Georgie gave her a strained smile and took her change from the shopkeeper. The thrill of a secret romance dissolved in the reality of inconvenience.

37

Piana di Caiazzo
December 18, 1943

How on earth could he get to Naples? Hutch set the scales back in their case for the night. He needed Kaz's signature on a three-day pass for the Pharmacy Corps exam, but Kaz had made it clear he wouldn't do Hutch any more favors.

Hutch hadn't seen his CO since the accident, but Captain Sobel said his burns weren't too serious, and he'd be back to duty after Christmas. Perhaps by then, he'd have softened. Or perhaps Hutch could take advantage of his hospitalization and go directly to Colonel Currier. But that might be deemed disrespectful and make things worse in the long run.

"How was the day shift?" Dom sloughed off his mackinaw.

"Busy." Hutch wiped the back counter with a rag. "Lots of casualties from the

Winter Line, trench foot, pneumonia. But Ralph and I kept up. You're in good shape for tonight."

"Got a Thermos full of coffee. I'm ready."

"Great." The sooner he escaped to quarters, the better. The nurses from the 802nd were coming up to the 93rd tonight for the officers' Christmas dance, and he wanted to distance himself from the music. The woman he loved would be dancing. But not with him.

He pulled on his mud-splattered mackinaw and lifted the tent flap.

Georgie burst inside, all grins and swishing silk and perfume.

"Georgie." He stepped back, in desperate need of a shower, a shave, and a clean uniform.

She waved to Dom and set a box on the front counter. "Hi, Dom. Would you please give us five minutes alone? We'd appreciate it."

"Sure thing." He winked, grabbed his jacket, and stepped outside.

Hutch cleared his throat. "This isn't a —"

"Nonsense. Let's get you out of this dirty thing." She unbuttoned his mackinaw. So beautiful with her curls pinned up, plenty of red lipstick, and that intoxicating perfume. "Lillian's standing guard outside. Bergie intercepted Chad and will keep him busy as long as he can."

"Chad." He pulled off his jacket.

"Captain Chadwick." She slipped off her raincoat, revealing a deep blue dress that brought out her eye color. "Don't you worry. He might be pompous, but he's a gentleman, and Bergie will keep him in line. He's not as bad as you think. He rides. His family has horses at their country place in Connecticut."

Of course they did. Hutch stiffened.

"Oh, sugar." She sighed and took his hands. "You know my heart belongs to you."

"I know." Why was he ruining one of their few moments together with a bad mood? He drew a deep breath and kissed both her pretty little hands. "You look beautiful. Really beautiful."

Georgie dissolved into a smile. "You do too."

He chuckled. "Hardly. And I stink."

She wrapped her bare arms around his neck, pressed close, and burrowed her nose under his chin. "You smell wonderful to me."

His eyes flopped shut, and his head spun. With Georgie in his arms, he felt like a real man again. He pressed his lips to the warm skin of her arm, then gathered her near for a long kiss, her dress silky to his touch. If only he could spend the rest of the evening like this, holding her, dancing with her, hearing her lilting voice.

She pulled back and rubbed her thumb over his lips. "That color looks better on me than on you."

"I disagree. I'm going to steal every molecule of that lipstick." He gave his best attempt at a rakish grin and bent down for another kiss.

She stopped him with a firm hand to his chest. "As much as I'd love that, we don't have much time, and I want to give you your Christmas present."

He grimaced. "I gave mine to Bergie to give you."

"I know." She darted away and pulled the wrapped present from the pocket of her raincoat. "Let's open them together."

How could he not love her? All dressed up, she looked like a Hollywood glamour girl, but the light in her eyes reminded him of a six-year-old under the Christmas tree. "All right," he said. "You go first because you'll burst if you don't."

"I will." She ripped open the brown paper. "I'm the baby. I always go first."

"Of course you do." He frowned at his meager offering. "It's not much. I couldn't go shopping."

"Oh! This is so much better than something from a store." Georgie held up a tin star ornament he'd made, then an angel, a bell, a nightingale. "Look! These are darling. There must be a dozen, all different, all beautiful."

"I'm glad you like them."

"I do. I'll hang them in our tent, and it'll be so cute and festive." She wrapped them in the paper, then pointed to a leather case on the counter. "Now open yours."

"That's for me?" Looked expensive, whatever it was.

"Sure is." She clasped her hands together in front of her chest and lifted her shoulders. "Hurry. I can't wait to see your expression."

He'd rather look at hers, which was too cute for his meager words.

She waved him to the case. "Hurry."

"All right." He flipped open brass clasps and lifted the lid. A telescope, new and shiny. "How . . . where . . . ?"

"The most wonderful little store in Naples. He had all sorts of things."

Hutch stared at it. If he ever got to Naples, he couldn't afford something so nice, not on his sergeant's salary, not with almost every penny going into savings so he could open his own store after the war.

Georgie chattered about the charming shopkeeper and all he'd said about the telescope, incorrectly — but sweetly — filtered through Georgie's lay vocabulary.

He fingered the eyepiece. What kind of man was he? His gift to Georgie looked pathetic. He should have given her jewelry or something, but he was trapped in the hospital complex and couldn't afford anything expensive anyway.

She laid her hand on his forearm. "You don't like it?"

He glanced down to her eyes, swimming in hurt. "Of course I like it."

"Are you sure?"

"Of course." He wrangled up a smile. "It's real nice. Better than the one I had before."

"Really?" Her eyebrows drew together. "I wanted to make you happy."

"You did. I just — I wish I had something nicer for you."

"Oh, baby!" She threw her arms around his neck and kissed his chin. "Your gift is perfect. I know those ornaments took you hours to make, and they're beautiful. I'll treasure them always."

"I hope so." He held her tight. While making the ornaments, he'd imagined decorating Christmas trees with Georgie together through the years, holding up curly-haired tots to hang the star high, reminiscing about how they met, enduring the teasing of teen-age children, and someday lifting their withered hands to trace the shapes against the glow of colored lights.

"Hutch! Georgie!"

He sprang back. Lillian poked her head inside the tent and beckoned to Georgie. "Hurry. They're coming."

"Bye, sweetie. I love you." Georgie planted one last kiss on his lips and dashed for the entrance, tugging on her raincoat.

"I love you too." His arms felt cold and empty.

Dom stepped back inside the tent. He pointed to his cheek and waggled his eye-brows. "Lipstick."

Hutch rubbed his cheek, hating to remove the touch of the woman he loved. He threw on his mackinaw and peeked outside. About fifty feet away, illuminated by tents glowing from electric light, two women in long gowns strolled away from him. Two officers approached in full dress uniform.

Bergie took Lillian's hand.

Chadwick swept a low, dramatic bow to Georgie. "Milady, your beauty has utterly captivated me. I am rendered helpless by the power of your enchantment."

Hutch's stomach felt sour. What was it *he*

had said to her? "You look beautiful. Really beautiful." As pathetic as his gift.

"That's very kind of you." Georgie sounded polite but unmoved. Good.

Chadwick kissed her hand. Hey, Hutch had kissed it only moments before!

The jerk stepped close. "May I have the supreme honor of escorting you this evening? Although I'm afraid you'll be my undoing."

Georgie, bless her, stepped back. "We certainly wouldn't want that, would we?"

Hutch grinned. He'd thank her later.

"Please." Chad held her hand to his chest. "I'm a perfect gentleman and promise to behave myself."

"I'll make sure of it." Bergie spoke in a loud voice, probably for Hutch's benefit. "Lillian and I will stick close and keep him honest."

"I wouldn't have it any other way." Chad tucked her hand under his arm. "A lady's honor is a precious treasure."

Georgie tilted her head. "As long as you behave as well as you speak, you may escort me."

For one brief moment, Hutch hoped Chad wouldn't behave so Georgie would slap him good and hard.

The foursome headed to the officers' club,

where engineers had laid a wooden dance floor. Hutch stepped outside and watched. He should be part of that group. He should be with his best friend and his girl, off for a fun evening.

Georgie glanced over her shoulder at him. He could feel the remorse in her gaze. But it wasn't her fault. He raised a hand in farewell and walked hard in the other direction.

The enlisted men wouldn't get a dance. Nope, they'd get a turkey dinner with all the fixings, sure they would. And an officer in a Santa hat would pass out candy. Happened every single year. But no dance. No women in long dresses. No chance to twirl his girlfriend around the dance floor in public.

The sourness in his stomach turned into gnawing pain. He popped a sodium bicarb tablet in his mouth. How could he concentrate on writing letters when the music reminded him that Georgie danced in another man's arms, the arms of his nemesis at that?

Maybe she'd be better off with Chad. He could adore her in the flowery words she deserved. He could give her the horses and land she deserved. He could be seen with her in public, for heaven's sake.

Hutch stopped and glanced up to the pitch-black sky. This wasn't doing him any good, and it wasn't fair to Georgie. He needed to take his mind off the whole stinking situation.

He charged down the pathway and into Lucia's ward. The little girl sat up in bed with a blanket over her shrunken legs. The casts had come off earlier in the week, and the staff had fashioned crutches and braces for her, but she couldn't stand yet. Bergie held out hope, but then he always did.

Lucia grinned. "Signor Ucce! Look!" She stretched out a string of paper dolls.

"Pretty. Did the nurses make that for you?" He sat on her cot.

"Yeah." She'd already picked up some slang. She waved her hand in the air. "Pretty *musico.*"

The strains of "Moonlight Serenade" drifted through the canvas. Medics worked the ward tonight and older, married physicians, freeing the nurses and single doctors to go to the dance. Dozens of patients stretched out on cots or sat in wheelchairs. None of them could go to the dance either.

Well, why shouldn't they? Why shouldn't they have their own dance? Hutch stood, took Lucia's hand, and swept a bow even lower and grander than Chadwick's. *"Balle*

412

con mi, per favore?"

"Yeah! Yeah!" She bounced on her cot and held out her arms.

He picked her up, set her on his hip, and took her hand in the dancing position. Down the aisle they danced, swinging and swaying, her giggles sweeter than the music.

The song finished, but Lucia shook her head. "No. Again, again-a."

A medic tapped Hutch on the shoulder. "May I cut in?"

He had no choice, so he passed on his tiny partner. A set of vigorous chords announced "Sing, Sing, Sing."

The medic broke into a jitterbug, hard and fast. Lucia's braids whipped around, and her giggles broke up as her jaws banged together.

The patients sat up now, all who could, and they clapped, sang, snapped fingers to the beat. One man drummed on the rim of his cot, another mimed blowing a trombone, and another conducted the band as if he were Benny Goodman himself.

When the band switched to "Brazil," Lucia was passed to an ambulatory patient who rumbaed her down the aisle.

Hutch stood back, his heart warm. The little girl's cheeks glowed, and her laughter blessed every man on the ward.

The music changed again, to the plaintive notes of "The Story of a Starry Night."

Back in August, that song played while he sat on the beach at Termini next to Georgie in her pink dress, with her bare arms draped over her knees. Half an hour ago, he'd kissed those bare arms. Now they were wrapped around Captain Chadwick's scrawny neck.

A heavy weight pressed his chest, and he tapped Lucia's latest partner on the shoulder. "May I?"

"I guess you're the guy who brought her."

"Yep."

"My Ucce!" Lucia's big brown eyes sparkled, and she reached for him.

He settled her in place and led her in a gentle dance, her head resting on his shoulder. His tongue felt gigantic in his mouth. The war had introduced Hutch to Georgie, yet kept her out of his arms. The war had orphaned and crippled Lucia, yet placed her in Hutch's arms.

How could anyone make sense of such insanity?

38

Pomigliano Airfield, Italy
December 25, 1943

A low rumble beneath Georgie vibrated through her backside and feet. That meant the tail landing gear was up.

She opened her eyes and released her breath. Although she'd made progress, takeoffs and landings still bothered her.

When the plane leveled off, she stood. Succumbing to temptation, she glanced out the window. The dark bulk of Vesuvius rose to the south, puffing smoke. Scuttlebutt pointed to an eruption brewing. Almost two thousand years earlier, Vesuvius had killed every living creature in Pompeii. And Pomigliano Airfield lay not much farther north of Vesuvius than Pompeii lay to the south. That fact did nothing to settle her nerves.

Nervous or not, she had a special job.

"Merry Christmas, gentlemen." She

headed down the aisle of the C-47 with her musette bag, ducking Hutch's darling ornaments, which she had strung between the litter racks. On her way, she handed out tiny packages tied in gauze. "We have a little present for each of you. Wait until I pass them out, then you can open them all at once."

"Sealed with a kiss?" Private Hodges winked the one blue eye peeking from under a wad of bandages.

She waved him off. "I wouldn't want to make my boyfriend sad on Christmas."

Yet she'd done exactly that. She passed out the rest of the packages while uneasiness writhed in her stomach. Why did she go to that stupid dance? Chadwick had acted like a gentleman, if a pompous gentleman, and Bergie would certainly tell Hutch all had been innocent, but she'd longed to be in Hutch's arms and ached from the sadness in his eyes.

The dance confirmed the gulf between them, and she hated it.

At the front of the plane, she threw a bright smile in place. These men had been wounded in battle or suffered from illness far from home. This could be their worst Christmas ever, but she was determined to give them pleasant memories. "All right, gentlemen. Open your presents."

The men untied the gauze, and Georgie and Sergeant Ramirez helped those with casts or bandages on their hands.

"Fudge!" someone cried.

"Hey, watch your language. A lady's present."

Georgie laughed. "A square of fudge for each of you. I don't want to ruin your carefully designed hospital diets too much."

"Ruin to your heart's content, ma'am." An ambulatory patient on the right side of the plane popped his piece in his mouth. "Heaven."

"Mm-hmm." The man next to him nodded. "A morsel of joy."

The nurses would be so pleased. Last night they'd worked hard over their little Coleman stoves, making batch after batch for their flights — and for themselves too.

"Speaking of joy . . ." Georgie waved her hand like a choir director. " 'Joy to the world!' "

The men joined in the singing, only a few at first, since most had their mouths full, but then in unison. Sergeant Ramirez had a strong bass voice, and he dipped into the harmony. Soon a chorus overpowered the engine noises and resonated through the plane.

Rose would be pleased. She loved Christmas caroling. If only she could be here.

Georgie blinked back tears, took requests, and caroled her way through her duties.

A sense of fulfillment nudged grief aside. This was why she'd returned overseas. Her lifelong gift to lighten people's hearts and her new nursing skills combined to ease the pain of the hurting.

If only she could make Hutch feel better.

Her voice faltered, but she dove into "White Christmas."

She'd had a long talk with Mellie last night. Hutch wouldn't be content until he became an officer. But was that right? Didn't the Lord want him to be content where he was, regardless of his circumstances? After all, what if he never got a commission?

She shuddered and launched into "Hark! the Herald Angels Sing." After all this time, all this work, what would he do if he lost his dream?

The C-47 jostled and dropped a few feet.

Georgie let out an embarrassing cry and grabbed onto the litter support rack.

"Just some turbulence." Sergeant Ramirez took hold of her elbow. He wasn't much taller than Georgie, but he was built like a tank. "Are you all right, Lieutenant?"

She smiled, although her pulse hammered. "Just startled me, that's all."

"Yeah." He returned her smile, but with concern in his eyes. Everyone knew of her disastrous performance in the plane crash.

Georgie set her hands on her hips and assumed an expression of mock outrage. "Turbulence on Christmas Day? What kind of outfit is this? We ought to be ashamed of ourselves. Fine way to treat our holiday guests."

Ramirez chuckled and headed to the rear of the plane.

Her mock outrage floated away, replaced with anger at herself. She'd been through turbulence before, plenty of times. Why did she let it affect her?

She took Private Hodges's pulse and recorded it in the flight manifest.

She still had a long way to go.

Pozzuoli, Italy
January 11, 1944

Hutch glanced at the clock and drummed his fingers on his completed examination. Half an hour remained, but he'd already gone over the test twice and knew he'd done well. Numbers were his lifelong friends.

Asking Colonel Currier for the three-day pass had been a smart choice, but he barely made it. The 93rd had closed at Piana di Caiazzo on January 5 in preparation for an upcoming amphibious operation, somewhere higher up the Italian boot. They were staging in the Naples area, a clear sign God wanted him in the Pharmacy Corps.

Hutch arrived in Caivano outside of Naples on Sunday, and the test was in nearby Pozzuoli on Monday and Tuesday. Since he already had approval for a third day, tomorrow he'd see Pompeii with Georgie and her friends, acting as their tour guide to justify the fraternization.

This might be the last time he saw her for a long while. Since July, Georgie had followed him from shore to shore, but would she follow him to the next beach?

Only one other applicant sat in the tiny room, Lt. Pete Cameron from San Francisco. Pete nibbled on his pencil, then scratched down an answer. Nice fellow, Pete. He'd attended Officer Candidate School and now served as an artillery officer in the US 3rd Infantry Division, which was preparing to ship out in the same convoy as the 93rd Evac.

Since he already had a commission, Pete didn't need this as badly as Hutch did.

Pete closed his exam book, puffed out a breath, and stood.

Hutch got up too and turned in his test. He smiled at Pete. "How'd it go?"

He ran his hand over close-cropped curly blond hair. "Don't know. I'm rusty. Haven't practiced in two years, thanks to Uncle Sam. Maybe I should have done what you did."

"If you did, you'd have to 'yes, sir' all day long to men who have the same education as you do and call you 'boy.' "

Pete shook his head. "Pharmacists get a raw deal in this Army, don't they?"

"Glad we finally have our own Corps. I've been waiting for this."

The officer administering the exam tucked the tests in a manila folder and stood. "You and nine hundred others."

Hutch frowned. "What do you mean, sir?"

"They've received nine hundred applications for the Pharmacy Corps, I'm told."

Pete let out a low whistle. "Lousy odds."

"Look at the bright side." Hutch tapped his foot. "Nine hundred men have the same vision. That'll make the Army take notice. Think what we could do. Nine hundred officers could staff every fixed and mobile hospital, both stateside and overseas."

Half a smile from Pete. "But only seventy-two of us get a shot at it now."

"Twelve." The officer headed for the door.

Hutch's gut clenched. "Twelve?"

He held open the door. "They're only commissioning twelve officers at this time."

"But — but Congress approved seventy-two."

"The Army decided a gradual implementation would be best. Twelve now, more later."

Pete whistled again and headed out. "I just wasted two days of my life."

Two days? Hutch had wasted over three years. He couldn't move.

"Sergeant?" The officer waved him to the door.

"Yes, sir." His voice splintered on his wooden tongue, and he forced his feet to move.

Twelve positions? Nine hundred applicants? For the first time in his life, numbers betrayed him.

39

Pompeii, Italy
January 12, 1944

Georgie stood outside Pompeii's arched gateway and scanned the crowds arriving from the train station. What if Hutch didn't make it? The invasion force could sail any day, and who knew when she'd see him again.

She rolled the guidebook in her hands.

Was that him? A tall dark-haired man walked alone and with a familiar gait. He wore an enlisted man's service uniform in a lighter shade of olive drab than the officer's dress uniform.

Her heart flipped over. She stretched up on tiptoe and waved. "Hutch!"

He raised a hand in greeting. Not the enthusiastic reception she craved.

She dashed down the pathway, weaving among the servicemen, both American and British.

Hutch stopped and gave her a smart salute. "Good day, Lieutenant."

She rolled her eyes and saluted him back with a grin. He had no choice but to follow protocol. "I'm glad you made it."

"Barely." He headed up the pathway, keeping a proper distance from her.

It wasn't like him to be terse, but she could cheer him up. "I've never seen you in dress uniform. You look so handsome."

His jaw jutted forward. "More like an officer?"

Her step faltered. "That wasn't what I meant."

He grimaced and faced her. "I know. That wasn't fair."

Georgie's breath solidified in her lungs. Something was wrong. "Sugar, are you all right?" She reached for him.

"Don't." He sidestepped her and glanced over his shoulder. A military policeman stood guard at the gateway. "That MP would love to get his hands on me if I got my hands on you."

"I'm sorry. I forget sometimes. Are you all right?"

He groaned and marched up the path. "Let's just get this charade going. I'm supposed to play tour guide for you and your friends, right? The only way I can legally be seen in your presence. Do you have the guidebook?"

Georgie breathed hard, and not from the exertion of catching up with his long-legged pace. "What's going on?"

He held out his hand as he walked. "The guidebook? I need to convince that MP."

"Sure." She slipped it into his hand.

He glanced at the booklet, creased from folding and rolling. "What happened to it?"

"I was kind of nervous waiting for you." Not as nervous as she felt right now though.

Hutch chewed on his lips and shifted his gaze to her. A host of emotions swarmed in his brown eyes. "It's fine. Really, it is."

No. It wasn't fine. He was facing another invasion, separation from her, the Pharmacy Corps exam, and leaving Lucia. "Please tell me what's wrong. Is it Lucia? Were you able to take her to the orphanage?"

"Yeah." He continued up the path, saluted the MP, and handed his dime to the Italian man in the ancient arched gateway. "They let me go with her. It's a decent place, spartan but clean. The Red Cross will take good care of her and help her write me."

"That's good." Georgie paid her ten cents and pushed through the turnstile. "Does she like it?"

Hutch headed forward, looking straight

ahead, and his Adam's apple rose from his knotted tie to his jaw. "She cried."

"Oh, sweetie." More than anything, she wanted to take his hand and snuggle close, but she gripped her shoulder bag instead. "That must have been hard on both of you."

"Everyone she loves deserts her."

"You'll come back for her."

"Yeah." He squinted at the ruins. "Where are your friends?"

"Up ahead. We agreed to meet at the Forum." Time to explore the next issue. "Were you able to take the exam?"

"Yep." He gripped an imaginary baseball bat and swung. "I hit that ball so far out of the park, they won't find it till March."

So why the dark tone? "That's good."

He passed neatly spaced columns of an ancient temple and didn't even glance at them. "Doesn't matter."

Despite the chill in the air, Georgie wiped moisture from her palms onto her skirt. "Why wouldn't it matter?"

"Some bureaucrat decided seventy-two pharmacy officers would strain the system. They're only commissioning twelve now. You know how many men applied? Nine hundred. That gives me a whopping 1.3 percent chance."

"Oh my goodness." No wonder he was in

a bad mood. "I'm so sorry. But I know you'll be one of the twelve."

He let out a scoffing laugh. "One point three. Might as well be zero."

"Please don't get discouraged. I'm sure —"

"Don't bother." He opened the guide-book. "Let me get my bearings so I can play my role."

Georgie's teeth ground together. He had every right to be angry, but no right to take it out on her. Besides, this was supposed to be a fun, romantic day, and if he didn't cheer up, he'd ruin it.

"Georgie! Over here!" Mellie waved at her. "You have to see this view. It's the most incredible thing I've seen in my life."

Maybe her friends' enthusiasm would be contagious or at least shame Hutch into a better mood. She tossed him a little smile, but he just motioned for her to lead the way.

Georgie joined her three friends in their gray-blue skirt uniforms. "Hutch, you remember my friend Mellie."

"Lieutenant Blake." He saluted her.

"Kay and Louise, you haven't formally met Hutch yet. Hutch, these are my friends Kay Jobson and Louise Cox."

"Lieutenant Jobson. Lieutenant Cox." A proper, unsmiling salute.

Kay grinned and extended her hand. "You can call me Kay."

"No, ma'am. I can't." At least he shook her hand.

Louise shook his hand too. "So you're the antiquities expert. Georgie said you'll be a great tour guide."

"I'm no expert, and I've never been to Pompeii. But I'll do my best."

"I'm sure you will." Georgie gave him a sweet smile. "Where are we now?"

"The Forum." Mellie laughed. "Even I know that. Would you please turn around and savor that view?"

Georgie did so. A long plaza stretched before her, framed by broken columns of varying heights. The remains of a temple sat at the far end, and beyond that Vesuvius rose, its smoking top concealed in the clouds.

She twisted her purse strap. "Sometimes I wonder if this is a safe place to be stationed."

"It's war." Kay sauntered down the Forum. "Nothing's safe."

How embarrassing to be caught wallowing in her old fears, and in front of Hutch, who'd helped her rise above them. But he seemed absorbed in the guidebook.

"That's the Temple of Jupiter." He pointed

straight ahead. "Temple of Apollo's to our left, Building of Eumachia to our right."

That was all? Where were the stories, the details, the color? She followed the group down the Forum and threaded through the columns. Hutch remained silent, as dark and forbidding as the volcano itself.

He led the way past the Temple of Jupiter and through an arch, with the ladies scampering to keep up. Why did he have to be a grouch on what could be their last day together in ages?

Kay sidled up and leaned close. "Remind me what you see in him."

Georgie pressed her lips together. Right now she had a hard time remembering that herself. She let out a long breath. "He's had some bad news. He's not usually like this."

"I'd hope not. He makes Ward look like fun."

Several feet ahead, Mellie crossed the street on high stepping-stones. "Aren't these interesting? Hutch, what does it say in the guidebook?"

He continued down the raised sidewalk. "Says they flushed the streets every day."

"The stepping-stones would keep your feet dry. How clever." Mellie perched on a stone and peered down at the road. "Look at the chariot ruts in the pavement. My goodness."

Louise gave her a playful push into the street.

Mellie laughed, then studied the stones. "It looks like the chariots could straddle them. I wish Tom could see this. Such a clever design."

Georgie followed the ladies across the stones, not easy in a straight skirt and heels. If Tom were here, he'd help Mellie across. He'd be in a good mood, laughing and enjoying himself. But oh no, not Hutch.

He turned right onto another street, approached a building on the left, and motioned for the women to head in first. "The House of the Faun. Ladies?"

Georgie passed through the doorway and raised one eyebrow at him, but he didn't even meet her eye.

The group stepped into a wide paved courtyard. All around, remains of walls jutted up, their porous volcanic stone exposed.

"Isn't that charming?" Mellie stood before an empty rectangular pool with a mosaic of diamond-shaped stones on the bottom. In the center stood a small statue of a dancing faun.

At least one man in the building looked happy.

The nurses explored the vestibules, but

Hutch remained at the entrance. Fine. Even if he wanted to ruin his own day, he wouldn't ruin hers. Georgie stayed with the women and tried to enjoy herself, but how could she when her boyfriend embarrassed her in front of her friends?

Mellie headed for the entrance. "What's next, Hutch?"

"More houses." He led them down the street and into the remains of another home.

Louise exclaimed. "Just look at those paintings."

Vibrant frescoes of classical figures in rusty red, ocher yellow, and milky blue covered three walls of a little side room.

"Astounding," Mellie said. "The same ash that killed thousands preserved this art for millennia."

"What's this painting about?" Kay asked.

"Don't know." Hutch didn't even look in the guidebook.

The ladies exchanged a glance that curled Georgie's toes — surprise at his chilly tone and sympathy for Georgie. That was enough.

"Excuse me, ladies." She gave them a fake smile, gripped Hutch's elbow, and led him out onto the street paved with stones as white as her anger.

She crossed her arms. "Why'd you even

come today? This was supposed to be a fun outing, but you're ruining it for everyone."

His brow furrowed under his service cap. "Let me get this straight. I found out all my work these past three years is probably in vain. The goal I've worked for is being stolen from me. And you're annoyed because your tourist excursion doesn't meet your expectations?"

She sniffed. He made her sound selfish, which wasn't true. "You could at least try to be pleasant. You didn't even look happy to see me."

He glanced away, sank his hands in his trouser pockets, and tapped his foot on the paving stone.

Her lower lip pushed out. "You aren't happy to see me."

"What?" He turned back, his eyes darker than she'd ever seen them. "How am I supposed to show I'm happy? I'm not allowed to fraternize with you, to hold your hand, even to call you by your first name, Lieutenant Taylor."

"You could at least smile."

"Smile? You want me to play happy when I've had a lousy week and things might not get better for the rest of this stinking war?"

She adjusted her stance on the uneven stone. "What if they don't get better? Are you ever going to let it go? Are you going to sacrifice your peace of mind for your goal?"

"What? Do you want me to give up?" His upper lip curled. "I thought you supported me, thought you understood, considering what you went through."

"What I went through?"

"With Ward. Isn't that why you broke up with him? Because he didn't support your dreams, your goal?"

Georgie's sweaty fingers slipped over the purse strap. "What's that have to do —"

"You're doing the same thing." He knifed his hand through the air. "The Corps is my dream, my goal. I thought you supported that."

"I — I —"

"Why do you want me to give up? I need to fight for my goal."

Georgie gave her head a firm shake. "I just want what's best for you."

"What's best for me? The Corps is best for me. Finally getting a little respect for once."

She studied his furious face. "This has become more than a dream. It's an obsession. And you're getting bitter."

"Obsessed and bitter." He shifted his mouth to one side and nodded a few times. "Thank goodness an officer's around to tell me what's what."

"Oh, that's real nice, Hutch." She whirled around and marched down the street. "I don't want to talk to you when you're like this."

"Fine. Don't talk to me at all. The last thing I need is more disrespect."

"Why don't you go home and mope in private?"

"Is that an order, Lieutenant?"

"Maybe it should be." She pivoted to face him. "I'm sick of your foul mood."

"Yeah? Well, I'm sick of all of this." He flung out his arms. "I'm sick of lying and hiding and sneaking around."

She set her hands on her hips. "I'm sick of being blamed because the Army likes my profession better than yours. If I hear one more gripe out of you . . ."

His arms settled to his side, and he stood tall and still, his expression a strange mixture of sadness and anger. "You'll what? You'll end it? For a single gripe?"

For the second time in only a few months, she felt the foundation cave beneath her. But now it rattled her like an earthquake. With effort she kept her legs beneath her and shook back her curls. "If you're going to be grouchy for the rest of the war, then I don't want to be with you."

He stood even taller if that were possible. "If you can't respect me, if you can't support my goals, then I don't want to be with you either. It's over."

"Over and done."

"That's for the best."

"Absolutely for the best."

Hutch snapped his heels together, saluted, turned smartly, and marched away, the tails of his jacket flapping with each strong step.

Georgie groped for the wall and leaned against the rough ancient stone, once lashed by volcanic wind, then buried in ash, now exposed to the elements.

If this was truly for the best, why did her soul scream?

40

Anzio, Italy
January 23, 1944

Good-bye and good riddance to *LST-242.* Four nights sleeping on the heaving cold steel deck under an Army truck and almost two days of enemy air attack made Hutch long for terra firma.

Even if terra firma was Anzio, the birthplace of Roman emperors Nero and Caligula, of evil itself.

Hutch gripped the side of the DUKW amphibious vehicle as it cut through the waves. The shore looked quieter than the day before when the Allies made the main invasion, with the British landing north of Anzio, and the Americans taking the twin towns of Anzio and Nettuno.

Operation Shingle was the Allies' latest gamble. By landing about forty miles south of Rome and sixty miles past the Cassino front, they hoped to break the stalemate, cut off the Germans, and make them retreat north of the capital.

Beside him on the DUKW, Bergie whooped. "What a ride!"

"Yep," Hutch shouted over the clattering engine. He wiped sea spray from his face with his mackinaw sleeve.

"We'll get a nice vacation at the shore, I've heard. Almost no resistance yesterday. We can race for the Alban Hills as soon as General Lucas unleashes us."

"Yep." White and tan buildings cringed by the waterline, and far away across the Anzio plain, the Alban Hills ripped a jagged line through the blue sky.

"On to Rome!"

"Yep."

Bergie held one hand on his helmet and glanced at Hutch. "Don't strain your vocabulary."

Hutch adjusted his field pack on his shoulders. Since he left Lucia and broke up with Georgie, every word felt like a sword in his throat.

"Are you ready to talk —"

A medic cussed and pointed skyward. Three German Junkers bombers crossed the bay.

Hutch crouched low in the cramped boat, oddly free of fear, just glad to distract Bergie from dissecting his problems.

Bullets spat out and splashed in the surf behind the DUKW. Lousy aim, thank goodness.

Antiaircraft fire boomed from the shoreline, and the planes wheeled out to sea. With a familiar whine, bombs fell, missing *LST-242* and sending waterspouts a hundred feet into the air.

Bergie wiggled himself back up to standing. "I'm glad the nurses aren't coming for a few days."

"Yep." Why did he choose that word?

Sure enough, Bergie's gaze homed in, and his mouth opened to drill Hutch with questions.

Hutch pointed ahead. "Shore coming. Don't want to miss this."

The DUKW driver turned around. "Hold on!"

The men obeyed, and the DUKW rode the wave to shore like the surfers Hutch had watched when he was stationed in Hawaii. With a bump, the wheels hit the sand and carried the vehicle onto the beach. Water poured from every surface and carved gullies through the sand.

The DUKW ferried them about a hundred feet inland. The driver motioned the men out of the boat. "Everyone out. Gotta go back for more of youse."

Hutch sat on the edge, swung his legs over, and thumped to the ground. He found a patch of dry sand, pulled a glass vial from his pocket, and scooped up fine beige sand for his collection. If he had his way, he'd never collect another vial again.

He joined the dozen men from his DUKW and followed them toward the town. For once, the 93rd Evac was supposed to set up in actual buildings, a sanitarium by the Anzio pier.

Hutch marched in the cool air, and the firm sand barely clung to his combat boots.

Bergie dropped back to walk with him. "I'd kiss the ground, but I don't want sand between my teeth."

"Nope."

"A new word."

Hutch rolled his eyes.

Bergie nudged him. "It's taking you longer to get over two months with Georgie than it did five years with Phyllis."

His chest felt tight. "I loved her."

"Are you finally ready to talk about it? Remember, I'm the relationship expert now. Six months with Lillian."

"She's good for you."

"I thought Georgie was good for you."

"I did too. I was wrong."

"How's that?"

The blue bay was marred by dozens of LSTs, destroyers, and landing craft, and overshadowed by the Luftwaffe. "She doesn't support my goal. Says I'm obsessed and bitter."

"You *are* obsessed and bitter."

Hutch glared at his friend's grinning face. "Thought you were on my side."

Bergie hiked up his overcoat belt, loaded with equipment for once. Even the officers had to carry their own gear since the 93rd could only bring twenty-three trucks in this first wave. "I'm trying to be on the side of reason. It's a stretch for me."

"So don't stretch."

Bergie drew a deep breath. "Why do you say she doesn't support your goal?"

"She told me to let it go, give it up. Easy for her to say. She already achieved her goal."

The column of men entered the town of Anzio, filled with two-storied buildings with red tile roofs. Allied shelling had demolished some of the structures. Under a heap of brick, limestone, and plaster in the street, two feet clad in German boots jutted out.

Six months in a combat zone, but the sight of violent death still slammed Hutch in the chest.

Bergie cut a wide path around the scene. "I hate this war."

"Who doesn't?"

Another body lay crumpled next to a burned-out donkey cart. The man still clutched his rifle.

Bergie pointed his thumb at the German. "What would've happened if he'd surrendered?"

"He'd be alive. Such a waste. Such a stinking waste."

"Sometimes giving up is better than fighting."

Hutch stopped and stared. "Are you saying —"

"What'll you do if you don't get a commission? What then? How long are you going to be angry? That's no way to live."

"No way to live? *This* is no way to live."

"You're right. War is a horrible way to live."

Hutch's jaw clenched, and he blew a hot breath out his nostrils. "You know that's not what I meant. I'm talking about the position I'm in. I have to take orders from a florist who knows nothing about my work. I can't eat a meal with my best friend. I couldn't date the woman I love. How would you like it if you couldn't be seen with Lillian — or even call her Lillian?"

"I love her. I'd make do."

"Baloney. You've never had to try. You never will."

"No." His voice came out low and strained. "So, let me get this straight. Georgie got on your case about being bitter. Remember when you told me you loved her? You said you liked how she encouraged you to grow. Sounds like that's what she was doing."

Hutch kicked away a chunk of concrete. "Don't you get on my case too."

"Why not? You're turning into a grump. Georgie was tired of it, and so am I."

"Are you now? You don't have to listen to it. You're not supposed to talk to me anyway . . . sir."

Bergie turned to him, his blue eyes cool. "You know what? That's a good idea. You need to work things out. After you do, let's talk again."

"Yes, sir." He whipped up a salute. "Whatever you say, sir."

Bergie walked away and flipped a wave over his shoulder, leaving Hutch alone.

41

Pomigliano Airfield
February 9, 1944

Georgie sat cross-legged on the tarmac and scanned the letter from Ward. He'd actually written a full letter, not an itty-bitty V-mail.

He pined for her. He was remorseful. He still loved her. Pearline meant nothing to him, and he'd do anything to win Georgie back. He'd wait out the war, proud of his little nightingale. He'd take her traveling, anywhere in the world. He'd do anything if only she took him back.

Right on the heels of her sister Freddie's letter, begging Georgie to come home. Her pregnancy was sapping her energy, and she couldn't run both the store and her home. Desperate for help, she believed only Georgie would do.

Home. The old longing pulled at her. If she returned home, if she went back to Ward, could she still be strong? Should she take him back? She'd be needed and pampered, and was that really so bad?

Hutch certainly never pampered her. He thought she was spoiled. Thank goodness she was rid of him.

To the south, smoke snaked from Vesuvius's crater. No matter how many times she said it, she couldn't make herself believe it. Why did she still love that grouchy old bear? Why did she miss him? Why did she worry about him?

He had to be at Anzio.

She shivered and returned Ward's letter to its envelope. She couldn't go back to Ward until she broke the hold Hutch had on her heart.

"They're having a rugged time up there."

Georgie looked up. Roger Cooper and Bill Shelby sat about ten feet to her right, waiting to see if they'd fly today. Three other C-47s were already loading, but the staff hadn't decided if Coop's plane would join them.

"Yeah, rugged." Roger tapped a rhythm on a wooden crate with his drumsticks. "Two weeks now, isn't it? We still haven't taken Cassino."

"Nasty business up there." Shell took a drag from his cigarette. "Jerry's sitting up there in that abbey, you know he is, and we

444

aren't allowed to bomb him out. He's up there, calling down artillery, ripping our troops to shreds every step they take."

Georgie shuddered. For the last two weeks, flights overflowed with men bloodied and broken by the many failed attempts to cross the Rapido River and seize Cassino and its mountaintop abbey.

Roger changed the rhythm, now low and steady as machine-gun fire. "Anzio's no better."

Georgie stretched a smidgen closer. The first few days of the invasion had gone easily, but since then she'd heard nothing good.

A long puff of smoke from Shell. "Don't know why General Lucas didn't charge for the hills when we had the chance. Now the Germans are dug in."

"Forget that. They're counterattacking. We're trapped on the beachhead."

"Did you hear about that hospital?"

Georgie sucked in her breath. "What hospital?"

The men turned and stared at her.

"Sorry." Her cheeks warmed. "I didn't mean to eavesdrop. But . . . but what about the hospital at Anzio? Which hospital? What happened?"

"Don't know which one." Roger turned to Shell. "You know which one?"

He shook his head.

Roger tucked his drumsticks inside his leather flight jacket. "The Luftwaffe bombed them. The hospitals are on the beach, marked with giant red crosses on every single tent, and the Luftwaffe bombed them. Three —" He made a face and glanced to Shelby.

The copilot shrugged his slight shoulders. "She'll hear anyway."

Roger readjusted his pilot's "crush" cap over his auburn hair. "Sorry, Georgie. About two dozen people were killed, including three nurses."

Two dozen? Her lips tingled. If two dozen were killed, several times that many had been injured. Had Hutch been hurt? Killed? Any of his friends?

"You all right?" Roger's brown eyes narrowed with compassion.

"I have . . . friends up there."

"Sorry 'bout that. Guess you dames all know each other."

She nodded. Why mention Hutch when he was out of her life anyway?

"Lieutenant Taylor?" Lieutenant Lambert beckoned from down the tarmac by the tents of the 58th Station Hospital, which served as a holding unit at Pomigliano.

"Excuse me, gentlemen." Georgie stood,

brushed gravel from her backside, and went to the chief nurse.

Lambert frowned. "We have a delicate situation. A patient who should be evacuated, but some of the men refuse to fly with him."

Georgie disliked flights with POW patients. "A German."

"No, one of ours. A pilot. He lost both legs below the knee when his P-40 crashed under Luftwaffe attack. He earned a load of medals."

"So why . . ."

Lambert's mouth twisted. "I wish Mellie were here. You're not my first choice for this case, but we'll see. You have the final say whether you'll take him or not. He can always wait for tomorrow when another nurse is available, maybe find enough patients willing to fly with him."

"Why wouldn't . . ."

The chief headed into the tent. "Come see."

Georgie followed. Had the poor man been badly burned in the accident? Was that why the men didn't want to share a plane with him? The smell often caused strong men to retch.

"Lieutenant Taylor, may I introduce Lt. Roy Cassidy?" Lambert stepped aside.

The patient lay on a cot, and he turned his mahogany face to Georgie. "Good morning, ma'am."

He was . . . colored. And an officer. "Good — good morning." She was supposed to say "sir," wasn't she? But to a colored man? What a strange war this was.

"You're from the South, ma'am." His accent hailed from the North. A slight smile, and he turned his gaze to Lieutenant Lambert. "Looks like I'm waiting another day. That's fine. I'm in no rush, ma'am."

Georgie pulled herself together and closed her dangling jaw. "Lieutenant Lambert, may I speak with you in private?"

She nodded and returned to the tent entrance. "You don't have to explain. I saw your face. I know the Army is supposed to have segregated facilities, but with the small number of colored patients, evacuation poses problems since we don't have colored nurses."

Mama used to have a colored girl help with the cleaning and cooking, and Daddy hired the men as farmhands. Georgie had associated with Negroes all her life, but never as equals. "He — he's a pilot, you said?"

"Yes, with the 99th Fighter Squadron. The Tuskegee Airmen."

"I've heard of them."

Lambert crossed her arms and tapped long fingers on her upper arm. "They had to fight for recognition, for acceptance, for respect. The Army didn't think black men could fly — just like they didn't think women could handle the rigors of air evacuation."

The man's legs came to an abrupt end. So had his dreams. "Is it true what they say about the Tuskegee Airmen over Anzio?"

"Why ask me? You can ask him."

Georgie nudged her feet back in his direction. What would Daddy say? Segregation had always worked. It was best. Mixing the races wasn't natural.

A woman in a combat zone wasn't natural either.

She stood at the foot of his cot and twisted her hands together. "Excuse me. I have a question."

"Yes, ma'am?" His eyes twitched.

"Is it true what they say you fellows did over Anzio?"

"Depends. What do they say?"

"That you shot down thirteen German Fw 190s in two days."

"Yes, ma'am. That's true. Claimed one myself."

She tried not to glance to the collapsed

blankets where his feet should have been. "Those German planes — they're the ones who strafe our troops and bomb our hospitals."

"Yes, ma'am."

"You colored boys are flying to protect white boys?"

His deep brown eyes flashed with understanding. "Ma'am, I don't care what color they are, as long as they fight for freedom."

She swallowed hard and spun to face the rest of the ward. "Excuse me, gentlemen. Which of y'all don't want to fly with Lieutenant Cassidy here?"

Four hands went up.

A patient across the aisle sat up in bed. "It isn't right, ma'am. I'm sure you agree."

"I do. It isn't right at all." She put on her best Southern belle smile. "It isn't right that Lieutenant Cassidy lost his legs saving the lives of men who can't see fit to share an airplane with him."

The patient blanched even whiter.

Georgie looked each man in the eye. "If y'all don't want to fly with Lieutenant Cassidy, then I don't want to fly with you."

"Ma'am!"

"That's my decision." She met Lambert's gaze. "I'll take Lieutenant Cassidy on my flight. Any of these fine gentlemen who wish to join us are more than welcome. If they don't wish to, they can fly out another day, and Lieutenant Cassidy will enjoy a private flight."

"Hey! Since when do girls get to make the decisions?"

"This war turned our world upside down, didn't it?" She faced Lieutenant Cassidy and saluted him, her throat suddenly tight. "Thank you for your service . . . sir."

"You — you're welcome, ma'am."

Georgie crossed the tent to where Lambert stood. "Shall we load?"

"Yes. Captain Zimmerman has the flight manifest. You can scratch out certain names." Lambert's eyes crinkled around the edges. "A fine decision, Georgie."

"Thank you, ma'am." Her shoulders felt lighter and straighter. She'd made lots of decisions lately, and this one was wise. But were all of them?

Georgie took the flight manifest from Captain Zimmerman and followed him around the tent as he relayed each patient's condition and medical needs. She took careful notes.

Returning overseas was right, but she doubted some of her other decisions.

A romance with Hutch had not been smart at all. Yet for some reason she didn't regret their short time together, the sweet taste of what love could be. Even if it ended badly.

Sadness swamped her. It ended so badly. She really had acted in a childish manner, hadn't she? Demanding Hutch be cheerful on a bad day? Now he was at Anzio. Under fire. With a broken heart.

What on earth had she done? Tonight.

Tonight she'd write him.

Georgie finished her notes on her patients. Two men still refused to fly, and she crossed their names off the manifest.

No, she would not write Hutch. Twice lately she'd lifted her pen to do so, twice she'd prayed, and twice the Lord stilled her hand.

Georgie sighed and flipped the pages into place on her clipboard. What would be the cost of her next decision?

42

Hardly a good time to take an afternoon off, but orders were orders.

Hutch sat on the shore and glanced behind him to the beachhead that had earned nicknames too impolite to mention in his letters home.

In the distance, artillery boomed and American B-17s and B-24s roared. Each day the Germans inched closer, compressing US and British forces into less space.

The hospital's location by the pier in Anzio lasted only six days until enemy artillery drove them out, to a site south of Nettuno, where all four American hospitals clustered by the sea.

The rumble of jeeps and ambulances, the cries of the wounded, and the hum of generators — Hutch was supposed to get away from all this, Kaz said. An order came from high up that all the hospital personnel needed regular days off so they wouldn't join the ranks of patients with "Anzio anxiety" and "Nettuno neurosis." Today was Hutch's turn.

The brass kept a close eye on Hutch since Sgt. Bob Knecht with the 95th Evacuation Hospital had been killed on February 7. Hutch had met him just a few days earlier — another pharmacist serving as an enlisted man, a graduate of the Cincinnati College of Pharmacy, an instant friend. And he was dead.

Hutch was supposed to get away? How could he get away when he had no place to go?

He faced the bay. American ships floated in the cold gray waters under a cold gray sky. He hadn't seen the sun in ages, and he couldn't remember when he'd last seen the stars, much less watched them. The telescope sat in its case with all mementos from Georgie, including the embroidered handkerchief. He should enclose it in his next letter to Lucia, but that would mean opening the case and remembering Georgie.

He groaned and rested his elbows on his knees, his Bible in hand. Every time he saw that telescope case, he saw Georgie providing for him because he couldn't provide for himself, Chadwick kissing her hand, Kaz reprimanding him for fraternization, Georgie calling him obsessed and bitter.

Hutch flipped open his Bible to Romans, which he'd been trying to read since landing almost three weeks earlier. Finally in chapter 5.

Down to the third verse. "We glory in tribulations also: knowing that tribulation worketh patience; And patience, experience; and experience, hope."

Air from his nostrils curled into steam in the cold air. He'd had plenty of tribulations. He'd been patient for three and a half years. Didn't he have enough experience? Where was his hope?

He slammed the Bible closed and bowed his head. "Lord . . ."

But prayer wouldn't come. Just like the Bible didn't bring him peace. It only irked him. As if God didn't understand what he was going through, as if he wanted Hutch on a different path.

Why? God started him on this path in the first place. Prayer and Bible reading helped him decide to take a pharmacy position and work hard to establish the Corps.

Look what that got him.

Hutch stood and checked his watch — four thirty. Too early for dinner, too early to retire, but Kaz promised to write him up if he went to Pharmacy.

Anzio didn't have recreational facilities. The first time hospital personnel had tried to organize a baseball game, they drew enemy fire. Looked like a rest camp apparently, and rest camps were fair military targets.

Hutch unbuttoned his mackinaw and stuffed his Bible inside his field jacket, layered underneath the mackinaw.

A loud whistle overhead.

He jammed on his helmet and dropped to the ground, curled up as small as possible.

A thump to the north, another, and another. Not too close. The ground barely shook. But definitely in the hospital area.

He pushed up on his elbows and glanced up the beach. A flickering glow lit the sky, and columns of smoke drifted inland.

"Stinking Nazis." On February 7 when Bob was killed, a Luftwaffe pilot jettisoned his bombs under fighter attack. An accident. But this artillery attack was on purpose, targeted to tents marked with enormous red crosses.

A shell whined to the north and sent up a geyser of sand near the 33rd Field Hospital.

Hutch's survival instincts told him to find a hole and hide, but something deeper told him to go help.

He scrambled to his feet and ran up the beach. The closer he got, the louder the shouts, the cries, and the thunder of falling Nazi shells.

Dozens of fires rose from the hospital site. How many had been killed this time? How many wounded? How could he help? The top priorities were to aid the wounded and put out the fires that served as beacons to German artillery spotters.

He dashed into the complex for the 33rd Field Hospital. A tent lay crumpled, in flames, and cries rang out underneath. Men swung at the flaming canvas with tent poles. Hutch grabbed a pole, tugged it free from its loop, and joined in, heaving scraps of canvas to the side, off the wounded and dying.

He stomped on the smoking scraps, kicked sand on them.

Men screamed, their blankets and clothing on fire. Hutch flung off the blanket from the patient closest to him, whipped off his mackinaw, and pressed it over the flames. "You'll be all right."

Wild eyes stared up at him, but Hutch didn't have time to comfort, only to save. After he extinguished the flames, he went to the next victim — a man beyond help.

A sergeant ran up. "Take the wounded to the 56th. We can't deal with them here. Too much damage. Move them right on their mattresses."

Medics grabbed mattresses. Hutch turned to find a patient to transport, but all were taken.

He jogged down the pathway, looking for another way to help. He passed two nurses in embrace, in tears.

"She was so young, so full of life," one said.

Another nurse killed? Embers burned in Hutch's chest. This war stank. It stank, it stank, it stank.

He dodged medics and doctors and nurses, heading for the next fire. He turned a corner and slammed into someone.

"Sorry." He noted the surgeon's garb. "Sir."

The man wheeled to face him. Captain Chadwick, fire in his gray eyes. "You? What do you think you're doing here, boy?"

"I'm helping, sir."

"You're a druggist." His words spat into Hutch's face. "Go rearrange the cosmetics display or something, but get out of here. You're in the way — again."

The embers in Hutch's chest sent off dangerous sparks. "Don't need to be a physician to put out fires and save lives."

"Save lives?" His whole face twitched, shot through with pain. "Druggists are better at taking lives. Get out of here before you kill someone."

Hutch stared, dumbfounded. Taking lives? What on earth was this man's problem?

"Did you hear me, jerk? Get out of here."

"Yes, sir." Hutch saluted, his hand banging his helmet. Jerk? Chadwick was the jerk, but he wasn't allowed to say that.

He wheeled away, his stomach in flames no bicarb could put out. He was forbidden from returning the insults, from refuting the lies, from defending himself and his profession.

Stupid, stinking Army. Stupid, stinking war.

He strode toward the road that connected the hospitals and he passed the pharmacy tent, shredded by shrapnel.

Hutch paused, checked behind him for Chad-jerk, and stepped into Pharmacy.

One of the shelving units had fallen off the counter. Broken glass and powders and liquids covered the dirt floor. Three technicians looked up at Hutch.

"John Hutchinson from the 93rd Evac. I'm a pharmacist. May I help?"

"Yes!" A tech sprang forward and pumped

Hutch's hand. "Lloyd Parker. Two tents down, Receiving took a direct hit. The concussion — you see what it did. We need to get this place up and running."

"Sure do." Hutch tossed aside his charred mackinaw and assessed the situation. First they had to clear out the broken glass and the worst of the spills so they could work safely. Then they could prepare burn solutions for the wounded and take an inventory of the damage so they could order. The 93rd could help in the interim.

Supplying the beachhead presented a continual challenge, with cargo planes unable to land on the battered airstrip and ships shelled at sea.

"All right. Let's clear out the glass." Hutch grabbed an empty crate, wrapped a rag around his hand, and picked up shards of glass. "Lloyd, why don't you find a shovel? We can dig a hole and bury the spilled meds."

The hard work quenched the sparks in his stomach. Pharmacy wasn't flashy, but it had worth. He healed with chemicals rather than the scalpel, but he still healed.

If only the Army agreed.

43

Outside Naples, Italy
February 14, 1944

Miss Carpino, the Red Cross worker, held open the orphanage door and motioned in the flight nurses with their boxes full of goodies. "It's so kind of you to come. The children are excited to have a party."

Mellie hefted up her box and smiled at Georgie. "Great idea."

"Thank you." Throwing a party for orphans seemed a more noble use of her skills than her usual birthday parties for the nurses.

Spartan but clean, just as Hutch described the orphanage. What would he think about her visit? Would he be grateful she'd thought of Lucia or would he think she'd disrespectfully usurped his place in the child's life? The way he'd been acting before they broke up, who knew? Sometimes she was glad to be rid of him, and sometimes the pain of missing him ripped her up inside.

The Red Cross girl led them into a dining hall with two long tables and benches. Several dozen dark-haired boys and girls sat at the tables, supervised by two nuns in long black habits.

"Buongiorno." Georgie grinned and waved.

"Buongiorno." The children wiggled in their seats. If the nuns hadn't been present, Georgie had a hunch the nurses would have been mobbed.

The Red Cross girl, an American with Italian heritage, made an introduction in Italian, complete with swooping airplane hand motions.

Georgie scanned the orphans until she found Lucia at the end of the far table with crutches propped next to her. She wore a shabby brown dress, and Georgie's next sewing idea zipped into her mind. Why, all the children looked like they could use a new dress or shirt or sweater. If Georgie had her way, no hands in the 802nd MAETS would be idle for some time to come.

The Red Cross girl turned to the six nurses. "Go ahead and introduce yourselves. *'Mi chiamo'* means 'my name is,' and *'tenante'* means 'lieutenant.' "

The ladies went down the line ending with

462

"*Tenante* Taylor."

"*Signorina Giorgiana?*" Even from across the room, the light in Lucia's eyes shone.

A nun gave the girl a soft reprimand, and Lucia responded in excited Italian. At the mention of "*Signor Ucce,*" Georgie's heart jolted.

Before Lucia could get in trouble for talking back, Georgie approached the nun. "It's all right, Sister. I know her."

The Red Cross girl translated, and the nun nodded to Georgie and stepped back.

Lucia stretched out her hand. "*Signorina! Signorina!* Signor Ucce ask you come?"

"No." Georgie squatted by the table and took Lucia's hand, smiling over her pain. How could she tell the girl Hutch hadn't asked or told her anything for a month? A month and two days. "But he would come himself if he could. I know he'd like you to have a party. Do you understand?"

"Yeah." She turned a grin toward the Red Cross girl. "*Signorina* Carpino teach me English."

"Good. Let me get the party started, and I'll come back to talk to you."

The nurses passed out a square of fudge for each child. After they finished, Mellie, Kay, and Louise took the more active children outside to play baseball.

Grief stole the breath from Georgie's lungs. Rose would have organized the baseball game if she were here. She would have loved this outing.

But Rose wasn't here. And the purpose of the party was to cheer up the children, so she pulled herself tall and helped Vera and Alice set up paper and paint and scissors for the quieter children and those who couldn't walk.

She gave Alice a smile. "Thanks again for giving up your paint set. I know you planned to capture the landscape."

"I can get more sent from home." A fall of blonde hair concealed her expression. "These children don't have a — a home."

Most of the children seemed chipper, but one little girl sat alone, rocking back and forth, a red roof tile clutched to her chest. And a boy around nine painted a picture of a house — with a swastika-bearing tank barreling into it. These children had seen things no child should see.

"*Signorina! Tenante* Taylor. See me walk." Leaning heavily on her crutches, Lucia edged forward with short uneasy steps.

Georgie resisted the impulse to help. "You're doing so well."

"*Signor Ucce* like?" She plopped onto a bench at the art table.

"I know he would." Georgie slid a piece of paper in front of her. "Do you — do you write to him?"

"*Si.* Today I paint him."

"He'll like that."

Lucia lifted wide eyes and a grin. "Please read me."

A smile tickled Georgie's lips. "What do you mean?"

She dug in the frayed pocket of her dress and pulled out a wrinkled letter folded in half. "Please read me. Signor Ucce. I no read well."

Pain crushed her chest. When he wrote this letter, he certainly didn't intend for Georgie to read it. Yet how could she resist Lucia's plea? And how could she avert her eyes from the open window to Hutch's world?

She flattened the letter on the table.

Dear Lucia,

How are you, little star? I miss you very much, but I know the nuns take good care of you. I hope you are happy and making lots of friends.

The hospital is busy. All the doctors and nurses miss you, but we're glad you have a roof over your head and a soft bed and lots of good food.

Our hospital is right on the shore. If it's quiet at night, I can hear the waves from my tent. When I have time off, I like to sit on the sand and watch the funny little birds hop up to the water, then skitter away when a wave comes in.

Someday this would be a nice place for little girls to build sand castles and play in the water. Have you ever been to the shore? I know you'd like it. Did you know there are stars in the ocean too? They're called starfish, and they walk on little tube feet that tickle your hand if you touch them.

Keep learning to read and write like a good girl so you can write to me all by yourself. I like your letters very much. Please tell me what you've learned and all about your new friends.

Now, let's sing together, my little star: "Twinkle, twinkle . . ."

Georgie's voice broke, but she pulled herself together for Lucia's sake and sang with the child.

"Thank you. Thank you." She tugged on Georgie's sleeve. "Please write me."

Heavens, no. He couldn't receive a letter in her handwriting. "Signorina Carpino —"

"No. She is nice but she is busy always.

Please?"

That wouldn't do. She waved to Vera. "Could you help me please? This is Lucia, and she wants a letter transcribed. I can't do it. Please don't make me explain."

Vera raised one perfect eyebrow, but then smiled at Lucia. "Of course. I'd love to write a letter for you, Lucia."

"Thank you." Lucia flipped one black braid over her shoulder. "Dear Signor Ucce."

"Oo-chay?"

"U-C-C-E." Georgie's voice caught, and she turned to show a boy how to rinse the paintbrush before switching colors.

Hutch was at Anzio for certain. Somehow receiving secondhand news deepened the sense of distance, of separation, of loss.

Her eyes stung. The letter showed her everything good and lovable about Hutch. Had she made the wrong decision to break up with him? Had she been too hard on him? What if he needed her comfort and encouragement and cheer?

Her sudden laugh amused the little boy with the paintbrush.

No, the last time she'd seen him, Hutch had rejected every attempt to cheer him. She needed to stop questioning her decisions.

Howling laughter rose from outside, and Georgie glanced out the window. Kay and Louise doubled over laughing. A group of boys kicked the baseball around with fancy moves, and the bat lay on the ground. Mellie played along. Apparently they preferred soccer to baseball.

Georgie smiled and circled the table, saying, *"Bella, bella"* for each painting.

One boy gazed longingly out the window. He had no feet. He'd never play soccer again.

Georgie swallowed the lump of pity and sat next to him. "Here. Let me show you something fun." She folded a piece of paper into eighths like a pie, then snipped out little triangles and squares from the edges.

He watched skeptically until Georgie unfolded it. "See. A snowflake."

Interest flickered in his dark eyes, and Georgie handed him the scissors and a piece of paper. "Your turn."

For the next hour, she helped with art projects and then assisted with the cleanup.

When it was time to leave, she hugged Lucia. The little girl wouldn't let go of her waist or her heart. Had it really been only a few weeks since she hoped to form a family with Hutch and Lucia? Now that would never happen, and until Hutch found someone else to marry, he wouldn't be allowed to adopt and Lucia would stay in this orphanage.

She gritted her teeth, closed her eyes, and forced out the necessary prayer. *Lord, please let Hutch find the right woman to be his wife and this child's mother.*

Lucia pulled back and wiped away a tear. "Please write me?"

Georgie's smile quivered. "I will."

"Come back?"

"Lord willing, we will." And with a pile of pretty dresses and neat shirts and warm sweaters. Mama could send her more cloth and yarn and notions.

"Promise?" Pain lurked deep in those big brown eyes.

Georgie knelt beside the bench and took her hands. "Sugar, I won't make a promise I can't keep. But I promise to write, and I do want to visit again very, very much."

Lucia nodded and shut her eyes. She'd lost so much, poor sweet thing — her family, her home, the strength in her legs, and even Hutch.

"You be good for the nuns now, you hear?" She squeezed the girl's hands.

"*Si.* Yes. I promise."

"Good girl." After she pried herself free, she joined the other nurses outside under a cloudy sky.

Mellie slipped her arm through Georgie's as they walked down the road to the train station. "Was it hard to see Lucia?"

"She asked me to read a letter from Hutch."

"Oh dear. Do you want to talk about it?"

She sighed. "I learned he's at Anzio as I suspected. But he didn't say anything I wanted to hear, like how he's really doing."

Walking on Mellie's other side, Kay wrinkled her nose. "Are you still pining for him? Don't. Tall, dark, and handsome does not make up for grouchy."

She reined in her irritation. "I'm not pining for him."

"Good. A cute thing like you can find a new man like this." Kay snapped her fingers. "What about that doctor from the dance? Chadwick, wasn't it? A looker, and he sure had his eye on you."

Drips from last night's rain fell from an umbrella pine, and Georgie dodged them. "He's not my type."

"Oh, and he's at Anzio too, isn't he? Too bad they won't let us fly in there. If you're not interested, I am. I don't have a physician on my roster."

A different man every day of the week, with an out-of-character exception for

Sundays. "Why so many men?"

"It's fun." She shook back her strawberry blonde hair. "You've heard about sailors having a different girl in every port? Well, I have a different man in every airport."

"But why do you *need* so many?"

Mellie's fingers dug into Georgie's arm, but Georgie ignored her. She'd been too caught up in her own life's drama to focus on Kay as her project. That needed to change.

Kay's chin elevated. "It's not a need. It's just fun, no commitment. The boys know that from the start. Any man gets too serious and he's gone."

Mellie's grip intensified, and Georgie dropped the subject, but only for now.

What was fun about a lack of commitment?

Of course, commitment hadn't worked that well for Georgie. She'd ended a relationship destined for marriage, and then an even better relationship that seemed destined for an even better marriage.

The ladies entered the railroad depot and stood in line for tickets.

Now Georgie was unattached, and for the longest time in her life.

As much as she hated the void, she couldn't fill it yet. Not until she evicted the

471

notion that only Sgt. John Hutchinson belonged there.

93rd Evacuation Hospital, Nettuno
February 18, 1944

Hutch wasn't sure he'd ever be able to stand straight again. He headed for his lunch at the mess doing the "Anzio Shuffle," hunched in a duckwalk to avoid decapitation by enemy shells. He lived in his helmet, even sleeping with it balanced over his head.

Dozens of personnel at the four American hospitals had been killed or wounded. The US Fifth Army had made noise about evacuating the nurses, but when the women protested, the Army backed down.

They might change their minds this week.

The sound of metal scraping on metal pricked Hutch's ear. Incoming shell. He raced for the nearest foxhole and leaped in. He landed with a splash, and chilly water soaked his trousers and feet.

He grimaced. The water table on the Anzio beachhead lay only a few feet below ground this time of year, so the hospital couldn't dig in for protection.

The shell landed to the west and shook the ground, but it missed the hospital.

On his right, a pudgy man in pajamas shivered. "I was under the opinion that the appropriate treatment for trench foot was to keep the feet dry and elevated."

"It is." Hutch smiled. "Here. Put them up on my knees."

The man swung dripping feet up over Hutch's knees. "This is the most undignified situation in which I have ever found myself."

"Undignified?" A young man with an arm in a sling cussed. "Plain dangerous. It's safer at the front. I swear I'll go AWOL and return to my unit."

Dozens of patients had done just that.

Two loud whines overhead, and the men hunkered close to the earthen wall. Hutch braced himself, but the shells landed far away.

The trench foot patient readjusted his muddy helmet. "Trapped between the devil and the deep blue sea, with the Nazis, as always, playing the role of the devil."

"Yep." The Germans were on the move again. Last he'd heard they'd broken the final defensive line and were within six miles of the shore. The Allied forces could all be in POW camps by the end of the week. At least today's overcast blunted the rumors about German paratroopers dropping onto the beachhead.

Some hoped for a Dunkirk-type miraculous evacuation, but most realized the only plan was to fight to the end.

"I feel like I'm fighting Pop's war." The younger man propped up his bandaged arm with his healthy hand. "It's like World War I trench warfare."

Hutch leaned his head against the sandy wall. "Bombarded without stop. Can't go forward. Can't go back. A microcosm of my life."

"Microcosm?" The trench foot patient sat up a bit higher. "A fellow man of education?"

"Bachelor's in pharmacy. Not that it does a fat lot of good around here." He pointed to the stripes on his sleeve.

"I understand." He held out a wet hand. "Robert Prescott, Ph.D. in European history and private first class in the infantry. No demand for professorial types in Uncle Sam's Army."

Hutch shook with his equally wet hand. "Watching history being made."

"And I'm unable to record it. I'm not even allowed to keep a journal."

"What a waste."

"In many ways. I could be writing scholarly books — very well. Instead I'm shooting a rifle — very poorly. But we all have our dreams on hold for the duration, don't we?"

Hutch studied Robert's round earnest face. He had to admit the truth. He wasn't alone in disappointment and frustration. "Yeah, we do."

"Know what you mean, pal," the man with the sling said. "You're looking at Dick Engelhard, the man meant to be the star of the US Olympic swim team in 1940."

Hutch gave him a wry smile. "Games were cancelled in '40."

"Yeah, and prospects don't look too good for '44."

A shell whizzed overhead and thumped to ground in the distance.

"I'd say not." Robert glared toward enemy lines.

Dick's light eyes took on a faraway look. "And in '48, even if this blasted war is actually over, I'll be past my prime. Life's passing me by."

Hutch sighed. "Me too. My fiancée couldn't wait and married another man. The Army won't —" He was tired of explaining it. "Back at home, I'd have a bustling drugstore and be a pillar of the community. Here it's nothing but hassle and disrespect."

Dick grumbled in affirmation. "Nothing

you can do about it. Just got to do your best."

" 'Whatsoever ye do, do it heartily, as to the Lord, and not unto men,' " Robert said.

Hutch stared at him. His mind tingled — from the cold or from the memory of a truth forgotten? "What was that?"

"It's in Colossians, chapter 3." Robert wiggled his wet toes. "The apostle Paul addressed that to servants."

Servants? Hutch sagged against the wall. Servants had to do what they were told without question. They had no control over their lives. They didn't even have the luxury of dreams and goals. Who was he to complain?

He'd lost sight of the importance of doing his best without complaining. Not for the sake of man. Not for respect. For the Lord.

The truth tasted as sour as the acid in his stomach. He'd thought disrespect was eating him up from the inside, but disrespect came from outside. Bitterness came from inside. Bitterness was chewing a hole in his stomach, in his soul, destroying his relationships with Georgie, Bergie, even the Lord.

He pressed his hand over his abdomen. *Lord, help me find my way out of this mess.*

44

Pomigliano Airfield
March 6, 1944

Rain pelted the tent, and Georgie's needle flew through the fabric. Between her scraps and what she'd purchased in Naples, she had enough for a dozen dresses and a dozen shirts for the orphans, a good start.

Kay Jobson slouched on her cot and frowned at her knitting needles. "If I wanted to 'knit my bit,' I'd have stayed on the home front."

"It's for a good cause." Mellie pinned a little sleeve onto a bodice. "We might as well keep busy since we can't fly in this weather."

"Remember Pearl Harbor . . . Purl Harder!" Kay held her knitting needle to her forehead in a salute.

Georgie smiled. "That's the spirit."

"I'm being sarcastic."

"So am I." She seemed to be the only nurse who welcomed the rain. On February

24, an evac flight had crashed in Sicily. Two nurses from their sister squadron, the 807th, had been killed.

Her insides jumbled up like the yarn in Kay's lap. All her memories of Rose's death had come back in a rush. She hated how her old fears wormed back into her soul, how she took comfort in the hominess of sewing. How she wavered.

Letters from home didn't help. Her sister Freddie had been placed on bed rest for her pregnancy, and now Bertie and Mama joined the call for Georgie to come home and help, and Daddy insisted she patch things up with Ward out of mercy for the poor, inconsolable man.

The tent flap opened, and Lieutenant Lambert stepped inside, rain dripping from her coat. "Gracious. When will this let up?"

"Take off your coat and sit a spell." Georgie held out a shirt. "You can sew on buttons."

"Giving orders to your chief, are you?" Lambert smiled and tossed her coat onto the crate by the entrance. She took the shirt, needle and thread, and a handful of buttons. "I do like this project, Georgie."

"I do too." She tied off a knot and snipped the thread. She liked it far better than braving the skies.

"I have news for the three of you." Lambert squinted at the needle and poked the thread through. "At the end of March, six replacement nurses will arrive from Bowman. We'd like to rotate some of the original gals stateside. By then, even accounting for your furlough, you'll have served a full twelve months overseas. The Army Air Force thinks that's enough, and you should have a chance to go home."

Georgie's heart seized. Home.

"Nonsense." Mellie held up the little dress for inspection. "The men on the front lines don't get to go home after twelve months."

"No, but the airmen have limited tours." Lambert pulled the needle through a button. "You ladies face most of the dangers our airmen do."

"I'd rather stay if it's possible." Mellie laid the dress in her lap and leaned closer to the chief. "I love this work. Besides, the nurses at Anzio — they don't have a chance to go home."

"No, they don't." Lambert gave Mellie a warm look. "I'd love to keep you."

"I want to stay." Kay took a stitch. "After all this flying, ward nursing would be dull."

"Wonderful," the chief said. "Vera's staying too, and Alice is thinking about it."

Georgie's needle weaved along the seam

line like an ocean wave. Would it be wrong to go home if it were her decision? Her family needed her, Ward needed her, and Hutch didn't want her. She'd handled crises with grace and quick thinking, and she'd made decisions leaning on the Lord. Perhaps her purpose overseas had been accomplished.

"What about you, Georgie?" Lambert gave her a careful look. "You've done so well since your return, but I'm offering the chance to all the original girls."

All that remained. She swallowed hard. Several were gone due to illness, pregnancy, transfer — or death.

"When do I have to decide?" Her voice came out shakier than she liked.

"Not until the replacements arrive. I'll make a list of the girls who are interested, but I'll leave a spot on top for you because of all you've been through."

Her needle stilled. "I'll pray about it."

But already her answer seemed clear.

93rd Evacuation Hospital, Nettuno
March 12, 1944
Ralph O'Shea stepped down into Pharmacy. They'd managed to dig down one whole foot and stack sandbags around the sides of the tent for a smidgen of protection from air raids. "Sick of this rain." He shook water

480

off his mackinaw.

"Hey, watch it." After a day plagued with shortages and artillery fire and a bout of dysentery, the last thing Hutch wanted was more mud.

"Ought to give you some sugar pills instead of those bicarb tabs."

Hutch's jaw clenched. What did everyone expect? Bombarded night and day, goals thwarted, no respect. After meeting the professor and the Olympian, he tried to spend time with the Lord, but every time he opened his Bible, he fell asleep, exhausted.

Just as well the Army Air Force had abandoned the airstrip at Nettuno due to constant shelling. He didn't want to see Georgie in his current state, hear her nag him to smile and be happy.

"How were things on the day shift?" Ralph joined Dom and leaned back on the counter.

"Crazy."

"You'd think now that the Germans are driven back and dug in on the defensive, things would quiet down around here."

"Nope. But we got another shipment of penicillin. Put it in the icebox in the lab."

Hutch wiped down the counter. That penicillin was the only good thing that had happened today. Finally a new manufacturing process increased the supply and made it available in all hospitals. "Remember — 100,000 units per ampule, and the dose is 50,000 units every four hours."

"We know. You've told us." Ralph rested his elbows behind him on the counter, his head too close to a large bottle lying on its side on the shelf. According to Kaz, it belonged up top because it started with a *B* or *C*. According to good practice, it belonged with the bulk items on the bottom shelves, where it could stand upright.

But Hutch bit off a reprimand, tired of being the stern policeman.

"Busy here, huh?" Ralph tilted his head back. "On second thought, I feel a touch of pneumonia coming on. Think I'll let you work a double shift."

"No, you don't." Dom swatted Ralph in the shoulder.

Ralph's elbow slipped. His head jerked back and bonked the shelf.

The bottle tipped over the edge and shattered on the counter. White powder flew everywhere.

Hutch thumped his fist on the counter. "Now look what you've done."

Ralph swore and rubbed the back of his head.

"What was it? Better not have been the

boric acid." Hutch picked through the shards for the label. Sure enough: Acid, boric, 5 lb. His last bottle. He bit back a cuss word he'd never spoken in his life and had rarely thought.

"You know how hard it is to get this stuff?" He pointed at the mess. "I've had an order out for over a month."

"Sorry," Dom said.

"Sorry." Hutch waved his arm toward the tent entrance. "That's what I'll have to say next time the docs need boric acid solution for a burn patient. They'll think it's my fault for not ordering enough."

"Said we're sorry." Ralph's eyebrows drew together. "Not like we did it on purpose."

"No, it was an accident, because you two forget you're working with dangerous chemicals, with expensive medications, with items in short supply."

Another incident that begged to be told to his father. But since he and Bergie weren't speaking, Kaz censored his letters. Hutch was gagged, powerless.

Ralph cast a glance at his fellow tech. "What do you expect from uneducated yo-kels?"

Hutch's heart lurched. He'd gone too far. "That's not what I said."

"Not in so many words." Ralph jerked his

head toward the tent entrance. "Go on, Dom, I'll clean up. Your shift's over."

Dom faced Hutch and raised a rigid salute. "If that's all, sir, I'll be leaving, sir."

"Sir? I'm not a sir."

"That's what you want, isn't it?" Ralph swept boric acid and glass shards into an empty cardboard box. "You want everyone to 'sir' you."

"No." His stomach squirmed. "I just want some respect."

"Because you deserve it." Dom pulled on his mackinaw. "We, on the other hand, don't deserve it because we don't have some fancy college diploma."

"That's not what I think." His voice came out low, but his thoughts tumbled lower. "I'm sorry I did something that made you think that."

Dom exchanged one last look with Ralph before leaving — a look that said it all. Hutch had done plenty.

His mind whirled. What was wrong with him?

He fumbled into his mackinaw and headed out into the wet evening. Rain stung his eyes, but not as much as the technicians' words stung his heart.

What was his true motivation in wanting a commission? So others would "sir" and salute him? So he could prove he was as good as the others?

Did he really think he was better than Dom and Ralph because he went to college and they didn't?

Pain wrenched through his insides, the old stomach problems and the new dysentery cramps combined. He had to get to the latrine and fast.

The poison begged to get out of his system. But what was more poisonous than pride?

It was nothing but pride to want others to look up to him.

He headed for the latrines. No, pride didn't drive him. He wanted a commission for good and noble reasons.

What were they?

His mind, slowed by pains, tried to remember. Better health care, wasn't it? For all patients in all hospitals.

"Yeah, that's it." And the Army — the Army stood in the way.

45

Pomigliano Airfield
March 22, 1944

For the first time in weeks, Georgie wanted to fly.

Mount Vesuvius had erupted on March 18, with earthquakes and giant billowing clouds, bulging with ash and death. Last night, furious red lava spouted thousands of feet into the air and slithered down the slopes, menacing Italian villages already pummeled by war and poverty.

For once, the sky seemed safer than the ground. In the air she wouldn't be turned into a statue like those poor souls in Pompeii, frozen in their death poses for tourists to gawk at almost two thousand years later.

After Roger Cooper and his crew had dusted ash from their C-47 and the mechanics assured them the engines were clean, Georgie and Sergeant Ramirez loaded ten patients eager to escape from Italy to Tunisia. Since the ash delayed their takeoff until late afternoon, they'd stop over in Palermo, Sicily, for the night.

The plane lifted into the air, and Georgie sighed in relief. After they leveled off, she began her rounds. Three litter-bound patients on the left side of the plane, and the rest sat in canvas seats toward the front and along the right.

Using the stirrup-shaped foot under the middle litter, Georgie hoisted herself up to take vital signs on Private Stowe in the top litter. Blinded and burned in an exploding tank in one of many attempts to take Cassino, Stowe couldn't see Vesuvius's fireworks.

"One step closer to home." She wrapped her fingers around his wrist.

He turned his bandaged head away from her. "What? So I can start my new life? Hardly. My life's over."

"I'll have no such talk." Georgie squeezed his arm. "I won't lie to you. Life won't be easy. But with persistence, ingenuity, and hard work, you can accomplish much. I'll allow you exactly five more minutes to feel sorry for yourself, and that's all."

"You sound like my mother." The bandages on his face shifted as if he were trying to smile. "Six minutes, and we have a deal."

"Oh, all right. Six. But I'll check on you to keep you honest."

"Yes, ma'am."

The plane banked sharply to the right.

Georgie lost her footing, her grip, cried out. She tumbled to the floor and whammed back into a patient's knees.

He grabbed her shoulders. "Ma'am! You all right?"

"I'm fine." Other than a sore backside.

What was going on? Roger Cooper never made drastic maneuvers like that. She struggled to her feet and braced herself on the right side of the fuselage over the patients' heads.

The plane continued a steep climbing turn, and Georgie fought her way uphill.

Something bonked the fuselage, shook the plane. Another hit, loud and sharp.

Every drop of Georgie's blood turned icy cold. They were under attack? The Luftwaffe rarely ventured as far south as Naples anymore.

"Everything's fine, gentlemen. Lieutenant Cooper's an excellent pilot." She held on and looked out the left windows.

Large dark chunks dropped from the sky. What on earth?

One hit the left wing, tipped the plane out

of its climb.

She bit off a scream. Her patients needed her calm.

Sergeant Ramirez sat on the floor at the back of the cabin, his hand pressed to his temple, blood oozing between his fingers.

Georgie froze. She should help him, but first she wanted to find out what was going on. "I'll be there in a minute, Sergeant."

"It's not that bad. Go talk to the crew."

She plunged forward, upward as the plane spiraled high, and she pulled herself through the door into the radio room. The radioman-navigator spoke into his headset, and the aerial engineer leaned through the doorway into the cockpit.

"What's going on?"

The radioman glanced up at her. "Vesuvius remains loyal to the Axis cause. It's throwing flak at us."

"Flak?"

"Volcanic rocks. Coop didn't want to fly today, thought it was dangerous. He's trying to get up out of range. Then we'll check for damage, decide if it's safer to proceed to Palermo or venture back into the maelstrom."

"Oh no."

"Just keep the patients calm."

"I — I can do that." If she could keep

herself calm first.

From the shivering recess of her heart, she prayed for wisdom and strength. She worked up a smile, closed the door behind her, and faced the patients. "Gentlemen, we're in for an exciting ride, something to tell your children about — the time you got caught in the eruption of Vesuvius."

The men sat forward, shouting questions and comments.

She held up one hand. "Lieutenant Cooper is taking us up out of danger. Now, was anyone other than Sergeant Ramirez hurt on our roller-coaster ride?"

Since no one claimed new injuries, Georgie made her way to the back of the plane, the men holding her hand to keep her from falling.

Sergeant Ramirez sat on the left side of the plane by the cargo door and wore the interphone headset. "Listening in on the chat up front."

"Anything new?" Georgie flung open the medication chest.

"Coop thinks we're clear."

"Here, stop the blood." She handed him a gauze pad and pulled out iodine.

He pressed the pad over his temple. "Not that bad. You know how head wounds bleed."

"I know. But we'll want to clean it up and take a closer look."

Ramirez's dark brows wrinkled. He raised a hand to silence Georgie and stared straight ahead. After a minute or two, he looked up to her. "Coop says number one engine took some damage but is functioning okay. None of the crew wants to return. They think it's safer to go to Sicily. But just in case . . ."

Georgie's stomach felt queasy, and she wrapped her arms around her middle. "Just in case what?"

He pursed his lips. "In case we have to ditch, they're making preparations, radioing RAF Air-Sea Rescue."

Ditch? The word stuck to the roof of her mouth.

"Don't worry, Lieutenant. You know they have to prepare for the worst."

Georgie gripped the side seams of her jacket in her fists. "Of course."

"We've leveled off. Why don't you finish your rounds while we wait for the bleeding to stop?"

"Yes." She blinked too many times, recognizing his attempt to distract her with activity.

Still nothing but a helpless baby who needed someone to show her the way.

"Well, go ahead."

She nodded and obeyed. Her clipboard and flight manifest had fallen when she had, and one of the ambulatory patients handed it to her.

For the next half hour, she made her rounds, noting elevated heart rates for most patients. Her own pulse had to be high as well. Her voice sounded tinny, and her fingers trembled. She thought she'd grown the last few months, but she still unraveled in a crisis. What good was she? Whatever made her think she could succeed as a flight nurse?

And she didn't like the look of things. She'd flown in a C-47 often enough to recognize normal engine sounds. Engine one ran rough and choppy, and engine two worked harder to compensate. Her ears popped a few times. They were descending.

After she'd filled in her manifest with shaky handwriting, she returned to the back of the plane. "Let me see that wound, Sergeant."

"Yes, ma'am." He removed the reddened gauze pad.

Georgie inspected the cut, about three inches long. "It isn't deep. You won't need stitches. I'll bandage it for you."

"Thank you." He sat in silence as Georgie cleansed the wound and applied a bandage.

His silence made her more nervous, as if he were waiting until she was done to relay bad news.

But delaying bad news didn't make it any less bad. "What's the latest?"

"We're heading for a lower altitude. Engine one won't last, and they're descending so we can ditch safely in the Mediterranean. We need to prepare."

"Pre— prepare?" She sank to her backside and winced from the pain in her tailbone.

"Yes, ma'am. We're about halfway between Palermo and Naples, and we can't make it either way. We need to plan."

Plan. Plan. Plan. The word bounced through the dark emptiness of her mind.

"What's the first thing we have to do?" Ramirez narrowed his eyes at her.

"Do." She pulled her knees tight to her chest.

"Come on, Lieutenant." He put one hand to his bandage and got to his feet. "I'm one of the surgical techs Major Guilford recruited from an evac hospital in Algeria. I never went to the School of Air Evacuation, never got ditching training. You did. What do we do first?"

Thoughts sloshed in her mind, drowning. Ditching training? She took that. She passed. What was the first thing to do? She hugged her knees tighter. "G— group the patients. Ambulatory patients who can't swim. Ambulatory patients who can swim. Litter patients."

Ramirez picked up the flight manifest and gave her a long, hard look. "If you don't pull yourself together, Lieutenant, a lot of men could die." He headed down the aisle.

Georgie rocked back and forth. The plane was going into the ocean. If they survived the impact, she had two minutes at most to evacuate the patients. Perhaps as little as thirty seconds.

A flight nurse was supposed to be calm and collected, quick-thinking, decisive.

Daddy had told her she was in over her head, and Ward said Georgie being decisive was like a thoroughbred trying to be a big old draft horse.

Her throat swelled shut. Why had she been so stupid, so vain, so headstrong to think she could do this?

Today, due to her incompetence, a lot of men would die.

93rd Evacuation Hospital, Nettuno

In the waning light of a pointless day off, Hutch lounged on his cot, alone in his tent with the *Stars and Stripes*. The Allies on the Cassino front wouldn't relieve the troops at

Anzio anytime soon. The Army Air Forces had bombed the living daylights out of the abbey of Monte Cassino over a month ago and the town of Cassino a week ago, but the infantry couldn't cross that line.

"Sergeant Hutchinson?" A corporal peeked inside the tent. "Mail."

"Thanks." He set down the newspaper, fetched two letters, and returned to the cot.

A letter from Lucia, which he savored. She'd written half of it herself, in large handwriting and decent English. Miss Carpino wrote the rest, where Lucia raved about another visit from Georgie and her nurse friends, who brought dresses, shirts, and sweaters they'd made.

A strange thought — two girls he loved, two girls he'd lost, enjoying each other's company. Without him. Jealousy twisted inside, but he shoved it away, thankful Lucia had someone to brighten her life. Wasn't it just like Georgie to do the brightening?

He'd lost so much.

Hutch sighed and picked up the letter from Dad, postmarked February 15. Over a month earlier. Maybe he had some news about the Pharmacy Corps. The Army had dragged its heels so much, a ditch a foot deep had to extend halfway across Washington DC.

Hutch jabbed his finger under the lip of the envelope and pulled out a sheet of stationery in Dad's firm, careful script.

Dear Son,

I don't believe in idle talk when bad news awaits. The Army commissioned twelve officers for the Pharmacy Corps in January, before your examination even arrived. Your exam score was outstanding, but it was too late. For the past two weeks, I've pulled strings and called on every favor. In vain. John, I'm afraid there's nothing to be done.

The cruel injustice of the matter is that you weren't selected because you're overseas, and yet your overseas work helped create the Corps.

Hutch couldn't even read the rest of the letter. He crumpled it up and ground it into the dirt with his heel.

"For nothing. Nothing. All for nothing."

His chest heaved, his stomach writhed.

Because he chose to serve as a pharmacist, he got sent overseas and lost Phyllis. Because he chose to pursue his goal, he lost Georgie. Because he chose to practice his profession, he lost his chance to serve in that profession's own Corps.

Everything, everything had been stripped from him. All respect, all control, all love.

What did he have left? The makings of a stomach ulcer.

Hutch groped in his pocket for his pillbox. Not there. Must have left it in his other pair of trousers.

He grumbled and dug into his barracks bag until he found his trousers. Where was that pillbox? The day he needed it more than ever?

There. His fingers felt the cool metal, but it slipped away and down through the crevices in his bag.

Hutch fisted his hands, and a growl emanated from deep in his tortured stomach. Couldn't any single thing go his way? Just one thing? Just for once?

He plunged his hand into the bag until he reached the bottom. There it was, lying on a leather case.

The telescope.

Rage ripped through him. He yanked and tugged until the case rested on his cot, taunting him.

His breath tore out his nostrils in hot bursts. That telescope represented everything the Army had done to him, emasculating him.

He never asked for a new telescope.

Georgie thrust it on him and he had to take it, had to take everything the officers dished out. He definitely didn't want a telescope purchased by his officer girlfriend out of pity.

Why would he want to watch the stars anyway? The stories behind the constellations now repulsed him.

Stories about cheating lovers and defeated warriors and flying horses and fickle gods.

He picked up the case. His fingers dug into the smooth leather. He couldn't control any bit of his life. But he could get rid of the telescope forever.

46

Over the Mediterranean

The fog of fear. The paralysis of panic.

Georgie hugged her knees to her chest, lost in the familiar hated emotions.

She would die. All these men would die. Because she was silly and weak and indecisive. Her parents were right. Ward was right. She never should have left home.

She would die. She'd never see her family or friends again.

She would die. Just like Rose.

Her eyes drooped shut, and moisture seeped out. Except Rose didn't die from incompetence, only from being in the wrong place at the wrong time.

Georgie groped next to the medical chest for her musette bag. If she couldn't see her loved ones again, she'd have their mementos with her when she died — photos, the stuffed nightingale . . .

She clutched the bag to her chest. Rose

believed Georgie could be a good flight nurse and so did Mellie.

Through the khaki canvas she felt something round and hard. The tin punch from Hutch.

She gulped back a sob. She'd already said good-bye to him forever, but would he mourn her? Would he regret encouraging her to stay in flight nursing? *Oh Lord, please don't let him feel guilty.*

Her finger traced the design through the canvas, the undulating waves, the nightingale above. How ironic that this nightingale was about to die in the waves.

Because she wavered.

" 'If any of you lack wisdom,' " she whispered, " 'let him ask of God . . . and it shall be given him. But let him ask in faith, nothing wavering. For he that wavereth is like a wave of the sea driven with the wind and tossed.' "

Georgie lifted her chin and focused on the medication chest. "Nothing wavering. Nothing wavering."

Could she do it? She'd been through the training. If she had her wits about her, some of these men, if not all of them, stood a chance.

"Almighty Father, Lord of the wind and the waves, save these men's lives. Give me wisdom. And now, please. I wasted too much time."

Footsteps thumped down the aisle, and Georgie scrambled to her feet.

The radioman-navigator set a briefcase by the cargo door and lashed it in place. The aerial engineer joined him and tied down the emergency equipment — life rafts and ration containers and radios.

Georgie swallowed hard. Her training swirled together in her head, random thoughts coalescing into a plan.

Tension billowed in the plane, darker than Vesuvius's ashen clouds. Ramirez had a heated discussion with a patient, and men talked in tones of anger or worry or stoicism or false cheer.

Georgie grabbed the bag of "Mae West" life vests from under the bottom litter and headed to the front of the cabin. "Gentlemen! May I have your attention?"

Voices quieted, and the men looked to her.

"Thank you." She smiled and cocked her head. "As I'm sure you already know, we're going for a little sail in the Mediterranean this evening."

Questions, outcries, and Georgie raised her hand.

Ramirez let out a sharp whistle. "Your survival depends on listening to the lady.

Now listen, or I'll knock silence into you."

"That won't be necessary, Sergeant, but thank you." She handed him a pile of life vests. "Gentlemen, please fasten your seat belts and put on a life vest. If you need assistance, raise your hand, and the sergeant and I will help you. Also, if you're able to help your neighbor after you put on your own vest, please do so."

Georgie passed out life vests to the ambulatory patients, then put on her own as a demonstration. She hiked herself up to the top litter to put a vest on Private Stowe and check his securing straps. "Listen, gentlemen. It's crucial that you follow our instructions. When the plane lands, stay in your seats until we tell you. The crew needs to come down the aisle first to get the life rafts inflated and the emergency equipment stowed."

She hopped to the floor and put a life vest on Lieutenant Cameron in the middle litter. "We'll assign who goes in which raft, based on your medical needs. Patients who can't swim will be evacuated before those who can."

"That's not fair." An ambulatory patient leaned forward in his seat.

"It's perfectly fair." She fastened a vest on Corporal Travinski in the bottom litter.

"You can swim to a raft while the others can't. And remember, Lieutenant Cooper is the aircraft commander. You'll follow his orders without question, and I operate under his authority — and as an officer myself, may I remind you?" A sweet smile softened her words.

"Yes, ma'am." He sat back, his eyebrows tented.

"Everybody secure?" Georgie strode to the front of the plane and checked each patient's seat belt and life vest. "When we tell you, assume the ditching position. Hook your hands under your knees and lean over with your head down. Please show me."

The patients demonstrated.

She set her hands on her hips and smiled. "Oh, you'll do just fine. Sergeant Ramirez, please come with me and bring the flight manifest."

My goodness, she was calm. She hardly recognized herself.

In the back of the plane, Georgie ran her finger down the list of names. "Stowe and Cameron will go in my raft, since they need the most care. Travinski and Bard in yours because they need care too. Who can swim?"

Ramirez jabbed his finger at three names. "And these two are strong and cooperative. They agreed to help with the litter patients."

Georgie marked numbers by the ten names, one through five in loading order. Each raft would hold two patients and a crew member. The first two rafts would be for the four non-swimmers, the third for two swimmers, the fourth for Travinski and Bard, the fifth for Stowe and Cameron, and the last for the pilot.

She handed the manifest to Ramirez. "You tell each patient his number. I'll gather meds and supplies."

He nodded, his dark eyes appreciative.

Georgie grabbed her musette bag and opened it. Not a very large bag, and full of necessities and mementos. She tossed out her change of clothes and toiletry kit, then pulled out framed photographs of her family and her horse. A lump threatened to cut off her breathing and her reason. She coughed it away and set the frames aside.

Photographs could be replaced. Lives couldn't.

That left her Bible, the stuffed nightingale, and the tin punch.

If they were stranded at sea, she'd want her Bible more than ever. She couldn't bear to part with the little bird, and the tin punch took no room at all.

Georgie sifted through the medication chest. Morphine and codeine and aspirin for pain. Phenobarbital for anxiety. Epinephrine for shock. Sodium bicarbonate for seasickness. Sulfanilamide and a box of plasma in case anyone was badly wounded in the landing. Bandages, scissors, alcohol, syringes, IV tubing, flashlight, towels.

She stuffed the meds in her musette bag, then tied up the supplies in a towel with the knot around the strap for the musette bag.

"You done with that?" The engineer pointed to the chest. "Can I pitch it out? We need to get rid of as much weight as possible."

"Yes. Here." She tossed her clothing, toiletry bag, and photos into the chest. Never in her life had she been so cold-hearted, but it was for a good cause.

The engineer flung open the cargo door and heaved out boxes and equipment.

Cool air whipped Georgie's hair around her face, and the orange light of sunset spilled inside.

She took an empty seat to the rear of the plane and fastened her seat belt. Ramirez sat next to her, his face beaded with sweat, and he handed her the flight manifest. After she wiggled it down into her musette bag, she looped the bag over her leg with the bundle of supplies behind her feet.

Georgie's hands trembled, and her pulse

raced. Yet she had done her best.

Live or die, she'd fulfilled her duties and well.

The alarm bell rang six times.

"Assume the ditching position!" The engineer took his seat, and everyone leaned over their knees.

Georgie did too, staring at the vibrating floor. Would that be the last sight she ever saw?

She closed her eyes, prayed, and filled her mind with images of her family, friends, and even Hutch. She'd rather die with her loved ones before her.

Nettuno

Hutch marched through the hospital complex, plotting his course around doctors and nurses and medics and equipment, upright for once, in defiance of German shells and the Luftwaffe.

The telescope case fried his grip, as hot as the sun burning the horizon, as hot as the pains in his stomach, as the knowledge that he had failed in his quest.

He broke free from the rows of khaki tents and strode across the sand.

Dad was like Abraham, the leader setting forth into new professional lands, and Hutch was meant to be Isaac, the son of the promise. But he'd failed to grasp hold of that promise.

He'd lost his Rebekah, the woman hand-selected for him. He'd climbed onto the altar in faith that a ram would appear in the thicket and rescue him. But no ram. No commission. He was still tied up on the altar and would be for the duration of this lousy, stinking war.

The sand grew damp and firm under his combat boots.

Only one story of the biblical Isaac still resonated with Hutch — when the herdsmen of Gerar stopped up Isaac's wells. Isaac dug a new one, and they stole it too.

Hutch growled, the only sound that felt right today. Other people drank from the wells he dug. He'd labored for nothing. Nothing.

He had no control over anything in his life.

But he could control the stupid, unwanted, emasculating telescope.

Hutch strode to the water's edge, the ocean scalded with flaming streaks of orange. With a mighty growl, he swung back the telescope case to hurl it into the ocean.

Two clicks. A thud.

He whirled around. The stupid case had

popped open, spilling the contents onto the sand.

The case fell from his hand. He couldn't even do that one little thing.

Hutch dropped to his knees. Pain slashed through his belly, and he doubled over. He had nothing — no love, no voice, no respect. And without respect, what was he?

He was nothing.

47

The Mediterranean

The largest splash Georgie had heard in her life. A jolt banged her into the patient beside her, and Ramirez bumped her other side.

"Stay seated!" the engineer cried.

The second jolt was worse than the first, as Georgie learned in training, and Ramirez shoved her shoulders hard to the side. She cried out, then stopped herself.

The plane bounced forward, jiggling the passengers, until it finally came to a rest. Rising and falling. Tossed by the waves.

Georgie's breath rose and fell in synchrony. The plane was intact. They'd survived the ditching. But her job was only half done. She had to evacuate these men before the C-47 sank.

The engineer bolted from his seat to the cargo door, where he unlashed equipment and heaved life rafts into the water to be inflated.

Georgie moved to stand. Her seat belt. She fumbled it open and stood. Her legs buckled, and she grabbed Ramirez's shoulder.

"No time to wait for sea legs," he said with a partial smile.

"Nope." She slung her musette bag across her chest and cradled the bundle of supplies in one arm. "Anyone hurt?"

A few bumps and cuts. Nothing serious. Thank goodness.

"All right," she said. "Unfasten your seat belts but stay seated until your group is called. If you need assistance, tell us. Group one, head to the cargo door. The crew will tell you when to board. Group three, please help Sergeant Ramirez with the litters."

Georgie unfastened seat belts for a few patients, then led group two to the door.

The engineer sat in a raft with his emergency equipment, and the radioman helped the first two patients into his raft. Back in the cabin, Ramirez and his helpers unclamped the litters from the racks.

Georgie motioned the second group to stand out of the way while the radioman boarded and stashed the equipment. Was it her imagination, or did the plane sit lower in the water? Panic fluttered in her chest, but she blew it away.

Roger Cooper charged down the aisle from the cockpit. "Shelby's out through the roof hatch onto the wing. Plane looks steady, but let's keep moving."

Georgie helped the second group board, and all three litters rested on the floor. "Group three, your turn," she called.

After Cooper loaded the copilot's raft, he and Georgie assisted two more patients out. Shelby would join them after he completed his duties.

The plane did ride lower. The tips of the waves sloshed into the door.

"Sergeant, you're next." Coop motioned Ramirez forward.

Georgie and the tech carried Travinski's litter to the door. Ramirez got in the life raft, and he and Cooper maneuvered the litter across the bow of the raft, with help from Shelby, who crouched on the plane's wing. Then the last ambulatory patient stepped in.

A wave splashed through the door and drenched Georgie's feet with chilly water. Her breath congealed in her throat. The plane was going down. They had to hurry.

Cooper pulled an empty raft close, and Georgie took a wide step into the raft and knelt. Far too squishy and rocky for her taste.

The pilot slid Stowe's litter to her, and Shelby helped her heft the patient into position across one end of the raft. Then they tied the litter into place.

"Get the patient!" Coop cried.

Georgie spun around. Water rose above the rim of the cargo door and swamped Lieutenant Cameron on his litter. He'd drown! With all her might she dragged the man out of the aircraft.

Up to his waist in seawater, Coop shoved the litter until it lay safely across the raft.

The plane dove down, inappropriately graceful and elegant. Heavens, no! Roger Cooper was still inside.

Georgie leaned over, heart pounding, but she had to stay with her patients. "Get out!"

"Coop! Get out of there!" Shelby leaped off the wing and paddled forward. Only the tailfin protruded from the water.

"Cut the lines!" the engineer cried, and everyone threw off the ropes that tied the rafts to the plane before they could be dragged under.

A man bobbed to the surface. Roger Cooper's dark red hair shone in the last rays of sunlight. He shook off water like a dog. "That was refreshing."

Georgie savored the men's relieved, nervous laughter. Shelby socked Coop in the shoulder, and then they swam to their rafts and hauled themselves inside.

They all survived. Thank God, they all survived.

But for how long? The sun joined the C-47 beneath the waves. The six rafts looked tiny and lonesome on the giant twilit ocean. An ocean where German U-boats prowled.

They had water and rations and supplies, and they weren't terribly far from land, but all she could think about was those news stories of men stranded at sea for weeks, slowly giving in to starvation, insanity, and talk of cannibalism.

She'd just have to keep herself occupied. Stowe and Cameron had sopping wet dressings to be changed, and nightfall would soon make work difficult.

The crew lashed the rafts together in a circle and tossed out the sea anchor, which acted like a parachute in the water. They needed to stay close to the coordinates where they'd gone down so Air-Sea Rescue could find them, which wouldn't be until morning at the earliest.

Georgie worked hard and fast, changing dressings and distributing evening meds.

No moon lit the sky. Other than the stars, the only light rose far to the north — an eerie red glow from Vesuvius, gloating in its victory.

Nettuno

"Nothing! Nothing!" Hutch knelt, doubled over, one fist pressed over his burning stomach, the other fist pounding the firm, damp sand.

"Why, God? Why?"

No one respected him anymore. The Army never respected him. Phyllis married someone else. Bergie and Dom and Ralph gave up on him. Dad had to be disappointed in his failure. Georgie bought him a stinking telescope out of pity.

He glared at the spilled contents of the telescope case, and a spasm seized his midsection. Had she really bought it out of pity . . . or out of love?

He blew off the pain, and truth filled his mind. She did it out of love. She never cared about his rank. Instead she loved him for who he was. She'd respected him.

And he drove her away with his bitterness.

In the strange orange-blue light after sunset, the telescope lay on the sand with a piece of cloth pinned underneath — the embroidered handkerchief.

He pulled it out and shook off the sand, picturing Lucia chattering in her charming mix of English and Italian about *il orso* and the star-zay, picturing Georgie presenting it, shrouded in grief for Rose yet still thinking of him.

He missed Lucia. He missed Georgie. He missed all the light in his life.

Hutch traced the embroidered pattern of Ursa Major with the mortar and pestle forming the bear's belly. Georgie said it was part of his constellation, like pharmacy was part of him.

Pharmacy had always been part of his identity, but had he made it the *only* part?

In Georgie's design, the mortar sat deep in the belly of the bear, weighing it down. Did Hutch do the same thing? Carry the weight of his profession in his belly? The burden, the disrespect, the bitterness all chewed away the lining of his stomach.

He fingered the embroidered North Star, the knot of dark blue thread firm and unmovable as Polaris itself. "Lord, I didn't waver from my goal, and it was a good goal. I did it for you, for the patients, for my profession."

Yet his labor was in vain.

Or was it? He pressed the heel of his hand to his forehead. His work did help establish the Corps. If he'd done it for noble reasons, for the patients, for his profession, he wouldn't mind if he weren't included.

But he minded. He minded deeply. Because he'd done it for himself.

He groaned. His goal started well, got tangled up with pride, and swallowed him with disabling and alienating bitterness.

A stab of pain, and he clenched the handkerchief. Why? Why had he pursued his goal so doggedly? So others would respect him, look up to him, treat him like he was worthy? Did it even matter what others thought of him? Or only what God thought?

And what did God think of Technical Sergeant John Hutchinson?

Hutch's eyes slipped shut. The Lord loved him as a sergeant. The Lord would still love him if he were a private or if he were the commanding general of the entire Allied Armed Forces. God's love didn't depend on rank, or how hard a man worked, or whether a man succeeded.

God loved him for the sole reason that Hutch was his child.

With his elbows on his knees, Hutch rested his forehead in his hands, and the handkerchief dangled before him in the growing darkness.

Since the North Star shone above Ursa Major, the bear had to raise his heavy head to see it. Hadn't Hutch once told Georgie to focus on the Lord and not to waver?

"Lord, I've been a fool. I made my goal my guiding star instead of you. I lost all light in my life because I took my eyes off your Light. Please forgive me."

He clutched the handkerchief from the woman he loved, who had once loved him. He'd lost her. The Army wasn't to blame, only him.

"Lord, help me. Help me accept my lot in life and find contentment. I'm alone. No one respects me. I have nothing — except you. And you — you're all I need. I remember."

He opened his eyes. One by one the stars blinked on, and a verse came to mind: "Whatsoever ye do, do it heartily, as to the Lord, and not unto men."

Hutch sat up straighter. Something remained in his life after all.

48

The Mediterranean
March 23, 1944

Georgie lay on the floor of the raft while the two litters rested across the top of the raft on either side of her. How could she sleep in a damp uniform in the chill night air with a full bladder, knowing the only thing that separated her from the ocean depths was a piece of rubberized canvas? Knowing her friends would be terrified for her when the flight didn't arrive in Palermo? Knowing her family might receive a telegram in the next few days?

But why worry? Worry accomplished nothing but robbing her of sleep.

She rolled over and sighed.

"Can't sleep?" Lt. Peter Cameron peeked over the side of his litter.

"Afraid not." She spoke in a low voice.

"I hate to be a bother, but the pain's coming back."

Georgie pushed herself to sitting. Six weeks earlier, the poor man had been injured by a shell at Anzio, causing severe abdominal and chest wounds. He'd come through multiple surgeries and had a good prognosis — if he survived the ordeal at sea. "Would you like something for the pain?"

"Yes, please. I don't want to waste the MS — save it for the others. I can take p.o. now. Do you have codeine?"

She blinked at his dark figure. "MS? P.o.?"

He chuckled. "Yes, I know the secret code. I'm a pharmacist."

Georgie's heart leaped, then settled back to its sad and painful place. "Did you — you didn't serve in a hospital then."

"No. Took a commission in the artillery. I wanted to be an officer, and in the Army the rating of pharmacist is enlisted."

"I know." Ignoring her heavy heart, she found the flashlight and rummaged through her musette bag for the bottle of codeine. "You made the right decision."

"I thought so until my gun emplacement took a hit from one of those Nazi railroad guns."

She shuddered. Word of giant German artillery guns pointed at the trapped souls at Anzio had spread throughout Italy. "I still think you chose right. I know . . . someone.

A pharmacist. He chose to serve as an enlisted man. He wanted to join the Pharmacy Corps."

"Yeah? I took the exam with a fellow . . . what was his name?"

Her chest tightened. "John Hutchinson?"

"Yeah, that's him. Funny we know the same guy. Too bad though."

"Too bad?" Terror seized her. Had he been hurt at Anzio? Killed? "What do you mean?"

"We didn't get into the Corps. Our exams arrived after they'd already knighted the chosen twelve."

Georgie gripped the bottle of codeine. "Oh no. Poor Hutch. He — he really wanted that."

"I could tell."

He wanted it a bit too much. Georgie frowned, screwed off the lid, and handed a tablet to Lieutenant Cameron. "Do you want some water to wash it down?"

"No, I'm fine. We'd best save the water."

"True." She didn't want to think about what would happen if Air-Sea Rescue failed to find them.

She also didn't want to think about Hutch. How did he handle the news about the Corps?

The old longing to reach out to him returned. If only she could listen and hold him and comfort him.

But that wouldn't help. She couldn't kiss away his bitterness any more than he could kiss away her fears. They each had to turn to God alone.

Georgie curled up with her head resting on the side of the raft, and she closed her eyes. Her friends couldn't get her through this ordeal. Neither could her family or the love of a good man. Only the Lord.

Nettuno

Last night's humbling brought Hutch his best sleep in months. If today's humbling went as well, he hoped to wean himself off sodium bicarbonate in the near future.

In the early morning light, he pushed back the tent flap and hopped down two feet into Pharmacy. They'd been able to dig a bit deeper. Ralph was still there, thank goodness, waiting for Hutch and Dom to relieve him.

"Good morning." Hutch joined Ralph at the back counter. "How was the night shift?"

"Fine." Short and stiff.

Hutch missed the old joking and camaraderie, and it was his fault. From the crates that formed the front counter, Hutch removed two empty ones and set them upside down.

Dom entered the pharmacy.

"Good. You're both here." He pointed to the crates. "Please sit down. I have something to say."

Dom and Ralph exchanged a look, then sat. Ralph sighed. "What did we do now?"

"Nothing." Guilt made him wince. "Look, I know I've been difficult to be around lately."

Another look between the techs said he'd been very difficult.

Hutch sank his hands into his pockets and took a deep breath. "I apologize. I treated you with the same disrespect I hated, and I'm sorry."

Ralph arched one red eyebrow. "All right . . ."

They needed more. Of course they did. He tapped his foot on the ground. "Goals are good, but I let my goal take over my life. I became so . . . obsessed with getting respect that I forgot to treat others with respect."

"I'll say," Ralph muttered.

"I'm sorry." He stared at his tapping toe, forced it to be still, then glanced up at his techs. "All work done well is good work. And you guys are the best. You're smart and hardworking. You deserve my respect and you have it, even if I've failed to show it.

That'll change from now on."

"Okay." Dom raised his chin and narrowed his eyes at Hutch as if checking for sincerity.

"Even if the Army doesn't agree, my work has value, and your work has even more value." Hutch pointed his thumb to his chest. "Because you've had to put up with me."

Ralph cracked a smile. "They ought to give us medals."

Hutch laughed, as rusty as an old bike chain. Had he laughed, even once, since he and Georgie broke up?

"All right, Ralph, get out of here. Catch some sack time." Hutch motioned him to the door then went to the back counter. "Let's get to work, Dom."

As he launched into the morning routine, Georgie's sweet face remained in his mind. She'd played an important role in his life, even if it was shorter than the lifetime he'd hoped for.

Georgie would be pleased with his change of heart. Should he write and tell her? What if she thought he was trying to manipulate her affections? Trying to earn back her love?

No, he'd lost that forever, and deservedly so.

■ ■ ■ ■

The Mediterranean

Georgie's bladder woke her up. Around the circle of rafts, soft voices indicated the men were stirring.

While trying to sleep, she'd thought up the most ladylike solution to her predicament. After she took off her shoes, socks, and jacket, she sat on the side of the raft, held onto a handle, and lowered herself into the ocean on the outside of the circle. Her eyes slipped shut in blessed relief, but her cheeks warmed. What would Mama say?

Nonsense. If Mama were stranded at sea with fifteen men, she would do the same thing.

The only part she hadn't thought out well was getting back into the raft. That took some effort. Finally she swung one sodden leg over the edge and hauled herself, panting, inside.

Now she had to sit shivering in sopping wet trousers, but the sun would eventually dry her off.

Georgie took her bearings. She couldn't see land in any direction, but Vesuvius still glowed to the north.

"Listen up, boys. Here's the story." Roger

Cooper pointed to the radioman's raft. "Pettas is transmitting our coordinates over and over. Air-Sea Rescue should be here before long."

"Thank goodness," Georgie said, and the men erupted in cheers.

Roger held up his hands. "Don't get too excited. I don't know when. In the meantime, we'll follow standard procedures. The crew will pass out your morning food and water ration, and we'll maneuver the rafts so Lieutenant Taylor and Sergeant Ramirez can take care of you. After that, we'll rig shelters so the sun won't spoil your creamy complexions."

Georgie decided the best cure for anxiety was a combination of prayer, keeping busy, and being cheerful for others. As the sun rose, the circle of rafts warped into a variety of shapes so she could administer medications, take vital signs, check casts, and change bandages. Her cheer seemed to alleviate the men's anxiety too, and she didn't touch her supply of phenobarbital.

By nine in the morning, her flight manifest looked as full and neat as if they'd made a routine flight. All patients cared for, assessed, medicated, and at ease.

"Do you hear that?" Private Stowe pointed to the north. "Sounds like a plane."

Georgie strained to listen over the men's chatter. Perhaps it was true that blind people had better hearing.

"Hey, you hear something?" another patient called. "Shut up, you numbskulls, so we can listen."

The men quieted, but all Georgie could hear was the lick of waves against the raft and her own pulse, oscillating between joy that they would be rescued and fear that the enemy had found them.

The Luftwaffe rarely ventured this far south, but what if today was the exception? The rafts wouldn't stand up to bullets, and the sicker patients wouldn't survive long in the water.

A deep breath and a quick prayer, and Georgie sat tall again. After all she'd been through, it'd be ridiculous to fall apart now.

"I see it!" Shelby pointed north.

Georgie squinted and made out a long dark silhouette. She'd studied aircraft recognition at Bowman Field, but all the lessons about wing structure and tail configuration ran into a blur.

She bit her lip. A fairly large two-engine plane similar to the C-47, but not exactly like it.

The men engaged in a spirited discussion about the identity, the worst being a German Junkers bomber, the best a British Vickers-Armstrongs Warwick Air-Sea Rescue plane.

The plane headed straight to their position.

"Please, Lord," Georgie whispered. "Let it be ours."

Roger Cooper whooped and waved his flight jacket over his head. "It's a Warwick ASR. God bless the RAF."

Sure enough, Georgie spotted the red, white, and blue RAF roundel, and she cheered along with the men.

The Warwick waggled its wings at the survivors and entered a circular flight pattern over their position. It would stay there until the British rescue boats arrived.

Georgie laughed and cheered until tears ran down her face. All her patients would survive. With God's help, she'd gotten herself and ten patients through the worst crisis she could have imagined.

She grinned and hugged herself. Silly baby Georgie no longer existed.

49

Nettuno
March 29, 1944

Why had he never used the telescope before? Despite the spill onto the sand, the adjustments were smooth and the magnification clear. Orion stood high over Anzio Bay, his arm cocked, his bow bent, his belt in place, the hunter ready to fell his prey.

"Aim at the Luftwaffe, why don't you?" Hutch smiled, pleased to be able to joke again.

Orion wanted to fight, but Hutch found peace in surrender. Now that he'd resigned himself to his situation, even embraced it, a sense of purpose and satisfaction energized him.

He was an enlisted man, but so were the vast majority of servicemen. He had to deal with a supervising officer who knew nothing of his job, but Kaz deserved respect as a human being, and Hutch gave it to him.

Respect was a man's lifeblood, and Hutch had no right to deprive anyone of it, even if deprived himself. His peace and his determination to give respect, combined with a bland peptic ulcer diet, had almost completely eliminated sodium bicarbonate from his life.

A cool dark night on the beach, at least an hour before the moonrise, and a first-rate telescope. All he needed was someone to enjoy it with.

His chest felt heavy, but he shook it off. Yes, he would be alone for the rest of the war, and after the war, it'd take a long time to find a woman as good for him as Georgie had been.

Even if he didn't find the right woman, he'd take care of Lucia. He'd knock himself out finding a couple to adopt her. Maybe his sister Mary and her husband, or his parents, or Bergie and Lillian. He wouldn't mind being Uncle Ucce if Lucia had a good home.

He peered through the eyepiece at the Great Orion Nebula at the tip of the hunter's dagger. It turned off as if someone had flipped a giant light switch.

Hutch frowned. That wasn't normal star twinkling. It lasted longer, as if something had passed in front.

Like a plane. Like a Luftwaffe bomber.

The faintest throbbing sounded to the northwest, too soft to be heard over hospital noises. Why hadn't the general alarm blasted its warning?

He'd come back for the telescope later. "Red alert! Air raid!"

Hutch sprinted up the beach, shouting at full voice, onto the hospital complex. "Air raid! Red alert!"

An officer lifted a whistle and blew it three times. The alarm was picked up, carried by whistles throughout the hospital, and within seconds the air raid siren blared on the loudspeaker at the 56th Evac next door.

Overhead, the planes circled and fired flares, lighting up the sky. White circles and red crosses glowed from the roof of each tent.

A whistle rose from above.

"Dirty rats! This is a hospital!" Hutch resisted the urge to fling himself next to the sandbags lining a ward tent, and he jumped down inside. The nurses and medics were moving patients' litters under the cots for protection, and Hutch pitched in.

A blast hurt his eardrums, and the concussion wave slammed him in the chest and sent him staggering back. Screams and shouts a short distance away. The 93rd had been hit.

Hutch recovered his footing, shook his ears clear, and shoved a few more patients to relative safety.

Another whistle, keener, closer.

A nurse yelled — Lillian — and fell over a patient on his cot to protect him.

Hutch threw himself over Lillian.

The blast kicked them so hard the cot collapsed. Jabbing, burning. His entire back. He cried out.

Screams all around him. He had to help. He'd only taken some shrapnel.

The lightbulbs winked out, and the only illumination came from fires outside, sending orange-yellow light through gaping holes in the tent.

Hutch lurched to his feet and held out his hand for Lillian. "Are you all right?"

"Yes. Thank you. Hutch, is that you?" She peered at him, then wheeled to her patient — shaken but unharmed.

Others hadn't fared as well. A medic pulled a blanket over one patient, and three men cried out in agony — two medics and a patient.

Hutch's breath raced. He stepped forward to help.

Another blast — from the ground outside — shot out blue-white chunks.

He crouched low, shielded a patient. Blazing metal flew into the tent, onto the cots, burned holes in the tent.

A patient shrieked and tried to kick off his flaming blanket. Hutch pitched off the blanket and crumpled it up to smother the fire.

"Incendiaries!" a man shouted and called the Germans several choice names. "They're using fragmentation incendiary bombs. On a hospital."

More choice names erupted, even from the nurses. Hutch shared their opinion if not their vocabulary. This broke all laws of warfare and decency.

Men wrestled back the burning canvas. Hutch hefted up a sandbag, slashed open by shrapnel, and poured sand on glowing chunks of magnesium. Only smothering put out magnesium fires.

His back protested each movement, warm and wet, with dozens of prickling pains, but his wounds could wait.

The fires were out, but the next tent over was ablaze. Hutch ran over and slung streams of sand at the flames. Others aimed fire extinguishers or pumped water from a water tanker.

When the sandbag was empty, Hutch grabbed another. Leaning, bending, moving his arms — all sent pain skittering over his back, but he worked despite the pain, through the pain.

They killed the flames. Canvas hung from the poles in charred shrouds, and voices rang from inside — shouts, cries, orders.

Hutch charged inside. Doctors and nurses and medics worked frantically among the wounded. He touched the arm of the closest physician. "Can I help, sir?"

It was Bergie, his eyes stark white in a face smudged by soot.

The men stared at each other. They hadn't spoken since landing at Anzio.

"Sir," Hutch repeated. "What can I do?"

Bergie blinked. "We need help. We've got to get these men to pre-op and stat."

"I can do that." He spun around, recognizing men from laundry, mess, lab. "You guys! Are you fit to carry litters? They need help."

The men sprang to action. Hutch and the lab tech grabbed a litter.

"Follow me." Bergie led the way. "I'll be needed in surgery."

"Come on, men." Hutch kept up with Bergie's brisk pace, although the strain of carrying the litter sent warm trickles down his back.

At pre-op, they laid the wounded inside the tent, also marred by scorched holes.

Bergie sent them back to the ward tent. "Captain Sobel will tell you which patients to bring."

Hutch and his crew made two more runs. He breathed hard. Sweat ran down his neck and stung the wounds on his back. But he kept moving, fueled by adrenaline and the knowledge that he was doing great good.

When the last patients had been delivered, Bergie met them in pre-op. He shook hands with the litter-bearers, ending with Hutch, a penetrating look in his eyes. "Thanks."

"You're welcome, sir."

"I'm not needed in surgery. We have more doctors than wounded. And we have about three dozen wounded. One more if we count you."

"It's nothing." Hutch shrugged and regretted it when fresh hot pain rippled down his shoulder blades.

"Stop being pigheaded. Your jacket's shredded, and you're a bloody mess."

Hutch ventured a smile. "You already knew that."

Bergie studied him then marched out of the tent. "Come with me."

"Yes, sir." Now he had an opportunity to make amends.

The physician led him into Receiving, deserted and relatively undamaged, and he lit a lantern. The 94th Evac had opened at Anzio earlier that day and had taken all new admissions — ironically to lighten the load at the 93rd so the engineers could dig them in deeper and protect them from air raids. A bit late.

Bergie motioned to a cot. "Sit down. Take off your jacket and shirt." He opened a medical chest and gathered supplies on a tray. "How'd it happen? A bomb hit near your tent?"

"Nope." Hutch took off his jacket, gritting his teeth. "I was stargazing at the beach, saw the planes come in. I ran back and raised the alarm."

Bergie faced him. "I heard someone shouting. That was you?"

"Yeah." He unbuttoned his shirt. This would hurt. "Ran into a tent to help. A nurse threw herself over a patient, and I shielded her. That's when I got hit. Better me than her. Your Lillian."

He spun and stared. "My Lillian? Is she okay?"

"She's fine. Hard at work last I saw her."

"Thanks." He waved his hand at Hutch. "You have to take off your shirt. If you don't, I will."

Hutch braced himself and peeled off the shirt, grunting as the fabric separated from his torn flesh. A cry escaped despite his best efforts to stop it.

"Lie down on your side, your back close to the edge." Bergie set up two stools, one for himself, one for his tray, and he pulled on rubber gloves. "Let's see what we have here."

Hutch eased himself down, facing rows of empty cots, the cool air stinging his wounds. "By the way, you were right."

"Yeah? About what?" He tucked a towel under Hutch's right side.

"About my goal becoming an obsession, about how sometimes surrender is better than fighting."

"Mm." Bergie plucked something from Hutch's back, and it tinkled into a basin at his feet. "What prompted this?"

He gripped the edge of the cot. "I didn't get into the Pharmacy Corps."

Hands stilled. "I'm sorry. That meant a lot to you."

"It meant too much. Somewhere along the line, I let pride take over, and it made me bitter." He fought to keep his voice even.

"Stop squirming. Gotta find the shrapnel in this forest of hair."

"I don't have hair on my back."

"That's what you think."

Hutch's grin turned to grimace as pain

sliced into his left side. He bit off a cry.

"Sorry. It was in deep. Got it."

"Thanks." Sweat dribbled over the bridge of his nose, and he blew out a deep breath. "Wish you could have cut out my bitterness. I lost Georgie. I lost your friendship."

Bergie paused in his work. "You didn't lose my friendship. You misplaced it."

"Can you forgive me?"

"Depends. You back to normal?"

"I hope not. Hope I'm somewhere new and better."

"Mm. Good. I'll forgive you if you lie still and stop whining like a girl. I'll get you cleaned up and bandaged, then send you to X-ray to make sure I didn't miss anything. I rarely do."

Thank goodness for the change in subject. This kind of talk hurt almost as much as the wounds.

Bergie cleaned his back with moistened gauze. "You don't need stitches. All surface wounds. It'll hurt like the dickens but won't get you out of work."

"G-good." Hutch shivered from spasms of cold and pain.

"Baby."

"Butcher."

He laughed. "Careful. I'm the one with the scalpel."

The tent flap swished open, and footsteps thumped down the aisle.

"Hiya, Chad. You hurt?"

"Just a small burn. Got hit by magnesium from the incendiaries. You can't stop the burning from that. I pulled it out though, so the damage is minimal."

Hutch steeled himself. Capt. Al Chadwick would test his resolve to show genuine respect when shown none in return.

Chadwick sat on the cot in front of Hutch and rolled up his left sleeve.

"I'll take care of that as soon as I finish here." Bergie dabbed at the wounds.

"Good evening, sir," Hutch said.

Chadwick acknowledged him with a brief glance. "No need, Berg. I can handle it."

"Let me know if you need a hand." Bergie pressed Hutch's shoulder. "Onto your stomach so I can apply sulfanilamide powder."

Hutch rolled over and rested his head on his forearms, facing away from Chadwick.

"Injured in the back, was he?" Chadwick snorted. "Running away. Should have known."

Though Hutch tensed, he didn't take the bait.

"Actually . . ." Bergie drew out the word in a strained tone. "He ran *to* the hospital.

538

He's the one who raised the alarm. He was injured protecting Lillian. He saved her life."

Another snort, some rummaging through supplies. "That's revolutionary — a druggist saving lives for once."

Bergie's hand tightened on Hutch's shoulder. Hutch raised one hand to silence him and turned to face his nemesis. Something ran deeper here than mere professional rivalry.

Even if he got in trouble for insubordination, he had to speak. "Excuse me, sir. That's the second time you've made a comment about druggists and saving lives. May I ask what you have against my profession?"

"Your *profession*?" He smeared petrolatum over an angry red mark on his forearm. "Your profession is nothing but snake-oil salesmen masquerading in white coats."

"Chad —"

"No, Bergie, let him speak." Hutch watched the man's jaw shift from side to side. " 'Snake-oil salesman' is a strong term, sir. Would you care to explain?"

Those gray eyes pierced like shrapnel. "Why not? The truth will bring you down a peg."

The smell of sulfanilamide powder filled his nostrils. "I've been brought down several pegs lately. I can handle it, sir."

Chadwick placed a square of gauze over his wound. "When my little sister was five, she had digestive problems. My father prescribed a mild tonic of nux vomica."

Hutch drew in a sharp breath. "Strychnine."

"Yes." He tore off a piece of tape with his teeth, then secured the gauze pad. "The druggist increased the strength tenfold. Isabella died a horrible and painful death."

Compassion replaced the last trace of animosity. That explained everything. Such tragic loss, such deep pain, such betrayal often failed to submit to reason or forgiveness.

"I'm sorry, sir. For your sister, for you, for your whole family. I can see why you don't trust pharmacists."

"I understand too, buddy. I do." Bergie applied bandages to Hutch's back. "But isn't that like little Lucia hating all IV fluids because her brother received some before he died? Isn't that like the patient back in Sicily who said all physicians were quacks because a surgeon mistakenly amputated his dad's good leg back in World War I? The poor man was left with no legs."

"That's not the same." Chad tore off another length of tape.

"Sure it is. All professions have good and

bad apples, you know that. Even the best physician — the best pharmacist — can make a mistake. Judge each man on his own merits." Bergie thumped Hutch in the arm. "Sit up now, but slowly. Don't want to pop off the bandages. I'll walk you over to X-ray, where they'll praise my stupendous surgical skills once again."

He eased himself up to sitting and met Chadwick's eye. "Thank you for telling me, sir."

The physician's eyes glazed, and he gave a brisk nod.

Hutch pushed himself to standing. His vision darkened, and he wobbled. "What'd you do, Captain Bergstrom? Carve your initials into my back?"

Bergie took his arm and guided him out of the tent. "My initials? I carved my entire given name."

Hutch laughed and paused, lightheaded. Sweat tickled his upper lip. "I'm glad our friendship is no longer misplaced."

"Me too, buddy. Me too."

50

Marina Piccola, Capri, Italy
April 5, 1944

Georgie picked her way along the rocks on the shore in her new leather sandals, and a cool wind ruffled her pink sundress.

A dozen shades of blue and green shimmered in the water, and to her left, the Faraglioni, three large rocks, jutted out of the ocean.

A week's R & R on the island of Capri served as her reward for the ditching incident. But what kind of reward was solitude? A party — that would have been a reward.

With a huge, multilayered decision to make, she missed her friends, not so they could decide for her, but so she could discuss her options with someone — aloud.

She passed three soldiers lounging on the rocks, and she angled her straw hat as a shield. Plenty of men begged for her company this week, but she didn't want that kind of company. Even the handful of nurses she'd met wouldn't do. She needed someone who knew her well.

Behind her, the Via Krupp wound down steep limestone cliffs in stacks of hairpin turns, braced by stone walls overflowing with bougainvillea. Whitewashed homes with red tile roofs dotted the green hillsides, unmarred by war. A carriage had brought her down from her luxurious hotel in the town of Capri to the Marina Piccola, led by charming horses with plumes on their head-dresses.

She'd seriously considered discussing her decision with the horses.

Georgie stood on a spit of land poking into the bay and tugged her cardigan tighter around her waist. "Lord, it's you and me."

If she could survive a ditching, she could make the decision the ditching sparked. The Army smelled publicity, and they wanted to send her on a one-month bond tour. A cute, plucky nurse who had saved ten lives at sea could sell tons of war bonds and bring attention to the flight nursing program. After that, they'd give her a nursing position at Walter Reed Medical Center in Washington DC with full weekend leaves to visit home.

A year ago, her decision would have been easy, but not now.

She pulled a notepad and pencil from the pocket of her dress and perched on a rock, far enough away from the water to keep her toes dry from chilly waves. This choice called for Hutch-like rationality.

She drew a T-shaped chart on the paper and labeled one column "Virginia" and the other "MTO" for Mediterranean Theater of Operations. Her decision had multiple layers, so she marked four rows — comfort, professional, people, and spiritual.

For comfort, Virginia won — no air raids, no strange diseases, soft beds, and good food. The MTO side was empty. That felt wrong, and she knew why. "I don't care about comfort." She wrote it down.

The professional aspect was a wash. Either way she'd use her talents and skills to care for the sick and wounded. Either way she'd aid the war effort.

People. She nibbled on her pencil. Her family wanted her. Freddie's need for bed rest stretched the family thin as they cared for Freddie's children and grocery while running their own homes and farms. Georgie would only be home for the weekends, but every bit would help.

And Ward. At regular intervals, his letters declared his undying love, his wish to marry her at the time of her choosing, and his willingness to fulfill her every wish. She could do worse than to marry a good man who adored her.

As for people, who would keep her in the MTO? She wrote down the names of her friends, but they didn't truly need her. Once-shy Mellie had plenty of good friends. Kay hadn't opened up, and if she ever did, it would be to Mellie, not Georgie. The other ladies had lots of friends. They would do fine without her.

What about Hutch? She slowly wrote his name, remembering his warm eyes, his passionate kisses, his gentle humor, his wise advice. Love alone wouldn't bring him back into her life. With a deep sigh, she drew a line through his name. No, she wouldn't let that lingering dream sway her decision.

"Spiritual." She jabbed her pencil in the next box, tearing her thoughts from the man she shouldn't still love.

Her smile rose. This was where the MTO won. "Challenges me," she wrote. "I'll continue to grow." But in all honesty, she had to write in the Virginia column, "I proved myself."

The ditching incident showed how much she had grown. She'd overcome her fears and been strong and capable in a life-threatening crisis. More importantly, the change felt permanent. Back in Virginia, she wouldn't revert to the pampered baby role, no matter how hard her family tried to make her. And they'd try.

Georgie held the notepad at arm's length, and the page fluttered in the wind. The Virginia column was longer and more convincing. Maybe she was done in Italy, her lessons learned, her job finished, free to go home and seize her lifelong dreams.

If so, why did she feel a strong urge to pad the MTO column?

Georgie tapped her pencil against her chin. "Are you thinking what I'm thinking, Lord?"

Deep down inside, she wanted the MTO side to win. Because she wanted to stay. Because she needed to stay. Her work here was not done.

Naples, Italy
April 8, 1944
The strains of "Star Eyes" floated out onto the circular terrace of the Orange Club overlooking the Bay of Naples, and Georgie blinked rapidly. If she and Hutch were still together, that song would have been perfect for them.

Instead she tried to concentrate on Lt. Larry White's dissertation on how many crates of rations his battalion had unloaded today. Never again would she let Kay Jobson set her up.

Kay insisted Georgie couldn't be the seventh wheel. Mellie danced with Tom, Louise Cox laughed with Tom's friend Rudy Scaglione, and Kay was fending off the advances of Lt. Hal Heathcock, who served with Larry White in Quartermasters.

The entire 64th Troop Carrier Group had left the MTO for India on April 2, taking half of Kay's flyboy boyfriends. The Quartermasters fellows filled the gap.

"A 45 percent increase over last month. But we're keeping up." Larry folded his napkin with long tapered fingers.

"That's wonderful." Georgie nestled her chin in her hand and tried to focus on his gray-blue eyes. A good-looking man, but not for her. Her gaze drifted over his shoulder to Vesuvius, dark and solid in the twilight across the bay, and still sending up plumes of smoke, but no longer menacing.

"That new penicillin. That gives us headaches." Larry pressed his hand to his temple. "It has to be refrigerated. You can imagine the challenges."

Georgie's smile faltered. "I can imagine." Why all the reminders of Hutch? She was trying to celebrate. Her flight of six nurses had all decided to stay with the 802nd.

"Star Eyes" ended, and Tom and Mellie breezed onto the terrace, flushed from dancing.

Tom held out Mellie's chair for her, then sat beside her. "Have I ever told all of you why I love bridges?"

Mellie smiled but raised one eyebrow. "Okay . . . ?"

"You know why, Mellie." He tucked her hand in his on top of the table. "But do your friends?"

An odd topic of conversation. Georgie gave Mellie a faint smile. "You said Tom wants to build bridges all over the world."

"I do." His blue eyes lit up. "Bridges connect people, and the best bridges are also works of art that inspire the soul."

"True." Georgie glanced around the table at the polite smiles.

Mellie patted his hand. "Are we to be blessed with a lecture on the differences between suspension and cantilever bridges?"

Tom laughed. "Not today. Unless you want one."

"That's all right." Kay shrugged Hal's arm off her shoulders. "Though I'm sure it'd be fascinating."

It would definitely be more fascinating than Larry White's inventory of supplies.

Georgie smoothed her uniform skirt.

Tom gathered Mellie's other hand into his grip. "I met you through a thin paper bridge of letters. That bridge grew stronger when we met in person, and our love made it into a work of art that inspires my soul."

Mellie's eyelashes fluttered, and she lowered her chin. "You're embarrassing me."

"I'm not done yet."

Georgie's heart squeezed. Thomas MacGilliver Jr. wasn't talking about bridges. She had a hunch she was about to observe one of the most important events in Mellie Blake's life.

"One more thing I like about bridges." Tom's voice thickened. "Their permanence."

Louise let out a soft gasp.

Tom got out of his chair and went down on one knee.

"Oh, Tom." Mellie wouldn't raise her chin, and tears glistened on her cheeks.

Georgie's eyes filled with joy for her friend and bittersweet wistfulness for her own happy ending.

"Look at me, sweetheart." Tom nudged up Mellie's chin.

"I — I need a handkerchief."

Kay laughed and handed her one. "Stop blubbering. This is the happiest moment of your life."

"I kno-o-ow." Mellie dabbed at her eyes, sniffled, and looked into Tom's beaming face.

"The love between us is strong," Tom said. "It's been tested. It's proven solid. Would you do me the honor of making our love officially permanent? Would you please be my wife?"

"Oh, Tom." She leaned forward in her chair, threw her arms around his neck, and burrowed her face into his shoulder. "Yes. Oh, Tom, yes, yes, yes."

"Thank you." He closed his eyes, almost as if in pain, and held her tight.

Georgie's heart squeezed again, this time out of guilt, out of compassion for him. When Mellie found out Tom's identity, Georgie had urged her to let him go so she wouldn't be burdened with an infamous name for life. Tom probably thought no one would ever take on his name, and now sweet Mellie would wear it gladly and proudly. That was love.

"I have a ring." Tom's voice came out scratchy. "You want it?"

Mellie let out a shaky laugh and pulled back. "Do I want it?"

"Well, do you?"

Everyone around the table laughed. Tom

took a little box from his trouser pocket and slipped a ring on Mellie's finger.

Georgie stood with the others. She hugged the engaged couple, admired Mellie's ring, and pressed her handkerchief into Mellie's hand, since Kay's hankie was no longer dry.

Hal and Larry stood to the side, talking to each other, and Kay stood alone by the edge of the terrace. Georgie joined her. "So, who's next, do you think? You and Hal?"

"Oh, please." Kay shuddered. "He won't get one more date out of me. All hands."

"Well, it won't be me and Larry. The man's as interesting as an Army manual."

"Sorry. Thought you liked them quiet and dry."

Because of Hutch. "Quiet isn't always dull."

Kay swept her hair off her shoulder. "I suppose not. Appearances can be deceiving." A breathy tone hinted at sadness.

Georgie stared at the redhead. What was going on? Gingerly, she threaded her arm through Kay's. "Do you miss the flyboys?"

"India," Kay whispered, her gaze fixed over the moon-dappled ocean. "Can't believe he's gone."

He? Only one? Who had broken through? "Grant?"

"Grant?" Kay made a face. "I broke up

with him weeks ago. Getting too serious."

"Then who — ?"

"No one." She gave Georgie a firm hard look. "No one at all."

That was a whopper of a lie, but Kay Jobson certainly wouldn't tell the truth tonight. Georgie raised a soft smile. "I won't pry. But I'll pray for him and for you."

"There is no him." Her chin high, she turned away, letting Georgie's hand fall. Then she turned back. "But thanks for the prayers."

Somewhere, down on the terrace floor, lay Georgie's lower jaw. She closed her mouth. Well, well, well. What was happening with Miss Kay?

A full moon illuminated the beauty of Naples Bay and the deeper beauty of her friends on the terrace. Oh yes. She had definitely made the right decision to stay in Italy.

51

Nettuno
April 14, 1944

Hutch's gaze circled the six other men from pharmacy and lab sitting on crates and camp stools. "You heard the order. We leave the day after tomorrow, and the 11th Evac will take our place."

"Eighty-three days at Anzio is enough," Dom said.

"But who's counting?" Ralph grinned, his fair face yellow from Atabrine. The forces at Anzio had started the antimalarial med two weeks earlier.

Hutch glanced around the tent, finally dug in six feet deep and reinforced with boarding and sandbags by the engineers. "Our equipment stays here, and we'll take theirs in Casanova back on the Cassino front."

Dom nudged Ralph. "Casanova — great place for lovers."

"Guess we'll have to leave you here."

Hutch laughed and held up his hands. "Okay, men. I called you together for a reason. As you know, Kaz's organization is . . . different."

"It's stupid," one of the lab techs muttered.

"I'd like to switch it back for the fellows in the 11th," Hutch said. "They'll have a hard enough time adjusting to air raids and artillery. They need to be up and running immediately."

Ralph leaned forward on his knees. "On the other hand, if we leave it as is, the men from the 11th will raise a stink. Kaz will get in trouble."

Hutch gripped his hands together. "That's the other reason I'd like to switch it back. Kaz acted in good faith that he was helping us. He shouldn't get in trouble."

"But —"

"But he deserves our respect as a man and as our supervising officer. I'd like to protect his reputation." Hutch glanced behind him toward the door. "Now, he's under the weather today, so he won't know what we did."

Ralph grumbled. "Too bad we'll have to waste time in Casanova setting up Kaz's way again."

"I don't think so." Hutch patted his hands

554

on his knees. "That's the second part of my proposition. I want to run it past all of you. We'll decide together."

"What do you have in mind?" Sergeant Paskun, the lead lab tech, said.

"Simple. We're taking over the 11th Evac's tents and equipment and supplies. In a sense, we're borrowing from them. We tell Kaz we don't feel comfortable changing the organization of another hospital. It's like visiting someone's house and rearranging the furniture. We wouldn't want to be rude, would we?"

Dom's eyes lit up. "That might work."

Murmurs of agreement swept the circle.

A sense of accomplishment warmed Hutch's chest. "If we're united and make a big enough fuss, I think we'll prevail. If not, I vote we go en masse to Colonel Currier and state our case. I'd rather not involve him, but —"

"I agree," Paskun said.

"Me too." Ralph thumped his fist into his open palm. "Let's do it. Who's with Hutch?"

All six hands shot up, and Hutch smiled. If this worked — and he'd prayed plenty about it — then they could practice as they'd been trained, in a safer and more efficient environment. And they could do so while treating Kaz with respect and kindness.

"Okay." He clapped his hands. "Let's put this place back to rights."

Casanova, Italy
April 16, 1944

Hutch dropped his gear beside his new cot and stretched up to his full height. Felt good to stand straight for once. His back prickled, and he scratched the network of scabs that itched like crazy. Thank goodness Bergie wasn't there to tell him to stop scratching.

He headed out to search for the pharmacy and laboratory tent. The 11th Evac had a slightly different layout from the 93rd.

Rolling green hills surrounded the hospital under a partly cloudy sky. No rumbling artillery, no roaring aircraft, no crashing waves. Would his ears ever adjust?

He'd adjust quickly to not wearing his helmet. His garrison cap felt flimsy, the warm air ruffled his hair, and his head floated light and unburdened.

So many burdens lifted. The name Casanova needed one extra letter — if it were Casa nuova, it'd mean "new house," a new start.

As he walked, he read Dad's letter again. The Pharmacy Corps had opened six more positions. To reapply, Hutch needed to fill out the short form Dad enclosed. Dad said with Hutch's high test score and excellent application, he'd get the commission. Within a month he'd be stateside.

In the Bible, when the herdsmen of Gerar fought with Isaac, the patriarch gave up his first well. They fought again, and Isaac surrendered his second well. But when the third well gushed forth and he prospered, the herdsmen realized God was on Isaac's side and begged for a treaty with him. Isaac finally kept a well.

This second chance at the Corps could be Isaac's last well, Hutch's reward for seeing the light, learning his lessons, and surrendering.

Hutch unfolded the application form, read it through, and ripped it in half.

Dad wouldn't be pleased, but this was for the best. Hutch needed to find contentment outside of recognition. He had peace, a renewed passion for his job, and satisfaction in it.

He'd joined the Army to provide excellent patient care, and that's what he did at the 93rd. Doing an important job well was plenty for him.

Hutch ducked into the pharmacy tent and almost stumbled. Level earth. No drop into dugout conditions.

Lieutenant Kazokov stood in front of the counter, studying the shelves, hands on hips.

Hutch tensed. Time to implement his plan, with full respect.

Kaz turned. "Ah, Sergeant. There you are."

"Good day, Lieutenant." Hutch gave him a genuine smile. The man really did try hard, had the best motivation. "I'm glad to see you're feeling better."

"Thank you. One more bout of dysentery might do me in." He frowned at the shelves and ran his hand along a line of bottles, neat and orderly.

"I've been thinking, sir —"

Kaz held up one hand. "No, I've been thinking. You fellows gave it a try. You went along with my modernization. But I'm a man of careful analysis, and I don't see that the reorganization increased efficiency. That was the purpose in the first place."

"I know you had the department's best interest in mind, sir."

Kaz turned his small, dark eyes to Hutch. He was more than a caricature. He was a good man who wanted to make a difference.

Hutch smiled at him. "Where would our country be without innovators, men willing to take a chance and make changes?"

The lieutenant set his hand on the counter by the scales. "Did you know when Thomas Edison invented the lightbulb, he tested three thousand filaments before finding one that worked?"

"Yes, sir."

"If Edison can admit failure, so can I." He thumped the counter and faced Hutch. "I trust you and Paskun to come up with the best organization for your departments."

Hutch couldn't contain his smile. "Thank you, sir. I appreciate the vote of confidence."

"It's earned." He headed for lab. "I'll go tell Paskun."

What was better — the unexpected respect or the pharmacy setup, the blessed setup? Bulk items on the bottom shelves, topicals grouped with topicals, injectables with injectables, orals with orals.

First thing, an inventory. Hutch sifted through the paperwork and found a WDMD Form 16a to order Class 1 Medical Items. He pulled the first bottle off the shelf, acetone, about half full. Fine. Acetic acid, glacial, almost out. Better order some.

Bergie jogged into the tent, cheeks flushed. "Hiya, Hutchie. Stop scratching."

"I'm not . . ." He was. He forced his hand back to the task.

"How's pharmacy?"

"Great." Acetylsalicylic acid, bulk powder, order one more pound. "Got a fresh, organized start and permission to keep it this way."

"Good." Bergie leaned his elbows on the makeshift counter. "Say, did you decide?"

"I told you last night I'd stay here. It's final. Ripped up the application. I wrote to Dad last night, and I'll mail it as soon as the PX is open."

"Are you sure it's the right decision?" Concern lowered his voice.

Hutch hefted the bottle of aspirin tablets. "Absolutely certain. This is where God wants me for many reasons."

"You also said you were going to write a letter to Georgie. Did you?"

"Yep." That was harder than the letter to Dad. He had to express his gratitude without sounding romantic, pathetic, or manipulative.

"Why don't you just hand it to her?"

Hutch spun to face him. "What?"

Bergie wore a small, satisfied smile. "She's in Receiving. She and Captain Maxwell didn't know we switched places with the 11th and that we don't have patients yet."

His heart jumped around untethered in his chest and turned his head toward Receiving.

"She asked about you, real sweet and concerned, and I told her you were better than ever, happy and peaceful. You should have seen the smile on her face."

Hutch wished he could have seen it too.

"I told her to come over and say hi, but she thinks you don't want to see her."

He didn't want to see her. And yet he did, more than anything.

"What are you waiting for? Get over there. They won't stay long since we don't have patients."

Hutch's feet felt as if he'd poured the hospital's entire supply of numbing procaine into his boots. But he had to go. It was part of his humbling.

He had the letter as an excuse. Even better, she'd see his face when he delivered it. She'd see his sincerity and understand he wasn't trying to win her back.

With great effort he popped his knee forward and moved his foot. He patted his chest to make sure he had the letter in his field jacket, gave Bergie a croaky "thanks," and headed out.

He strode down the path to Receiving, dodged men and equipment, and wet his mouth and lips.

What would he say? He hadn't planned to see her, just to mail the letter. But the thought of saying good-bye in a more gentlemanly manner than at Pompeii — that quickened his pace.

Hutch burst into Receiving. Empty, except for four medics rearranging the cots. Where were they? Had they already left?

The other receiving tent. Hutch charged out and into the tent next door. A nurse and a medic rummaged through the medical chest.

His hands splayed out, groping for what he'd lost. "Excuse me, ma'am. Have you seen Captain Maxwell and Lieutenant Taylor from the air evac squadron?"

"Sure." She pointed to the other entrance to the tent, the front entrance. "They left a minute ago."

Oh no. He dashed through the tent. *Please, Lord, let them still be here.*

He shoved aside the tent flap, got it tangled around his arm, and shook himself free. Straight across the main road, a jeep backed out. He'd recognize that curly head anywhere.

Hutch ran to the jeep. "Lieutenant Taylor!"

Georgie whipped around, mouth and eyes wide.

He stopped a few feet from the jeep and saluted Captain Maxwell. "Excuse me,

Captain. Please pardon the interruption. I have something for the lieutenant."

A frown puckered his forehead. "All right, Sergeant. Proceed."

Hutch turned to Georgie, and his entire chest caved in on him. She looked stunned. Pale. Beautiful. With all his heart, all his soul, he still loved her.

Captain Maxwell cleared his throat. "Yes, Sergeant?"

Hutch's gaze flicked to him, then back to Georgie. In that split second, she composed her face into hospitable, polite distance. He'd lost her forever, thrown away her love in exchange for wallowing in bitterness. The stupidest mistake of his life.

But he wanted her to know she'd made the right decision in breaking up with him. "I have a letter for you."

"You do?" The delicious way she turned two syllables into four. How he'd missed it.

"Yeah." He pulled out the letters, made sure he had the right one, and held it out to her.

She reached for it and hesitated, her fingers curling. When he poked the letter closer, she nodded and took it. If only he could have grasped her hand and pulled her up into his arms and held her forever.

But she would have slapped his face and

rightly so.

Hutch stepped back but fixed his warmest gaze on her. "I wanted to thank you. For everything you've done."

Her lips parted. Her eyes had never been bluer.

He pulled himself tall and gave her half a smile and a full salute. "Good-bye, Lieutenant, Captain."

"Good — good-bye." Georgie fumbled through the salute.

"Good day, Sergeant." The captain shifted the jeep into first gear, and the vehicle churned down the road.

Georgie didn't look back, but Hutch held the salute until she disappeared from his sight.

From his life.

52

"What was that about?" Captain Maxwell turned the jeep onto the road south toward Naples.

Georgie fingered the letter and recovered her breath. "That's — Sergeant Hutchinson. He's the pharmacist. He was thanking me. I used to bring him supplies — oranges and things. For compounding medicines."

Maxwell grunted. "He had more than gratitude on his mind. Don't let him get the wrong idea. He's an enlisted man."

"I know that, sir." She turned to watch the scenery and to hide her expression. She hadn't been prepared to see Hutch, for the rush of emotion, the intensity of his eyes, the richness of his voice — it overwhelmed her. How could he communicate so much with a simple gaze? Remorse, peace, and the heartbreaking message that all was over between them.

Was it only the longing of her imagination

or did she sense he still loved her regard-less? If only she'd had more time. If only she could have formed words and questions. If only she could go back.

But she couldn't. They had to return to Pomigliano by nightfall, only thirty miles, but on a rutted road clogged with trucks and jeeps and troops and mules.

What had he written? Her finger slipped under the lip of the envelope, but she yanked the naughty digit back out. She couldn't read this in front of Maxwell. She'd turn into a blubbering idiot, and he'd know the relationship involved more than oranges.

What if Hutch *did* still love her? What did it matter anyway? Love alone wasn't enough.

But what if Bergie was correct? What if Hutch had found contentment? Were the answers in this letter?

She lifted up on one hip and sat on the envelope. Away with temptation.

Maxwell honked the horn at the truck in front of them. Even though the Cassino front had been in a stalemate for three months, activity teemed on the road. The units constantly switched position as if a change in scenery would change the results. The flow of supplies in one direction and sick and wounded in the other never stopped.

The truck rumbled forward and spewed a black cloud of exhaust in Georgie's face.

She coughed and swatted the exhaust away, and Maxwell hit the accelerator.

The jeep lunged forward, then pitched down at a crazy angle.

Georgie yelped and caught herself on the dashboard.

Captain Maxwell cussed and climbed out of the jeep. Georgie climbed out too, grabbing the letter so it wouldn't blow away.

The jeep's left front end rested in a deep pothole. The truck must have straddled it, but in the blindness of the exhaust cloud, the little jeep fell right in.

"Blew the tire." He kicked at the ground.

"Oh dear. Do you need help changing it?"

"Hardly a job for a woman."

"Have it your way." Georgie sauntered over to an olive tree about thirty feet off the road. No need to tell him Daddy had made her change tires since she was twelve. Even in the Taylor family, pampering only went so far.

"Need some help, sir?" Half a dozen soldiers piled out of the truck behind them.

"Yes. Thanks, boys."

While they shoved the vehicle out of the pothole and off the road, Georgie made herself comfortable on a rock under the olive tree.

She drew in a big breath and opened the envelope. His handwriting was so . . . Hutch-like. Square and neat in orderly rows, with a lift to the taller letters that appealed to her for a reason she couldn't place.

Dear Georgie,

I'm sure you're surprised to hear from me, but it's time. After three months of literal and spiritual bombardment, I've made changes in my life, and I want to thank you for the role you played.

Please know this is not an attempt to woo you back. I don't mean to say hello again, but to say good-bye in a better way.

First, let me tell you what's happened lately. A few weeks ago, I found out I did not get into the Pharmacy Corps. I reacted in bitter rage.

That evening, the Lord brought me to the painful realization that my goal had become my idol. The handkerchief you embroidered helped show me. In my quest for acceptance from man, I'd forgotten I had God's love. Nothing else matters.

The Lord is forgiving, and with his

help, I've found contentment where I am. I'm determined to do my best work and respect others, whether or not they respect me.

Second, thanks for having the courage to tell me I was racing in the wrong direction. Once I told you it's important to have someone in your life who helps you grow and who's hard on you when you need it. You did that for me, and ironically I rejected it. But now I appreciate what you did.

Please forgive me for allowing my obsession, bitterness, and pride to destroy our friendship.

Third, thank you for taking Lucia under your wing. She writes fondly of your visits to the orphanage, the parties, and the new dress you made her. I can't be there, but I'm thankful you are.

Another reason for this letter is to encourage you. You used to doubt your ability to make decisions, but you made excellent decisions in regards to me. You acted in kindness and strength and truth. Even your decision at Pompeii was right. Please don't ever doubt your strength in the Lord.

Again, this is not an attempt to win you back. I only want to express my gratitude and bolster you. Even in your absence, you helped me.

With kind regards,
Hutch

Georgie groped in her pocket for a handkerchief like the blubbering idiot she was.

Now she knew two things for certain — his peace was genuine, and she loved him more desperately than ever.

But now she doubted her earlier assessment that he still loved her. He didn't want to woo her back. He wanted to say a better good-bye. She'd made the right decision at Pompeii. Those did not sound like the statements of a man in love.

She blotted her face dry and hiccupped.

For goodness' sake, now wasn't the time to be a crybaby. Now was the time to meld her old and her new talents.

She knit together an idea in her mind.

53

Casanova
April 24, 1944

Hutch scraped his spatula across the top of the wooden capsule mold, making sure each capsule half had an equivalent amount of the aspirin, phenacetin, and caffeine mixture. The hospital hadn't opened for patients yet, but Captain Chadwick had ordered APC capsules for his own headaches. Hutch smiled. Chadwick might not like Hutch, but at least he trusted him now.

Dom hadn't returned from lunch, and Hutch savored the quiet. He nestled the top halves of the capsules in place, then tapped them out of the mold onto a towel. Each capsule received a quick roll on a moistened piece of gauze to seal it shut, then Hutch gently rolled the batch in the towel to remove fingerprints and traces of powder. Into the amber vial they went, and he affixed the label square in the middle. Nice.

"Hello, Hutch."

He almost dropped the bottle. "Geor— Lieutenant Taylor."

"What did I tell you? Call me Georgie." She grinned and set a paper bag on the counter. "I brought you two surprises."

With great concentration, he set down the bottle of APC capsules. What was she doing here acting as if nothing had changed between them? "Surprises?"

"This is the first. Come see." She beckoned him over.

He urged leaden feet forward, although his heart twisted in pain as her sweet face drew nearer, lit up as he remembered.

He peered inside the bag. "Oranges. Thanks."

"I figured you might be running low."

"I'm out." His voice sounded dull, as if he didn't want to see her. He smiled, although it did a stupid twitchy thing.

"Not many at Anzio, I imagine." She leaned crossed arms on the counter. "I worried about you up there. Was it as bad as they say?"

"Yeah." He rotated the bag of oranges on the counter. He sounded like an idiot. Whatever was going on, he needed to play along. Perhaps she wanted to be friends again, and that would — well, that would be enough. "How are things in your squadron?"

"Hectic." She tossed a glance up and to the side, completely adorable. "They're treating me like royalty all because my plane took a dip in the Mediterranean."

Hutch's mouth dropped open. "The evac flight that ditched? Was that you?" The article in the *Stars and Stripes* hadn't named names.

She pointed to the red, white, and blue ribbon of the Bronze Star on her jacket. "I prayed and didn't waver. Your gift helped."

"My gift?"

"The tin punch with the nightingale over the waves."

He'd forgotten about that. "You still have it?"

"I'm thankful I had it that day. Even in your absence, you helped me." She held his gaze, her eyes serious and grateful.

His tongue dried out. Her words . . . that was a line from his letter. He should know; he wrote five drafts before he got it right.

One side of her mouth puckered in concern. "I'm sorry you're not in the Pharmacy Corps."

He chuckled and took the bag of oranges to the back counter. "I'm not."

"Seriously? You mean it?"

She thought it was only bravado, so he gave her his most content smile. "Last week I turned down a genuine second chance to join the Corps."

Georgie gasped and leaned forward. "What? But why? That's what you wanted."

"I don't want it anymore." He stashed the bag of oranges in an empty crate next to the counter. "I have satisfying work here with people I like. And humility is good for me. The last thing I want is a commission."

Her silence drew his gaze. Her expression glowed with . . . admiration? Adoration?

Hutch's heart slammed into his throat. Could it be possible? Could he ever gain back her love? More importantly, was that what God wanted? Because Hutch wanted it deep down at the cellular level.

"I'm confounded, John Hutchinson." She gave him a teasing look.

"Con— confounded?" He hadn't said one intelligent sentence since she arrived.

"I said I brought two surprises, and you haven't even asked about the second one."

He'd lost count after one. "I'm — well, what is it?"

"Not what. Who. Honestly, I'm quite perturbed at you." She leaned out the doorway. "All right, Lillian."

Lillian was a surprise? Hutch stepped

from behind the counter.

Georgie and Lillian held back the tent flaps on either side, and a little girl hobbled through the door on a single crutch.

"Lucia!"

"My Ucce!" She bounced up and down on her braced legs. Her crutch fell to the ground.

"La mia Lucia." He scooped her up and pressed her to his chest. *"La mia bella Lucia."*

She hugged his neck so tight he could barely breathe, but he didn't mind at all. She felt heavier, less skinny.

After he blinked away the moisture in his eyes, he met Georgie's gaze and mouthed, "Thank you."

She dabbed a handkerchief at her cheeks and mouthed, "You're welcome."

He pulled back to look at Lucia. "The nuns feed you well. You're nice and fat."

"Si." She giggled and pointed into her mouth. "I lost a tooth."

"How do you expect to eat food if you keep losing your teeth? Where did you put it? We need to screw it back in."

"Silly Ucce. I get new one."

"You do? Well, I'll be. What'll they come up with next?"

She pulled on the collar of her dress — dark blue with little white dots. "Like my new dress? Signorina Giorgiana make it. My 'Twinkle, Twinkle' dress."

It did kind of look like the night sky. Wasn't that just like Georgie to think of the perfect gift? His heart full, he sent her a smile. "It's beautiful."

Lucia bounced on his hip. "Now go sure?"

"Go sure?"

She frowned and tapped her temple. "The water. The sand. The starfish. The sure."

"The shore," Georgie said.

In his letters he'd mentioned taking her to the shore someday, but someday wasn't today. "I'm sorry, little star. I have to work today. And there's a war on. The shore will have to wait."

"No, it won't." Georgie smiled and fiddled with her fingers. "One of the advantages of being the heroine of the day is you can ask for things and people give them to you. Colonel Currier gave you the rest of the day off, and I came up here in a jeep. You can use it. There's a nice beach only ten miles from here."

He stared at her. "You did that for me?"

"And Lucia."

Something was wrong. "What about you?"

"What about me?" Georgie's cheeks turned pink.

"If I take the jeep, what — how will you . . . ?"

Her cheeks went red, and she fluttered her hand toward Lillian. "I can visit with my friends here. I haven't seen them for ages. Lillian's tent is almost empty, and she's letting me and Lucia stay the night, so you can take as long as you wish."

When Hutch mixed ointments, some were stubborn. He'd mix and mix, and it seemed they'd never combine. The substances were just too different. Then in one beautiful moment, the ingredients snapped together into a smooth mixture.

Hutch's thoughts snapped together just as smoothly. Georgie had designed the perfect plan. She'd made it possible for Hutch and Lucia to go to the shore alone. But he knew as strongly as he knew his pharmacopoeia that Georgie hoped to join them.

"Lucia?" His voice rasped, and he swallowed to wet his throat. "Wouldn't it be more fun if Signorina Georgie came with us?"

"Si! Si!"

"Oh! Goodness." Georgie pressed her hand over her chest. "I wasn't fishing for an invitation."

Lillian crossed her arms and arched an eyebrow at Hutch. "No, but she brought her sundress and sandals."

"Lillian!" Georgie stamped her foot.

"Bye now. You drop by my tent to change when you're ready." Lillian wiggled her fingers in a wave and ducked out of the tent.

Hutch fought back a laugh, both at Georgie's embarrassment and from his own joy. She definitely wanted to come, and this rang of romance, not just friendship.

"Honestly, Hutch, I didn't —"

"I know." He set Lucia down and handed her the crutch. "I have to wait until Dom comes back. It'll be soon. I should clean up my mess too."

"Yes. Of course." Her voice sounded tiny.

"The weather's nice for a change. At least seventy degrees and clear." He returned to the back counter, grabbed a rag, and brushed up a bit of spilled APC powder. "Should be a clear evening too. Perfect for stargazing."

Her feet shifted on the dirt floor. "I suppose it would be."

He returned the box of capsule shells under the counter, and warmth expanded his chest. "I have a new telescope. Fine piece. Saved lives at Anzio."

"What?"

He winked at her. "Earned me the Bronze Star too. Pinned on by Gen. Mark Clark

578

himself. I could tell you about it today if you'd like."

"I'd like that." She'd never looked so shy in all the time he'd known her. "I — I brought a picnic. No steak this time."

If he could have her love again, he'd be happy with K rations. "I don't need steak."

Her cheeks flamed, brighter than ever. "That's not what I . . ."

Their secret code. For heaven's sake. His own cheeks warmed, and he laughed. "That wasn't what I meant either."

She laughed too, and Lucia joined in, not knowing the joke of course, and that made Hutch and Georgie laugh even harder.

He waved them out the door. "Go get ready and I'll finish up in here, grab my telescope."

Georgie took Lucia's hand. "Meet you here in half an hour?"

"Yes." It would be the longest half hour of his life.

54

"Presto! Presto!" Lucia sat on the blanket, and her legs wiggled in front of her.

Georgie wrestled with a buckle on the braces. "Sweetie, I could work more *presto* if you held still-o."

Beside her on the blanket, Hutch laughed and rolled up his trousers above his knees. "You heard her, Lucia. You have to obey. She's an officer."

"I don't want to be an officer today. That's why I wore my sundress." Her face heated. Again. She wiggled off the first leg brace. Goodness, everything she said sounded forward.

"But you *are* an officer. And a fine one," he said, his voice husky.

Oh, the expression on his face. The affection, the strength, the respect. She wanted to bottle it up to store in her musette bag so she could bask in it whenever she wanted.

He broke the gaze and shrugged off his shirt.

How was she supposed to concentrate with him walking around bare-chested? She frowned at the last leg brace and fumbled with the straps. "You don't have to take off your stripes on my account."

He chuckled and scratched his lower back. "I don't mind the stripes. I mind the fabric. It's so warm today. Feels great."

Lucia wiggled her leg. "The water, *per favore.*"

"*Si, signorina.*" Georgie slipped off the second brace. "Can you walk without the braces?"

"A little. I stronger."

Hutch growled.

Georgie stared at him, but Lucia giggled.

He got to his feet, growled louder, and leaned over the child, hands raised. "The big hairy bear is going to steal Lucia and dump her in the ocean."

She shrieked with laughter. He swung her up and ran down to the water. Sand flew behind his bare feet, and Lucia's braids bounced every which way.

Georgie stood, brushed sand from her skirt, and followed. He would make a wonderful daddy. Each moment she loved him more. And he still loved her. She could see it in his eyes even if they hadn't spoken the words.

On the drive from the hospital, they'd discussed their Bronze Star experiences and everything else that had happened in the last three months. But not their relationship. Not their feelings. They circled the topic from a wary distance.

At the waterline, the turquoise sea washed up onto creamy sand, and Hutch crouched next to Lucia, holding her by the waist while she stabbed at a spent wave with her toe. Georgie's chest ached at the beauty of the scene, and even more so when Hutch glanced over his shoulder and smiled at her.

"Could you take my place with Lucia for a second?"

"Sure." She stepped closer, the sand changing from dry and warm to moist and cool.

Dozens of pale scars covered his back. "Your back! Oh, Hutch!"

He craned his head over his shoulder. "I suppose it looks bad."

"You said you took a little shrapnel."

"I did." He measured an inch between thumb and forefinger. "Each piece was little."

"You poor thing." She clasped her hands so she wouldn't try to caress away those scars. "That must have hurt."

He transferred Lucia's hand to Georgie. "The itching now is worse than the pain then."

"Well, don't scratch. You'll get infected."

"You sound like Bergie." He pulled a clear glass vial from his pocket and scooped up sand.

"What are you doing?" A gentle wave chilled her feet, and Lucia squealed.

He held up the vial for inspection as if it were one of his formulations. "I take samples from every landing, every shore. I think . . . yes, this is my favorite."

Because of the sand or because of the company?

His gaze swept back to her, rich with meaning.

The breeze ruffled the skirt around her knees and blew curls into her face. Why now? She brushed them back so she wouldn't break the connection.

"Beautiful," he said, his eyes smoky, his voice throaty. "The water, the sky, Lucia . . . you."

Her lips parted, and the words "I love you" floated in her mouth, waiting for the faintest puff of air to push them out. Instead, she smiled and turned to Lucia.

"Let's go out just a little bit farther, shall we?"

This time he'd have to say it first.

"I didn't think she'd ever fall asleep," Hutch whispered.

"Me, neither." Georgie's heart warmed at the silhouette of sleeping child against the starry sky.

Once Lucia grew accustomed to the water, she'd splashed with glee, then built dozens of sand castles. After the picnic, she splashed and built some more.

Georgie sat on one hip with her feet tucked to the side, and she adjusted the damp hem of her dress. "The nuns will need to give her a thorough bath tomorrow."

"No kidding." Hutch adjusted dials on his telescope. He wore his shirt again but loose and unbuttoned.

Everything within her wanted to snuggle close, but she held back, and a tiny flame of annoyance lit inside. He hadn't said one word about love, hadn't so much as reached for her hand. Would the man ever speak his mind?

He pointed to the north. "I thought long and hard about which constellation to show you tonight."

"Oh?" Her voice sounded crisp.

"Lyra, the lyre that belonged to Orpheus." He traced a pattern with his finger. "See that bright star, low to the horizon? Then four stars below it in a diamond shape?"

Georgie scanned until she found the little constellation. "It's pretty."

Hutch dug his feet into the sand and rested his elbows on his knees. "Orpheus married a woman named Eurydice. On their wedding day, she was killed. He was heartbroken and followed her to the underworld. He played such beautiful music on his golden lyre that Hades and Persephone were persuaded to let him bring Eurydice back. On one condition. He had to lead her out, and he couldn't look back at her until they were both up in the land of the living. As soon as his feet touched the upper world, he turned back, anxious to see if she was still behind him. She was. But she wasn't up in the land of the living yet. She disappeared, right before his eyes, forever."

"What a sad story."

"Mm-hmm." He faced her, his eyes luminous in the starlight. "I don't want that to happen to me."

"Oh . . ." Her sigh tingled over her lips.

He reached out, hesitated, and twined one of her curls around his finger. "I already lost the love of my life once. I couldn't bear to lose you again."

"Oh, Hutch." The full realization of his love rippled into her soul. She shifted closer and leaned her shoulder against his.

He cupped his hand around the back of her head and pressed his lips to her forehead. "My Georgie. I love you so much. I was such a fool."

"And I was a spoiled brat." She wrapped her arm around his waist, his warmth and strength seeping through, stirring her emotions into a whirl.

"Nonsense." He tipped up her head and gazed into her eyes. "Can you ever love me again?"

"I never stopped loving you. Not for one minute. You'll never — you'll never lose me again."

Finally, finally, he dipped closer for a kiss.

But playfulness bubbled up inside. After making her wait so long, he could wait a moment himself. She turned away. "On the other hand, you'd make a striking constellation."

"What?" A laugh burst out. "Okay, now you *are* being a brat."

"See? Right there." She rested her head on his shoulder and pointed to the sky. "Those two stars are your eyes, and I just want to live in them forever."

"Do you?" His voice rumbled, and his embrace tightened.

He made it hard to concentrate, but she was determined to finish her piece. "Those two are your shoulders, which are mighty fine, by the way."

"Is that right?" He eased up her chin, his fingers caressing her cheek, his gaze locked on her lips.

"That one." Her finger waved somewhere near the sky. "That — that's your — your mouth —"

A slight nod, and he lowered that mouth to hers in a kiss longer and sweeter and more passionate than ever before. The most savory, juicy steak of a kiss.

She pulled back to catch her breath, and a tiny laugh escaped. "You said you didn't want steak."

He laughed too, and he kissed her again. "You said you didn't have any steak. But then you flopped one onto my plate. I'd be a fool to turn it down."

"I'm glad you gave up your foolish ways."

"Me too." Hutch sighed and leaned his head against hers. "You know this will still have to be a secret."

"I know."

"It won't change for the duration of the war. We can write, have a few private moments, but evenings like this — they won't happen often, if at all."

"That's all right." She squeezed his waist. "Most couples are separated now, aren't they? At least we can see each other sometimes. And when the war is over . . ."

"Then we can make plans." He settled a kiss above her ear. "Like where to live."

Her eyes drifted shut at the joyful thought of sharing her life with him. "It's too early to talk of such things, but I want you to know I could live anywhere. If I'm with you, I'll love the big city."

"I had another idea. Charlottesville needs pharmacists, right?"

"Well, yes." She straightened up to look him in the eye.

He patted the poor abandoned telescope. "You can't see the stars well in the city. I've always had to drive to the country to stargaze. I'd like to buy some land outside town — not too close to your family, mind you — and I could watch my stars, and Lucia could romp in the grass, and you could have a horse or two —"

"You'd do that for me?"

He grinned. "Are you kidding? It sounds like a dream."

"It does." It sounded like her lifelong dream of home and family and a horse of her own, but with this gentle, funny, steady man she adored, whose love would encourage her to grow.

Georgie brushed a kiss over his lips. "The sweetest dream I could imagine."

Dear Reader,

Thank you for joining Hutch and Georgie on their journey. If you'd like to see interactive maps of Sicily and Italy with accompanying photographs, please visit my website at www. sarahsundin.com.

The 802nd Medical Air Evacuation Transport Squadron was a real unit, the first to fly a true air evacuation mission. Although all characters in the 802nd in this story are fictional, with the exception of the commanding officer, Maj. Frederick Guilford, their movements, locations, joys, and challenges are real.

Likewise, the 93rd Evacuation Hospital was real. Real-life people in this story include Col. Donald Currier, Major Etter, and Sergeant Paskun. The incident with General Patton did occur at the 93rd, one of two slapping incidents within a week. Patton's "dialogue" in the novel is adapted from Colonel Currier's account.

I am indebted to Dennis Worthen's fine book, *Pharmacy in World War II* (New York: Pharmaceutical Products Press, 2004), for many of the details on the Pharmacy Corps and the state of the profession in the wartime military. While Hutch and his father are fictional, the frustrations they faced are real. The "any intelligent boy who can read a label" comment was spoken in Congressional hearings. On a sad note, Robert Knecht is listed among the pharmacists killed in action. Mr. Knecht served as an enlisted pharmacist with the 95th Evacuation Hospital and was killed at Anzio on February 7, 1944. His service and death are poignantly described in Evelyn Monahan and Rosemary Neidel-Greenlee's *And If I Perish: Frontline US Army Nurses in World War II* (New York: Anchor Books, 2003). He was secretly engaged to an Army nurse. His name is included in this story as a tribute to all pharmacists who served their country.

ACKNOWLEDGMENTS

What a joy it was to write this book! But it couldn't be done alone. Highest thanks go to the Lord, for giving me courage to face my fears and for smacking me upside the head whenever my goals veer toward obsession.

My family deserves much more than mere thanks. Living with a writer is strange. Thank you, Dave, Stephen, Anna, and Matthew for putting up with me and supporting me. And thank you, Stephen, for sharing your knowledge of astronomy and doing an "astro edit."

I had the joy and honor of talking to Dorothy White Errair, president of the World War II Flight Nurse Association and an actual World War II flight nurse (807th MAETS). Her daughter, Melinda Errair Bruckman, is dedicated to collecting and preserving these amazing women's stories. Please visit their beautiful website at www

.legendsofflightnurses.org. If you have information about any of the flight nurses, they'd love to hear from you.

Thank you also to Warren Hower of Hower Research Associates, who located the entire detailed unit history of the 93rd Evacuation Hospital in the National Archives. A treasure trove!

Many thanks to Bruce H. Wolk, author of *Stars on My Wings* (unpublished), the story of Jewish-American airmen. Bruce let me read his interview with a C-47 radioman-navigator who ditched in the Pacific on a medical evacuation flight, an invaluable aid — and a harrowing account.

Thanks to my nephew, Adam Groeber, a reenactor in the 82nd Airborne WWII Living History Association, for practical information on C-47s.

Special thanks go to Sarah Hamaker, Carrie Fancett Pagels, Nanci Rubin, and Andrew Winch for answering my questions about Virginia.

I couldn't have written this novel without my amazing critique partners, Judy Gann, Bonnie Leon, Ann Shorey, Marcy Weydemuller, and Linda Clare. I appreciate your keen eyes and your prayerful hearts.

I'm beyond blessed by my supportive church, small group, and women's Bible study group. I love you guys!

I say it in every book, and I mean it in every book. My agent, Rachel Kent, and my editor, Vicki Crumpton, and the entire team at Revell Books — you are the best! I couldn't have imagined a better group of people to work with. Your knowledge, professionalism, and talent are outstanding. Plus, you all make me smile.

And dear reader, I'm so thankful for you! Please visit my website at www.sarahsundin .com to leave a message, sign up for my quarterly newsletter, read about the history behind the story, and find tips on starting a book club. I look forward to hearing from you.

DISCUSSION QUESTIONS

1. Georgie thinks she's gotten herself in over her head as a flight nurse. Do you agree? Have you ever been in a situation where you felt you were in over your head? What did you do?

2. Hutch struggles with disrespect in his position. How does he cope at first? How does that change during the story? Have you ever felt like your work wasn't respected? How did you cope?

3. Both Hutch and Georgie are blessed with deep, long-term friendships. How do these friendships help them? Do you have a friendship like that?

4. Hutch and Bergie say they balance each other out. How do you see that in their friendship? In your closest relationships, do you prefer lots of similarities or a bal-

ance of differences? Some blend?

5. How does Georgie deal with grief? How does grief change her?

6. Hutch has an interfering supervisor and a rude coworker. How does Hutch deal well, how does he come up short, and how does he improve? How have you dealt with unpleasant workplace relationships?

7. In what ways is Georgie's family deeply loving? How do they stifle her? How can we avoid locking family members into roles and help them grow?

8. Hutch and Georgie find themselves in an uncomfortable situation, with the woman outranking the man. How does this create difficulties? How do they try to work through these difficulties? Today it's not uncommon for a wife to earn more than her husband. How can modern couples deal with this?

9. Hutch starts with a good goal, but it turns into an obsession. Why do you think this happened? Do you agree with his decision at the end of the book?

10. How does Georgie handle fear at first? How does she handle fear at the end? Do you ever find fear holding you back?

11. In what ways does Lucia demonstrate the resiliency of children? The vulnerability? How are she and Hutch good for each other?

12. Both Georgie and Hutch find their dreams have changed by the end of the story. Has that ever happened to you?

13. How are stars symbolic in the story? What do they mean to Hutch? To Georgie?

14. Why do you think Vesuvius (which erupted from March 18–23, 1944) is pictured on the book cover?

15. If you read *With Every Letter,* did you enjoy watching Tom and Mellie's story progress? The last book in the Wings of the Nightingale series (summer 2014) follows Lt. Kay Jobson and Lt. Roger Cooper. From what you've seen of these characters, what might you anticipate?

ABOUT THE AUTHOR

Sarah Sundin is the author of *With Every Letter, A Distant Melody, A Memory Between Us,* and *Blue Skies Tomorrow.* In 2011, *A Memory Between Us* was a finalist in the Inspirational Reader's Choice Awards and Sarah received the Writer of the Year Award at the Mount Hermon Christian Writers Conference. A graduate of UC San Francisco School of Pharmacy, she works on-call as a hospital pharmacist. During WWII, her grandfather served as a pharmacist's mate (medic) in the Navy and her great-uncle flew with the US Eighth Air Force in England. Sarah lives in California with her husband and three children.

The employees of Thorndike Press hope you have enjoyed this Large Print book. All our Thorndike, Wheeler, and Kennebec Large Print titles are designed for easy reading, and all our books are made to last. Other Thorndike Press Large Print books are available at your library, through selected bookstores, or directly from us.

For information about titles, please call:
 (800) 223-1244

or visit our Web site at:
 http://gale.cengage.com/thorndike

To share your comments, please write:
 Publisher
 Thorndike Press
 10 Water St., Suite 310
 Waterville, ME 04901